PRAISE FOR ROBERT J. SZMIDT

"With the right tech, it's easy to be a god. But as Robert J. Szmidt points out in this impressive novel, to be a god for the right reasons, sometimes you have to spend a few years in Hell, first."

—David Weber, author of the *Honor Harrington* series.

"An exciting beginning to an epic saga of space exploration. Morrisey and his crew of daring, corrupt rogues will hold you breathless as they loot the wrecks of spaceships—until they find the one that could change everything in the galaxy."

—Nancy Kress, author of *Beggars in Spain*

"A fast-paced tale of a piratical salvage crew who find more than they expected when they discover an ancient Alien artifact. An engaging story."

—Jack Campbell, author of *The Lost Fleet* series.

EASY TO BE A GOD

THE FIELDS OF LONG-FORGOTTEN BATTLES, BOOK 1

ROBERT J. SZMIDT

WFP
WORDFIRE PRESS

EBook ISBN: 978-1-68057-236-0
Trade Paperback ISBN: 978-1-68057-235-3
Casebind ISBN: 978-1-68057-301-5
Library of Congress Control Number: 2021951082

Cover design by Janet McDonald
Cover artwork images by Adobe Stock
Kevin J. Anderson, Art Director
Published by
WordFire Press, LLC
PO Box 1840
Monument CO 80132
Kevin J. Anderson & Rebecca Moesta, Publishers
WordFire Press eBook Edition 2022
WordFire Press Trade Paperback Edition 2022
WordFire Press Hardcover Edition 2022
Printed in the USA
Join our WordFire Press Readers Group for
sneak previews, updates, new projects, and giveaways.
Sign up at wordfirepress.com

DEDICATION

*With thanks to all the great SF masters
who have read* Easy to Be a God
and supported me all along.

PART ONE
THE NOMAD'S MISSION

ONE

THE SOLAR SYSTEM, ALPHA SECTOR

06/22/2354

"Time to get up, my lord..." whispered Monicatherine, still sleepy, and stretched herself sensually between the rustling sheets.

"Not just yet, the sun's barely rising," said Nike very quietly, making himself heard, but not disturbing her blissful idleness.

He sat, or in fact reclined, in a shallow armchair draped with a tiger fur, eyes fixed on the narrow bay window. Sipping tangy wine from a crystal goblet, he watched the treetops being tossed by the strong wind and the gray-blue mountain range looming in the distance. Although the first rays of dawn had just lit up the horizon, it was bright enough to make out every detail of the landscape. Wispy clouds drifted lazily across the sky like wreaths of smoke from a dying campfire. Among them frolicked slender, winged silhouettes racing the wind. Too distinctive to be confused with birds. Too swift and lithe. Too glistening. An entire wing of fiery red dragons had left their nests to greet the day in the air.

"Why didn't you awake me, master?"

The question came from behind his armchair so unexpectedly

that he started involuntarily, dropping the goblet. Either Moni-catherine had crept up so quietly, or he had been so wrapped in thought. The crystal vessel—fortunately already empty—fell directly onto the furs carpeting the stone floor. It didn't smash, and only a few drops of scarlet liquid splashed on the long, snow-white hairs, however …

That's not a good sign, Nike grimaced.

"What's bothering you, darling?" The girl was crouching alongside now. She rested her head in the crook of his shoulder, letting him slide his fingertips over her long golden hair.

"You know very well what." He leaned over to kiss her, but she stood up right at that moment.

She passed by him naked, still sleep-warm and dreamy, stood in front of the window obscuring the whole view, and then bent forward sensually, resting her elbows on the narrow windowsill.

"Dragons … look how many there are today, darling," she said, knowing that his attention was not focused on the winged giants.

"I like dragons," Nike responded, trying to sound unruffled. "They're so dignified, but at the same time so carefree."

Monicatherine smiled. A moment later, she knelt by the window and together they watched the distant, whirling glim-mers. The pale red dawn continued to swell on the horizon.

"I'll miss them," Nike added. At the same time a sudden flash made him snap his eyelids shut. He kept his eyes closed tightly, but it did not help much; he still felt as if the naked sun had blazed straight into his pupils.

"It's seven already," he heard Monicatherine's words. "Your last parade … You're gonna be late."

The blinding flash made him realize she had turned off the illusioner. The image of the stone wall with the narrow bay window vanished, and with it—the trees, mountains, sky, and the dragons dancing in the wind. The panoramic screen occu-pying half the cabin now showed the boundless blackness of space and the home world suspended in it. Precisely synchronized with the illusion, the Sun had emerged from behind the edge of the blue and white globe. The photochromic crystallite darkened instantly, yet Nike was dazzled anyway—all it took was the blink of an eye.

"I'll make it." He groaned, partly with pain and partly because it was their last shared illusion.

"It sounds as if you don't want to go to the parade." She walked over to him rolling her hips, but stopped beyond his reach. "Are you sure everything's all right?"

"You've seen my grade book," he answered evasively, still rubbing his eyes. "I've got the fourth best score in my year."

"And I told you it's enough, didn't I? Trust me."

"I do, darling." He reached out to grab her waist, but only caught thin air and that unique—though somehow elusive—scent of warm skin.

Monicatherine stepped back nimbly and continued to look intently at him, as though to imprint his image in her memory; his elongated face, straight, proportional nose, high cheekbones lending him the alpha male look, deep-set brown eyes, and jet-black short hair only growing at the back of his head.

"You seem so downcast today," she began as he was getting up from the armchair.

"C'mon. It's not every day you graduate from the Academy."

"Being inducted isn't a sentence," she retorted. "Nothing's really going to change. With your grades you're sure to stay within the Solar System. You might even get a post here in orbit."

"Yes, nothing's gonna change between us," he assured her, knowing that his words were at least as false as the illusion they had been watching a short time before.

"Get going," she said, throwing him a jumpsuit—the dress uniform for last-year cadets—the same one he had so meticulously folded the evening before. "There's only fifteen minutes left till the first whistle, and I'd like to—"

She didn't have to finish. He knew what she wanted. He also knew he would miss that the most.

"Attention!" Three equilateral formations of uniformed figures straightened up in a split second.

In this place everything appealed to the imagination: the semidarkness of the immense hangar, the streamlined contours of the fighters looming in the distance, the massive bulk of assault ships, and more than anything—the omnipresent cold, which reminded the participants in the ceremony that they were only separated from endless space by a layer of porous helon a few yards thick.

"And finally, Admiral-Rector Damiandreas Dreade-Ravenore," the duty officer announced, then saluted the lecturers occupying seats in the honorary grandstand and left the rostrum, giving his place over to a well-built man.

Dredd, even though bald as a coot, wasn't at all old. He may have notched up a hundred sixty years, of which a hundred and thirty-three years he had spent in active service, but he still looked like a young god thanks to almost eight decades of forced hibernation. He was as tall as a basketball player, had a square jaw, broad shoulders, the muscles of a bodybuilder, and limber but dignified movements. All the cadets envied the Admiral his fitness, but none of them would have confessed—even under torture—that during the six long years of training they had felt even a trace of affection toward him. Damiandreas Dreade-Ravenore was a supercilious, sadistic clone-of-a-bitch and liked nothing better than to give speeches. He loved to torment the cadets physically but also verbally. They had experienced both kinds of harassment many times—firsthand and first ear, so to speak—and long before had sworn that none of them would utter the slightest sound during his farewell speech.

"At ease, cadets!" he began customarily, holding up a thick sheaf of papers, which contained notes for his speech.

He then fell pointedly silent, counting on the murmur of despair he so relished. This time, though, the cadets stayed true to their word and disappointed Dredd. Those in the middle of the front row could see the Admiral's eyelid twitching.

"I have no doubt that more than once you've asked yourselves why we trained you in such tough conditions," he said in an angry tone, putting the script down on the rostrum. "Why you had to carry out the most complicated warning procedures with your eyes closed, when—"

Here he stopped and shifted his gaze over the regular formations, before picking up his speech with a repetition, a favorite rhetorical device of his that allowed him to lengthen his address.

"—why you had to carry out the most complicated warning procedures with your eyes closed, when for a hundred and eighteen years no vessel of the Federation Fleet has been involved in combat. We have no enemies today, I agree. The first and the last colonial war was an absolute and unequivocal success. But it was a Pyrrhic victory, there's no denying it. Every family lost loved ones in that conflict. However, that immense blood sacrifice ensured our civilization a century of peaceful existence and unprecedented development. Never has peace been so enduring in the history of Humankind.

"We reached the stars barely three centuries ago. The beginnings were humble. The colonization of the Moon lasted forty-five years, following the first flights to the Silver Globe picked up again in the initial decades of the twenty-first century. Things went more swiftly with Mars, but we still needed thirty years in order for the domes of cities and industrial installations to spring up among the rust-colored sands. The beginning of the twenty-second century finally brought a breakthrough, a huge breakthrough. The invention of FTL drive—for the first time in history, fully efficient—allowed the human race to reach the stars.

"Events gathered pace. Thousands of space probes hurtled

toward distant systems, extending the borders of the known Universe. The final frontier had been overcome; the final obstacle keeping us on Earth, the cradle of Humankind, had been surmounted. People had left the home world and in less than a hundred fifty years had colonized one thousand and fourteen planets in eight hundred and seventy-two star systems within a one thousand nine hundred light-year radius of Earth. They had also investigated a further eighteen thousand dead star systems, unsuitable for colonization. That's a great deal, a really great deal for almost three centuries of expansion, and were it not for the period of civil war—" The Admiral made a short rhetorical pause again.

"That's a great deal, a really great deal for almost three centuries of expansion, and had it not been for the civil war we might have added to that list hundreds—if not thousands—of other worlds. But what is our Federation in the grand scheme of things, since even ten times as many colonized planets would be a mere drop in the ocean of the Galaxy? Tens of billions of new stars still await exploration in the center of the Milky Way, not to mention those in its remaining spiral arms. We haven't got the slightest idea how many habitable, Earthlike planets orbit them. Neither do we know how many civilizations as powerful as ours, or even mightier, may exist there.

"The fact that we have not yet discovered advanced forms of life in the one arm of the Milky Way we have so far explored, that we have not come across any signals or artifacts left by Aliens, doesn't mean in any way that they do not exist. That they aren't out there," he nodded toward the bulkhead, "just beyond the frontiers of knowledge. And that they haven't been observing us for a long time … That they won't threaten us in the more distant or quite near future … The Universe is immense; some even say it's infinite. We will not be safe, while even one system in the farthest corner of the Galaxy remains unexplored. And the end of the exploration will only be possible in thousands—and who knows if not tens of thousands—of years."

He stopped again, ran his hand over the naked skin above his left ear, as if he wanted to smooth down some nonexistent hair. His fingers touched the long red scar, which extended as far as the root of his nose, transforming his face into a warning of what might befall any one of those present in the hangar out there in space, when the true test comes.

"We've been unified for a hundred and eighteen years. For the first time in the history of Humankind there are no states, no nations; the concepts of races and borders have lost all significance. Our great-great-grandfathers shed their blood and laid down their lives to unite all people under a single banner. However, the Federation will still need at least another century to compensate for the losses incurred in that war. Many worlds are awaiting repopulation, many planets can no longer be our home—"

He fell silent. This time, he didn't glance at the cadets. Once again he had drifted off into memories of the times he had looked at the dying colonies as a soldier, an officer, and finally the commander of one of the fleets. Scores of planets had been turned into eternal cemeteries; hundreds of colonies were still licking their wounds. That was the cost of the ultimate union. All the cadets knew that look on the admiral's face, and were aware that his pondering over the past would soon be over.

"Today you complete your training in the most elite school," the Admiral spoke again. "Tomorrow you begin service in front-line vessels. You will be dispersed throughout the Universe, across dozens of sectors, and hundreds of systems. Some of you, however, will be granted the honor of serving here, on Earth. Yes, I have seven such assignments."

When the Admiral waved some cards he had taken out of his pocket, from the ranks standing in front of him came soft murmurs of satisfaction, acknowledged—of course—by Dredd's wry smile. No one had expected him to show so many gold cards.

"For the first time in five years such a large number of graduates will take up service in High Command on Earth. Seven assignments for the seven top students, for best of the best. Before I award them, however, I have something less felicitous to communicate."

A deathly silence fell. All cadets knew what would be said, but none of them wanted to hear it.

"I have received from High Command official orders—" The Admiral-Rector paused to emphasize the gravity of the words he was about to utter. "I have received from High Command official orders for fifty-three cadets to serve honorably and responsibly in the craft of Recycling Corps."

A dull groan swept through the hangar. Dredd did not react, but looked down triumphantly at the sour faces of the cadets standing in the rear row. They had the greatest chance of "honorable" service in the Recycling Corps, where the death toll was still heavy.

"A great adventure awaits you, gentlemen. You weren't committed to your war studies, so now you'll be able to see the wartime effects for yourselves. Here are your invitations to the fields of long-forgotten battles," concluded Damiandreas Dreade-Ravenore, not without satisfaction, activating the screen of his reader. "But first allow me to commence my speech ..."

––––––––

Nike toyed with the small, oblong piece of plastic inscribed with his future. Or actually the absence of a future. Following Dredd's speech—which lasted more than an hour—the ceremonial awarding of assignments took place and another academic year officially ended. Not many people remained in the hangar. A few lecturers saying goodbye to their favorite students and around a dozen cadets still waiting for the liaison officers of minor vessels, who apparently had been delayed. In fact one could have said "around a dozen condemned men." Service onboard the heavy wreckers of the Recycling Corps was far from safe. This year's fifty-three posts meant that at least as many crew members had departed this life since the last parade.

"Statcherskee!" The distorted sound of his surname brought Nike out of his reverie.

He looked up just as Dredd, who was talking to a short, fat man in filthy mechanic's overalls, pointed at him. He picked up his kitbag and threw it over one shoulder.

"You're Statcherskee, are you?" A red-haired officer with a puffy face walked over and held out a hand stinking of chemicals to take his card.

"My name's Stachursky. It's a Polish name, so you pronounce the 'CH'—"

"Shut it, boy."

"Yes, sir!"

Only when he drew closer did Nike notice a modest stripe with the rank of captain of the Fleet and the name "MORRISEY" sewn on beneath the faded gold lettering of "FSS NOMAD" on the worn-out, stained overalls.

His card was at once shoved into a reader, but Morrisey, rather than turning on his heel, whistled softly and glanced at the cadet. Nike didn't notice it, for he was gaping in horror at the metal fingers gripping the case of a small comlink.

"Are you taking the piss?" asked the astonished captain of the *Nomad* without looking up. "I see from the exam results here that you're one of this year's top graduates. Fourth best score. Your sort don't wind up with us."

"Sir, it's not a mistake, sir." Nike clicked his heels in accordance with regulations.

"Really? So how do you explain it then, boy?" Morrisey asked, nodding at the reader where, next to a hologram of his face and personal details, one could see the results of all his exams and the almost perfect final grade.

"Let's say he penetrated something he shouldn't have, and too deeply at that." Dredd approached them and answered for the nonplussed cadet.

"What?" Captain Morrisey looked surprised.

"I beg to report, sir, that I fucked the Admiral's youngest daughter!" Nike explained to his new superior slightly louder than the situation demanded.

The laughter of the lecturers standing nearby died out in an instant.

TWO

"DID HE REALLY SAY THAT?" asked Heraclesteban Iarrey, the *Nomad*'s skinny beanpole of a first officer, wiping the sweat off his neck with a paper towel and throwing the wet tissue straight onto the deck.

The extractors began to recycle the thin paper the moment it touched the metal grille. Someone had decided that the temperature on the bridge of the wrecker would imitate the tropics. It must have been the captain, because none of the regular crew were protesting.

"Really." Morrisey, sitting in a chair with his legs crossed on the table, continued to examine the files of the five cadets who were standing meekly in a row by the wall beside the food dispenser.

They were all more or less the same height and build, as if those criteria were the reason they had ended up onboard the *Nomad*.

"And Dredd didn't kill him?" Iarrey said in amazement, taking another paper towel.

"He would have, as God's my witness. But the boy was already under my command." Morrisey waved Nike's card.

"You were lucky then, son." The *Nomad*'s chief navigator,

cornet-pilot Annataly Davidoff-Rozerer, the only woman onboard, examined the new arrivals as though they were goods displayed for sale. "If our good old boss wasn't such a martinet—"

"I promised the old man that for a small fee the turd won't survive his first job," Morrisey added casually.

Loud laughter roared through the mess hall. Even Father Pedroberto, the *Nomad's* chaplain, chuckled. Only the cadets maintained prescribed silence.

"All right, I owe you a welcome, so here goes—" The reader was finally put away in a pocket and the feet of the *Nomad's* captain touched the deck. "My name, as you may well know by now, is Henrichard Morrisey and the rules are very simple and easy to remember.

"Firstly, onboard this vessel I'm more important than God the Father, the Son, and the Holy Spirit. Secondly, if you thought that Admiral Dreade-Ravenore was the worst cunt in our sector, you'll soon find out that you didn't have a clue what real cunti-ness is. Thirdly, the work we've got to do is in no way easy or safe. The fact that the *Nomad* needed five new cadets this year ought to tell you a lot about the tasks awaiting us, or rather, I should say, you.

"Recycling Corps third wing, of which we are part, has received from High Command the order to clean up the noto-rious Victor Sector. So far we've managed to do roughly half the job. Now we're just reaching the Victor 3A13 system, if that name means anything to you. Well?" He glared at the cadets, who nodded fervently. "In that case I'd like to hear a short summary of major battles in this system," he said and pointed at the first one in the line.

"We gave them a good kicking, sir!" Peterasmus De'Vere had the sixth score—counting from the wrong end, of course, which came as no surprise considering his appearance alone suggested a total absence of gray matter.

"We gave them a good kicking, you say? A very interesting

statement … though if you think about it a bit longer, totally wrong."

"They gave us a good kicking, sir!" The cadet grinned triumphantly.

Morrisey shook his head in disbelief. De'Vere was struck dumb.

"Was it a tie?" he asked in amazement.

"Ties, you pathetic excuse for a cadet, are what judges from the space league call. Perhaps *you* will tell us about it?" The captain's finger passed Nike over and rested on the chest of Christopherasmus Carre-Four.

The foolish smile faded from the narrow lips of the aristocratic slim face the moment the cadet understood that the order didn't apply to Nike.

"I don't think I'll be able to—" mumbled the fourth clone of an aristocrat from a second-rate planet.

"You think right, you clone-of-a-bitching spawn!" Morrisey interrupted him unceremoniously, and, ignoring the crimson spots which had appeared on the cadet's cheeks, roared at the top of his voice, "And what do you, slobs, have to say for yourselves?!"

To that question neither Josephilip Kolczuk, a pimply and taciturn midget said to be the bastard son of a prominent bigwig from Earth, nor his total opposite, Yukitaro Domita, the fourteenth child of a serf from a planet with such a complicated name that no one dared utter it in its entirety, could come up with an answer. Which was actually not so surprising, since—like the first pair questioned—they represented the Academy's lowest intellectual level and would never have graduated, had it not been for positive discrimination and pressure from the governments of lesser sectors. Not to mention the High Command's plans regarding the replenishment of Recycling Corps' crew.

Finally, Morrisey pointed at Nike.

"Victor 3A13 is the catalogue name of the system known in

astronavigational atlases as New Rouen. It consists of a single G4-type star and eight planets. It is distinguished by an extremely high concentration of hyperspace tunnels," recited the recent high-flyer of the Fleet's best school, standing as stiff as a ramrod.

"For that reason, during the war, New Rouen was one of the most important transfer points in the Victor Sector. The Federation planned to take control of it at the beginning of the conflict in order to cut off some of the enemy's distant planetary systems from hyperspace supplies. To that end two strike teams were sent, which were supposed to attack at the same time the installations on Delta, the only inhabited planet in the system, and an orbital transit station, built before the rebellion of the outer colonies. That operation unfortunately resulted in the utter defeat of the Federation's forces. The enemy, for the first time in the history of space conflicts, planted mines at the predicted entry points around the gateways, thus breaking all known conventions. Moreover, the rebels had gathered considerable space forces to protect the defense command of the entire subsector, which was being established right then on Delta. Admiral Tahomey led his striking force out right onto one of the minefields and lost almost half of his frontline vessels immediately after leaving hyperspace.

"The second task force had more luck during the first stage of the operation, but as it soon turned out, four squadrons of battleships defending the headquarters and the transit station were a tough nut to crack even for the Federation's most modern vessels. It could be said that no clear victor emerged from the battle. Most of the system's defensive installations were destroyed, but control over it was not regained. The two fleets inflicted heavy damage on each other in the battle, which lasted almost thirteen hours, and—"

"All right. That's enough!" Morrisey interrupted the cadet, and placed his feet on the table once again. "Cadet Stachursky has done his homework, which can't be said about the rest of your little gang. Which is why from now on the remaining honorable cadets will have numbers instead of names. You"—he pointed at De'Vere—"will be One, you"—he aimed his finger at Carre—"Two … No, wait … Mother Nature has already given you a number, you clone-of-a-bitching spawn, so you'll be, as God and Daddy—forgive me—the Donor wanted, Four. That makes Kolczuk Three, and Mr.—urgh—Sodomita Two. Cadet Stachursky remains Cadet Stachursky, unless and until I have a yen to change it, and will be the liaison between the captain and the numbered crew, meaning that none of you will ever address me directly without my express permission. All of you will communicate with me exclusively via Cadet Stachursky. Furthermore, none of you numbers, unless you are ordered to, have access to the upper deck. Is that clear?"

"Yes, sir!" they answered in unison.

If nothing else, at least the Academy instilled discipline into all its cadets.

"And in case anyone wonders what these numbers mean, I'll explain it right away," continued the captain. "It's an old custom in frontline vessels. When I issue the order, for example, to go into open space, I won't have to point a finger, or call anyone by name. Number One goes first, and if he fucks up—meaning he buys it—he's followed by Number Two, then Three and so on. Is that clear?"

This time, the response was not quite so unanimous.

"Bog off!" yelled Morrisey. "Cadet Stachursky will stay with us for a moment longer, though."

———

"Do you know, son, why I ordered you to stay?" asked the captain after the other cadets had left the bridge.

"No, sir!" answered Stachursky truthfully.

"You really don't know?"

"Really, sir!" Nike tried to think something up on the spot, but he had no idea what his new commanding officer was getting at.

Morrisey put the cadet out of his misery.

"I've seen your file, so I know you're one of the aces of the fucking orbital Academy. It's unfortunate that you chose the wrong hole and fucked, ha-ha"—the captain's laugh turned out to be infectious—"literally fucked up your own life. But you aren't stupid, quite the opposite, so you'll quickly find out that not everything they say about the Recycling Corps is true. And since this is the way things are I'd rather suggest a deal right away."

Iarrey, the navigator, the chaplain, and the lieutenant responsible for the weapons systems, who seemed to be called Bourne —that much could be deciphered from his dirty name tag—and who up till then had been silent, surrounded the disorientated cadet.

"What kind of deal, sir?" Nike inquired tentatively.

"Do you know why all the battles of the Unification War and generally all the skirmishes in space occurred in the vicinity of the Lagrangian points?" the captain asked out of nowhere.

"In theory—" Nike began, deciding to play safe.

"Go on."

"During our lectures we were told it had something to do with tactics, but the truth is probably that no one was thrilled by the thought of a slow and anonymous death in a cosmic void far from any routes. For which reason the captains preferred to fight in places called libration points or Lagrangian points in honor of—"

"Keep it brief, son," the captain cut in.

"—to fight in gravitational zones where damaged and annihilated craft will remain for a long time, creating something like asteroid fields or belts, somewhat resembling the rings of Saturn, owing to which one can hope with a fair degree of probability for search and rescue operations. That is also why, since the beginning of the conquest of space, all tactics have involved static warfare. No heavy vessel joined battle at speeds exceeding zero point zero zero four standard light speed, in order not to break out of the Lagrangian point following destruction."

"And what does it mean in practice?"

"In practice it means that almost all the vessels destroyed in battle are still orbiting in L-points, assuming they haven't broken out of the gravitational trap as a result of unforeseen circumstances and fallen onto the surface of nearby planets."

Nike thought of Dredd and his eighty-year odyssey in a rescue capsule. Had it not been for that tactic, the Admiral would long ago have become a lump of frozen meat drifting through the unending void, or a gorgeous meteor slicing through the sky of a distant planet.

"Excellent," Morrisey laughed heartily. "A very apt conclusion, Cadet Stachursky. And what does that mean for us?"

"We don't need to work our backsides off."

"That's true, but—"

"—but a smart, pretty boy like you ought to know by now that one can make a good living out of it."

That was the moment Nike understood why the lieutenant responsible for the weapons systems seldom spoke. Bourne's high-pitched, squeaky voice was particularly hard on the ears.

"We'll offer you a small share of the profits in exchange for total and complete obedience, and looking after that trash." The captain nodded toward the elevator door through which the remaining cadets had disappeared a moment before.

"A share of the profits, sir?" repeated Nike.

"You really don't get it, do you?" Morrisey, just like the other crew members, seemed sincerely amused. "If you play by the High Command's rules you live a quiet life. If you play by ours, the job may be fucking dangerous"—he held up his hand, showing his electronic prosthesis—"but fucking profitable, too. You'll do your time onboard the *Nomad* and a tasty bonus to your pension will be waiting for you."

"And the numbers will do most of the dirty work for us anyway," added Iarrey.

"The fact is we have specialized robots," explained the captain, "but they are bloody expensive. Destroying a machine like that means tons of detailed reports, which often go beyond the investigative department. The death of a lowest rank cadet means only a letter to the parents, a medal, and, very rarely, some paltry financial compensation—"

"Plus, the greater the losses in action, the better," whispered Annataly almost sensually, leaning toward Nike's ear.

"The more dead, the more moronic are the people willing to work in the Recycling Corps," Morrisey took up the subject. "But no one weeps over the casualties, particularly not top brass who get a tidy bonus from our scam. Especially considering that we save them a bunch of hassle with … let's not beat about the bush … academic refuse."

"If I understand right," said the candidate for shareholder in Nomad & Co., "first we penetrate and then we destroy?"

"*Penetrate?* I like the way your mind works, Nike." The captain smiled at his own thoughts. "Spatial archaeology is a wonderful field of science, particularly if you have backup in the form of top-secret maps and access to all the Fleet's archives …" Morrisey trailed off. "Are you in or not?"

"What will happen if I turn the offer down?" Nike asked cautiously.

"I made Dredd a promise, and I'm a man of my word." The calm, even humorous answer was a clear threat. "I only break a promise when it's in my interests to do so."

"I get it." Nike looked his commanding officer in the eye and nodded. "I'm in. That only leaves one matter—"

"Two," the captain interrupted him bluntly.

"Two?" Nike said in surprise.

"Yes. First of all, the financial aspect. To avoid misunderstandings. You know what they say: let's love each other like brothers, but reckon up like clones. You'll get ten percent of the profit from all joint operations and fifty percent from your own."

"Okay." The offer seemed fair, and anyway in his current situation Nike would have agreed to any deal, even much worse.

Morrisey suddenly grew serious.

"Second, boy ..." That *boy* sounded ominous. "Lieutenant Davidoff-Rozerer is the only woman onboard, and as you probably realize, she's mine, and only mine. I'm not good ol' Uncle Dredd and I won't spend half a semester wondering how to whip your arse in a sophisticated manner. If I discover just one— never mind how tiny—trace of your presence in her, I'll—" He made a gesture with his prosthesis which might have meant anything. "Got it, Mr. Daughterfucker?"

Nike glanced furtively at the navigator's jumpsuit—or more precisely at the body, which the tight piece of shiny material was covering. Then he looked straight in Bourne's twinkling eyes. He did not smile back.

"Got it," he nodded, and reached for his kitbag. "By your leave, sir."

"Just a moment ..." The captain's searching gaze was still on him.

"Yes, sir?"

"Your name. Nike. Why don't you have a standard double-barrel, like every decent person?" Morrisey asked.

"I do, sir," Nike answered.

"So why don't you use it then?" Annataly looked genuinely shocked.

"I do. It's formed from Nik and Ike.

"Ha, I know an Ikenneth, but I'm sure Nick's spelt differently," Iarrey butted in.

"My father's family came from the New Russian sector, which is why the first part's spelt differently," Nike explained. "After some famous—God knows how many 'greats'—grandfather. He was supposed to have been a successful author on Earth around the end of the Old Era."

THREE

THE NEW ROUEN SYSTEM, VICTOR SECTOR

06/27/2354

They left hyperspace a long way from the star shown on the Federation's maps as Victor 3A13, a dozen or so degrees beyond the ecliptic plane, at the edge of the calculated safety field. The *Nomad*'s captain preferred to enter the system at a neutral point, in order to fly to the distant Delta, keeping well away from any deep-space debris. Today, when state-of-the-art navigational systems could calculate jumps with the accuracy of the location of the departure point from subspace close to a billion miles per light-year, they could approach any system without the need of using wormholes and the risk of coming across the remains of battles waged ages ago, or flying straight into a trap set by long-dead defenders. All they needed was to travel down a traditional route to the neighboring planetary system and make the last jump using tachyonic hyperspace drive. There was a downside to this, though, and a serious one at that—the flight at subluminal speed had to be longer, because the points of departure were usually located very far from the destination.

On the third standard day after arriving in the system, Morrisey showed up on the upper deck and right away dropped into the worn-out commander's chair. Annataly was still reading off data from distant reconnaissance probes, which had been shot off toward all the libration points in the system two days earlier. Iarrey was cataloguing the results, and Bourne and Nike were biding their time at the spare control panels, occasionally checking selected readings. The chaplain and the other cadets had still not been woken. Before the rest came out of hibernation, the *Nomad*'s automated systems had examined the entire planetary system. Now all that was left for people to do was to analyze the data and get to work.

"When will we have the full picture?" Morrisey asked, having fastened his seatbelt.

"In around five standard minutes," Iarrey answered.

Morrisey nodded, stuck a lump of something olive green into his mouth and started to chew on it.

"I'm waiting, First Officer," he said suddenly, and then spat into the grating beneath the main screen.

"It hasn't even been a minute," Iarrey replied, slightly ruffled.

"All depends on how you look at it," the captain retorted enigmatically, activating the panoramicon.

The curved walls of the bridge changed color and in a few seconds became transparent. During so-called transparent flight close to a planet, disorientation affects a few percent of experienced astronauts, but in space it's not a problem. Nothing disturbs the inner ear, particularly when the equipment on the bridge allows one to establish reference points, hypothetical vertical and horizontal planes.

The center of a planetary system with a single G4-type star was directly in front of the ship's bow. The screens displayed the iridescent green orbits of all the planets and their satellites, and the routes of most heavenly bodies passing through the proximal space in their eternal trek through the Universe, which were marked in red. There was some deep-space debris, but not enough to spoil the impression of being out in a vacuum.

"We have the proper cluster in orbit of the system's fourth

planet," Iarrey said. "The parameters agree with the baseline data. Most of the wreckage, around ninety-seven percent of predicted mass, remains in the zone. However, I have a few readings outside the L-point. Some of the scrap is already beginning to get out of the gravitational trap. Just a few more years, and—"

"Don't get carried away, Iarrey," the captain interrupted him. "What about the mines?"

"The probes were sent forty-seven hours ago, and we've localized traces of sixteen of the twenty fields mentioned in the intercepted reports of the colonists. The four remaining ones may not exist any longer."

"As far as I know, no entire minefield has ever disappeared or been detonated," the captain murmured, clawing his prosthesis. "I'm not moving my arse from here until you have all the obstacles located."

Iarrey shrugged and continued to check the data on his control panel.

"What do we do with the fields we've located?" he asked a moment later.

"What do you think? Get rid of the shit."

You can't hear anything in a vacuum, but the views are gorgeous was how the Academy's lecturers praised the system navigation. Now their words took on a new light. The myriads of nanoscouts accompanying the probes entered the nuclear minefields, which had been planted a hundred and thirty years earlier to prevent access. The inky-black void suddenly flashed with an explosion of colors. It wasn't anything like a firework display, but it was nonetheless enchanting. Dozens of explosions merging with one another, slowly waning plasma, a halo with colors much more vivid than a rainbow's. Had today's technology existed a century before, strike team number one would have cut through the minefield like a laser beam through paper. Unfortunately, Admiral Tahomey could only rely on luck, which is why today some one hundred and eighty wrecks of various kinds were orbiting a planet whose original name no one remembered anymore.

"We've got coordinates for the remains of the four minefields, which were entered by strike team number one," announced Annataly, who had also begun processing the data. "Actually they don't exist. The wrecks detonated most of the mines left after the first pass, and the ones that didn't explode then are sure not to go off now."

"You can never be sure, honey bunny," Morrisey muttered. "Do you have any readings for active mines left inside the junk belt?"

"No more than ten," Annataly replied.

"Do we have visuals?"

"Sure."

On the panoramicon appeared images showing the distribution of hypothetically undetonated mines. All the representations were calibrated so as not to disorientate the viewers. Suddenly, the Delta grew much bigger, as though in a fraction of a second they had traveled millions of miles. Then they "moved" quickly around the globe, switching to the frequencies used by different probes.

"Mr. Bourne?"

The short question was enough for the officer to treat everyone to a brief lecture on how to neutralize each mine. It was packed full of technical terminology and mathematical formulae, but the point was straightforward and could have been expressed in a few words: they couldn't use the collapsars for remote gathering in of all the wreckage without running the risk of random explosions and spreading the remains outside the zone.

"When will the H-probes be in place?" Morrisey asked.

"The first wave is already in orbit, the mapping of the libration point was finished fifteen minutes ago," Iarrey answered calmly as usual.

The microprobes of the holovisualization network allowed

them to create a 3D map of the whole zone and to assess the situation.

"Let's have a look." The first officer switched the panoramicon over to the view transmitted by the probes' synchronized cameras.

In the blink of an eye they were right in the center of the junk belt. The wrecked ships and flotsam created a dense field spreading out over an area of thousands of cubic miles around the Lagrangian point, in the form of an amazing—and quite solid—metal and plastic structure. Only shreds remained of the majority of the vessels, particularly the smaller ones; destruction initiated by the enemy's lasers had been completed by Nature itself. Endless collisions with neighboring wrecks had transformed the once proud ships into a scrap heap. The crew members of the *Nomad* watched a series of similar images in silence. From time to time they could make out the torn-open and disemboweled hulls of corvettes and destroyers. Too damaged, however, to be worth taking a closer look.

"Welcome to Monsieur Lagrange's hell," Morrisey commented sarcastically. "Here the treasures of the past await their discoverers, and death—losers."

While the probes were transmitting almost identical images of the field of a long-forgotten battle that had been fought a hundred and thirty years earlier, Iarrey was localizing further mines and preparing to remotely detonate the ones which didn't have bulks of scrap in their vicinity.

They scoured the zone systematically, but it was fifteen minutes before anything caught their eye. The plump hull of an ancient battleship sailed majestically out of the planet's shadow cone. Morrisey, who was just entering the activation codes for more nanoscouts, immediately ordered the image to be projected onto the main screen and had less important information removed from it. The nearest probes were only a few miles from the well-preserved bow of the battleship, which meant that Nike could easily read off the clearly visible number and even part of the name, which for many people was still a symbol of the victorious fight for unification. The huge battleship seemed untouched. Even the impact of the heavy fragments of other vessels couldn't damage such a powerful sheathing—and they hadn't yet seen any wrecks bigger than the flagship's in this part of the libration point. The battleship, revolving slowly around its axis, soon filled the entire screen. It seemed to be sailing right under the *Nomad*'s bridge, although in reality over a billion miles still separated the two ships.

Morrisey sprawled in his chair, smiling imperiously.

"Mr. Stachursky, what do we have here?" he asked.

"FSS *Odin*, pennant number BS 61, Admiral Tahomey's flagship," Nike recited from memory. "One million one hundred sixty thousand tons of displacement mass, actual hull length eight hundred ten yards, diameter at its widest point seventy-two yards, weaponry ..."

"That's enough," Morrisey interrupted, still grinning. "To put it briefly, this is our El Dorado! Timeworn, but not exhausted."

The captain's prosthesis pointed at the screen.

Right then they saw the darkened, jagged edges of just one of many immense holes in the sheathing, which extended from amidships to the narrowing of the propulsion section.

FOUR

LESS THAN A HUNDRED HOURS LATER, drifting at
the edge of the libration point with the deflectors at full power,
they watched up close the melted sheathing around the dark
hole leading straight into the wreck. The outer layer of frozen
helon took incredibly beautiful shapes. The evaporating white-
hot metal had hardened in a split second in contact with the
absolutely cold vacuum. Many of these fragile sculptures had
been destroyed during the wreck's century-long passage
through space, but several had been preserved remarkably well.
They could admire one of them in full close up now. A geyser of
molten metal had spurted from the wreck's innards and solidified in the eternal frost, creating a shape in which a human form
was clear even for someone devoid of imagination. The helon
giant was pointing its outstretched arms toward the perfect
blackness of space. There were more limbs than necessary, and
one might have caviled at the proportions, but nonetheless this
masterpiece didn't seem any more avant-garde than the sculptures gracing the fashionable contemporary art galleries on the
Federation's planets.

"Beautiful, isn't it?" Morrisey pointed at the crystal-white
melted helon. "As though Mother Nature wanted to warn us—"

The piercing wail of an alarm siren interrupted him. Iarrey lunged for the control panel and with one slap restored silence on the bridge; a silence that was immediately filled with the shouts of the crew members.

"Shut your traps, you clones-of-bitches!" Henrichard Morrisey's shrilling voice was as effective as Iarrey's hand a moment before. "First Officer, report!"

"Active mine on a collision course," whispered Iarrey. Everyone heard him quite clearly in the deadly silence.

"So what?" the captain snarled contemptuously at him. "It's not the first and it won't be the last. What is that junk anyway?"

"M7." The first officer still didn't raise his voice.

Morrisey blanched; all saw it.

"Patient Death," Nike murmured.

Thus had that kind of plasma mine been christened years ago and thus was it still called. Planted by rebels in the last phase of the conflict, chiefly in the proximity of the Federation's transport nodes, they were capable of lying in wait, perfectly camouflaged, for decades; and so they took a bloody toll on the stellar routes long after their creators had surrendered. They hung someplace in space, concealed in their designated positions, waiting for that one and only victim, even though the war was long over. Left to themselves, forgotten, but utterly self-sufficient, self-homing, and almost indestructible smart, powerful high explosives against which there was no defense.

"What are the readings?" Morrisey asked in a much less confident voice.

"It locked on to us eight seconds ago," Iarrey replied. "It's a classic rebel tech."

"Distance?"

"Seven hundred and fifty clicks to the blast zone and falling."

"Honey ..."

"I have all the coordinates. I'm slowing our approach."

"How much time left?" the captain asked.

"Seven minutes tops, if Annataly knows what she's doing." Iarrey needed a few seconds to answer the question.

"Watch your own arse," cornet-pilot Davidoff-Rozerer pouted.

Morrisey, who had already put himself together, looked at the cadet.

"Any suggestions?" he asked.

"The best tactic in this case is to reduce approach speed to a minimum, send out a distress signal, and abandon ship in the stern rescue capsules before the craft enters the blast zone, sir!" Nike trotted out obediently.

"Sure, sure." A grimace somewhat resembling a smile appeared on the captain's face. "That's what the textbooks say. We love this tub like our own home and we'd rather die than let it be damaged, wouldn't we?"

The rest of the crew nodded, without much conviction, though.

"So what would the army do in this case?"

Nike said nothing. The captain spat on the grille, activating the extractors.

"Number One, put on a spacesuit," Morrisey said after a moment of awkward silence, "and go to the bow airlock. Numbers Two and Three will wait in full kit in the port and starboard secondary airlocks. Number Four will go to the hold by the rootler. Kitted out in a full spacesuit, too. We'll defuse the mine during our approach. You've got a minute to carry out my orders."

Morrisey got up from his chair before finishing. Nike didn't even flinch when the *Nomad*'s captain disappeared behind his back. The foul odor of grease mixed with the spicy smell of the stuff he never stopped chewing told the cadet his new superior officer had stopped right behind him.

"But waking them will take—" Nike felt a shiver run down his back.

"True, Cadet. The problem is the numbers are still sleeping

soundly and the only crew member we can sacrifice right now is you." He heard the captain's voice just behind his right ear.

"I beg to report, sir, that the use of inexperienced cadets to defuse smart mines of this class would be suicide," Nike answered, trying to stay calm.

He was aware of his abilities, which weren't much greater than those of the other four cadets. He also precisely knew the parameters of the mine standing in their path. That combination didn't leave a shadow of doubt.

"True." This time, Morrisey's voice was behind his left ear. "Have I never mentioned I really am one nasty bastard?" the captain asked and suddenly snorted with laughter.

Surprised by his reaction Nike shuddered involuntarily, feeling a slight spray of saliva on his ear and the back of his cropped head. He glanced nervously at the other crew members. They didn't look as worried as they had a moment earlier.

"M7, Patient Death, armed and dangerous," the captain continued, amused, appearing in Nike's line of vision again. "Do you know what it *really* means?"

Nike shook his head.

"It's an absolute guarantee that no one has ever rummaged around in our giant's bowels," Morrisey smiled meaningfully. "The Mark Seven is a terrifying weapon, which sowed terror in the hearts of our crews. A ruthless killer you can't escape from. Unless you happen to have ..."

He turned and raised an eyebrow inquiringly.

"... the deactivation codes?" Nike finished the sentence timidly.

"Excellent, my young friend!" the captain slapped his back and laughed aloud. "High Command was kind enough to supply us with the available set of code tables, both ours and the rebels'. All we have to do is decipher the code sent with the localization signal, give the appropriate response sequence, and our M7 will become a regular pile of scrap, and our numbered buddies won't wake up before we're back from rifling through our untouched haul of treasure. You won't be asking for time to change your underwear, will you?"

"Treat that joke as a baptism of fire," Annataly added. "We usually do it to the numbers, but sometimes one has to make do ..."

Nike smiled, seeing the amused expressions of the others, but frowned just a moment later. If they wanted some fun they'd get some.

"You mentioned the available set of tables. Does that mean we don't have all the codes?"

He noticed with unalloyed pleasure that sweat beaded the forehead of the gorgeous navigator, Iarrey rushed to the control panels, and Morrisey paled once again. This time, the captain didn't even have to pretend.

FIVE

THEY ENTERED the wreck through the widest breach. Two teams of two plus transport robots. Bourne was with Iarrey. Their job was to investigate the lower decks, or actually the only section in that part of the ship that hadn't been totally destroyed. The other team, consisting of Morrisey and Nike, had to check the bow part of the battleship's upper decks. Annataly was monitoring the operation from the *Nomad*'s bridge.

They searched cabins, passageways, and holds, loading on the transport drones everything that hadn't been sucked into space after the crash. Morrisey didn't seem to attach much importance to searching and opening successive cabins; before Nike had finished loading up the required objects, the captain would disappear into the next passageway, checking the readings on his holopad.

Two standard hours after boarding the wreck, having moved along elevator shafts, they reached the main passageway connecting the bridge to the officers' living quarters. The arched, undamaged vault stretched away for fifty yards, ending in a massive bulkhead.

"Bingo," Morrisey muttered, gliding farther down the passageway and shining his torch onto the ceiling, section by section. "The bridge seems unharmed. Give me the coder and a mobile reactor, right now."

The captain, staring at the wall of solid helon, didn't take notice of the cadet's silence at first. Eventually he realized Nike hadn't heard his instructions. "What the fuck ..."

He started to turn around and only then did he see what the beam of light from his partner's suit torch was pointing at. The door of the nearest elevator wasn't closed: a boot of a spacesuit was sticking out, the electromagnetic studs on its sole clearly visible.

"Nike?" Morrisey sounded serious. "Can you hear me, boy?"

There was no answer. The cadet hadn't even moved.

"Nike, you clone-of-a-bitch!" the captain roared, achieving the desired effect.

"Yes, sir?"

"What are you staring at? Never seen a dead body?"

"No, sir, I haven't."

"Well, that's one debut out of the way." Morrisey flew up to the door, stuck both gloved hands in the gap and tried to move it. It would not budge.

"Annataly, can you hear me?" he switched to the bridge's frequency. "I need a repair drone."

There was no response for a few seconds, but the navigator answered before the captain became impatient.

"Iarrey's breaking into some chambers, he'll be done in five minutes."

"Five minutes, galacticunt!" The captain turned around and looked at the bulkhead. "Okay, get me another coder and a reactor. I also have a little door to open."

"I'm on it, sir." This time, the answer was fast and concise.

"And you—stop twiddling your thumbs." Morrisey slapped the cadet on the arm. "Use the scope to check there aren't any more of these inside."

Reluctantly, Nike did as he was told. He flew over to the gap, cautiously, and fed a telescopic camera into the cylindrical cage.

A moment later, he had an image of the interior. The man whose boot they had seen was in the elevator alone. His suit appeared to be intact, at least on the surface. Nike communicated the information to the captain. It was ignored, just as he had expected. Morrisey, whistling merrily to himself, was unscrewing the casing of the scanner panel by the lock. Nike resumed his observation of the elevator's interior. In spite of being trained to fight, he shuddered at the presence of a dead person, or, to be more precise, the corpse lying literally at arm's length. Many people had died in that battle, some sucked out of the mutilated hulls, others burnt alive or vaporized in reactor explosions, but this man must have had a lingering death. He continued to live, imprisoned in the wreck, until the air in his tanks ran out. Six or even ten hours …

"Well?" Morrisey's voice brought Nike out of his reverie again. "Show me what we've got here."

The captain steered the camera for a while and then suddenly whistled. He looked down the passageway where the coding robot was just plugging into the bulkhead's panel. The massive cube of the mobile plasma reactor had already been connected up and all the lights in the entire section came on. Morrisey smacked the glowing red call button on the elevator, but it still didn't react. The mechanism had frozen over a hundred years earlier, so there was no chance of it working.

"Ann!" the captain yelled into the comlink, as though he'd been bitten in the backside. "Get me that drone down here!"

"But Iarrey's still not—"

"And he's never going to. Tell him to cut a passage through with your nail file. I've got something awesome here and I need that drone right now!"

"You've got it, sir."

Nike looked at the irate captain in confusion.

"What did you see there, sir?" he finally asked.

"It's one of Tahomey's staff officers," Morrisey answered, and added at once, "If you'd looked closer at what's sticking out from under the body, you'd have seen what might be the last ship's hololog. And that, my dear, is worth an unbelievable fortune on Earth. And I saw it first. You snooze you lose." He poked a metal finger into the cadet's chest.

"Yes, sir!"

A moment later, the shaft through which they had reached the main passageway lit up in a pale-green glow. A massive repair drone emerged from inside and froze two feet away from them. Morrisey plugged the end of his programmer into the reader and the huge robot began moving again. Its long pincers plunged into the gap. For a while nothing happened, or at least it seemed that way. Sound didn't carry in a vacuum, but the chips of paint floating away from the oval door told the two men that immense force was being applied to its surface. Just in case, Morrisey pulled the cadet farther into the passageway, yet still nothing happened. The mechanism had either jammed for good, or something else was blocking the door.

"We'll cut it," the captain decided, and the drone obediently extended a burner.

Twenty seconds later, almost half of the metal plate blocking the way to the elevator was hanging by the wall of the passage-way, and Morrisey was dragging the body from the cage through the freshly cut opening. The captain's triumphant expression vanished in an instant when he saw what the corpse was holding.

"Shit!" he said throwing the obsolete electronic notebook toward the deck. "The diary of ..." He looked at the name tag. "Major Visolay, fucking moron, who couldn't even get into an elevator properly. What kind of name is that anyway?"

"Perhaps it's worth something." Nike caught the gliding notebook and connected it to his power pack, but the display remained blank. "I'll be able to open it up on the *Nomad*."

"Who gives a damn what that asshole wrote?" Morrisey snarled.

"I might find something interesting—"

"Strip him," the captain suddenly ordered.

"Say what?"

"I said, strip the body. Get his suit off him."

"But …"

"But me no buts. Time is money. An antique, undamaged suit will fetch a good price on Earth."

"I can't …" Nike felt genuine horror at the thought of having to touch a dead man. "We can't just—"

"Yes, we can," Morrisey interrupted him. "Move it, we still have to check the bridge."

"No. I won't do that, sir!"

"You're starting to piss me off, Cadet. And anybody who pisses me off comes to a sorry end."

"I … I just can't …"

It seemed as though the captain would hit the ceiling, but instead he plugged into the drone and when it set off again toward the bulkhead with burners heating up, he seized the corpse's arm and began to fiddle around with the helmet seal.

"We ought to give him a funeral in line with—" Nike began.

"Don't teach your grandmother to suck eggs," the captain cut him off. "We'll give him a funeral, but he'll have to pay for it first."

The *Nomad*'s captain deftly pulled the mummified remains out of the spacesuit. In the ghastly flashes of rapidly setting fountains of plasma from the bulkhead being torn open, Nike saw the non-regulation long hair on the major's shriveled head. He turned away so as not to see the dead man's face, but couldn't ignore Morrisey's behavior. The captain threw the spacesuit into the transport drone's container and leaned over the corpse once more. He didn't go for the dog tags, as might have been expected, but began to struggle with the dead man's hand. He was pulling off the officer's ring!

"Don't say anything!" Morrisey snapped, seeing the expression on the cadet's face. "Now me and Mr. Visolay are quits."

He stood up, threw away a piece of finger he had torn off

accidentally, and examined the ring, lifting it up close to his visor. "A brainiac, just like you."

Nike didn't answer, still feeling contempt for his new commanding officer, but decided not to exacerbate the situation. The Academy had taught him obedience, among other things.

"Oh, yes," muttered the captain, looking at the plans of the ship on his holopad again.

He pointed at the irregular breach cutting the hull at a sharp angle and marked in red. "If that impact hasn't depressurized all the chambers on the command subdeck, we have a really big deal in store. The bridge, Tahomey's cabin ... Do you know how much his private archive will be worth?"

Nike shook his head inside his spacious helmet, although he doubted that moony Morrisey could see it.

"Boy, we have the chance of getting our hands on a fortune, the size of which no one has ever dreamed of."

"How much?" Nike asked, more to keep the conversation going than out of curiosity.

Standing idly in a passageway of the moribund ship, lit up by showers of sparks, sent shivers down his spine, particularly now, in the company of Major Visolay's corpse.

"They won't pay less for the Admiral's logs on Earth than—"

Morrisey didn't manage to say anything else because Annataly's voice drowned him out.

"Captain, we've got a problem," the navigator said in her usual expressionless tone.

"Be more precise, honey," Morrisey snapped.

"A large lump of a rebel corvette is on a collision course—"

"Get out of its way, or do some target practice and don't bother me with crap like that!" Morrisey said furiously and returned to watching the bulkhead being ripped open.

"But, sir ... It's a collision course with the wreck of the *Odin* ..."

"What?!" the captain roared. Even through the fogged-up crystallite his eyes could clearly be seen shining. "We're going to be on the bridge in five, six minutes. Can't you destroy that shit? Or at least knock it a few degrees off course—"

"I've done the maths three times already. No chance," the navigator retorted. "It's a gutted, but almost complete Samurai class corvette. Two hundred and fifty thousand tons of fucking helon composite, and going at a fair lick—"

"Do something!" Morrisey yelled. "I'll give you an extra three ... no, wait, five percent!"

"You have eight minutes to get back into space," Annataly's voice was flat as though a computer and not a living creature were speaking.

"That's an order—" the captain began.

"Seven minutes, fifty-five seconds ..."

"Galacticunt! We're so close!"

"Seven minutes fifty seconds to impact."

"Why didn't you tell me about it sooner, bitch?!" Morrisey roared.

"Because the object entered the collision course literally two minutes ago, after hitting a fucking asteroid which turned into a cloud of dust in front of my eyes, you stupid prick!" That response from the *Nomad* was much more emotional, at least the latter part.

Annataly got a grip on herself and added calmly, "The second team are already withdrawing, sir."

"Give me ten minutes, just ten fucking minutes and we'll be on the bridge!"

"You won't manage to search it in three minutes, and then it'll be too late to spend what you've collected in your swag bag. You won't just be losing a hand this time."

A little anxious, Nike flew over to Morrisey and placed his hand on the commanding officer's armored shoulder.

"We can come back after the impact," he suggested. "Perhaps we'll be able to—"

"Like fuck we will," Morrisey bristled. "Do you know what a quarter-ton lump of metal will do to this wreck?"

"Not much, maybe," Nike calmly replied. "It depends on how fast it's flying and what the angle of approach is."

"Knowing Ann, that bloody corvette's flying fucking fast," the captain muttered, looking down at his prosthesis. "Otherwise she wouldn't have made such a fuss—"

"Extremely fucking fast, or even faster," the chief navigator interrupted him. "The impact will probably destroy both wrecks. At best, the remains will be pushed out of the zone; at worst they'll end up in Delta's atmosphere. Get your asses out of there while you still can. Six minutes twenty seconds."

Morrisey spat, quite simply spat inside his crystallite helmet, and then keyed in the sequence to stop the robot's work. Finally, he kicked the major's mummified remains with all his strength.

"It's your fault, you cretinous clone-of-a-bitching stiff. It's your fault ..."

For a moment Nike didn't know what to do. Fly after the soldier's body gliding down the passageway, or help to disconnect the robots. Morrisey solved his dilemma by pulling him onto the repair drone, which was already moving toward the elevator. They both seized its arms and shot down the arched passageway toward the nearest breach. Nike turned the comlink volume almost all the way down, so as not to hear the captain's colorful oaths, cursing the conspiracy of the late major, his lame crew, and all the gods known to Humankind.

They entered space a minute and a half before the collision of the two giants. Morrisey, continuing to curse through clenched teeth, didn't even turn around to look at the incredible spectacle. Nike, on the other hand, could not take his eyes off it.

SIX

"WHY DIDN'T our computers calculate the possibility of the impact earlier?!"

Almost an hour had passed since the crash, but Captain Morrisey was still savaging.

"How can you calculate in advance the outcome of the interaction of a million elements?" Iarrey repeated for the fiftieth time. "I've analyzed the final minutes data several times. There's no way we could have predicted it. It was a sequence of collisions, which began—I'm sure you'll find this funny—with the *Nomad*'s entry onto the edge of the junk belt. The pieces pushed away by the deflective field set off the process which ended up with that."

He pointed at the sorry-looking remains, which had once been two proud warships.

Morrisey looked at him reproachfully. He said nothing, but his expression was enough to quieten Iarrey. On the screen they could still see the whirling cloud of dust, within which the two wrecks had disappeared and with them the hope of finding the objects belonging to Admiral Tahomey. Most valuable objects which would have guaranteed all the members of the crew an affluent life for many years to come.

"We have plenty of loot in the hold," Bourne murmured in a conciliatory manner.

"It's a pile of shit!"

"A pile of *antique* shit, worth a tidy fortune," Annataly corrected the captain. "We've never cleaned up like that earlier. You'd said so yourself before the impact."

Morrisey looked at her in anger.

"Do you know what we could have found in Tahomey's private quarters?" When she shook her head, he added grimly, "For his private log, certain individuals would have paid the equivalent of the value of this ship ... or more."

"You should have started the looting on the bridge then," the navigator jibed at him.

"Don't piss me off, Annataly!" the captain roared, dropping into his chair. "Beginning with the bridge is like ... like starting your dinner by eating the dessert."

Nike smiled blandly. The navigator was right; Morrisey only had himself to blame. If he hadn't been robbing the dead so zealously ...

"Bad luck, plain bad luck," Iarrey said, trying to calm things down. He'd hidden behind the nearest control panel, just in case. "There was nothing we could do, sir. An act of God."

"What act of God?" The captain shook his head and suddenly burst out laughing. "Don't you fucking know who's God *here*?"

"You are, sir," mumbled Annataly.

"Correct," Iarrey seemed to agree with her.

"Don't blaspheme, Henrichard," bridled Father Pedroberto, who had been quiet up to then. Bourne had woken him after the collision. "Let's do our duty, and be happy with what we have. What's done can't be undone, as the Good Book says, and there'll surely be other opportunities to make money. Most importantly no one got hurt."

Morrisey turned away from the screen, where more fragments of the battleship and corvette began to burn in the upper layers of the atmosphere of the fourth planet of system V3a13. He looked like a little boy who had just been told he wouldn't get the toy he'd seen in a holonet ad.

"Amen," he said, clenching both his good hand and his prosthesis.

Nike watched him with a mixture of disgust and fascination. Captain Morrisey never ceased to puzzle him. In just a few seconds an old man despairing at his loss turned back into the vigorous officer he was.

"Get to work!" Morrisey yelled, letting go of his armrests. The one on the right bore the clear marks. It probably wasn't the first time it had been molested by Morrisey's metal fingers. "Tidy up this mess, before the rest of it disperses."

"The collapsars are configured and ready to go," Iarrey reported, smiling and winking at Annataly. "According to my calculations, two medium-strength ones should be enough to collect up all that trash from the L-point. I've already keyed in the coordinates."

Morrisey sat up straight in his chair and quickly scanned the data passing across the holoscreens.

"What are you waiting for? My blessing?!" he shouted, and the crew instantly knew their good old captain was back. Capricious, yes, but at the same time very down to earth. Even Nike had to admit the guy had great charisma, although he could be a vicious bastard, too.

Shocks were felt as they cast off the two collapsars. The *Nomad* had eight of them. Two light, four medium, and two of maximum power. Until that moment Nike hadn't heard much about those incredibly efficient—but also simple—devices, which weren't used beyond the Recycling Corps. Created as an element of orbital defense, the collapsars only served one purpose today; positioned in the proximity of space garbage dumps they attracted like magnets—or perhaps more like black holes—every atom of matter around: from space dust to the biggest asteroids to the wrecks of antique battleships. When the collapsar's gauges registered that the quantity of attracted mass had stopped increasing, it set off toward the nearest star, and some time later—could be even after many months—it burned up, vanishing from the Universe forever.

The medium collapsar could attract from the libration point and then bind up a mass of a hundred million tons. The strongest ones were ten to twenty times more powerful, although they weren't used near inhabited planets anymore. However, they were useful when it came to destroying well in advance large asteroid concentrations approaching inhabited systems.

Right now two such devices, visible on the *Nomad*'s screens, were gliding majestically to their assigned positions. They only needed another ten minutes or so to attain full power when around them would begin to emerge miniature models of spiral galaxies, with specks of cosmic dust representing stars and the fragments of the wrecks forming nebulas.

Fascinated by this sight, Nike focused his entire attention on one of the golden pyramids, around which smaller fragments had begun to gather. It did not last long, though; the image suddenly sparkled and where a moment earlier there had been a whirling cloud of dust there was now clean space and a dead planet suspended far away.

"—what the galacticunt is that supposed to be?" Coming back to his senses, he heard the end of the sentence hissed out by Morrisey.

"I carried out a routine check on the data from the remaining L-points in this system," Iarrey explained. "The probes found another wreck graveyard near Theta."

"What are you talking about?" the captain stormed. "That fucked in the fractal chunk of frozen rock is a billion clicks from the central star. No one fought over Theta, because there was nothing there. The fight was here, over the only fucking gateway in the sector."

He poked a finger into the control panel. "We don't have anything about the other place, no records, no mentions; not from the High Command's archives nor from the rebels themselves. I've never ever heard of any battles in that region!"

"I know, sir, I prepared the reports for you myself, but readings don't lie." The first officer was quite clearly unconcerned by the captain's speech or mentions of High Command's archives. "The probes located over seventeen million tons of garbage in the Theta's L-point."

"It probably intercepted some bloody asteroid field," Morrisey said disdainfully.

"I've only just started gathering readings now, but the preliminary data point to a very high metal content," Iarrey informed, not backing down.

"Have you never heard of ores?" The captain collapsed into his chair and spat on the floor. "Perhaps it's an iron moon shot to fuck by an asteroid."

"I've been checking, sir," Annataly cut in. "The system's schema totally match the data from the period of its registration."

"Honey, perhaps that bird brain of yours hasn't registered it, but this Big Bang butthole-shafted Universe is a squillion fucking times older than our oldest atlases." Morrisey groaned. "A battle in which both sides had lost such an immense tonnage would have resounded throughout the known Universe. If you ask me, they're regular iron asteroids orbiting some half-baked clone-of-a-bitch pretending to be a planet."

The number of curse words per sentence indicated Morrisey's growing irritation. Although he'd stopped talking, no one wanted to take up the subject, at least not for the next few minutes.

"You're right, sir," began the incandescently furious navigator finally. "Still, we have to hang around here until both collapsars finish their work."

"Which ought to take"—Iarrey made some rapid calculations —"at best, two hundred and seventy-two hours until the moment we put the collected mass on its terminal course."

"We can leave the numbers in orbit or send a few probes to monitor the process," the cornet-pilot suggested eagerly. "We'll manage to reach Theta and return before that pile of scrap moves away from Delta's orbit for good."

"We can't leave that shit unattended," Nike decided to speak up. "According to the directives, that planet is scheduled for repopulation."

"Fine, so we have twelve days to lounge around," Annataly summed up. "Twelve days of boredom, hibernation, or checking that L-point."

Morrisey snorted.

"We aren't going to race around the entire system chasing rainbows."

"And what if there's something valuable?" she asked with an ingratiating smile. "Something that'll compensate us for the disaster with the *Odin*?"

The captain stared at the central screen as though he hoped he might spot something at such a great distance.

"Nothing could compensate me for the loss of Tahomey's log," he said after a moment. "You can trust me, honey, that in this part of the Universe there's never been anything more valuable from our point of view. But all right, if it makes you feel better, we'll go there. Stachursky, get back to the archives and check all—and I mean *all*—available information about this system's history. In particular any records regarding the gateway. That includes private correspondence of people who'd served here before the war. Bourne, study the data from Theta's libration point. Before we get into its orbit I want to have complete reports on my terminal ..."

He stopped for a moment and scanned them all grimly. "I know we're wasting time, which is why there's one more proviso: if we don't find anything interesting, you all get docked three percent of shares from this expedition."

"And what if we do?" Nike asked, surprising everyone.

SEVEN

REACHING the fringes of the system took a bit longer than Annataly had predicted. After two hundred standard hours, they had only passed Zeta's orbit. Captain Morrisey visited the bridge less and less frequently. He concentrated on doing what he liked most. He, Iarrey, and the chaplain began to catalogue their haul.

Two days later, the first officer announced—albeit only unofficially—that provisional estimates of the value of the objects found in the wreck led them to conclude they had gathered a veritable fortune aboard the *Odin*. The sum he mentioned after he'd arrived in the mess hall stunned Nike. The cadet almost choked on a piece of meat cultured on the *Nomad* when the confidential whisper reached his ears. The news didn't make quite such an impression on the other members of the crew, however. He left them in excellent humor and went to his cabin with another set of data to analyze and his vacuum-packed supper. He slept on the lower deck, as did the other cadets, except he had been given a cabin in the central section, a long way from the still sleeping "numbers," as he had begun to contemptuously call his recent companions in misfortune.

Everything aboard the *Nomad* revolved around money and

antiques. Nike had never been interested in antiquities before. As far as he could recall, in his house there were no remnants of the distant past. No portraits of his ancestors or mementos from before the war. As was the case with most current inhabitants of Earth, Nike's forebears had come from distant sectors and in acknowledgement of their service had been transferred right after the war to a deserted center of civilization. Nike was born into a wealthy family, but spent his early childhood far from Earth, on planetoids, where his father was on the board of a mining company. Life was mundane there. The miners generally came from poor planets where no one cultivated traditions, or knew stories about events preceding their birth. He spent a lot of time among those people, as hard as the rocks they crushed. Oftentimes he checked the contents of personal containers before they ended up in the incinerators following their owners' bodies. Apart from a few old holos, mostly stills, showing their family or their homelands, he never found anything special. He wondered why the miners didn't leave any valuable stuff behind, considering they made good money. Although rumor had it that the other miners divided up the belongings of their dead colleagues, and only threw useless junk into the containers, he didn't quite believe it. Now such behavior seemed to him more than probable. And possibly in its own way understandable. However, he still wasn't prepared to accept it, for moral reasons.

Immediately after receiving his orders, Nike plunged into the archives again. He did not show up in the open-access area of the ship for several days in a row, apart from at mealtimes and during rare briefings. He chose the privacy of his cabin, where he could examine virtual files. As work it was unproductive, to say the least. Delta had been settled five years before the outbreak of war, and only owing to the ideal location of the transit station, the construction of which became necessary following the start of the colonization of the Galaxy's new sector. The planetary system had not been thoroughly researched, except for a narrow band of the habitable zone which embraced two planets of a, to be honest, secondary category; also, fairly cursory reconnaissance flights had been carried out around the three—nearest the system's center—of altogether five gas giants. They were not even given proper names, as was customary, but were left with the catalogue numbers from the general astrophysical atlas.

Several probes had indeed been sent to the periphery, but they had not transmitted much data before the war broke out. The archives contained scarce information confirming the existence of Theta, the most distant planet of the system, but that was it. Nike did not find any detailed reports or any remarks. A few months after the planet, or actually the planetoid, had been added to the central register, further exploration of system V3A13 ceased to have any importance for anyone on either side of the conflict.

Scouring the terabytes of private correspondence of the transit station's crew, even with such incredible search engines as High Command's operating systems possessed, didn't yield any results either. The colonists were more interested in the fate of the distant worlds they originated from than in their nearest surroundings. Even Delta did not arouse their interest—although in their defense it could be added that in the initial phase of terraforming it cannot have been especially hospitable—never mind the most distant recesses of the system.

Nike looked at the clock; it was already long after midnight according to ship's time. He'd spent hours poring over the records. His eyes were stinging, his eyelids drooping. He was unable to focus on the contents of further letters, memos, and reports selected by the computer. He put his reader down on a pile of mobile recorders, turned off the light, and settled down on his bunk. In the surrounding gloom, again he saw the stone wall and narrow bay window, and behind it: the sky and dragons frolicking among the clouds …

"Move over."

He didn't react. He never reacted the first time Monicatherine provoked him.

"I said, move over."

This time, the words were accompanied by a light nudge to his shoulder. He obediently turned over on his side. He heard the slight rustling of the bedclothes and a moment later, felt the gentle touch of her fingers, which glided over his thigh drifting over each hair. The familiar warmth of her skin spread over his legs and back, where their bodies were pressed together most tightly. That familiar warmth he yearned for so much, and that unmistakable scent of warm skin …

He got up, reaching for the light switch. Astonished by his sudden reaction, Annataly fell out of the narrow bunk, in spite of the railing around it, and landed on the floor with a loud thud. Nike heard her stifled cry.

"What are you doing, you jerk," she hissed a moment later, trying at the same time to rub her bruised elbow and shield her eyes from the bright light in the cabin. "Turn that damn thing off."

He didn't react. He looked at her with his eyes wide open. She was sitting completely naked in the center of the cabin, now sucking a grazed finger for a change. He saw her clearly in the bright sub-xenon light. In spite of her fifty-something standard years she still had a young woman's figure. A narrow waist, long slim legs, flat stomach, and quite ample and still firm breasts: everything that an attractive woman ought to have in order to attract a man's attention. Perhaps she was just a little too muscular, lacking that layer of fat beneath the skin, which made Monicatherine's body seem so …

"Had a good enough look, Roaring Romeo?" she asked in a whisper, having stopped sucking the index finger she had cut during the fall.

"What are you doing here?" he parried her question with one of his own.

"What do you think?" she burst out laughing as quietly as

she could manage. "I'm just checking if it's not worth swerving off course a bit—"

"Not a chance." Nike sat up in a corner of his bunk and pulled his knees up. "You'd better don your clothes and evanesce before the old man starts looking for you."

The navigator got up, but didn't reach for the loose-fitting shirt lying by the door.

"Don't you feel like finding out why I mean so much to Morrisey?" she asked, and stretched herself sensually.

Too sensually ...

He forced himself to look away. It was difficult particularly now, when the part of her body most exciting men's imaginations was framed in the gap between the railing and the top bunk.

"What I feel like doing doesn't matter much," he replied cautiously and licked his lips, which she fortunately did not notice.

"You surely aren't afraid of Henrichard's threats?" she asked, leaning forward to see his face. He was still staring at her breasts. They were swinging right in front of him.

"Of course not. He's just a softhearted old guy. What could he do to me?" Nike giggled. "In which case, why are you whispering?"

The expression of amusement vanished from her face. If looks could have killed ...

"You won't get a second chance," she hissed, but didn't move an inch.

He would have sworn that the closely trimmed triangle of her pubic hair was as black as the hair on her head. And it was also there for the asking.

"Perhaps it's better this way," he murmured. "I've got used to this fucked-up world and I'd rather not leave it right now, especially considering I've just become pretty rich."

This time, she bent to pick up her shirt. She put it on and then reached for the panties, which were lying alongside. Nike was amused to see that they didn't resemble regulation fleet under-wear, not in the slightest.

"I don't get you," she said, fastening the top buttons of her shirt. "Do you prefer that machine?" she nodded toward the cabin phantomator.

"No, to tell you the truth I prefer real-live women," he replied with a mysterious smile on his face. She would probably have been surprised to find out which model he usually loaded into the device. "Under different circumstances, at a different time, in a different place, it would be my pleasure—"

"Under different circumstances? Are you counting on your turtle dove waiting for you?" Being a woman, she struck where it would hurt most. But she didn't hit the target. She was well wide.

"No, I'm not counting on that, actually," he answered without a second thought. "I'm sure she doesn't wake up by herself any longer. Who'd wait around for a garbage collector?"

"So why don't you make the most of the chance to have a real adventure?" Strangely, she sounded honest.

Her nipples, however, may have gone erect from the cold of the nighttime cabin temperature.

"Because it's a one-way ticket," he said, resigned. "I've tasted forbidden fruit once already—"

"And did it teach you anything?" There was more sarcasm in the question than curiosity.

"Sure ..." he said, nodding toward the door.

He didn't watch her leave. The hiss of the sliding door told him he was alone. For a short while he sat in the same position he had frozen in for a better effect, then jumped down onto the cabin floor, went over to the door, and hesitantly placed his hand on the panel by the lock.

It was much brighter in the corridor and he had to squint. But anyway he saw her almost at once. She was standing right in front of him, hands on hips and a triumphant smile on her face.

"Our lord and master is drowning his sorrows after the loss

of the treasure trove in such quantities of booze it would be very risky to light a match near him," she whispered, lifting her right hand so he would see the lacy panties swinging on her index finger.

"Annata—" he began.

"Call me Smiley."

Instead of a reply, he just pulled her unceremoniously into the cabin, closing her mouth with a kiss.

———

Nike opened his eyes and ran his hand over the bare sheet. There was no one beside him. No dent in the pillow, no warmth emanating from the material. He sniffed the air, but couldn't smell the merest trace of a strange scent. The cabin was as sterile as ever.

"Hm ..." he murmured, swinging his legs over the edge of the bunk. A hurried look around the small cabin betrayed nothing of Annataly's recent visit.

He jumped down onto the floor and stretched. *Holy shit! If only I could have such beautiful dreams every night,* he thought, moving toward the sanitary facility and rubbing the sleep out of his eyes. Back to drab reality. There were letters, reports, and terabytes of pure shit about nothing still awaiting him in abundance. He activated the faucet and washed quickly, and then raised his eyes to the mirror to look once more at the gray face of a guy who had literally fucked up his life ... Suddenly he smiled. The crimson print of full lips in the very center of the polished crystallite surface left no doubt about the events of the previous night.

"You little ..." Muttering under his breath, he smudged the imprint of Annataly's lips with a wet hand, and then wiped the shapeless smear off with a paper towel.

Morrisey might have never dropped by, but it was better to be safe than sorry, as Carre-Four used to say in the Academy.

Christopherasmus was a total dick, but even he occasionally managed to say something smart.

Nike returned to his cabin after popping out for breakfast, collapsed onto his bunk and groped for the reader. When he was shoving the next mobile recorder into the device he noticed it was Major Visolay's battered notebook. He twiddled with it, hesitating shortly, and then reached for the universal dock. For a second nothing happened; the notebook, which hadn't been powered for over a hundred years, looked utterly inert. *Not too surprising*, thought Nike. The data stored on the crystals ought to have survived intact, but the electronics might have flipped after such a long time, even though it was standard military equipment, and supposedly indestructible …

Suddenly there was a soft buzzing and the 3D display lit up for a split second. But no image appeared. There was only a flash after which the device went blank again for a few long seconds. Nike watched in growing fascination as more lights on the casing lit up. Half a minute later, he had in front of him the slightly blurred image of a virtual keyboard and a box for entering a password. A century ago, 512-bit codes seemed unbreakable, but today any computer could unravel them in fifteen minutes. And the *Nomad* didn't have just any old equipment, but the most efficient quantum monsters. Even the auxiliary core Nike was using cracked the old notebook's security in less than thirty seconds.

Over thirty terabytes of data were stored on the device's crystal. Most of them were archived messages sent by the major to his family and their replies. Nike ignored those files, as well as the countless photographs, and went straight to the memory segment where Visolay stored his text files. Only one piqued the cadet's curiosity. Chiefly owing to the code used to protect it. Nike waited another twelve seconds for the old protection system to be removed. Then a folder labeled with a long sequence of digits appeared on the device's holographic display.

Nike found two files in it. One extremely small and the other almost a hundred times bigger.

He opened the short one first and whistled under his breath after scanning a few lines of text. It became apparent that Morrisey had been wrong; very wrong.

Nike closed the major's file and froze with his finger hovering over the other icon. The moment of hesitation was short, though.

"Fuck Theta," he muttered, dragging the file with the short name *Forge* into the screen's field.

———

A few hours later, Nike stared at the last sentence of the major's account in speechless disbelief. He might have expected anything of the long-dead officer, but definitely not the salvation from Dredd.

EIGHT

THETA TURNED out to be an irregular lump of rock with a mass twenty times smaller than Earth's. It orbited its star at such a distance that it could only be seen as a spot against the constellations of the central part of the Galaxy's arm with difficulty.

Morrisey, chewing constantly, looked at the planet through bloodshot eyes and listened to the reports as they came up. The probes, sent an hour earlier, should have been transmitting direct information from the libration point any time soon. Nike's several days long research confirmed that the cluster in question had already existed when the colonists started to populate the V3A13 system. The data obtained from the only probe that had reached Theta orbit before the destruction of the transit station suggested the existence of a wreckage, similar in mass to the one in Delta's Lagrangian point. A hundred years before, no one had been interested in analyzing these data, which at first had been treated as an indicator of just another asteroid field and then been lost in the terabytes of coming in information, and quite simply forgotten.

"I said it was a pure waste of time!" the captain interrupted after the first officer had barely begun his presentation of the available data. "In a few minutes you'll see for yourselves that it's some fucking lump of rock packed with iron ore."

"I don't think so," Iarrey responded with his customary calm.

"Oh?" The amusement flickered across Morrisey's face.

"I compared the data with similar results gathered from a few hundred asteroid belts, including those from the most high-yield mineral deposits we know—"

"And what did you discover, First Officer?" the captain asked, suddenly interested.

"The content of rare and heavy elements in this place is at least ten times higher than in the most concentrated deposits in open space, sir."

Morrisey turned around. One might have concluded from his expression that even a hundredfold difference wouldn't have made an impression on him.

"With all due respect, Mr. Iarrey, even if we're really dealing with asteroids which consist of metallic ores in their purest form, there's still too few of them. What company would build an entire mining infrastructure here for such a small amount of raw material?"

"I'm not saying that—"

"I've got visuals," Annataly interrupted, plunging the bridge into darkness again.

First they saw a panorama of the entire L-point. The visual representation of the space surrounding them was filled with small, difficult to identify fragments circulating around the immense irregular shape, which resembled a tuber covered in patches of lichen rather than an asteroid.

"I still think it's what's left after some sort of collision," Morrisey muttered. "Do a close-up of the edge. And now, Ann, choose one of the stones and maximize it."

"Yes, sir."

A second later, the cameras of several probes had homed in on the selected target.

"Up clone's—" They all cursed simultaneously.

On the screen whirled a fragment of some kind of structure. There was no doubt. In spite of the horrible distortions, one could still distinguish several elements. Nature doesn't create trusses, cables, or pipes inside rocks.

"Home in on something else," the captain requested.

They looked at around a dozen other similar fragments. Only one of them was an ordinary piece of rock; all the others betrayed their artificial origins to a greater or lesser extent.

"Let's find daddy," Morrisey said, suddenly animated. "Let's see who's sitting in the middle of that spider's web."

The cameras switched to the next target at once. An immense irregular lump occupied the screens' central fields. It revolved slowly around its vertical axis, in the same direction as all the particles surrounding it. After the general view they moved to close-ups of specific fragments—these, however, came as a disappointment. The object's surface was uniform and resembled the skin of a prehistoric reptile. An unending sea of blisters covered every bit of the lump except for six bulging rings distributed evenly over the entire surface.

"Weird, but seemingly inert piece of rock," stated Morrisey after seeing the next few identical images.

"I don't think so …" Nike said, carefully examining the regular bubbles covering the irregular surface of the object.

"Be more specific, Mr. Stachursky!" The captain graced Nike with one of his habitual looks.

"Have any of you noticed even one impact crater on that … that thing?"

"He's right!" Iarrey rushed to the control panel and began to enter some commands.

"What do you mean, he's right?" The disorientated captain glanced at the screen to check what Heraclesteban was doing.

"I mean that in open space there's only one kind of object that doesn't have collision scars … and that's ships protected with deflective field."

"You're wrong, Iarrey," Morrisey said coldly.

"I'm not wrong, sir," the first officer protested.

"Stars don't have craters either."

Annataly was the first to crack, bursting out in loud laughter. She was followed by Bourne, and a moment later, everyone joined in—including the astonished Iarrey.

"I beg your pardon, sir, you're absolutely right, sir. There are two kinds of objects like that," he admitted a moment later.

"Three ..." Nike managed to utter that word, still laughing.

"What?"

"The effects of impacts aren't visible on gas giants either. After some time, of course."

"That's enough of this yap!" Morrisey pointed at the object on the screen. "I want a full analysis of that shit, right now! If that rebel scum were capable of doing something like this, it can't—"

"It's not the work of separatists," Annataly cut in.

"Who did it then?"

"If I'm not mistaken, Nike has found some data suggesting that the probes registered a cluster near Theta during the colonization of the system."

"So who could have built something like that?" Morrisey laughed repulsively. "Not Aliens, for sure."

"Why not?" Nike asked.

No one was able to answer that question sensibly. No one protested either; Father Pedroberto was already sleeping soundly in his cryo-cabin, probably dreaming about the riches he had acquired. The chaplain always ended up in the cooler right after praying for those who had passed on, and counting up the loot. He only made an exception when something interesting was happening. The expedition to Theta's orbit was nothing special to him; he shared the captain's opinion on that subject. And anyway: if something were to happen, Morrisey ought to wake him up. However, there was nothing to suggest that the captain intended to do that.

"Look at that, guys!" Iarrey shouted a few seconds later, pointing at the screen.

The close-up showed one of the domed growths adorning the lump's entire surface. A small fragment of rock, or possibly a broken-off piece of the structure—it was difficult to judge precisely—unhurriedly drifted toward it. When it was still fifty yards away the dome suddenly brightened up a tiny bit and the intruder slowed sedately, coming to a halt, and then—as if repelled by a magnet—moved right toward the belt of similar objects.

NINE

"THIS WAS DEFINITELY NOT BUILT by human hands," said Iarrey six hours later, looking at a holographic model of the artifact. "The technology used to create that … that …"

"Let's called it a station," Bourne suggested.

"I don't think it's a station, Mr. Bourne," the first officer argued. "More likely a classic FTL spaceship."

"Where does your certainty come from?" Morrisey asked.

"It's not certainty, but a conclusion based on the comparative analysis. I think what we're looking at is an element of a larger vessel. It was the only survivor of a crash which must have taken place here around fifty thousand years ago."

The captain whistled and leaned back in his chair.

"Fifty thousand years ago? Are you sure, First Officer?"

"Annataly and I checked it three times on each of the samples we'd taken. The results were similar each time, ranging from forty thousand nine hundred to fifty thousand fifty years. That's standard error of measurement."

"If I've understood correctly, you're talking about that junk …" The captain waved an arm, putting his hand through the holographic image of the disc surrounding the artifact.

"According to our findings, a significant part of those remains belonged to the vessel we're interested in. We spotted pieces whose appearance suggests they come from identical sheathing to this." He pointed at the central element. "It was most probably an external propulsion module. In the lower part of the object, if we consider the surface around which the fragments are moving as a level plane, we've only found cavities and a whole lot of protruding and apparently melted elements. Similar technology was used in pioneer times of space conquest, before the discovery of FTL drive."

Iarrey changed the holo. This time, the pear-shaped artifact was displayed horizontally, and a long grille extended from its narrower end, on which there was the dome of a huge engine.

"Of course it didn't necessarily look like that, I used models similar to the ones known from our history; however, I think that it might have looked something like that. The main engines, reactors, and fuel tanks were separated from the main hull, that's for sure. The radiation is too high for it to be an accident."

"And what's that cavity?" Morrisey asked, pointing at the place where the projected girders emerged from the hull.

"No idea."

A silence fell. They all looked at the slowly revolving hologram.

"So … do we go in by ourselves, or report it first?" Bourne asked timidly.

"Go in?" repeated Iarrey, clearly astonished by the very idea. "What do you mean, go in?"

"Just like we do with every wreck," the captain responded.

"It's the first trace of an alien civilization we've ever come across, and you want to go right ahead and loot it?" the first officer dug his heels in.

"Who said anything about looting?" Morrisey bridled. "We just want to examine it thoroughly."

"Yeah, right!"

"You know very well, Iarrey," the captain continued, "that if we hand it over we'll never find out what was inside. For the next hundred and fifty years information about the discovery will be more secret than the identities of the joint chiefs of staff. Our artifact will simply disappear, vanish into space. And you'll be given the order to keep your mouth shut till you die, or else ..."

His meaningful gesture left no doubt that High Command knew how to keep its secrets secret. "If I am to be muzzled for the rest of my life I want to know why, at least. I'd also like to have some sort of souvenir, evidence that we were the first people to discover a trace of an alien civilization."

"Shall we vote?" Annataly decided to put an end to the debate.

"I'm in favor," Bourne volunteered.

"Of going onboard, reporting the discovery, or voting?" Morrisey asked. "Could you express yourself clearly just this once?"

"I'm for going onboard," the lieutenant stated.

"Me, too," the navigator supported him without hesitation.

"Mr. Iarrey?" Morrisey looked at the first officer expectantly.

"I don't think it's a good idea—" Heraclesteban began.

"I'm not asking about the quality of the idea," the captain interrupted him, "just if you're buying in."

"I'm against going onboard. God knows what—"

Morrisey interrupted him again.

"Nike?"

"I ..." the cadet stammered, recalling the scene from the battleship. "I'm with the First Officer. It's not our business ... We'd better stick to the rules."

"So it's a draw." Morrisey stood up. "As the commanding officer I have the right to the deciding vote. And I am telling you: whatever might happen, we're going onto that ... that ... whatever it is."

"I wonder how." The first officer pointed at the holographic image of the alien ship. "Can you see any hatches? And what do we do about the force field?"

"*We?*" Nike smiled to himself. Iarrey who had been outvoted immediately became a servile cog in Morrisey's machine.

"The force field's a piece of cake," Annataly said. "Whatever was powering it must be almost dead by now. We'll just smash into that cob a couple of times with a broadband laser and it ought to dissipate it for good."

"And what if it's an absorptive field?" Nike asked.

"Absorptive, you say ..." The navigator stopped to think. "Who the hell knows? For all *I* know, it may be an absorptive field, considering that after thousands of years their ship still has an active force field. Of course, if it *is* an absorptive field, there's no point shooting, we'd only be strengthening it. It's a huge vessel, several times bigger than our most powerful battleships. Even if we were to use all the firepower we possess, we wouldn't trouble her potential defense systems."

Annataly was silent for a moment.

"All I've just said is strictly hypothetical, because I don't have a clue how powerful that force field is and how it works," she added quickly, seeing the look on their faces.

"The safest thing to do would be to use the trash orbiting it," Iarrey butted in when she had finished. "Constant bombardment ought to exhaust the energy of the deflectors pretty quickly, whatever their type. According to my calculations, right now there are ten collisions with the force field every standard hour. If we go into the very center of the belt at full power, we could make that figure increase even a hundredfold—"

"But that would mean unleashing a shitstorm again," Morrisey cut in just to keep his first officer from ever fully expressing an opinion. "The belt would become unstable ..."

"... which won't be a problem if we set up the smallest collapsar at the edge of the zone. I can steer it manually, decreasing and increasing the power of the gravitron depending on what we need and how the situation develops," Iarrey gave as good as he got. "I can also program the objects leaving the zone to be intercepted. In less than six hours we'll be rid of most of the trash surrounding the artifact. Our lasers will easily deal with the rest."

"But what about getting inside?" Nike asked.

"We'll have a good look," Bourne calmed him, "and if we don't find anything, you ought to know that a C4 robot only needs thirty minutes to get through the reactive sheathing of a modern battleship."

Morrisey lounged in his chair, folded his hands behind his head, and closed his eyes.

"I doubt whether that something is more resistant. And even if it is, we aren't short of time."

"Except we'll leave tracks behind us," Heraclesteban observed.

"I have faith in you, First Officer. I'm certain you'll think of something."

"But it might not go down too well with the High Command experts, particularly considering that it's our first contact with Aliens."

"Right, it could be a serious problem," the captain said glumly. "We haven't thought about what top brass might say."

"If they find out we inspected the artifact we'll end up in quarantine," Bourne murmured. "Eternal quarantine ... We have to proceed with extreme caution."

The captain was visibly dejected.

"If we don't find a way to make a noninvasive entry, we'll have to forget it."

"There only remains the question of those in sleep." Bourne interjected. "What do we do with them?"

"Are you talking about the numbers?" Morrisey snorted contemptuously. "Let's leave them in their little coffins. We don't need witnesses. The holy man can also keep on snoring for a while. Unless you want to administer a ceremonial baptism to our Aliens."

———

Up close, the alien ship was oppressively large: pear-shaped, covered in growths, and with a perimeter of more than three thousand five hundred yards at its widest point. The *Nomad*— hanging at a distance, which allowed its connecting corridor to be spread out—seemed like a fly about to alight on a cow's backside, as Morrisey had colorfully described it a moment earlier.

Iarrey's plan turned out to be perfect. It took less than six hours to neutralize the force field, and another six to clear the surroundings of flotsam. At sixteen hundred according to ship's time, they went eyeball to eyeball with the greatest mystery and the most momentous discovery of their lives.

Bearing in mind Iarrey's words of warning, the captain did not immediately order the penetration of the hull, but first sent all the available robots to search the wreck's surface thoroughly for a hidden hatch or any other point of entry. The operation was not yielding any results; the ship's hull seemed a genuine monolith.

Hour after hour the entire crew pored over their screens, analyzing the data being sent by the robots. Finally, when they had lost hope, and Morrisey had begun to prepare a report for High Command, something bizarre happened. One of the symmetrically aligned domes on the upper part of the hull became transparent. The rough surface first went cloudy, and then literally in a few seconds grew as transparent as the purest crystallite. They could see it thanks to the probes' cameras.

For fifteen minutes they were inspecting the rest of the ship, but nothing out of the ordinary occurred. The robots painstakingly continued to search other parts of the alien craft's rough sheathing, but the crew gathered on the *Nomad*'s bridge lost interest in their work.

The transparent dome didn't reveal anything specific; the only thing that could be seen beneath it was a lustrous surface as flat as a tabletop, which might have been a wall or the floor, depending on one's point of view. There were no marks on it whatsoever; nothing apart from uniform wearisome greyness.

"Hm …" Iarrey murmured, tapping more commands into the computer. "I think our little ship is up to something … If you ask me, that glowing surface is a sort of a solar collector. We've exhausted the ship's energy reserves and someone, or something, wants to replenish them."

"Don't be ridiculous!" Bourne waved his hand disdainfully. "A spaceship using solar collectors? Not quite the required output."

"Really?" Heraclesteban became indignant. "Mr. Bourne, the well-known expert in alien technology, knows best as usual. Their output may be hundreds of times greater than ours."

"Sure …"

"Have you read the instructions for those collectors? Is that why you're so certain?" Iarrey snapped back. "They were traveling in space when Humankind was still using flints to start a fire. It just so happens that the ship's dome is aimed at the brightest point in the system. Straight at the central star."

Bourne shrugged and went back to his duties.

"That would explain how the force field endured so long," Annataly said.

"I don't agree," Heraclesteban retorted at once. "We're too far from the central star for this method to work, even if the efficiency of those cells is a thousand times greater than ours. I'd say we seriously depleted the reserves of energy, which that something—for reasons unknown to us—needs very much. That explains the dramatic and ineffective attempt—"

"That's all well and good, First Officer," Morrisey said, turning around in his chair. "But what the hell does it mean?"

"In my opinion the core of the ship's central section, or whatever they used there to generate power, is still active. At least partially. Apparently, no living creature is in control, for a sentient being would know that such attempts are useless. A machine doesn't think; it just implements the most effective procedure needed to carry out its task. One by one, according to priorities and instructions ..."

"Meaning?" the captain asked again.

"What do you think I am, an Alien?" Iarrey laughed. "I don't have a clue, but let's wait, something's sure to happen."

TEN

IARREY WAS RIGHT. Three hours later, which they'd spent doing nothing, the crew saw one of the domes on the upper part of the hull expanding like a soap bubble. The surface did not change color as previously—the dome was simply growing upwards, although its circumference hadn't increased by even a fraction of an inch. It took exactly a minute until a circular opening with a diameter of well over thirty feet suddenly appeared at the top of the protuberance.

"Send the cameras inside!" Morrisey ordered excitedly.

The closest robots moved toward the opening and soon after three of them disappeared over its curved edge.

"Visuals!" the captain ordered.

"No readings," Annataly reported. "The ship's sheathing completely blocks out our frequencies."

"Position one robot above the opening; we'll use it as a relay," Iarrey advised. "If necessary, we'll make an entire chain of relays, using the other robots. We have several hundred more onboard."

"Good idea, First Officer ..." The captain raised his electronic prosthesis above the chair's armrest in a victory gesture.

Ten seconds later, on the screens they had a visual of a huge hall beneath the dome. The entire chamber was dark, only illuminated here and there by dim fluorescent light emanating from the fungi-like growths distributed at regular intervals over the spherical wall. The glow allowed them to discern the position of the "fungi," but did not dispel the darkness even in their proximity. However, it wasn't a problem for the cutting-edge night vision systems, which the *Nomad*'s reconnaissance robots were equipped with. The machines decoded the radar and infrared signals and changed them into a normal image, simultaneously creating a holographic model of the object under examination.

The chamber, now that the dome had risen, was shaped like a slightly flattened sphere. In its lower part there could be seen many strange constructions covering the curved wall, and clusters of phosphorescent "fungi" distributed around them. The robots' sensors had also discovered over a dozen openings of different sizes. Morrisey ordered the smallest probes to be sent into them, but it rapidly transpired that the corridors were too narrow or too winding and even worse, they blocked the transmission, thus not permitting direct contact with the probes. The first officer suggested examining them one by one, by means of a chain of probes functioning as relays. The crew left it until later, however. They had something much more interesting to look at.

A cylindrical installation, which may have served the ship's crew as turret mooring system, rose up from the lowest part of the spherical hall. It was divided into six segments of more or less the same length. Every one of them had six tubular projections with a lock at the end: the lower the segment, the longer the arms of the projections, to which small vessels were moored; their function could only be guessed at.

"What about that?" Morrisey asked, after they'd had a thorough look.

"I'd say we've found their hangar," Annataly volunteered.

"Yes," Iarrey agreed. "Clearly, their ship has implemented emergency procedures. The loss of power endangering the life support systems ought to result in a standard emergency procedure: evacuation in rescue capsules. In my opinion the spherical projections at the top of the mooring turret are capsules of that kind."

"But," the navigator added, "there's no one left onboard who could use them …"

"Let's hope you're right."

"Hope often blinks at a fool, Mr. Bourne." Morrisey got up from his chair and stretched until his vertebrae popped. "Let's move it. Iarrey, check all the unoccupied locks, I want to know how they work and if there are any mechanical security systems. We might be able to open one of them, which would be the easiest way to get inside. You have my permission to try anything as long as you leave no signs of forced entry. Nike and Bourne will help you. Let's reconvene in three hours, and you'd better have some hard facts. And you, honey, come with me. We have to talk …"

Davidoff-Rozerer nodded and walked toward the door without a word. Morrisey chivalrously allowed the woman through first, only to then slap her lecherously on her rear. The soft hiss of the closing door cut off the navigator's giggle. A silence fell on the bridge, punctuated by the beeping of the electronic devices.

"Right," Iarrey muttered, looking at Bourne's screwed-up face. "The old man's gone off for an in-depth conversation with Annataly, and meanwhile we have to do the 'open sesame' drill."

"Three hours isn't much considering the magnitude of the task," complained Bourne.

"And what does our whiz kid think about all this?" The first officer's smile was utterly sincere. Neither could a trace of irony be detected in his voice.

"Doesn't it strike you as curious," Nike asked, "that the alien ship's started evacuation procedures even though there isn't a living soul onboard?"

Iarrey's face darkened. The first officer frowned, and began picking at the day-old stubble and nervously chewing his lower lip.

"You know, Nike, you're damn right … I've tried to recall what procedures apply in the Federation Fleet in situations like this. The central computer has to monitor the whole lot of processes, including life support systems. If it has no contact with a living member of the crew, though, it would never initiate evacuation procedures."

"It seemed very suspicious to me also," Bourne interjected, looking concerned.

"On the other hand," Heraclesteban continued, "we really don't know what made that ship open one of its hatches. Perhaps it has nothing to do with evacuation. Or perhaps after such a long time the machinery's clapped out and not in control anymore, or the Aliens have other procedures than we do … We'll get a chance to think about all that when we get inside and investigate this frigging crate."

First they checked the unoccupied locks in the turret's upper section. It looked as though they were constructed similarly to those found on any Earthian spaceship. Unfortunately, all were shut fast, and they couldn't see any panels, controls, or handles on the smooth surface of the metal. Nothing at all that would have caused the opening of the locks' exterior hatches. Later they checked in turn the remaining sections where they had noticed unoccupied docking bays.

While Bourne and Iarrey were analyzing the construction of the locks, Nike supervised the work of six rootlers and drew up a detailed 3D plan of the "hangar," as they had christened the hall. He also examined some corridors they had discovered, but after checking three he was certain he was on the wrong track. All of them had been tightly locked, which did not surprise him. There was no air beneath the dome, and if the corridors had been connected to the ship's interior, they would have automatically sucked every single atom of gas from its chambers. So Nike left the laborious introduction of the robots to various tunnels until the very end and began scanning the lowest part of the hangar. And here he found a surprise waiting for him.

"Gentlemen," he called the two officers.

Iarrey didn't react; Bourne, however, went over to the cadet at once.

"I hope it's something interesting," he muttered, wiping sweat off his forehead. They hadn't lowered the temperature on the bridge, even though Morrisey was long gone.

"I think I've found a solution to our problem ..." Nike switched vision from the first robot's cameras to the main screen. "Here you go ..."

The lieutenant first looked at the turret's base, nestling among a tangle of pipes and curious installations of unknown origin, and then at the young man grinning from ear to ear.

"Well, what is it?" he asked uncertainly.

"Don't you see anything unusual?" Nike was genuinely astonished.

"To tell you the truth, I can't see anything but a heap of garbage."

A smile appeared again on the cadet's face.

"Doesn't that look familiar?" He pointed at one of the elements lying at the bottom.

Bourne squinted and pulled the virtual keyboard toward him. He carried out the same series of comparative analyzes that Nike had completed a moment earlier. And with exactly the same results.

"Would you mind coming over, Iarrey?" he asked, when the last pair of images had merged into one.

This time, the first officer dragged himself away from what he was doing. He walked over to them and had a look at the results of Bourne's work.

"My congratulations, son," he said appreciatively, and slapped the young cadet on the back.

———

"As you can see, sir, we'll be able to get onboard stealthily," Iarrey announced.

Morrisey looked in astonishment at the robot visible through one of the windows located in the corridor leading to the mooring turret.

"How did you get it in there?" asked the captain finally.

"All credit goes to our young friend here, sir," Iarrey answered, pointing at Nike. "Let him say."

"Come on then, son ..." Morrisey turned his chair toward the cadet.

Straight as a ramrod, Nike faced the commanding officer bravely.

"While I was putting together the scans for the hologram, I found a damaged rescue capsule with an open hatch at the bottom of the mooring turret. It must have come loose during the crash. Close scrutiny showed that the docking mechanisms are equipped with mechanical protection systems only. We used a few small antigravs and lifted the capsule up to the first unoccupied docking bay. After fitting the docking ring into the collar, the turret lock opened automatically. The robot, which had previously been put into the capsule, got inside, and we moved the capsule away, simulating a launch. The external lock closed automatically, but the other door was open."

"Here's the analysis of the composition of the atmosphere inside the alien ship." Iarrey handed his reader to the captain.

"Doesn't seem to differ much from the atmosphere on Earth," Morrisey noticed. "And the analysis of the bacterial flora?"

"We didn't find anything," reported Bourne. "The atmosphere seems to be as sterile as the inside of the booze bottle, but despite that and the similarities in the composition I wouldn't recommend unsealing our suits even in critical situations."

"No one's suggesting that." Morrisey thought for a moment. "The data you've gathered show clearly that the Aliens needed oxygen, just like we do. So we can conclude we're dealing with a protein-based life form."

"Possibly," Iarrey agreed. "Judging from the size of the hatches, controls, and handles, and the chair in the capsule, they're taller than us and more massively built. They might even be ten feet tall. While we're on the subject, the shape of the seat is interesting ..."

A view of the capsule's interior appeared on the screen. The chair was very long, rounded, almost streamlined, with two vertical grooves in its upper part.

"Any thoughts?"

"Unfortunately not. I've got too little data to be more specific, sir. So far we've been only operating within the corridor. The robot did reach the lock leading to the turret's main shaft and moved beyond to take samples of air, but then withdrew immediately. We waited for you before taking any further steps, sir."

"Excellent." Morrisey stood up. "Gentlemen, I think it's time for a small step of a man but a giant leap for mankind. Annataly, you stay here. Someone has to keep watch over us in case of misfortune."

"Bourne knows his way around this gear much better than I do," she protested, pointing at the equipment.

The captain quietened her with a gesture.

"Honey ..." he muttered, and walked over to her. "You're the pilot and the only one around here who handles a joystick with such deftness—"

He stopped short on hearing a snort of laughter from Iarrey, but did not turn toward him. "Back off. You'll have a chance for a trip once the coast is clear. I swear."

ELEVEN

THE FOUR OF THEM WENT: Morrisey, Iarrey, Bourne, and Nike. Surrounded by a swarm of robots and probes, they moved down gravitational belts into the corridor. The plan was simple. They were going to search the alien craft meticulously, chamber after chamber, leaving a chain of robots to extend their transmitters' range and blocking open all the doors they encountered. Annataly, who had remained on the *Nomad*'s bridge, controlled the probes and supplied reconnaissance information.

Thanks to the robots they had an accurate virtual map of the three next chambers in front of them. That gave them an adequate margin of safety. Morrisey may have been hotheaded, but he also had something of an obsession with safety. Losing a hand in an accident had taught him to be cautious.

They descended into the lower part of the turret, searching one vehicle on each level. However, they did not find anything that might have helped them even with an approximate identification of the creatures who had built the ship. They only managed to confirm that all the seats were of the same size and shape, meaning the Aliens—whatever they'd looked like—had belonged to one species.

"Clones-of-bitches," Morrisey muttered after they had left the last capsule. "Sterile clones-of-bitches."

The interior seemed impeccably squeaky-clean. In vehicles piloted by human beings there were always lots of objects reminding people of their families and homes. Not here, though. The inside of the capsules looked as if they had only just rolled off the assembly line.

"Perhaps they didn't feel the need to decorate their ship," Iarrey offered. "Or maybe they took everything with them when they left …"

"I don't give a fuck either way," the captain replied, flying after the robots toward the lock leading straight on board.

Nike projected a hologram of the next chamber. It wasn't very big, and from it emerged two identical corridors with elliptical cross section. The one on the left ended in armored bulkhead, and the one on the right led to something that resembled a berth deck. The glowing "fungi" were all over the walls, so the four men didn't have to switch on their lights and could save their suits' energy. Morrisey hesitated momentarily before he pointed to the right-hand corridor. He always took the easy way out, according to Annataly. That was fine with them—the lesser the risk, the greater the chances for a peaceful retirement.

When they passed a fork, the captain stopped suddenly.

"Annataly!"

"Yes, sir?" the navigator asked, a tad surprised by this unexpected call.

"Send …"—he quickly counted the machines accompanying them—"five robots and twenty probes to investigate the other corridor. And keep me in the loop."

"Roger that," she barked, and some of their machines turned back as if by magic.

The captain resumed walking when the robots were out of sight, then stopped in front of the next door and ordered it to be opened. The membrane furled as soon as one of the robots touched it. After it had closed behind them again, Iarrey ran his glove over its rough surface. A second later the door opened once more.

"Incredible," whispered Heraclesteban in solemn awe, positioning a robot so that the membrane could not close.

"Alien," Morrisey shrugged, clearly not impressed.

He looked down the corridor, which was bending sharply. The probes' cameras had scanned every inch of it a long while before. Nike projected a hologram of the corridor right in front of the captain's visor. From the readings it appeared that the corridor most probably ran around the hull and in that section had just one side door, the one through which they had entered.

"Right or left?" Bourne asked.

The corridor looked identical in both directions.

"Right," the captain replied.

They covered four more similar sections, from which they could reach further docks. For the moment they only registered the presence of side chambers, presuming them all to be identical, which was later confirmed when the returning probes fed new data into the computers.

In the fifth section they finally reached a side membrane, apparently leading to the ship's central part. However, it would not open automatically in spite of their considerable efforts. In the meantime Morrisey sent some robots to the farther sections of the corridor, in order to check whether there were any other similar membranes ahead. He could do it because Annataly'd already redirected the probes, which up till then had been—ineffectively—trying to force the bulkhead blocking the way at the first fork.

Having nothing else to do, the crew members sat down with their backs against the curved wall and watched further pieces of the 3D puzzle appear on Nike's holopad. In less than fifteen minutes the robots checked the corridor's remaining sections and found out that it indeed was a ring closed off at the opposite end by a heavy bulkhead, very similar to the one they hadn't been able to open. Clearly, the only way onboard the alien ship was through the membrane they were all sitting idly at.

"Hell," Iarrey murmured, when the holoimage was complete.

"Hell," Bourne repeated. "And so our adventure on the alien ship comes to an end."

Nike reached out to switch off the device, but Morrisey clutched his wrist.

"Gentlemen, do you really want to give up?" he asked. "We're sitting in the corridor of the first alien ship Humankind has ever encountered, and we aren't going to find out what's behind that fucking door?"

"The first we've ever heard of," Iarrey corrected him.

"What do you mean?" the captain demanded.

"I mean, we can't be sure it's the first alien ship encountered by Humankind," Iarrey replied calmly.

"I don't quite follow," said the commanding officer.

Bourne and Nike also looked confused.

"Just because we've never heard of the discovery of alien vessels, doesn't mean there's never been any contact. Can any of you swear High Command doesn't cover up findings like that?"

"What the fuck—" Bourne began, but the captain silenced him with a gesture.

"Do you have any proof for what you say?" he asked.

"Do you recall what happened to the *Vagabond*?" Iarrey parried the captain's question.

Everybody went silent. Nike glanced at the crew members uncomprehendingly.

"I don't."

Morrisey put a gloved finger to his visor, indicating that Nike should remain silent. Bourne lowered his head.

"The *Vagabond*," Heraclesteban explained, "was the *Nomad*'s sister ship. Years ago we were investigating the Oscar Sector. They were clearing up trash in the O2A7 System; we were doing the same in O2A6. Then we were supposed to move on to O2A8 together. Linden completed his work sooner than us. He reported that he would fly off to set the stage, and later sent information that he had two clear readings and was waiting for us. We had one more L-point to collapse. It was really dangerous there during the war. We finished a day later and were just preparing to jump when we received orders to return to base at once.

"And when we came back we found out that the *Vagabond* had flown straight into an unmarked minefield and the Fleet was blocking the O2E8 until further notice. Two weeks later we received new maps of the system and cleared up the mess. But there was only one reading this time."

Morrisey nodded his head; Iarrey clenched his fists.

"One fucking reading, get it?" Bourne said. "Linden had reported two, and that guy was accurate down to a click in cases like those. I served with him for three seasons, so I know what I'm talking about."

"Perhaps the Fleet sorted it out by themselves," Nike suggested, "and neutralized the minefields at the same time."

"Son ..." Iarrey pulled Nike toward himself until their visors were almost touching. "They send *us* to do that kind of work, and I assure you no one from the Corps cleaned out that system. I know every lousy skipper and every crate in Federation service. That aside, Linden didn't sail into a minefield; he spoke to us after taking his bearings, and while it's possible to hit a mine and not be able to react, it only happens when you're leaving hyperspace. Tadam said they had to take some additional readings because something wasn't right ... I've always thought that the other L-point was some kind of trick, and that the *Vagabond* sailed off to its death because of an amazingly interesting wreck they wanted to check out before we arrived."

"Clone-of-a-bitch!" Morrisey swore. "Either we're letting our imagination run away with us, or High Command really is trying to cover up contacts with Aliens. Which means that if we report—"

"Bang and we're six feet under," Bourne said, snapping his fingers.

"There's no over or under in space ..." Heraclesteban muttered.

"Who gives a shit," the lieutenant snapped. "With an extra hole between my eyes I won't much care!"

"So what do we do?" Nike asked.

"What do we do?" repeated Morrisey with indignation. "We blow this safe open." To the comlink he said, "Annataly, send a ripper to the other bulkhead, will you? Try to get through."

"But what about—"

He didn't let her finish.

"Honey, it looks like we're not gonna become famous, at least not this time."

TWELVE

THE RIPPER LOOKED like a huge spider, with its spherical abdomen and nine limbs—four for support, movement, and anchoring and five for operating tools. That sufficed to overcome every possible obstacle.

"What now?" Bourne asked, his fingers hovering above the keyboard. "Do we blow up the entire entrance, or cut cautiously and find out what's on the other side?"

"Drill a hole through that shit, just to be on the safe side," Iarrey said.

"Yeah ..." agreed Morrisey, who was sitting a few yards away and checking the data from the probes in the dock tunnels.

The ripper spread its support limbs wider. It could not anchor itself on such a hard surface, the electromagnets didn't work there either, and so it used suction cups. The plasma needle cutter approached the circular door, its point emitting a blinding light, and when the brightness became too much even for their helmets' visors, the arm moved toward the membrane blocking the passage. However, even before the plasma blade touched its strange surface the membrane furled all by itself, revealing a narrower, vaulted corridor.

"Oh, fuck," Bourne groaned, staring into the dark opening.

"Well, I'll be damned!" Morrisey leapt to his feet and flew over to the robot. "Lights, cameras!"

The small probes skittered between the spindly limbs, and a moment later, they were looking at a dead straight corridor, which ended with a membrane identical to the one that had just opened. Several smaller openings were visible in the side walls. Iarrey directed a camera toward one of them. The membrane furled the moment the robot flew up to it. The same thing happened with all of the remaining membranes, even the one at the end of the corridor. The four men stared in silence as another 3D image captured on the drones' cameras grew on the hologram.

On both sides of the passage linking the two ring corridors— outer and inner—there were only a few small rooms containing mostly equipment of the kind people use every day, but also a few completely strange things. Wherever they looked, however, they did not encounter even the tiniest shred of evidence of the beings which had built the ship. No images, no odds and sods, nothing; just the sterile chambers that had never been used— even the ones that seemed to be living quarters.

"Bizarre," Bourne commented, perching on the edge of a large seat and examining the streamlined surface of a table covered with peculiar controls. "Everything's integrated, impersonal. Like it had been designed by machines for machines."

"Perhaps it's some kind of unmanned—" Iarrey began, but didn't finish his sentence. The soft, but familiar bleeping coming from Nike's holopad quietened him.

They all gathered around the cadet to watch a red dot pulsating in one of the two accessible chambers on the other side of the corridor's inner bend. The probes had discovered traces of life.

"Visuals!" Morrisey demanded.

"There are none," Nike reported. "We've only got some scanning drones there and no other equipment. All the camera drones have been sent to search the shafts in the hangar."

"Get those pieces of junk back here! Right now!" the captain ordered.

"Yes, sir!" The cadet quickly fed in the appropriate commands.

Seconds went by, but none of them moved a muscle. No one said anything either; they were all staring hypnotically at the pulsating red dot. Annataly's raised voice sounded like a gunshot in the total silence. Even Morrisey jumped like a scalded cat.

"I've got a small problem here," she said.

"What is it?"

"I sent the additional camera drones to you, but—"

"Out with it," the captain ordered impatiently.

"There's something wrong with the holomap," she ended much more quietly.

"What do you mean?" Iarrey asked, confused.

"Take a look for yourself."

The grid recorded by the camera drones covered the iridescent green outlines of the ship's chambers, showing that one of the sections of the outer corridor was narrower than the first measurements had led them to believe.

"Perhaps the sensors are uncalibrated," muttered Bourne after examining the differences. "Most of our robots are museum pieces."

"So how do you explain that?" The drones had just reached the passage between the corridors. "It was straight according to the first readings, and now—"

Morrisey approached the membrane, which opened before him noiselessly.

"Clone-of-a-bitch ..."

The corridor was indeed bending gently—very slightly, yet discernibly.

"The difference is about a foot and a half in the middle section. The measurements can't be out by so much."

Bourne shook his head in disbelief.

"Say what you like …"

"We have visuals," Nike interrupted them.

They gathered around the cadet and his holopad. In the inner corridor there were no such differences; all the lines in both colors matched up perfectly. A moment later, the displays showed the inside of a cabin with gleaming cylinders arranged against the walls. There were a dozen of them, all looking the same and almost as high as the ceiling, with a diameter of over three feet. A thirteenth cylinder was in the center of the chamber, suspended above the floor or floating in the air. And the drone emitting an alarm signal was hanging right in front of it.

"Time to greet our hosts!" Morrisey shouted, and—not waiting for the others—glided toward the open membrane. They followed him, arming their weapons as they flew.

The inner loop, although a little smaller than the first, seemed to go on forever. Identical sections divided by elastic, self-sealing bulkheads, glowing with fungi-like growths, devoid of any distinguishing marks. The only sign that they were approaching their destination was the red dot on the hologram coming closer. They finally reached a dark-blue circle, beyond which—at least according to the readings—there ought to be something alive.

They entered warily, pointing their phasers at everything within view, but this cabin seemed just as empty as the others. Nike looked at the hologram, enlarging it to be able to see more details. The flashing red dot was inside the cylinder floating in the air. Seeing the captain's enquiring glance he nodded toward it.

Morrisey cautiously approached the cylinder and tapped it with the barrel of his phaser. Nothing happened, so he moved still closer and rested both hands on the shining surface, and then pushed down with all his strength. The cylinder dropped a little, but immediately returned to its previous position without apparent effort.

"Antigrav, stone me …" The captain knelt down and looked at the cylinder's bottom part.

Meanwhile, Bourne walked around the object operating the controls of the sensors.

"It seems to be perfectly smooth," he said. "No cracks, grooves, or temperature differences."

"Tough. We're gonna pry it open anyway," Morrisey muttered.

Iarrey was about to protest, but Annataly spoke first.

"We'll have cut through the bulkhead in a few seconds," she informed. "Here we go. The visuals of—"

Her voice was suddenly drowned by static. In the chamber the glowing growths flickered, and their light intensified. Morrisey jumped away from the cylinder. Bourne and Iarrey raised their weapons. Nike backed off and stood nearer the wall.

The cylinder was changing color; the upper part darkened very quickly, and its surface wasn't smooth any longer. Waves ran over it, as though the cylinder experienced combined stress.

"—ing on, for fu—" the navigator's distorted voice broke through the crackling for a moment, "—got to——ish—"

No one paid attention to Annataly's snatches of speech, or her evident anxiety—even when she started shouting. Suddenly the cylinder's surface bulged, as though something was trying to get out of it. And this was exactly what was happening. The shell—up until then as hard as helon—tore open under the pressure of almost human, six-fingered hands.

Someone fired. Nike didn't know who, but it certainly was not Morrisey. A gush of energy enveloped the upper part of the cylinder, blackening its entire width and burning a hole in one of the cylinders standing behind.

"Lost your fucking minds?!" the captain yelled.

Meanwhile, entire forearms appeared in the rent. They were horribly thin, considering their length. Gray skin, clearly visible gnarls of muscles working subcutaneously, and something like elbows. The creature seized the edges of the opening where the cylinder had remained solid, and began to pull itself up.

First they saw the Alien's head. Covering its crown were long protrusions, soft but thick as human fingers, the color of gold; they fell over its thin shoulders like hair. Seemingly, the creature's face resembled a human's. The eyes, nose, and mouth were in the right places, but everything was totally ... ALIEN.

The eyes, which were in whole as black as the darkness of space, lacked irises, the nose was underdeveloped and without any nares, the mouth so wide that its corners disappeared under the hairlike protrusions. But the strangest of all was a small growth in the center of the forehead, resembling lips squeezed tightly together. Something like a third eye, only closed.

The creature looked around the chamber. It did not seem astonished by the presence of the short beings surrounding it. It moved its mouth, and may have said something, but they couldn't hear anything through the crystallite anyway. Then it waved a hand, as though driving the intruders away. They did not react, just stood there, staring at the Alien as it straightened up. It was over nine feet tall, and standing in the cylinder it towered over the spacesuit-clad figures even more. Its head reached the domed ceiling. Its gray body was covered with a flowing tunic bereft of decoration. The clothing hung down over the cylinder's surface, obscuring the Alien's legs. The only other thing that could be discerned was a large bulge on its back.

Nike, fascinated, lost track of time. The Alien looked down on them from above, and they kept craning their necks to look up at it. Finally, Bourne took a step forward and raised his hand in the classic gesture of greeting. The being slowly turned its head toward him and tilted it, like a bird observing its surroundings. *Yes, just like a bird,* thought Nike and at that moment two curved shapes—furled wings—appeared from behind the Alien's back.

The being slowly spread them out to their full width, revealing complex patterns on a downy, snow-white background.

"It's an angel ..." Iarrey whispered, and genuflected, crossing himself reflexively.

A sort of a smile widened the Alien's lips. The being spread its arms and suddenly—

It all happened so quickly, the exact sequence of events wasn't clear. The Alien trembled. Its wings fluttered and the previously smiling mouth opened as if to scream. Nike saw the teeth; rows of even, conical fangs. Hundreds of them ... And that was the last thing he registered before his crystallite visor became covered in a dense web of cracks. At the same time, a split second before his visor shattered into tiny fragments, he heard the Alien's voice. It was an inhuman, ululating howl. Nike was standing farthest away, so he did not pass out at once, though he couldn't be sure any longer if what he saw was a real image or a delusion. Only a moment later did he realize he was breathing the air of an alien ship. He held his breath instinctively and almost immediately understood the absurdity of such behavior.

The Alien jumped down onto the floor and seized unconscious Bourne by the arm. It cleared his helmet visor of the crystallite shards, then lifted him up to his face. In his mind's eye, Nike saw hundreds of pointed fangs clamping onto the lieutenant's neck, but nothing of the sort occurred. The Alien and the human touched foreheads and remained so, motionless for several seconds. Finally, Bourne landed on the floor and the creature turned toward the exit, charging straight at Nike. The lump on its forehead, which had resembled pursed lips a short while before, was now open, but Nike didn't get a chance to peek inside. Flung by the Alien, he flew several yards down the corridor.

THIRTEEN

"ANNATALY! Come in, for God's sake!" When Nike returned to the chamber the captain had recovered his wits. He was holding the comlink headphones of his destroyed helmet in one hand, and was gently slapping the lieutenant's cheeks with the other. Bourne was covered in blood and had a large darkening bruise on his forehead. Iarrey'd already staggered to his feet and was throwing up by the wall.

"Did you see where it went?" The captain turned to face Nike. The cadet nodded toward the corridor without a word. "Is your comlink working?"

"I don't know ... I'll just check ..." He glanced at the panel on his sleeve. Most of the lights were glowing red. He reset the device. There was a slim chance that self-repair would work, so it was worth trying.

"Iarrey, grab your phaser, you take the lead," Morrisey ordered meanwhile, guessing the outcome. "I'll carry Bourne, and Nike will cover our backs. We're going back onboard the *Nomad*. Then we'll scorch the feathers of that screamer in the nearest sun."

No one argued. Nike brought up the rear, staring back into

the semidarkness concealing the farthest section of the corridor. That was why he didn't notice when Iarrey and the captain suddenly stopped.

"What is it?" he asked, bumping into them. A moment later, he saw what had made them stop.

Where there had been the membrane leading to the passage that connected both rings, now there was nothing. The smooth wall looked exactly like any other.

"Perhaps it's the wrong section."

"We passed four membranes," Iarrey said. "We're in the right place."

"Are you positive?" Morrisey asked.

"Absolutely."

The captain laid Bourne's limp body on the floor and walked over to the wall. He examined it carefully, then took two steps back, set his phaser at maximum power, and shot a gush of plasma. It hardly lasted a second. A large fragment of the wall vaporized, but when the cloud of acrid smoke dissipated they didn't see the inside of the corridor, which had been there a short time before. The hole was almost six feet deep, but for all intents and purposes it seemed to be just a dent in a solid matter.

"Captain!" Nike looked at the comlink panel. The lights were now glowing green.

"What?"

"I beg to report, sir, that my comlink is working."

"Terrific. Except that you don't need it to talk to me. And you can't make contact with the *Nomad* without open passages."

Morrisey cursed and pulled the trigger once more. Again they were enveloped in acrid smoke. All of a sudden Nike felt the floor shudder. As though the ship had felt pain; as though a tremor had passed through it. The cadet barely kept his balance. The captain also staggered, making a large breach in the ceiling before he managed to turn off his phaser.

This time they saw a familiar sight. It was one of the chambers they had explored a short while earlier in the connecting passage. Morrisey smiled wryly.

"Now we know why our measurements didn't add up."

"Astounding," said Iarrey, entering the opening. "The ship doesn't have a stable structure. It creates passages where they're needed at a given moment."

He looked around the chamber and pointed at the wall where once the entrance membrane had been. Now all he saw was the same smooth surface as there was everywhere else.

"I think it's led us to the place we were meant to get to …" He turned around and looked at the burnt edges of the opening. "Take a look at that, the matter is beginning to replicate—"

Indeed, bubbles, growths—whatnots—began to appear on the smooth surface which had been torched by the stream of plasma; the ship had already begun to rebuild its damaged structure.

Morrisey lifted Bourne and pushed Nike through the hole.

"Let's hope that the main corridors won't close up like the connecting passages. Nike, can you access the holomap of this part of the ship?"

"I've lost my holopad."

"Not good. Do you remember the layout of these chambers?"

"More or less … We're on the right, there were four small chambers here, of approximately this size."

"Four, you say …" Morrisey was silent for a while, as though he were calculating something. "The connecting passage was roughly fifty feet long. I'd say these chambers are probably about ten feet wide. So we have to cut through around ten more feet of wall to break through to the main corridor … My phaser's dead now, but we've got two fully charged ones … that ought to do."

"We can't risk using up all the plasma," Iarrey objected. "We might come across that … that angel again."

"We'll cross that bridge when we come to it," Morrisey put an end to the discussion. "Move out of the way—"

"No," Nike said softly but decisively.

"What do you mean, no?" The captain stopped and looked at him unkindly.

"You ought to think it through, sir." Nike gulped nervously. "That matter gives off a lot of smoke when it burns. If we all go in there, we'll suffocate."

Iarrey, who was still examining the edges of the opening, unexpectedly supported the cadet.

"The boy's right. This hole will close up in about six, seven minutes. You blast ahead, Henrichard, but we are staying here. We won't use up your oxygen," he added, handing over his phaser to the captain.

———

In order to cut through to the fourth chamber, Morrisey used up all the plasma from Iarrey's phaser. Their calculations showed that only three feet of wall were separating them from the main corridor. Unfortunately, the first opening had shrunk so much that they started to fear they wouldn't be able to get through it. Morrisey decided it was time to deplete the rest of the plasma from his phaser, which was the only weapon among the three men waiting in the inner ring.

Iarrey had managed to widen the opening by a foot or so before a soft hiss told him he completely ran out of plasma. That gave them another sixty—ninety at most—seconds. Morrisey had not wasted his time. Choking on the acrid black smoke, he had been obliterating another wall. Meanwhile Nike and Iarrey were fearfully looking down the corridor fading away in the darkness. Were the Alien to show up right then, none of the men would stand a chance. They preferred not to think what might happen if Morrisey had been mistaken and the outer ring no longer existed or had been moved somewhere else.

"It's now or never!" The first officer grabbed Nike by the arm and pointed at the rapidly shrinking hole in the wall. "We're going through."

They picked up the still unconscious lieutenant and dragged him in. It wasn't the easiest thing to do even in zero gravity. The billows of smoke, which made their eyes water and their lungs burn, stopped them from opening their eyes or taking a breath. They were bestriding the opening between the third and fourth chambers when something buzzed in Nike's headphones and he suddenly heard some words, heavily distorted by interference. Morrisey had got through to the place where the chain of drones was still in contact with the *Nomad*.

He lurched, choking, into the corridor.

"—re you? Over!" the navigator's voice, hoarse from shouting, sounded like heavenly choirs to Nike's ears.

"Smiley, we're alive!" he shouted between spasms of coughing. "Galacticunt, we're alive! We're in the main corridor—"

Morrisey, who was lying two yards from him with eyes as red as a vampire's, suddenly stiffened.

"What did you say?" he asked barely intelligibly.

"I reported that ..." Nike, still struggling to get his breath, smiled at the captain but only momentarily. The captain's face reddened.

"What did you say, you clone-of-a-bitching spawn?" Morrisey repeated and almost gagged, dry heaving.

"I don't get it—"

"You don't get it?" Morrisey lifted his phaser, its barrel still glowing red-hot. "What did you just call Annataly?"

Nike blenched. "Smiley." The only people Annataly allowed to call her that were the ones she ... He was careful onboard the *Nomad*, but now the sense of relief made him forget himself.

"It's not what you think—"

"Not what I think?" Morrisey could hardly speak, but his eyes expressed utter hatred. "I warned you, you little shit. The tiniest trace and ..."

Nike closed his eyes as the captain pulled the trigger. He didn't feel anything, though, just heard a piercing cry.

"Henrichard!"

Astonished, he looked down the corridor. A figure in a space-suit was standing there. Annataly, with no doubt.

"What are you doing here, you cloned slut?" Morrisey asked, equally surprised. He glared at the woman, then dropped his now useless, empty phaser in fury. "Who's looking after the fucking ship?"

"Slut? Cloned?" Annataly's voice sounded like the hissing of a viper. "Perhaps if you were more interested in me than the bottle, you wouldn't have such trouble getting an ere—"

"Shut your mouth, you whore!" roared the captain, turning blue. "I'll kill you and that … that …"

"You shut your mouth, Henrichard!"

The words didn't come from either Annataly or Nike.

"I couldn't give a fuck about your virility!" Iarrey continued, voiced raised. "We have a much more serious problem here. And I have no intention of dying just because you can't get a hard-on. Do you hear me, you old prick?!"

Morrisey's face turned purple. He was just opening his mouth to curse the first officer and the rest of them, but Annataly was quicker.

"I don't know what you've found, but you might like to see what I've discovered beyond those bulkheads." She threw the holopad toward them.

"I'll bet you won't trump us."

Morrisey caught the device in midair. He pressed play, but it was pretty apparent he would rather have torn the navigator and the cadet to pieces.

The ship's holds seemed humungous. It was hard to judge just how big they were. It was equally difficult to count how many bodies there were in its bowels—although the word "bod-ies" didn't apply particularly well to the situation. They saw thousands, tens of thousands of gutted, frozen humanoid beings hanging in orderly rows. Judging by their shapes and sizes there were women, men, even children …

"What the fuck—?" Morrisey whispered after a moment's silence.

"I don't know about you, but for me the pieces are beginning to fall into place," said Iarrey. "That dude with the wings, these bodies, the craft in the dock—"

"What the fuck are you talking about, Heraclesteban?" Morrisey asked. "What craft?"

"I carried out an analysis of those little ships moored to the turret in the dock," Iarrey reminded him. "I catalogued them all and … it's been niggling me since then. I had the impression I'd seen one of them before somewhere. So I decided I'd—"

"Get to the point," Morrisey hurried him.

"The Old Testament. The Book of Ezekiel," Iarrey summarized. "A wheel within a wheel."

"I asked nicely."

"A description of the angels which bore the prophet Ezekiel to heaven," Nike elaborated on the first officer's version, "and of the chariot that carried him away. And a wheel within a wheel …"

"I noticed the same design in the vehicles we found in the ship's dock," Iarrey concluded.

"Are you trying to tell me that this winged clone-of-a-bitch with a voice like an air-raid siren is the precursor of an angel?" Morrisey demanded.

"What winged clone-of-a-bitch?" Annataly asked, confused. Iarrey ignored her question.

"Yes," he addressed the captain, "this is exactly what I want to say. For thousands of years people have talked about angels, God's messengers. And here we have a spaceship with a winged creature straight out of a fresco from an ancient temple, and a hold full of eviscerated humanoids. I'm prepared to bet they're humans."

"You mean …"

"… we really are the food of the gods," Iarrey nodded.

"All right," Morrisey said, switching off the holopad. "And now may I ask who's looking after the *Nomad*?"

"When we lost contact I woke up Father Pedroberto," Annataly replied calmly.

"Well, let's pray that our winged friend won't pay him a visit before we get back." Morrisey sighed.

FOURTEEN

THEY WALKED TOWARD THE HANGAR, calling the *Nomad* the entire time—all in vain. They could not establish contact on any of the emergency frequencies. Nike was keeping his distance from the captain, just in case.

"I'll murder him, I'll throttle him with my bare hands," Morrisey said, furious. "Where's that sky pilot got to?"

"Knowing him, he's probably stuffing his face in the mess hall," Iarrey muttered.

"There's a PA system there as well," the captain slapped him down.

"You surely don't think," Annataly said, "that ... err ... this Alien has found its way onto our ship."

"How could it?" Morrisey snapped.

"An angel appearing before a priest ..."

"How could it appear before him?!" Morrisey yelled irritably. "Naked in open space? If it were such a daredevil, it wouldn't have had to maintain the atmosphere on its own ship."

"I was only thinking aloud," said the first officer, nettled.

"All you're doing is spreading defeatism. The Alien won't be able to open the locks without the access codes, and Pedroberto isn't very likely to see it."

"And have you by any chance wondered why Bourne has such a shiner?" asked Iarrey.

"Perhaps because he was hit fair and square on the forehead?" retorted Morrisey.

"By what?" countered Heraclesteban at once. "Nike said he'd seen the angel pressing its bump—"

"So what?" the captain interrupted him, annoyed, and tried to reach the *Nomad* again.

"And if it was probing his mind this way? Sucking out all the information it needed? Like the access codes to the lock."

"You're letting your imagination run wild."

"Maybe I am," Iarrey smiled nastily. "A few hours ago we didn't believe Aliens exist. Now we have a hold full of gutted people, a dude looking like an angel, and biblical chariots. I'd say it doesn't take much imagination to assume anything is possible. Even if it seems farfetched and totally ridiculous."

The captain did not reply; he began to call the *Nomad* with renewed vigor. Nike, in spite of his fear and aversion, deep down admired Morrisey's tenacity. He didn't believe that those efforts would bring any positive results, however, and when at the hundredth attempt some indistinct voice came on amongst the crackling, he almost whooped with delight.

"Father, it's me!" Morrisey yelled. "Do you read me, Father?"

"—es, I hear you loud and clear, my son."

The voice in the headphones was distorted but comprehensible. They all sighed with relief.

"It's an emergency situation," the captain said. "You have to wake the cadets and send them onto the wreck in full battle gear with spare helmets. Right now."

"I fear that won't be possible," the chaplain replied with great succinctness.

"Pardon me?" Morrisey was dumbfounded.

There was no response for a while.

"I was silent," Father Pedroberto finally said, "because I had to think the matter over ..."

"Father, what the fu—" started the captain, losing his rag.

"Don't say another word, Henrichard!" the chaplain quietened him. "I've tolerated your sinful actions, because I didn't have a choice. But now I do."

"Have you been watching us?" Iarrey asked in astonishment. "If so, you must've seen what the cameras in the wreck's holds recorded. You must've heard what I said …"

"Yes, indeed," Father Pedroberto confirmed. "If any of you think I have no vocation, then you're very much mistaken. I've always believed in the Word of God, in the Good Book. And if at times I behave otherwise …"

"What difference does it make?" Annataly asked in a faltering voice. "What does it have to do with sending a shuttle to get us?"

"Haven't you realized it yet?"

"No."

"What I've seen and heard today contradicts the fundamentals of my faith. A faith professed by tens of billions of people in hundreds of star systems. A faith which has shaped our civilization for millennia. You've found evidence that we may have worshipped beings which treated us like we treat … livestock. What do you think the result of revealing this truth would be?"

A silence fell and even Morrisey did not answer.

"It could shake the very foundations of our civilization. Or possibly even lead to another war."

"Don't talk crap, you lousy bastard!" Morrisey couldn't contain himself. "You managed to turn a blind eye to the slaughter of the innocents while you were coining it in and suddenly you're holier-than-thou—"

Father Pedroberto didn't let him finish.

"I was a sinner, that's true," he said, "but I've found a way to atone for my guilt in the eyes of God."

"What God, for fuck's sake?" Iarrey cried, exasperated. "You've seen what these creatures are really like. Now you should know your faith is totally meaningless …"

"I do," the chaplain calmly replied, "and you do, but the rest of humanity has no idea about any of it and won't ever find out."

"We won't tell anyone, cross my heart and hope to die," swore Morrisey sincerely on behalf of them all, horrified by a slow realization of what Father Pedroberto had in mind. Nike, Annataly, and Iarrey eagerly nodded in agreement.

"Don't underestimate me, my son," the priest retorted. "I know your weaknesses. You are too corrupted to keep this secret."

"Look who's talking," Annataly snapped.

"What do you plan to do, Father?" Nike asked sarcastically. "Do you intend to kill us all in cold blood? Doesn't that go against your commandments?"

"Commandments?" Pedroberto laughed.

"You don't want to atone for anything!" Morrisey exploded. "You're afraid they'll kick you out along with your mendacious lot!"

The priest's face showed that it was exactly the case.

"Do you intend to leave us to our fate?" Iarrey demanded. "With this monster at large?"

"I'm not insane," replied the chaplain. "You might still come up with something ... Which is why I've made sure this wreck will be wiped off the face of the Universe. And if you still don't know what I'm referring to, my son, the keyword here is: collapsar. In a moment I'll activate one of those goddamned devices. I'll dispatch you all to Theta. In a few hours not a single trace of your discovery will remain ... Godspeed, my children."

"I hope you burn in hell, you lousy bead juggler!" Morrisey cried.

Pedroberto looked at the captain as if he was an unruly boy, and then disappeared from the screen.

"In the light of recent events, I don't think fear of hell's much of a deterrent for him," Nike muttered, wretchedly.

"Precisely ..." Captain Morrisey's smile didn't bode well for the cadet. "And since I'm going to die today and heaven apparently can wait, it's time to keep my promise to Damiandreas, Mr. Daughterfucker."

PART TWO
THE COLONY

FIFTEEN

THE DEMETER SYSTEM, OMEGA SECTOR

07/14/2351

"How much more time do you need?"

Captain Henryan Darski didn't answer the question. He stood still at the center of the bulkhead, not taking his eyes off the white-hot hole and the sparks caused by a powerful laser drill. A finger-thick beam died suddenly, and the airlock went complete dark. The helmet visor needed two-tenths of a second to adjust to normal conditions. The crystallite brightened quickly, and so did the surroundings.

"Give the retractor here!" Darski yelled, waving his hand toward the rescuers waiting at the opposite wall.

They ran up to him immediately, carrying the thick jaws of the device in front of them. They fit it quickly to the hole, ignoring the fact that the plasteel was still red-hot. Every second counted for the people on the other side of the bulkhead. Rescuers knew it, so it was no wonder they acted nervously. The heavy retractor slipped out of their hands, and they managed to insert the four detents to the bloody glowing holes only on the second attempt.

Just to be sure, Henryan hit each end with the hammer, and

then raised his hand to signal for the operator to turn on the pumps.

"How long will this take?" The speakers of the comlink came to life again. This time the question was posed with a much more urgent tone.

"Two minutes, Major," Henryan said, not taking his eyes off the bulkhead. "Just two minutes."

"We don't have that much time!" barked Renaud, irritation in his voice.

"If everything goes according to plan, we will begin the evacuation in just—In just seventy-four seconds."

Darski went silent. A gap appeared in the middle of the bulkhead. The jaws of the retractor began to open the massive partition, battling the powerful pistons of the lock that pressed together four thick sheets of plasteel cutting off the access to the next section of the hull.

"It's working!" he yelled, forgetting the open channel of communication. "It's working!"

The technician attending the pumps smiled, and raised his thumb. On the other side, forty-two sailors and officers were waiting for rescue. Forty-two friends and comrades in arms.

"Captain, you will have to stop the operation in a minute," the commander of the ship, Commodore Benford, said. "The readings don't lie. If we don't put out the fire within this time, the oxygen tanks will explode and we'll have uncontrolled leakage of the hull, which means—"

"Sir," Henryan interrupted, knowing fully well that Commodore Benford hated it, "we'll manage to rescue them."

"I doubt it, Captain."

"Please keep Renaud away from the airlock controllers, and I guaran—" Darski stopped in mid-sentence. The retractor opened the sheets of the bulkhead enough for a small hole to appear between the jaws. "We have visuals, sir!" he reported excitedly.

"There's nothing to get excited about," grunted Major,

listening attentively to the whole conversation, even though the report was addressed to the commander of the destroyer. "Half a ship will blow up before you open this passage for good."

"We're not gonna open anything. We'll only fold the bulkhead back enough for a man to get through the hole."

"That's ridiculous ..." Renaud began, but this time Darski didn't let him finish.

"One more minute, sir. Just a minute!" he said into the microphone, turning to Commodore Benford again.

He clung to the bulkhead, switched the external microphones on and immediately regretted it. Behind the metal barrier swirled a crowd of terrified people. Screaming, crying, and cursing people. If he was to save them, he had to get in touch with someone who would establish order on the other side. Someone who hadn't panicked. He switched to the DFS—Department of Fleet Security—channel.

"Liambrose?!" he shouted. "Are you in there?"

A total silence answered him. The reply came only after several seconds that felt like an eternity.

"I am here, brother."

Henryan breathed a sigh of relief. "I'll pass you a rope in a moment. Make everyone form a queue, with the thinnest and the shortest at the front. Let them fasten tight to the rope every six feet. We will drag you to the airlock; it should speed up the evacuation."

"Got it."

"And calm them down, because every second counts."

"Sure."

Henryan opened additionally the general channel and almost immediately he heard the echo of a shot, coming from behind the bulkhead, then another one. That did it. The hallway of the adjacent section became quiet like the snow. Liambrose issued a series of quick orders, and a moment later, somebody's wiry hand appeared in the hole. Henryan looked at it a little surprised, but the unmistakable gesture immediately made him understand.

"We need the rope here!" he yelled over his shoulder.

The trapped man withdrew his hand as soon as he felt the touch of the rough material. The rope disappeared quickly in the hole, unwinding loop after loop like a line on the fishing rod with a very big fish on the hook. Henryan glanced at the display of his helmet. Fifty-four seconds had passed since he talked to Commodore Benford. The hole in the bulkhead was already eight inches wide, showing the terrified face and whitened hands of the first man waiting for evacuation. Ten, fifteen seconds, and this man will be in the airlock, followed by the others. Everything will go well, it has to ...

"Is Renaud in the control room?"

The unexpected question asked by his brother surprised Henryan.

"Yes."

"Damn. You have to stop him—"

The alarm signal drowned out Liambrose's next words. It also drowned out the cursing of the petty officer at the pumps.

"What's going on?" Darski jumped away from the bulkhead, seeing in the flashing red light that the thick jaws of the retractor began to bend.

"The power supply's been cut off," reported the technician, as much terrified as he was enraged.

"Why?" Henryan knew the answer before he asked the question.

The bulkhead behind his back slammed shut with a loud bang, severing the arm of the unfortunate man who was so anxious to survive that he had slipped it into the hole, even though he couldn't fit in the rest of his body.

"Renaud, you clone-of-a-bitch!" You can't ..." Henryan hissed, switching to the command channel.

But his receiver had already switched to the emergency mode and transmitted only the system messages.

"—ompression of Section Six, in five, four, three, two, one second. All the locks open. Pressure—"

Darski turned off the comlink. He slumped heavily down, next to the hand severed in mid-forearm, and pressed his hands to the helmet's visor.

They were so close.

SIXTEEN

WALLACEDRIC BENFORD LOOKED at him impassively as if he were staring into the void. The commodore wasn't of impressive height, but his broad shoulders were envied by every cadet. He was also completely bald, which at his age could be surprising, but not necessarily—especially for a man from the Outer Belt, where the ideas of transhumanism didn't enjoy much popularity. His oval face—difficult to read if he didn't want it—had very regular features, while the deep-set blue eyes gave it the appearance of gentleness, which not even his prominent nose could spoil.

"—and the heat shields of the oxygen tanks, closest to the origin of the fire, had been heated to six hundred degrees," the duty officer was reporting in the meantime, not taking his eyes off the screen. "Further deferral of a decision to decompress could lead to an explosion."

"Did you hear it, Darski?" Renaud asked.

"The critical temperature of these shields is six hundred and sixty degrees," countered Henryan, barely keeping his calm.

"Explain it to him, Tadam, before he gets my goat," Major asked overly politely.

Unlike Commodore Benford, he was very tall and terribly

thin. In the circles of people who weren't overly fond of him—which coincided with the most of the crew of the *Dragon*—he was called "The Skeleton." Also unlike Commodore Benford, he had a very malleable face, except that he didn't make full use of the opportunities it gave him. He rarely wore a smile; more often he displayed one of the hideous grimaces, known to the seamen all too well. Now he was fuming again. Even his wide-set hazel eyes seemed to be aflame, as well as the skin on his cheeks.

"You are quoting the norms regarding brand-new tanks, Captain," calmly explained the duty officer. "Ours are more than ten years old. Their resistance may therefore be lower than the theoretical by—"

"It may, but it doesn't have to," Darski cut him off scornfully. "I've done my homework, too. In the last seven years we've had three similar incidents in our fleet. In two of these, the tanks withstood the maximum temperature and didn't explode. One was seven years old, the other nine."

"But the third one—" the duty officer started.

"Tadam, please. If you had checked the logbook of the *Osiris* carefully, you would know that the tank we are talking about had malfunctioned a year before the explosion."

The duty officer winced. He didn't like it when his inaccuracies were pointed out—especially in the presence of his superiors. However, when Commodore Benford threw him a questioning look he nodded reluctantly.

"It doesn't prove anything," Renaud snorted. "The regulations—"

Darski interrupted him unceremoniously, "There were forty-two crew members there."

"But the regulations—"

"These people didn't wear protective suits, or have access to the safety zone."

"The regulations—" Major repeated much more sharply.

"—are nothing but a collection of unfeeling rules," Henryan finished for him.

Renaud was not to be deterred.

"The regulations clearly say that in such cases the safety of the ship is more important than the life of individual crew members."

"The regulations also say clearly what should happen to the officer who broke them," Henryan retorted.

He gave the impression of a man combining the best features of both his superiors. He was tall, but not as lanky as Renaud, and he had an athletic physique, although it was a far cry from Commodore Benford's body-build. His long face with regular features and a perfect profile could appeal to women, and many a female worker of the administrative department had drowned in his large green eyes before he followed his brother into space. Cropped blond hair adorning his temples completed the picture of a love interest.

"I beg your pardon?" Commodore Benford asked before Major opened his mouth.

"I have every reason to suspect that Major Renaud deliberately prevented the evacuation of those people."

"What the fuck are you talking about, you shithead?!" The accused officer jumped up from his chair.

"In Section Six," Darski explained calmly, "there was the investigation team looking into the death of Ensign Masters—"

"The one who overdosed recently?" Commodore Benford asked.

"Yes, sir. My brother uncovered circumstantial evidence, indicating that some officer or other is involved in the illicit trafficking in narcotic drugs." At these words Renaud's face turned dark red. "Strangely enough, the fire broke out exactly when the DFS officers were opening the locker with the evidence, sorry, hypothetical evidence. Just before the decompression procedure, my brother ... I mean Captain Liambrose Darski ... asked whether the man he suspected was in the control room, and when I said yes he told me to—"

He glanced meaningfully at Major Renaud, and that was it. Renaud exploded.

"It's a lie! A lie! I acted in accordance with regulations! I even broke the rules, giving you an extra minute!" He turned to Tadam, who nodded eagerly.

The regulations dictated decompression of the ship's compromised section when the risk of explosion of the oxygen tanks reached ninety percent. However, the bureaucrats hadn't thought of the possibility that the fire might cut the crew members off the special chambers, in which they should wait out the worst. Henryan didn't fail to mention one more thing: the fire appeared not only at the right time, but also in the right place for making the survival of those present in Section Six impossible. It was as if someone had a backup plan in case of the authorities' attempt to open the locker.

Commodore Benford finally showed his emotions. When he was looking at the officers—slowly, one by one, including those who hadn't spoken—a shadow of sadness appeared on his face. Undoubtedly, the superiors would kick his ass when the report of the death of one-seventh of the crew members reached the Admiralty. It could mean the end of his career … or a promotion and a medal. Everything depended on the interpretation of the facts by prosecutors investigating the disaster.

"We couldn't risk losing the ship," Commodore Benford said after a moment's hesitation, which was unusual for him. "If we had an uncontrolled explosion, casualties would be much more numerous and the damage greater. The *Osiris* case proves we could all have died."

At this point Henryan realized he was on the ropes. Commodore Benford would support Renaud because this guaranteed his survival as the commander of the ship. A few years before well-deserved retirement, this was worth turning a blind eye to inconvenient facts, even though so many good men had died.

"Sir, I'm sure that deferring the decision for another twenty seconds wouldn't have caused any harm," he tried again, although he was aware that his fate had been sealed.

"I gave you an extra minute!" Major Renaud snarled, gaining confidence.

"And that was your biggest mistake," Henryan retorted desperately.

"What?"

"If you hadn't lingered, my brother wouldn't have had a chance to ask me to stop you."

"His words prove nothing," Major Renaud said in a dismissive tone. "Had I been in his place, I would also have insisted on stopping anyone who was going to decompress the section in which I was trapped. Let me add: in perfect accordance with regulations."

"Maybe that's not what he meant ..."

Renaud's eyes widened.

"Then what?"

Without thinking much Henryan reached for his holster, which he'd managed to unfasten while everybody had been looking in the direction of the commodore, and having yanked the gun, he fired twice. At this distance he couldn't have missed. High-energy loads plowed through the chest of surprised Major Renaud, and blew his head off, killing him on the spot.

SEVENTEEN

THE STURGEON BELT, ZULU SECTOR

08/30/2351

Henryan woke up slowly, reluctantly, as if the cryogenic sleep wasn't going to relinquish its grasp on him. He felt a strange chemical odor and incredible heat. Drops of sweat were running down his forehead, but when he tried to raise his hand to wipe them, he encountered resistance. The hand did not move at all, even though he tensed all his muscles. At this point, he should have taken fright. His mind, however, was blank. A daze prevented him from embracing what was happening to him. He couldn't move his hand, so he just gave up. He couldn't lick his chapped lips, either. On his teeth he felt something thick, flexible, as if someone inserted a protector used in martial arts into his mouth. When he opened his eyes and finally looked straight ahead—that is, up, since he lay on something that slid along the dimly lit hallway—he saw a shiny, black barrel vault. The rock above him was as smooth as if something had polished or melted it. The rock and the lights, which he passed steadily, were the only things he could see.

A slight jerk made him realize that there was a stop. From the corner of his eye he saw the accompanying guards in shining armors. By now he'd sobered up enough to start thinking. The soldiers, reminiscent of archaic robots, had to make quite a racket, wearing so much metal, and yet even the slightest murmur didn't reach his ears. *There is no atmosphere in this corridor,* he thought. *Then how … ?* The terror subsided as quickly as it came. When he was being slid into the better-lit elevator car, he noticed the unmistakable reflexes in his peripheral vision. He was wearing a helmet with a very wide crystallite visor.

The way up or down—it was really hard to tell in the gravitational shafts—did not last long. Henryan found himself in another dark corridor, although not as long as the one leading to the elevator. Here it was a bit different. The platform passed a series of doors embedded in the raw porex wall.

Cells. They must be the prison cells, he decided.

There were dozens of them. At some point, the guards stopped again, letting the platform pass; it turned smoothly, slipped into a small niche behind the open door and immediately adopted the vertical position. The claustrophobically small room had no more than forty square feet. There was nothing in it; no furniture or windows. Henryan swayed slightly when the magnetic fetters let go. He would have fallen if not for the gyroscopes of his armor. Before he regained his balance, the display on his helmet came to life with a riot of lights and symbols, and the cell door slammed shut. Yes, his audio was also on.

"Number seven two one." He heard a mocking tone of a man in a shining colonel armor, standing behind the now transparent pane of the plasteel.

"My name is—" Darski began, surprised that despite the protector on his teeth the words came out clear. A slight pressure near the Adam's apple made him realize immediately that apart from a gag, he got also equipped with a simple speech synthesizer.

"You'd had a name before you arrived in our humble abode," the colonel interrupted him unceremoniously. "Now you are number seven two one and you don't speak until I let you. Understood?"

One flick of a finger and the body of the prisoner—zapped with a carefully measured electric charge—arched like a bow. It was meant to hurt and it did. Like hell, or even more. Surprised by the unexpected attack, Henryan couldn't help screaming. He howled like a wounded animal. The man behind the door waited for a long time, staring at the reader's screen, and when Darski pulled himself back together, at last he said, "I'm Colonel Marconrad Draccos, this penal colony's warden. Any questions?" He paused as if expecting the prisoner's reaction, but Henryan didn't bite the bait. "Great, seven two one. Some of our residents needed three or even more lessons to understand the first principle. Yes, the first, because it's not the only rule you'll have to follow here. Do you know, seven two one, the difference between this institution and the others?"

The warden paused meaningfully.

Henryan kept quiet. Still feeling the tingling sensation from the recent shock, he didn't want to provoke this man.

"That's rude, seven two one. You have to answer the warden's questions," a nearby guard said, and gave the prisoner another zap.

This one lasted longer; it was modulated and more painful.

Darski was taken by surprise again, and again he could not control his reaction. He howled as if he was getting skinned, because that's exactly how he felt. The fact that he should have been expecting torture didn't change much.

This time the pause in the conversation lasted much longer. Apparently, the armor was equipped with a built-in medical module, which monitored the vital bodily functions, because the warden spoke only when Henryan began to recover.

"Understood?" he asked, smiling politely.

"I thought …" Darski wheezed, the stiff tongue filling his whole mouth. If not for the synthesizer, probably no one could understand him.

Draccos shook his head.

"I'll give you some good advice, seven two one. Don't think, for here this process is very painful."

Although the prisoner knew what awaited him, there was little he could do to prepare himself for another dose of unspeakable pain. Fortunately, the third punishment lasted a blink. Perhaps Colonel Draccos didn't want the new resident to go straight to the urn. Or maybe there were built-in limiters, not allowing for the killing of the person protected by the armor.

"Now let's drop the jokes," Draccos said, genuinely amused. "I know you feel confused, seven two one, but believe me, that's just what we wanted. This is one of the harshest penal colonies, and you are a murderer, a man who cold-bloodedly shot his superior, and that in front of many officers. So let's be clear: you don't count on leniency here. No one is gonna go easy on you, not me and certainly not my staff. You've ended up here for …"

He checked the documents, as though he hadn't read them before, or didn't care about them, which was also a part of the process of busting the new prisoner up.

"For twenty-five years. Interesting. Not a very long sentence for such an abhorrent act. Why did the judge treat you so leniently?" He grinned at the sight of Henryan's widened eyes. "I give the detainee permission to speak."

"It was deemed a crime of passion," Darski replied truthfully.

"A crime of passion …" Colonel Draccos thought aloud. "A crime of passion would be for the captain of a ship to shoot his wife when he discovers that she's been whoring around with all his crew."

Henryan didn't answer until the warden nodded.

"I've given you permission to speak, seven two one. You can talk freely until I revoke it."

"Major Renaud, trying to cover up his involvement in the drug trafficking, caused the death of forty-two members of the crew, including my brother, the officer of the criminal division of the Security Department, who led the investigation."

Draccos looked up from the screen. He folded his hands, supporting his chin on two fingers as if in deep thought.

"Did they find any evidence proving his guilt?"

"They would have if not for—"

"So there was none."

Reluctantly, Henryan nodded. All the evidence was gone, together with everything that had been sucked into the void after opening the fire protection airlocks. No one was looking for it afterwards. Rescuers worked hard to recover the bodies of the victims, but even after they'd combed a huge area of space, barely half of the dead were found. Liambrose wasn't given a proper funeral, either. A plaque with his name and a diamond were sealed into the wall of the fallen, winding for miles in the Fleet Cemetery, except the gem had not been crystallized from the ashes of the victim, as tradition dictates.

"There was very clear and convincing circumstantial evidence …" Darski began, but the warden silenced him with a gesture.

"Let's stick to the facts. You shot an officer, a superior, because you feared that without evidence, no court would find him guilty. For this you got a twenty-five year prison sentence. On the one hand it's not much, considering the fact that somewhere out there, there are children who will never see their father again; on the other hand it's enough for you to understand that crime doesn't pay. The Sturgeon Belt is a unique place." He swept his free arm in a wide arc. "The local mines are among the most profitable ventures of the Admiralty. But that's not all. I'll tell you another secret, this one for your own good. There is no escape from this place. Not even in death. We have almost one hundred percent survival rate. I'm sorry, I haven't expressed myself precisely. Let me explain then: the average boarder of this merry guesthouse doesn't leave us until I permit it. As you will soon discover, life here is not a fairy tale. You've been sent to this penal colony to expiate your evil deeds, and we will do everything we can so that the justice is done."

He posed his index finger over the part of the display that activated electrodes, and grinned when he saw terror in the prisoner's eyes.

"There you go! You have been here for only a few minutes, and you already know that there is no joking around with us. I could torture you to death here and now; you'd suffer so terribly that eventually you would beg me to finish you off … No, I take it back, I don't know a man who would remain conscious long enough to beg for anything."

He rubbed the pad of his index finger with his thumb. "Do you know why I won't do it?"

Henryan shook his head slowly. This man was a sadist, and made it clearly understood that he didn't have to play by his own rules. And you can't beat pain—you're heroic until you suffer. Life is not a fairy tale, as Draccos rightly pointed out. Even the most resilient have the limits to their endurance, and those are not so difficult to cross.

"Right answer," the warden said. "Really. You are an intelligent man so I'm sure we will get along just fine. I'm not gonna kill you because I want to see you suffer day after day, month after month, I want to see you hit rock bottom … and then someday, twenty years from now, if I feel like it, I'll give you a chance. A chance at what, you ask? I'm certainly not talking about an early release. The judge was very generous to you, but here I am god. I'll decide … pardon me … I have decided your fate."

With these words he turned as if to leave, but he didn't make even a single step. He turned his head slightly so that Henryan could see his profile, and added, "There is, however, a small problem. In our sparse, but not very orthodox community, the murderer of an officer could be treated with respect, even considered as a true hero."

He nodded to himself.

"But I've just thought of a good solution. You will be the guardian angel of my rascals. When someone, not being able to stand the tension anymore, tries to harm himself … which, believe me, is almost impossible … you will stop him. At all costs, I should add. Failure, seven two one, is not an option. If you betray our trust, the punishment will be severe. In comparison, our today's trifles are … just trifles." He laughed maliciously, and disappeared from the prisoner's view.

A moment later, the door went opaque, leaving Henryan in the dark cell, alone with his gloomy thoughts.

EIGHTEEN

DRACCOS WAS RIGHT. Life in the colony wasn't a fairy tale. Above the entrance to the tunnel, through which the inmates went to work every day, some witty soul suspended a plaque with the inscription: ABANDON HOPE ALL YE WHO DO TIME HERE. This paraphrase best summarized the convicts' moods. It was the worst of the worst who ended up in the Sturgeon Belt, and more often than not they stayed there for good. Henryan belonged to a small group of "terminal" convicts, as those who'd received a specific term of imprisonment were perversely called. That's because nine out of ten residents were doing life without parole. And all of them dreamed of breaking free from this hell, even if to the afterlife.

Unfortunately, it was not possible to escape from the Sturgeon Belt. For almost the entire day, Draccos's prisoners were stuck in the Integrated Systems of Prisoner Protection, as the massive armor was called. Wearing it, no one could hurt himself. Besides, the inmates were never left unattended.

Every day in the colony was always the same. Sundays were no different from ordinary days, except for one thing. No holidays—even the most important, federal ones—were celebrated, either. The reveille was sounded at six thirty standard time; the mines were on the extra-systemic asteroid field, so the management didn't have to use the complicated time converters, necessary on the majority of the inhabited planets.

Immediately after the morning roll call, the prisoners went to the bathroom, where the armors were taken off for a short while to take a quick shower. Six days a week they were entitled to a three-minute dry bath, only on the seventh day they were allowed to use water—this brief, thirty-second contact with pure liquid hydrogen and oxygen was the single departure from the routine. However, it would be wrong to think that a bath was the perfect opportunity to take one's own life. The unarmored prisoners were bound with magnetic fetters and each illegal move was punished at once, and in the most painful way. There were no exceptions to this rule.

After performing their ablutions the prisoners were sent to the quartermaster's office, where they had their bodies sprayed with disposable underwear, and then they left for the mess hall to grab something to eat. This was the moment everyone was waiting for. Only there, and only for five minutes, they had direct contact with other people. They sucked cocktails at bulk food dispensers, called "confessionals" because in order to reach the tubes with nutrients, they had to kneel on special low benches. Then they walked to the locker room, donned occupational armors, collected the toolkits, and finally started a twelve-hour drudgery. At oh seven hundred sharp all shuttles unmoored from the docks on the penal colony dome.

When the prisoners reached the designated asteroids, they were allocated to all sorts of jobs and left for their workstations along the roadways. Although each team consisted of eight people—there were as many workstations at each extraction line —the prisoners always worked alone. Their comlinks were turned on only in the event of an emergency, and each instant of unwarranted use was punished. Ruthlessly and brutally, as always.

During the workday, the prisoners ate twice more, taking

nutrients from the feeders installed within the armor. Urination and defecation resembled relieving oneself at the dawn of spaceflight, which was another torture for the prisoners. The ancient heroes of space didn't have to spend the greater part of their lives walking around with a plastic tube in their rectum.

The inmates left the mine at nineteen hundred hours. Upon returning to the cellblock they handed in the toolkits, gobbled down some food at the mess hall, got rid of the spent underwear in the bathroom, donned standard armors, and then drifted away to their cells. Curfew sounded thirty minutes later.

Henryan quickly ceased to be surprised that almost every prisoner dreamed of breaking free from the hell of monotony, which could be done in only one way: by committing suicide. However, how to take one's own life, when the butchers—no one called them here otherwise—had left nothing to chance? The vast majority of those who died (during the three years Darski spent in the colony, he counted twenty-seven deaths) had Draccos's permission. The lucky ones were given an opportunity. One full minute. The magnetic fetters let go for sixty seconds, but even that was enough to tear the protector out of the mouth and bite off the tongue, or do something equally disgusting to off oneself. If the lucky sucker chosen by Colonel Draccos didn't manage to take advantage of this peculiar act of grace, he couldn't count on a reprise. Life's not a fairy tale …

At the beginning of incarceration, Darski often cudgeled his brains why the convicts wanted to commit suicide. In case of men sentenced to life, who had no hope of ever leaving the colony, this was understandable, but some suicides were "terminal" prisoners. Who kills himself a few years before the release?

Henryan learned the truth some time later, when the mills of colonial routine grinded his spirit and will to dust. After just two years of total isolation he became certain that if he was allowed to die, even in the most cruel and painful way, he wouldn't hesitate for one moment. Especially that the warden was also right about other things. Owing to the role which Darski played in the colony, the respect of the inmates quickly evaporated. Each prevented suicide attempt—albeit doomed to failure anyway—increased the aversion to the man who'd helped prevent it.

In his third year it got so bad that no one even wanted to talk to him. During those brief moments when the prisoners, bound with magnetic fetters, waited at the mess hall for their meal together, no one chatted him up. Henryan managed to withstand it for a week, plunging into the increasing apathy, and then he gave up. He simply gave up. He couldn't let this last bit of normalcy be taken away from him; these few moments of joyful chaos in the painfully orderly routine of the hell that was his home, and was going to be his home for a long time yet.

On average, suicide attempts occurred every week, while in Darski's team they happened once a month—at most. Still, he didn't have to wait long for the opportunity. Three days after he'd made his mind, the road header machine's cooling system failure led to the overheating of one of its cutting heads. The automatic safety system responded immediately, pushing the white-hot giant away from the wall being drilled. The operator saw his chance and took it without a second thought. He stood a step away from the mine face, and before anyone could react, he jumped into the hole. The armor had many safeguards, including the protective field, but even that could not withstand the prolonged contact with almost ten thousand degrees hot helon. The basic function, knocking the prisoner unconscious, wasn't of much help in this case.

The counter on Henryan's display indicated that less than a minute remained for the energy cells supporting the field to run out. He knew that after the force barrier was gone, the prisoner would be cooked alive. In just a few seconds, a dozen at most. If Darski acted immediately, as the procedures dictated, he would reach the accident site in forty-eight seconds, which would allow him to plug in the suicide to the external power supply and maintain the force field, so that the guards could shift the road header machine weighing several tons and detach the poor sucker from the white-hot cutting head. But Darski didn't move an inch. Five seconds later his comlink came to life. The supervisor asked why seven two one wasn't responding to the alarm signal. The lack of response had been understood correctly. Henryan braced himself for the unimaginable pain, which, as usual, didn't help him at all. He'd received such a dose of electricity that he lost consciousness, and when he came to, he was surrounded by impenetrable darkness. His muscles were still numb, every nerve seemed to be fried, and, in addition, he couldn't even move a finger. A moment later, he understood why.

He had been severely punished for his rebellion. He ended up in solitary confinement.

———

He spent there a week. He came out a wreck, but the very first visit to the mess hall showed he wasn't treated like a pariah anymore. No one turned away from him, no one spat at his feet. When asked, he answered frankly that he wasn't going to turn a blind eye again any time soon. The inmates didn't blame him for this.

Although he recovered within couple of weeks, he needed three months before he could disobey once again. It was the twenty-first suicide attempt in his team, counting from the last successful "escape." The triumph of the four two seven encouraged many. In the first weeks after his feat, there wasn't a single day that the rescuers replacing Henry—the rest of the inmates served this function on a rotating basis—didn't have to intervene. With time, however, the situation returned to normal. Several latest desperadoes didn't have too much brains, so Darski's activities were limited to guarding the stunned would-be suicides and transferring them into the hands of the supervisors.

The last felon had more luck than sense: he caused a short circuit in the drive of the transmission belt providing output to the shredder, and he was ordered to perform the diagnostics of the equipment. When he climbed the tray, it started moving as if touched by a magic wand, and the man, kneeling on it, fell straight on the rotating shaft that was crushing the ore. Darski pressed the blockade key only when the armor of four six eight turned into a piece of scrap splattered with bloody pulp.

Later, he claimed that he had been taken by complete surprise, although of course it wasn't true. He knew very well what was coming, since he'd checked the cause of the short circuit at the first sign of a breakdown. He immediately understood the suicide's plan, and estimated that it had a great chance of success. Moreover, he asked to be put through to the supervisor, and asked the guard whether as the rescuer on duty he should assist in the repair. Switching the comlink to the general channel, he not only lost sight of the suicide, but also absorbed the attention of the person responsible for this area. A few seconds of confusion was all that was needed for four six eight to die, and for him to obtain an unquestionable alibi.

He got away with it, if you could say so. He wasn't zapped on the spot, which was the primary method of discipline for any breach of the rules. He wasn't put in solitary confinement for the second time. Instead, he was called on the carpet. Draccos, not hiding his irritation, announced that the third successful suicide attempt on Henryan's watch would be "rewarded," regardless of circumstances, with something very special even for this penal colony.

Darski, shit-scared, was the model of integrity for the next six months. During this time only one inmate died, fortunately on a completely different asteroid. The inmates in Henryan's team still tried to take their own life, but they did it clumsily enough not to cause him any problems.

So it was until the week before the third anniversary of his incarceration. On Sunday evening, a stocky bald guy with pig eyes and scarred face knelt at a nearby confessional.

"You don't know me, rescuer," he said before taking a long sip of a cocktail.

Henryan looked at him.

"What do you want?" he asked shortly.

"You know what," the bald guy said, without a glance in his direction.

Darski realized that out of the two of them, the other man had a stronger death wish.

"Last time Drac warned me—" he began uncertainly.

He wouldn't hesitate a minute if he was sure that after his next insubordination, Draccos would kill him. Unfortunately, the warden knew quite well what the inmates dreamed of, and he wasn't going to help them in any way. The promise of the "reward" meant for sure an elaborate, lengthy, and painful torture.

"There is a way," the baldhead grumbled.

"Yeah, right."

"You'll see for yourself. Don't take the toolkit number six tomorrow."

The baldhead finished his cocktail, got up, and walked away without looking back even once.

NINETEEN

THE STURGEON BELT, ZULU SECTOR

08/26/2354

It was a piece of cake—all he had to do was to take any place other than the sixth one in the morning line and wait for the warehouse robot to do the rest.

Henryan arrived at the docks early. He watched five men from his team receive the equipment, then walked up to the tray, casually took another set of tools, and placed them in the appropriate pockets of his armor. He stood in the airlock within a minute, which the system gave every prisoner to prepare before the travel to the mine. Now he had only to wait for the arrival of the last two prisoners, and the opening of the compartment of the transport shuttle.

Darski worked just like the other prisoners. The only difference was that at every call of the supervisor, he had to drop the tools and do everything to stop the next suicide attempt. Integrated Systems of Prisoner Protection, despite the extraordinary technological advancement and the learning module of artificial intelligence, could not cope with critical situations, especially that the ingenuity of the inmates knew no bounds, and the basic method of automatic prevention, which boiled down to the electrical shock, was a huge threat to the prisoner.

Not having any idea at the time of the call how serious the situation was, Darski would have to immediately leave the assigned workstation and go to the accident site. He would assess the degree of risk along the way, analyzing the data flowing to the rescue module. He'd also make the first decisions on the way. During the three years of incarceration he took part in nearly forty such actions. He failed only twice.

Standing now in the airlock, he wondered what fate would await him, if he'd listened to the baldhead. Draccos promised him something special. He'd heard from the other prisoners that the repertoire of torture in the colony wasn't very wide. The warden put his vision of the penitentiary system into practice in cold blood. He considered pain a half measure; the true instrument of terror according to him was fear. Fear that was numbing, sucking both the soul and the reason. A week spent in solitary confinement made Henryan realize one thing: given a choice, he would rather stand pain—even inflicted every day, chronic and stronger than the suffering so far—than another week in a sealed armor that was additionally immobilized with the force field of the gravitational transport platform. Solitary confinement was, at least in his opinion, the worst possible torture. For more than twelve hours, the convict had to stand upright, staring at the perfect blackness of the cell. He couldn't even move his hand or foot. The isolation was to be complete, so nutrients were dispensed automatically, directly from the feeders in the armor. After curfew, the platform fell to a horizontal position, and returned to a vertical position at the reveille. The convict had a feeling of complete perdition. A few hours of such torture could be taken without much difficulty, but after a few days, even the toughest guys started to lose their sanity. They were willing to say and do anything to get out of the tenebrous abyss.

Henryan knew himself well enough to be aware that he couldn't stand prolonged seclusion. Were he to indicate the limit beyond which an irreversible madness awaited, it would be, at best, nine, ten days. He still remembered a panic attack that had overwhelmed him when he'd heard the wake-up signal on the eighth morning. He was on the verge of a heart attack or a stroke, and owed his life exclusively to the medical module of his armor.

The longer he stood in the airlock, the more he was convinced that he'd rightly opposed the baldhead. This attempt, like the vast majority of others, would have failed anyway. And he wasn't ready for the promised punishment, yet.

A few moments later, the last two members of the team appeared in the airlock. To Darski's surprise, the baldhead wasn't among them. At first he thought it strange, but soon he guessed that their evening conversation must have drawn the supervisors' attention.

Instead of the mine, the baldhead ended up in the interrogation room, or, more likely, in solitary confinement face to face with darkness.

———

Four hours of work passed nicely and quietly. Levitating in front of the display of the road header machine's dashboard, from time to time Henryan controlled the temperature indicators of the cutting heads, to avoid their overheating. The cable that connected him to the machine controller kept him in one position, about three feet above the cab's floor. Darski didn't turn the magnetic boots on, preferring to float freely. Thanks to this, he didn't feel the vibrations caused by the fast rotating heads and the powerful shredders, turning the excavated material into gravel, and then powder. A daily dose of such vibrations could shake a man to the bone, quite literally. That was the reason, among other things, why they took turns operating the road header machine. Over eight days, each of them worked at each workstation within a piece of primeval rock, drilled with helon heads. And when they tore the last ounce of ore from it, they would move to the next asteroid. There were millions of them in the Sturgeon Belt, so no one harbored fears that the next generations of convicts would run out of work.

"Seven two one, alarm in the hallway three."

Henryan reacted instantly. He ran his hands over the spectral controls of the display. He decelerated the rotation of the heads, retracted them synchronously from the face of the excavation, and then reached with a learned fluid motion for the plug of the cable connecting his armor to the machine controller. He pressed both fastening buttons at the same time, but it didn't do much good. He tried again, harder, and then grabbed the other end of the cable. The result was the same, that is, none. The slots had also been blocked. It was impossible!

Hearing the monotonously broadcasted call, he pulled himself up to the display to switch on the comlink.

"Supervision, I have a problem," he reported, his voice faltering. "The connecting cable got stuck in the slots."

"Unplug it anyhow, you fool!" the irritated guard yelled.

"I tried everything. It didn't even budge."

In the background, he heard a shrill whine, the patter of magnetic boots, and hurriedly issued orders.

"Cut it," the supervisor advised him.

"Yes, sir!" Darski said, reaching into the pocket on the right thigh, harboring the laser cutter.

Dozens of prisoners went to the hole after having tried to use this short blade to damage the armor. Henryan knew it was pointless. The focused beam was extinguished immediately after reaching the force field protecting the scrap into which they were pushed every morning. A cable, however, was something else: the shiny blue blade would get through it effortlessly, as if through butter. Darski put the plug into the socket at his waist, pressed the activation button ... and swore. The knife didn't work. Its tip remained black as the inside of the cell, in which he would soon end up if he didn't do something that would allow him to get out of the cab.

"The knife is cold," he said to the comlink.

"Are you kidding, seven two one?"

"No, sir. My tools are broken. Seriously." He showed the knife and the cable plugged properly in the socket to the camera, then pressed the activation key several times.

"Now you've done it, you scumbag," the supervisor hissed in the midst of a resonant silence.

The howling had died down. Henryan heard only the loud panting of the supervisor.

"But … I don't understand …" he stammered.

Suddenly everything was clear. The baldhead tricked him, knowing that the rescuer, trying to avoid the punishment, would reach for the toolkit he shouldn't take; the tools had been damaged on purpose by someone from the previous shift in order to immobilize the only person who could prevent the tragedy. This whine, this howl that died so abruptly … Someone broke free from the power of Draccos. Henryan tried to recall who was working that day in the third corridor. It had to be one of the new ones.

"I'm fucked," he muttered, heartbroken.

TWENTY

THE WARDEN'S office was located at the end of a tortuous corridor, melted inside the black rock. The air conditioning was even less efficient here than in the cellblock, occupying the highest levels under the outer casing of the dome. Just a few minutes outside the door—which was an integral part of the audience ritual—were enough to make the sweat run in streams down the unfortunate man's forehead and back. Draccos liked to humiliate his victims at every possible opportunity. Darski had understood this when he was called on the carpet after the previous successful suicide attempt.

This time he was spared the initial agony. The warden saw him without a ceremonious delay. An armed guard opened the office door at the sight of the arriving prisoner, who crossed the threshold of the air-conditioned room with relief, not slowing his pace. Draccos was sitting at his desk with a face devoid of expression. A sensitive man couldn't be a warden of the penitentiary unit; in this position were valued completely different qualities plus an additional priest's multilicence.

"Number seven two one's reporting to—" started frightened Henryan.

"Shut up, Darski, and sit down!" The warden kept a straight

face, but the fact that he referred to the convict by name, not by number, was more than striking.

Henryan obeyed, perching carefully on the rickety chair. It was hard to keep the required stillness on it, because the two opposing legs had been shortened by half an inch. Meanwhile, any wobble could result in imposing an additional penalty upon the prisoner.

Draccos leaned back in his chair and watched the convict, who waited for the verdict, with a sharp measuring look as if trying to penetrate his mind.

"Remember what I've promised you?" he asked casually.

Darski nodded. He preferred not to open his mouth, especially that the warden behaved strangely and this could only mean trouble.

"What's your excuse?" The warden made a permissive gesture.

"There was nothing I could do, sir. The tools that I received in the morning had been tinkered with. The guards can confirm my words. Someone put microcapsules with glue in both plugs and removed the fuses from the knife."

"You could have done it," Draccos said and straightened in his chair.

"Since the collection of the equipment I had been under constant supervision. Besides, I didn't have access to—" Henryan began to explain.

Since his release from the cab, he had been putting together a coherent version in his mind, trying to find an explanation for every detail. One hour was enough to find a number of arguments in his favor, which was satisfactory in his opinion.

But he didn't get a chance to voice anything. The warden silenced him with a raised hand.

"Enough," he said. "I don't really care if you had access to the glue, or if the recordings show you pulling out the fuses from the knife, or if the act of sabotage was committed by someone else. Whose fault it was, is now of the least importance. A convict died on your shift. The third one in a row. Someone has to pay for it."

Henryan raised his hand like a cadet who knows the answer to the question. He didn't want to interrupt the warden, but he couldn't let things escalate, either. He had a plan how to prevent this from happening.

Draccos looked at him angrily. After a moment's reluctance he let him speak.

"Maybe we should focus on catching the one who arranged all that?" Darski muttered. "Punishing me, you will release your anger, but—"

"You want to help me find the guilty party?" The colonel asked with a genuine surprise.

"I've been framed," Henryan reminded him.

Draccos shook his head, slowly, ominously.

"No, my friend. I'll get to the bottom of it without your help. Not another word!" He raised his voice when Darski opened his mouth to protest. "You keep quiet, I talk.

"Yesterday, I received the documents from the Admiralty. You probably won't believe me, but they asked about you." He smiled to himself as if he couldn't believe it, either. "In fact, they didn't ask, but demanded your immediate release."

Henryan felt a sudden surge of joy, but realized at once that the warden could be bluffing. It was one of his wicked games: to toss hope to a prisoner, and when he clutched at it, snatch it back together with the poor sucker's teeth and claws, and trample it in front of him. Darski didn't have friends in high places; moreover, none of the command would stand for him, even if the evidence of Renaud's guilt were finally found. Whether Major Renaud was indeed dealing drugs was now as irrelevant as Henryan's complicity in the last suicide. Once he understood that, he smiled to himself, which didn't go unnoticed by Draccos.

"You don't believe me?" the warden asked with a snakelike

voice. "You think I'm making this up so that your next punishment would be more painful to you?"

He leaned over his desk and activated the display occupying almost the entire tabletop. He set the virtual screen vertically so that both of them could see it well, and then opened one of the folders and enlarged the document in it. "Here, look."

Even from this distance, the document looked real, although in the age of holo you could falsify everything. Except one thing ...

Henryan raised his hand tentatively, and when he was given the right to speak again, asked, "Can I?"

Draccos hesitated, seeing the convict point at the display, but then a mischievous smile appeared on his mouth. He guessed what was going on. Aware that a refusal would be the confirmation of fraud, he quickly moved a virtual screen toward Darski, who found the source of the file within a few seconds.

"You thought I was bluffing," the warden teased, leaning back in his chair. "No, my dear. This time I didn't have to. And do you know what's best?" Henryan shook his head. "I haven't sent my reply yet. I have twenty-four hours for it."

Darski felt icy tentacles of fear slowly creeping up his spine.

"In any case, tomorrow I will be free," he said. He was surprised his voice did not falter.

Draccos raised his eyebrows. He looked amused.

"You think so?"

Darski nodded once, slightly. The wave of fear subsided. He knew there were only two ways out: the warden either orders to kill him, or he signs his release. He couldn't cripple the prisoner and release him in such a state. Contrary to what he insisted, he was not god. And the Admiralty hated it when someone stood up to them. A rotter like Draccos wouldn't risk his career to finish off an insignificant pawn.

"I think so," Henryan said.

"You know nothing about me, you scumbag!" The warden snorted, jumping up from his desk. "I don't ever let go. Never."

"I'm not worth what they will do to you, sir, if they discover the truth."

"You're not," Draccos admitted, looking at the prisoner with genuine disgust. "But I keep my word, even if it costs me a lot."

Henryan remembered their first conversation.

"Then give me the chance you were talking about." He dropped the "sir" since he had nothing to lose and was no longer going to grovel before the clone-of-a-bitch.

"With pleasure." Draccos sat behind his desk, switched the display to private mode, waved his hand a few times, and finally called the security. "Die in pain, Darski."

"Better this than having to look at your rat's snout," Henryan retorted and leaned back in his chair.

He didn't care anymore.

"It remains to be seen ..." Surprisingly, Draccos didn't lose control of himself. That, too, could be a bad omen. When the guards appeared at the office door, he added, "Before you say goodbye, I want you to have a look at another document."

Grinning, he opened another folder.

What appeared before Darski's eyes was the Admiralty's report on the investigation carried out on his former ship. He skimmed through the text, feeling previous uncertainty. When he finished reading, he looked up at the elated warden.

"So what do you say, murderer?" Darski swallowed so hard that his Adam's apple jumped. "How do you feel, knowing that you've killed an innocent man?"

Henryan looked down. This scum won on all fronts. For what he'd done, he deserved to die, not to spend twenty-five years in even the harshest penal colony.

"Escort the inmate out!" Draccos snarled, still grinning. "You know what to do with him."

The guards pulled Darski of the chair and without a word pushed him toward the door.

———

For the duration of the visit he was removed from the armor, the guards could, therefore, strike him with a hand taser. They did it for the first time right outside Draccos's office door; the second time when he reached the fork of the corridor on his still shaky legs. There, one of them kicked the prisoner toward the branch leading to the technical part of the administrative block. A moment later, they passed the sentry at the entrance to the docks. At this time, the only workers there were the robots unloading the containers with equipment and supplies. Henryan walked unsteadily, seeing very little through his watery eyes. The tongue was still stiff in his mouth and saliva dripped from between the numb lips down his chin and on the sweaty jumpsuit.

The guards took him to the wall of a great hall. There, one of them opened an internal airlock of the loading dock and the other pushed Darski inside.

"Stand on the second line," he ordered with a mechanical voice.

Henryan shuffled obediently to the indicated sign, then he turned awkwardly and tried to smile mockingly. They seemed to understand what this grimace meant, or maybe they didn't like the look in his eyes, in any case, they both smote him almost simultaneously. Darski was glad to see them aim their stun guns his way. He provoked them deliberately. Since they were told to tire him out before the execution, they could play with him in cold blood all shift long, and maybe even longer. If, however, he managed to piss them off … He hoped one of them would lose it, seeing that the battered victim was still mocking him.

Darski writhed on the cold grill for fifteen minutes, but to him it felt like eternity. Meanwhile, the guards stood there impassively, talking on a closed channel and waiting for him to recuperate. A chip, implanted behind the right ear of each prisoner and monitoring the vital bodily functions, informed the perpetrators that the victim's heartbeat was back to normal, and the muscles were finally limp again. They waited a bit more as if hoping he'd get up by himself, but he wasn't going to make their task any easier. The harder it was for them, the sooner one of them would go too far. That was the strategy he decided to stick to, but the torturers saw through his ruse. Instead of punishing him for the fourth time, one of the guards—without even looking in the direction of the airlock—said, "Get up, seven two one."

Henryan tried to get up, but he was still too weak. His hands were shaking so much, that he wasn't able to lift the body.

"Need extra incentive, scumbag?" the other guard mocked him.

"Somehow your wife doesn't complain about my abilities," Darski said, or rather mumbled, hoping that this insult would finally tip the scale.

It looked like they didn't understand. Apparently, his speech synthesizer got fried.

A moment later, one of them came up and set him on his feet unceremoniously. It seemed that they were getting bored. If they zapped him again, he wouldn't come to his senses soon. He knew that, and so did they. That is why he wanted so much to infuriate the bastards. He would have given anything for them to finish him off here and now, rather than start the game from the beginning, which, knowing their sadistic bent, was quite possible.

"Stand right there and don't even twitch!" the guard shouted.

Still standing outside the airlock, he waved at his companion. When both were safely in the dock, the airlock closed.

Darski breathed a sigh of relief. So, it's over. Just a few more moments and he will join his brother—of that there was no longer any doubt. In a second, an alarm would beep, yellow, then red lights would go on, and finally the pumps would begin to work. Whether he would still be alive at the time of the opening of the outer airlock, or whether he would die earlier, after a short fight for every atom of oxygen, would depend on the rate at which air would be sucked out from the airlock. One thing was certain: alive or dead, he would be sucked into the void, to freeze in a flash, and some time in the future, in a minute, or in one billion years, he would crash on any of the primeval rocks sweeping through space. Actually, he didn't care one way or another. He had come to terms with the thought of death, to which—after the news he'd learned today—he was looking forward more than ever before in the past three years.

The time passed, and he stood there, hunched over, his whole body still trembling. Fifteen minutes passed before Henryan even noticed. He was still too dazed to think of anything else than the excruciating pain. After another fifteen minutes, when he finally managed to straighten up, he began to have doubts. And what if this was not the end; if it was only a short break in the agony that awaited him? They locked him here so that he could recover his strength, because they didn't want to hang around and wait. They went to the mess hall to eat something, or to get new instructions, but they will return at any moment to torment him again.

Screw it, he thought. *Minutes, hours, doesn't matter. I will sneak away from them anyway. Today, tomorrow at the latest. They can't keep me here any longer.*

Encouraged by this thought, he spent the next three hours in the airlock. He stood on the second line with a defiant smile, in case they were watching him after all, which they should be doing if they'd wanted to make sure he wouldn't try to escape ahead of time. In reality, however, there was little he could do— the magnetic fetters hampered him so much that he wouldn't even be able to reach for his face with his hands, or to make two steps. He could only wait and battle with his own thoughts.

He shuddered when he heard the sound of sirens. Rhythmically flashing yellow light flooded the airlock. First, he got scared that it was all over, but then, almost immediately, he realized that in this game death was the prize. When red lights flashed thirty seconds later, he realized that something was wrong. The pumps should be started at the same time. But he didn't hear the unmistakable whistle of air sucked out through the numerous gratings. And he could still breathe. He glanced at the display on the wall of the airlock. Fifteen seconds to the opening of the outer airlock, pressure within the normal range. He turned unsteadily, facing the plasteel pane, behind which stretched boundless space.

They will shoot me into space like a bullet, he thought.

At least he could take comfort in the knowledge that this time he wouldn't feel any pain.

He looked over his shoulder at the display. Five seconds, four, three.

He wondered if he would have a chance to see the stars before—

PART THREE
THE STATION

PROLOGUE

08/17/2354

Karan Degard covered his eyes with the thicker eyelids. He waited for the familiar clatter of the arad, but not even the slightest murmur was coming from the tent. The silence lasted far too long. The swellings of the membrane came and went, but otherwise nothing happened. Fister was thus standing still, although the rim of the hubcap was cutting painfully into his parenchyma. Tahars, having sensed the growing tension of their host, moved nervously inside the porosity—both those feeding just below the surface, and the smaller ones, hidden at the cartilage that separated this part of the young warrior's body from the vital organs.

The dull clatter of the sacred bone restored his peace of mind. Karan Degard opened his eyes. He straightened up slowly, clutching with his claws onto the grips of his masticators, covered with an intricate pattern. The curtains separating him from the chief of the clan were still lowered, however—due to the radiance of the stronger sun, which was just rising behind the captured tent—he saw the silhouettes moving between sheets billowing in a lazy wind. The Supreme Suhur who'd just stepped on to the dais hunkered down.

"The Spirits of the Mountains have spoken again. They've fulfilled the promise made to us," Karan Degard wheezed with respect, and gestured for the bearers to approach.

The mennites standing closest to him moved aside, giving way to two almost naked youths covered with mud, carrying the curved limb of a sagr tree, an oblong object fastened to it with leather straps. It was impossible to determine the exact shape of the gift because it was tightly covered. One thing was certain: it wasn't much shorter than the most magnificent Suhurian spear. It also had to be very heavy because the thick branch was discernibly bent. The tishka skin that was thrown over it scraped the footworn ground with every step.

The fister gestured again, and another pair of youngsters emerged from the line of warriors. Passing by the bearers in fearful respect, they placed two low tripods in front of the tent. A hunched densha spread a hryll skin before them, adorned with the symbols of the clan, then he sprinkled it with the gore of a freshly killed Gurd. Blue drops soaked in quickly, joining hundreds of earlier ones that had formed dark spots on the skin's surface. When the condemned by gods turned to take his place behind the tent, the warriors could see a big bulge on his back. The intricate braid of dried tendons and small bones distended where a shriveled pelchavka was still stuck.

When the branch finally rested on the prepared scaffolding and the bearers got back into line, Karan Degard closed his thicker eyelids again. Next, without opening them, he reached for the tishka skin and uncovered the gift with a sudden movement. He didn't have to look either at the mennites gathered around, or the members of the clan crowding behind them, to know what impression he'd made on them. Murmurs died down abruptly. There was a silence broken only by the gurgle of the nestlings in a nearby pen. On the thick leather straps hung a strange, four jabber-blades long, silvery object.

A moment later, the densha pulled the front curtain of the tent. Tore Numa-Reh, one hundred and first chief of the clan of the Triple Pierced Shield, got up slowly, straightening the joints of his legs one by one. When the flat peak of his helmet reached the ceiling, he stepped down from the dais, but even then he looked down on much shorter warriors around him. Only when he left the shadow did he cover his main eye with the thinner eyelid. Karan Degard didn't know if it was the sun that blinded the Supreme Suhur, or perhaps the divine glow emanating from the gift offered to him.

Tore Numa-Reh strode proudly along the narrow lane between the tallest mennites, above whom he still towered by a few arrow tips. His gray skin, covered with a dense network of pyroglyphs and scars, shone as if greased; his side eyes were covered trustingly, but his tracheal membranes stuck out from under the border of the bone helmet. Karan Degard felt a warm thrill penetrating him to the core. The clan's Supreme Suhur seemed not only surprised, but also pleased.

At the chief's behest, the supporting straps were cut, and the gift of the Spirits of the Mountains was then carefully laid on the ground covered with a hryll skin. Tore Numa-Reh crouched near the glossy cylindrical object to examine the numerous details. He took his time, but Karan Degard didn't blame him. He himself had spent a lot of swellings of the membranes in front of the Bor Omot caves, delighting his senses with the view of the Thunder Sower.

"The Spirits of the Mountains have spoken to you," rumbled finally Tore Numa-Reh, not taking his eyes off the gift. "It must be the work of gods. No Gurd would ever create something so magnificent."

He slowly straightened his legs. "Do you know how to use this weapon?"

"Yes," Karan Degard answered truthfully.

"So, let our eyes relish the power of gods!" Tore Numa-Reh ordered.

Fister cowered anxiously, and his tahars began to fidget again.

"You who overtop the tallest Warriors of the Bone," he started gingerly. "The Spirits of the Mountains cautioned me not to use their gift prematurely ..."

The chief of the clan lowered the thicker eyelids on his side eyes, focusing his sight on the fister.

"Are you not allowed to show the power of this weapon, or you simply don't know how to do it?" he asked.

"I am allowed to do it and I do know how," the fister assured immediately, fighting once again the temptation to tilt his hubcap. "But before I get down to it, I would like you to listen to the warning given to me by the Spirits of the Mountains."

"Open your membranes, then!" rumbled Tore Numa-Reh, returning to the shade of the tent.

"This weapon has been stolen from the gods of Suns and Stars, who guard their secrets jealously, and therefore it can be used only once!" Karan Degard started the speech that he had memorized during the long journey back from the mountains. "When we use it, gods will know that we've acquired it, and will punish terribly those who committed sacrilege. That's why I was told to remember that we should keep this gift in secret until the day of the final battle. The Spirits of the Mountains call this weapon 'Thunder Sower.'"

He pointed to a massive butt.

"Here hides its unimaginable power. So great that the most powerful missiles hurled by Gurds will look as harmless as desiccated sagr seeds next to it."

A wave of quiet murmurs swept the ranks of warriors, as the weapons of the Bluebloods were famous for their destructive power.

"Thanks to it, we can change the fate of the upcoming war in one swelling of the membranes. This weapon could reach the enemy positioned twenty, or even thirty bowshots away."

There was another murmur of admiration, this time even louder. That was far beyond the Suhurs' sight distance.

"Well calibrated—and this is the part designed for this"—

Karan Degard quickly put on gloves in order not to soil the gift with his dirty claws, and touched reverently the protrusion at the top of the Thunder Sower—"it will turn into a bloody mess not only the chief of Gurds, but also all the accompanying Quadrupeds, and this in a radius of a dozen spears."

He pressed a red spot decorated with magical signs, and suddenly a spectral image appeared above the flat-ended protrusion.

Intrigued, Tore Numa-Reh left the shadow again—this time hurriedly, not keeping up appearances. Karan Degard moved a tiny lever, and when two slender supports slid out from the bottom of the weapon, he raised the Thunder Sower off the ground. Kneeling next to it, he pointed the thinner end of the weapon toward the watchtowers guarding the ford, located at a distance of fifteen bowshots. Everyone saw the outlines of tall tree trunks on the horizon, with bone watchtowers placed on them, but even the best observer couldn't tell whether they were occupied or empty.

The fister closed his side eyes, focusing on the space in front of him. After a moment, he stepped aside.

"On the death of my tahars!" Tore Numa-Reh raised his hands in astonishment.

The mennites shifted uneasily. The mysterious spectral image showed the top of the watchtower and an old warrior, leaning on his spear. Karan Degard turned a small knob, and at the intersection of the two dashed lines appeared a well-known figure of the honbut hunter. Despite his age, Hon Kon-Tamin was still vigilant. A red dot fell on one of his eyes, slightly below the border of the flat helmet.

"The tallest of the tallest, you can see for yourself how wonderful this weapon is," the fister continued, pleased with the impression his show had made. "Therefore I'm asking you again to accept the warning of the Spirits of the Mountains, and keep the existence of the Thunder Sower secret until the final battle, of whose arrival the tutelary entities warn us."

Tore Numa-Reh lowered his hands. His palp wound steadily around the rim of the hubcap.

"Why can't we try the weapon now?" The grunt came from the shaded tent.

In a hoarse voice of the highest priest there was disbelief, and something else that Karan Degard could not identify. Tikren Da-Deradha hadn't interrupted him until now, even though he felt like it several times.

"The wrath of the gods of Suns and Stars will fall upon the one who will use the Thunder Sower," the fister reminded hastily, taking a step back from the gift. "We must keep this weapon strictly secret. Thus spoke the Spirits of the Mountains."

"Not necessarily!" The priest left the pleasant semidarkness of the tent. Tapping the arad rhythmically, he headed toward the chief of the clan and the gift lying in front of him. "Gods gave me a sign today, after the sunrise of the first sun. I offered them six comely Gurds as the sacrifice. The gore ran down the altar grooves evenly, without foaming even once. No viscera were tangled while gutting, despite the fact that I chose the comeliest Quadrupeds recently captured on the plains."

Karan Degard humbly waited for the priest to finish.

"I'm only repeating what I heard from the Spirits of the Mountains," he wheezed.

Tikren Da-Deradha moved his blue-painted claws along the cool gleaming body of the Thunder Sower. It was evident that the unusual weapon from the otherworld made a strong impression also on him.

"The border clans' scouts say that Gurds are building new giant circles over there"—he pointed his arad at the ford—"on the lands we lost many clashes of the suns ago. Among them, they're erecting stone huts and making wonders with wood and iron. Reportedly, they've also possessed the ability to float in the air. They soar across the sky faster than kumaxes."

Tore Numa-Reh inflated his membranes as if to stop him, but

the highest priest silenced the chief with one slight tap of his arad at the cracked ground.

"I did not believe in these stories, like most of you, but today I don't know anymore whether I was right. The enemy has become insidious. For hundreds of clashes of the suns Gurds have been robbing us of our lands. Only in my lifetime we have lost the Valt Aram plains, full of prey. I came out of the pen there"—he pointed toward the mountains visible on the horizon —"in a hamlet at the foot of the Steep Scree, the same, on top of which we'd offered sacrifices since time immemorial. Many, many hundreds of bowshots from our present-day borders."

He shifted his claw toward the north. "We have nowhere to retreat anymore. Beyond the settlements of the last clans there are only rocky highlands and cliffs plunging straight into the foamy sea. There used to be more of us than the grains of redhusk in a shieldful; today we wouldn't fill a helmet, or even a hubcap …"

"What's your point?" asked Tore Numa-Reh, taking the opportunity of the priest's silent moment of reflection.

"I have seen enough wiles of the enemy in my life …" Tikren Da-Deradha replied, and fell silent again. "Doesn't it surprise you that the Spirits of the Mountains speak through a simple fister, instead of us priests?"

Murmurs grew louder. Even the mennites began to gargle among themselves and looked around as if searching for the answer to this question in the eyes of their comrades in arms. In the end their attention, as before, focused on Karan Degard.

"My venerable lord, even to me it seemed strange," the fister wheezed. "I never asked for this sort of recognition."

"That's what I can't understand. We beg for it every day, but the Spirits of the Mountains spoke to you—"

The chief of the clan took the fister's side. "The tutelary entities decide for themselves who they speak to."

"Really?" Tikren Da-Deradha wasn't going to give up easily. "Do you know of any other case of such grace?"

Tore Numa-Reh went silent for a moment, then denied, humbly folding his palp. Within his own lifetime no one except priests would hear so much as a whistle of the tutelary entities. After all, making contact with them required complex rituals and many offerings.

"I swear on my masticators—" Karan Degard started, but stopped immediately, rebuked by both dignitaries.

"Shut your membranes!" Tikren Da-Deradha ordered.

"Don't you dare utter even a screech until we allow you," added the chief, then turned to the priest. "Karan Degard has served me faithfully for six clashes of the suns; I've known him since he left the pen."

"Yes, I know," Tikren Da-Deradha cut him off. "You have tasted his tahars, as he's tasted yours. However, this doesn't mean he's telling the truth."

The last words of the priest raised bewilderment. Not only the chief's, but also the warriors'. Lying and deception had been alien to the clans until Gurds appeared in Suhurta. An exaggeration or understatement could happen to anyone, but a Warrior of the Bone had never been caught in a deliberate lie.

"What do you mean?" Tore Numa-Reh asked, visibly moved.

"It could be another trick of the enemy."

The chief of the clan and the fister folded their palps as one.

"I've burned scores of Gurdian circles, I've set out with the clan's fists as far as the foothills, but nowhere and never have I seen anything like this!" The Supreme Suhur pointed his claw toward the Thunder Sower. "Our enemy couldn't create something so perfect."

"You haven't seen much, the Tallest," Tikren Da-Deradha stated.

"Do you really think it's the enemy's trap?"

The priest did not answer immediately. He slid his palp under the bone robe, fumbled around the hubcap and pulled out a fat, squirming tahar. He immediately slipped its thicker end into the sucker.

"I believe that gods who created the two suns and all the stars wouldn't lower themselves to speak in the ears of a simple fister," he wheezed, crushing the tail of the symbiont with the corneous lip to suck its guts into the digestive bladder. "I also believe that the Spirits of the Mountains, who serve them faithfully, wouldn't offer us anything against the will of their masters. So I think," he ended the statement according to the custom.

Having absorbed the life-giving flesh of the symbiont, he tossed the empty shell on the ground.

The densha immediately leaned over, picked up the still squirming remains, and hid them in the satchel. What the old priest couldn't eat would go to the pen even before dusk.

Karan Degard couldn't defy this reasoning. But he had also heard a whistling sound of the Spirits of the Mountains. He'd heard it as clearly as if the tutelary entities hovered just above his helmet. And according to an earlier promise he had received a gift from the otherworld. Full of hope, he brought it straight to the clan's seat and laid it at the feet of him who governed all the fists. He believed that the Thunder Sower was the miracle Suhurs had awaited for generations; a weapon that would change the fate of the longtime and, what was worse, doomed war.

Gurds had been pressing on the Warriors of the Bone for more than a thousand clashes of the suns. Since the time their big bulky ships arrived at Suhurta's coast, far away beyond the horizon, at a distance of hundreds upon hundreds of bowshots from the settlement in which the Thunder Sower appeared. The clans put up a stout resistance. Once they even pushed the enemy toward the sea and forced them to leave the occupied territories. Countless rites praised the heroism of the bravest Warriors of the Bone and great victories in that war. This, however, was all in the past. A few generations later, a new, more powerful fleet of quadrupedal Gurds arrived, consisting of even larger ships. There came new legions of Bluebloods, who turned out to be much smarter, more numerous, and better armed than their ancestors. The outcome of the war had been sealed. Many clashes of the suns later, Gurds launched a final attack on Suhurta and since then pushed forward incessantly. First, they went straight to the east to wedge their armies between the Suhurs, and then, when they managed to separate the brave clans, they planted the poles with Gurdian knots near the cliffs on the opposite side of the continent, built the initial circle there and went to the south, leaving the wilder northern lands in a relative peace. But only temporarily.

Hundreds of clashes of the suns later, on a plateau beyond Seven Pinnacles, the two immense armies faced each other. The serried ranks of the united clans were five bowshots wide and two bowshots deep. At least eight shields of this world's bravest warriors outfaced Gurds. The enemy was defeated, although they were more numerous and had thunderous sticks. The plains, bathed in a shine of the setting suns, glowed blue. But the victory carried a steep price. Too steep. The plateau and the surrounding mountains were shrouded in smoke billowing up from the pyres, on which the fallen and the mercifully finished off were bidden farewell.

After this battle, the decimated clans had to retreat before the successive waves of the invaders, and flee to the mountains separating them from the northern highlands. The skirmishes lasted a long time, but in the end the Warriors of the Bone were driven out from even this inhospitable ridge. The enemy had not fought fair—whenever they could not win in an open battle, they starved the defenders to death or killed them deceitfully. Last Suhurs left their settlements across the river and their ancient altars during the lifetime of the current highest priest. Now, less than seven hundred bowshots separated them from the steep cliffs of the north and the waters of the ocean.

There was only one thing Tikren Da-Deradha wasn't right about: the number of the remaining warriors was smaller than the number of sagr seeds fitting in the claws, rather than filling the helmet or the hubcap.

The fister looked at the silvery gift from the Spirits of the Mountains, its rounded shapes and incredible alien ornamentation. It was hard to believe that Gurds were able to produce something so beautiful and complicated. Although ...

"Listen to me, everyone!" Tikren Da-Deradha got up, raising the arad high above his head. "There is only one way to find out whether the weapon was actually donated to us by the Spirits of the Mountains."

He paused as if wondering if he should continue. "We have to try it out! Here and now!"

"But—" Karan Degard opened his membranes once again, but fell silent immediately, before the chief or the priest could react.

Tikren Da-Deradha rolled his palp in a meaningful gesture.

"I don't think the Spirits of the Mountains had the courage to steal the property of the gods of Suns and Stars."

"I doubted it, too," the Supreme Suhur admitted, "but I changed my mind after Karan Degard had brought the Thunder Sower."

"Am I to believe that the winged favorite of our gods, hitherto not known from any rites"—he searched his memory for the name—"Lut Se-Ifer opposed the will of those who created the suns and then smashed one of them into tiny stars? That he rebelled when he was told that gods, unhappy with Suhurs, doomed them to extinction? That he was exiled and imprisoned under the mountains as a punishment? That despite the harassment, he and his followers intend to fight for us? Not only with Gurds, but also with the almighty Kored, Yabha, and Thub?"

Tore Numa-Reh waited for the highest priest to finish, and then he replied, "If it is a trick of our enemy, why haven't they chosen someone from the temple?"

"We are harder to deceive than a simple fister."

"You would succumb if the Spirits of the Mountains whispered in your head," Tore Numa-Reh insisted.

Though the chief's logic was unquestionable most often than not, the priest tried to undermine it.

"I'd notice the difference. I've talked to the otherworld hundreds of times."

"So you are suggesting that we disregard the warning of the Spirits of the Mountains, which you think in reality is coming from the enemy, and try the sacred weapon here and now?"

"Yes!" All the eyelids disappeared from the eyes of the priest.

"And what if Kored, Yabha, and Thub have left us in the lurch? What if we waste our last chance to be saved?"

"Use the Thunder Sower. You'll see for yourself."

Tore Numa-Reh nodded toward Karan Degard. The fister picked up the weapon dutifully.

"If it's the enemy's trick, I'd better move away many spears away from you," he wheezed.

"Words of wisdom," Tikren Da-Deradha praised the warrior. "Stand under that parchan tree, and aim at any of the watchtowers."

"But—"

"An empty one."

Resigned, Karan Degard withdrew without a screech and set off in the direction of the indicated plant, bending under the weight of the Thunder Sower. Following the instructions of the Spirits of the Mountains, he supported its massive metal body on the twisted branches so that he could aim calmly. When the empty cage of the watchtower appeared at the two lines' intersection, he pulled a "trigger," as Lut Se-Ifer called the small sheltered tab, with the tip of his claw. At the same time he said the brief silent prayer, which he'd also learned from the Spirits of the Mountains.

He didn't hear the roar typical for the thunderous sticks and trunks with which Gurds defended their circles. The silvery weapon jerked slightly in his clutches. The red lines, visible on the spectral image, still intersected at the center of the peaked structure made of bones. Karan Degard felt his membrane swell at an accelerated pace. At the end of the day, he was a fool; he had been tricked. The weapon didn't work, the tower was still in one pie—

The spectral image over the Thunder Sower's body suddenly disappeared, and was replaced with a dazzling whiteness. One of the mennites standing closest to Karan Degard gargled loudly in astonishment. The fister put down the weapon and looked at the horizon, where a big ball of fire and smoke was raising into the cloudless sky.

"On the death of all tahars!" he wheezed, and instinctively crossed himself with the gesture that the Spirits of the Mountains had taught him. For the three gods and their servant, sent away into the abyss.

He took the still warm body of the weapon in both hands, placed it on his shoulder the way Gurds used to do with their thunderous sticks, and walked back toward the settlement. He hadn't even made three steps, when he remembered the warning: the wrath of gods was supposed to come a moment after using the Thunder Sower. Elated by success, he forgot about the curse! As he'd already gotten out from under the twisted parchan branches, he was able to look up at the sky.

The lightning that hit him looked uncanny. It didn't have many branches, neither did it writhe or twitch. A straight column of the blinding light hit from the cloudless sky the place where the young fister stood. It burned a circle with a diameter of three spears, and set the crown of the sacred parchan on fire. The blast following the explosion that gouged a deep crater in the ground scattered the proud Warriors of the Bone the way a gale scatters the grain.

Karan Degard evaporated; not a single bone remained of him. With him disappeared the Thunder Sower.

TWENTY-ONE
THE XAN 4 SYSTEM, X-RAY SECTOR

09/02/2354

The shuttle docked smoothly to the central sleeve of the transit section. A sergeant, sitting in the last row, unbuckled his safety belts as soon as artificial gravity was turned on. He was tall and very slim although broad-shouldered; he had blue eyes, long, narrow, and tawny face, and a strand of black hair encircling the high-vaulted skull at ear level. The Signal Corps noncom's uniform hung loosely from his bony shoulders. When he reached for his hand luggage stored in the overhead locker, one could see his sinewy, muscular forearms. At first glance he looked like someone who was accustomed to wearing a combat armor or had spent much time on a high-gravity planet.

Three more people flew in to Xan 4 with him: a jet-black, portly lady captain, wedged in a tight suit of medical services, a New Russian, as indicated by her appearance and hard to pronounce name on her badge, and two young privates, for whom—judging from their reactions—it must have been the first deep-space travel. Moments after docking, the stewards changed the structure of the plasteel coating so that the passengers could take a look at the place they had been delivered to. The officers didn't pay the slightest attention to it, starting almost immediately toward the exit airlock, but the privates remained in their seats and absorbed the amazing view with an uncertain look on their faces.

The sergeant leaned over the youth sitting on the other side of the aisle.

"Have you been posted to Xan 4, Private … Gosse?" he asked, reading the soldier's name on the badge.

The chubby blond focused his eyes on the sergeant's face and nodded his head.

"Then it's your stop." The sergeant patted him friendlily on the shoulder.

He was accustomed to such sights. Since he started to serve he'd had six assignments. In ten years of stationing in space he had stayed at four orbital stations and visited a score of distant star systems. However, he still remembered the bewilderment that accompanied his first space travel, when he went to join his unit shortly after graduating from the Academy. In space, the concepts such as horizontality and verticality are relative. Your balance system gets confused whenever you enter the shuttle airlock, having the impression that you're about to climb a vertical wall. The disorientation is further aggravated by the fact that over your head, you see a huge, rapidly rotating structure of a space station, or an oval of a nearby planet. This time was no different. The long tunnel connecting the airlock with the terminal was tilted at an almost seventy degree angle.

At the hatchway, the sergeant looked at the steward, who was smiling goodbye.

"Better turn off the transparent mode," he advised, shaking hands with him. He jerked his thumb over his shoulder, pointing at the two conscripts who were still sitting in their chairs, staring at the construction that hung over their heads, the celadon-gold ball of the planet visible behind it, and the stars of this system, shining in the distance.

"I know what you mean," the steward said, opening the panel next to the hatchway.

The sergeant passed the hull before it turned gray again. He walked through the stabilization chamber and without stopping, quickly jumped onto the moving walkway. It was the best way to break out of the machine's gravitational field zone. The privates certainly didn't know this trick, but he didn't regret that he wouldn't see the aerobatics they would both perform in a moment.

The sleeve turned out to be damn long. Thanks to the transparent walls, the sergeant had an excellent view of the massive structure toward which he was heading.

The station resembled a monstrous wheel—the classic one, with a hub, spokes, and a rim. The body of the central part of this behemoth must have had a diameter of a thousand and five hundred feet, and consisted of three interconnecting spherical sections. The most distant one housed the reactors. The central one was a hub joining eight slender arms that connected with the rim at a distance of almost a mile and a half. The rim contained workspace and living quarters. The third sphere, the closest one, served as a spaceport. Bunches of sleeves protruded from its cylindrical surface. In all of them the sergeant could see the slowly moving silhouettes of people or the outlines of transported containers.

However, it wasn't the shape of the station that astonished the newcomer, but its size. During his many travels, the sergeant had seen several combat stations in the outer sectors of the Galaxy's arm, but even they seemed tiny next to the giant he was heading toward. The construction hanging high above the planet brought to mind one of the ancient orbital cities, which used to be placed in the initial period of colonization over the globes in the need of terraforming, so that pioneers had a place to live until the construction of ground stations was completed. Judging by the size of the rim, a few, maybe even a dozen thousand people could live there. Increased traffic around other sleeves of the transit section seemed to confirm the sergeant's suppositions. The place was buzzing with life. Scores of shuttles moved back and forth between the nearby Fleet's anchorage, the station, and the planet visible behind it.

It took the sergeant three minutes to reach the end of the sleeve. An unassuming welcoming committee was waiting for him behind the automated gate. Right next to the checkpoint stood a lanky slant-eyed officer in an immaculate gray uniform with lieutenant's insignia on his collar, and a little farther, inside the airlock, was a troop of gendarmes in full riot gear, guarding three prisoners.

The sergeant flinched involuntarily at the sight of the orange overalls. This place didn't look like a standard penal colony ...

He tightened his grip on the reader with transfer documents he was carrying as if wanting to make sure it was not a dream. The seed of doubt was still there. All the time he had the impression that the promise given to him by the Sector's command wasn't as generous as it might have seemed ...

———

"Sergeant Pry ... dein ... wraig?" the slant-eyed lieutenant stammered, trying to figure out how he should pronounce the exotic name.

"More or less, sir," said the sergeant, and saluted duly. "Teddie Prydeinwraig. It's a Welsh name. It caused me many problems in the Academy, which is why some teachers called me just Pry. This can make things easier for you, too, sir."

"Great, Pry. I know how difficult ethnic names are sometimes, although I don't have a problem with that myself. My name is Ngomobutu Mugabe. I am a deputy commander of the personnel department. Welcome to Xan 4." The lieutenant looked at his reader once more. "And where are Private Gosse and Private Adauer?"

"From what I noticed, they have problems with acclimatization," reported the sergeant. A moment later he added in a confidential tone, "They are rookies."

"I see." Mugabe winced, reaching for his comlink.

"It won't be necessary, sir." Prydeinwraig stopped him, jerking his thumb at the opposite end of the sleeve.

Both privates were already coming on a moving walkway. With their legs wide apart, supporting each other, but with their heads still upturned.

"Great," the lieutenant brightened.

A moment later, both privates tried to get through the narrow gate—at the same time, of course.

After all passengers had passed the checkpoint, Lieutenant Mugabe signaled the gendarmes. Their steel-shod boots pounded on the deck gratings when they moved toward the sleeve, herding the inmates among them. The convicts, dressed in orange overalls and shackled at the ankles with magnetic fetters, were desperately trying to keep up.

"What did they do?" the sergeant asked when the ominous procession disappeared in the depths of the sleeve.

"You'll find out soon enough, Sergeant," the officer replied enigmatically. "You're here to replace one of them."

———

The briefing room was small, low, and claustrophobically cramped. It was located in the central section of the hub, therefore had no windows, and only a narrow hatchway led to it. For the sergeant it wasn't a problem—he was used to much smaller and stuffier rooms—but both privates felt very uncomfortable. Stuck in their seats, they were sweating like pigs in spite of quite efficient air conditioning. When Teddie glanced in their direction, they smiled at him sheepishly, ineptly masking their anxiety.

"Attention!" The guard standing at the hatchway gave the command, and clicked his heels.

Prydeinwraig sprang to his feet and straightened in accordance with regulations; Adauer and Gosse also rose, but more slowly and awkwardly. Although almost thirty minutes had passed since leaving the shuttle, they still suffered from vestibular dysfunction.

"At ease!"

The colonel who spoke these words looked like a veteran. With a crew cut, flat, expressionless face, and small deep-set eyes, he was a classic incarnation of each cadet's nightmare. The impeccably tailored uniform, deftly concealing his excess weight, emphasized his rapacity. Teddie glanced at the privates. The conscripts still smiled; poor suckers didn't yet know with whom they were dealing.

"My name is Franciscollin Rutta," the colonel said succinctly, taking his place behind the rostrum. "I'm the commander of this station. Since you stepped onto it, you've been under my orders. Any questions?"

"No, sir!" the sergeant yelled.

"Great," the colonel snarled. "Sit!"

A slurred voice came from the back, "Actually ..."

"That's right, Private! Better the actual than the supposed." Colonel Rutta mocked Adauer. "I said, sit down!"

The conscripts fulfilled the command more or less at the same time. Luckily, they didn't try to take the same seat.

"Lieutenant," Rutta waved his hand toward the hatchway.

Another officer entered the room. Slim, tall, pale, with raven hair—of which he had less than the aging colonel—trimmed to one-eighth of an inch. A stiff salute made for their welcome.

"The head of the department of communications, Lieutenant Robertobias Valdez, will introduce you to your duties," said the commander of the station, then gave the newly arrived man a sharp glance, and marched out of the room, accompanied by a duly loud yell of the guard.

"At ease." Valdez sat down near the rostrum, and inserted his personal reader into the slot of a holoprojector.

He waited until the privates sat down again, and then called the roll. Prydeinwraig answered in accordance with regulations.

The rookies only stammered their names and the names of their native planets.

"I'm pretty sure you've never heard of Xan 4 or about this station," the lieutenant said when they were done with the presentations. "Our project is so secret that it's known to no one but those involved in it. Including the vast majority of admirals. But let's get down to the details. Consider your assignments indefinite, they will expire only when the project 'Two Suns' is completed, and it can take a while. In a moment you will receive the documents to sign, requiring you to maintain in strict confidence everything that you hear and see during your service in this system. This also applies to private correspondence, which is one hundred percent controlled by the counterintelligence cell of the DFS."

"Wild …" Gosse murmured. Either because of the acoustics, or because he couldn't quite control his voice, his words were heard by all present, including Valdez.

"Oh, yes," the lieutenant confirmed. "You have no idea. Or maybe you do?"

"Is this some kind of a penal colony?" the sergeant asked suspiciously, feeling chilly pressure in the pit of his stomach at the memory of the three prisoners under escort.

The lieutenant shook his head indiscernibly, and smiled to himself. As if he had expected this question, he didn't look at all surprised.

"We're testing new types of weapons on this planet?" one of the rookies asked.

"No."

There was an awkward silence. Prydeinwraig tried to guess what else might several thousand soldiers and civilians do in a foreign system—walking here along the corridors, they passed some people with badges indicating scientific and medical departments—but he didn't come up with anything sensible.

"Is it about the contact with Aliens?" Adauer asked finally, nudging Gosse with his elbow. Both burst into muffled laughter.

"No. It's not about the contact with Aliens." The lieutenant didn't share their amusement. "It's about observing them."

———

The briefing ended a few minutes later. The new soldiers, to their great disappointment, hadn't learned anything more. Valdez only collected their confidentiality statements, gave them a schedule of mandatory training, and finally handed in—against a signed and dated receipt, of course—their access cards for lodging and food vending machines.

"Please don't leave quite yet, Sergeant," the lieutenant said when Prydeinwraig reached for the documents and the key.

Gosse and Adauer went out with a springy step. Excited by the news about Aliens, they forgot about their labyrinth disorder. When the door closed behind them and the dismissed guard, Valdez put the reader aside, and then looked straight in the eye of the man that was standing in front of him and asked, "Why the weird name? If my memory serves me, you come from the Polish sector, Mr. Darski." The real name sounded oddly slurred in his mouth.

"This is the maiden name of my mother, who was proud of her Welsh roots, although ..." Henryan paused, not sure whether he should acquaint the officer with his family matters.

"Although ... ?" the lieutenant encouraged him.

"That's how the Welsh called English people."

"I don't understand."

"Never mind, sir. If it's a problem, please use the short form. Pry is much easier to pronounce than both of those names."

"Pry. Yes, of course," Valdez checked himself.

Henryan seized the initiative, taking advantage of the lieutenant's confusion.

"I've been assured in the Admiralty that—" he started.

The lieutenant raised his hands in a calming gesture.

"It's not like that. I am Colonel Rutta's right hand. Only the two of us know who you really are. To all other soldiers and scientists you will be Sergeant Pryde something-something ...”

“I hope so,” Henryan said, still resentful, then looked penetratingly at the new superior and asked incredulously, “Aliens? Seriously?”

Valdez nodded his head. “Of course. However, let's be honest, we're not talking about some highly developed civilizations.”

That much was clear. Darski knew that such a concentration of the Fleet at a relatively low orbit wouldn't escape the attention of the creatures on the level of nineteenth- or even eighteenth-century humanity.

“All of you will learn everything you need in the introductory courses,” the lieutenant added.

“We?” Henryan asked. “Are you saying that these two assholes had been brought here for the same purpose as I?”

Valdez shook his head.

“Relax. I was talking about Aliens. Colonel Rutta himself will introduce you to the rest of it when the time comes. For now, please make yourself at home, get your training sessions over and done with, and in three days we'll talk about your job.”

———

Henryan took the elevator going from the hub to the rim. According to the received schedule, he was supposed to go through arm H to sector 8 and block D. The mile and a half separating the terminuses took the cab more than five minutes. As usual these days, when left alone, he thought back to the moment in which he'd died in order to arrive in this place ...

———

The outer bulkhead was opening fast. The clang of the unbolted locks preceded by a blink the hissing of the pneumatic mechanisms, retracting the overlapping plates of plasteel.

Henryan stood with his eyes closed, waiting for a yank. Although he wanted very much to look at the stars once again, at the last moment he got scared of death and instinctively cringed, closing his eyes and mouth tightly, as if it could help him.

The hissing stopped, and he was still alive. There was no yanking, his body did not explode, nor did it turn into a block of ice. Surprised, he opened his left eye first, then the right one, and when the brightness emanating from behind the open bulkhead struck him, he shaded his face with his hand.

"Henryan Darski?"

Hearing his name, mispronounced as always, he thought it was a deathbed vision, one of those he had heard about so many times during his service on numerous ships. He nodded, unable to utter a word. He heard footsteps; someone came up to him, and then another one. The steps were quiet, devoid of the distinctive clang of the armor.

"Man, you look like shit," one of the newcomers said in an amused tone.

"And you stink like it, too," his companion added.

Darski felt them grab him under his arms and pull toward the light. *And I was so scared of the end,* he thought, when he was seated on something hard. No longer blinded, he could see bright spots around him and blurry shadows moving among them. He closed his eyes to squeeze the tears out, and when he opened them again, he saw a woman's face. She was quite ugly for an angel.

"I'm Commodore Ursulavinia Derrick. Welcome aboard the courier ship of the Admiralty," she said.

Henryan could already see well enough to make out the outlines of objects and silhouettes of people in unmistakable uniforms. Everyone looked at him with a mixture of interest and disgust.

"The Admiralty?" he repeated the last word involuntarily. "I've been released?"

"Looks like it," she said, grinning. "Something tells me we've arrived at the last minute."

He felt someone's hands under his armpits again. He was already conscious enough not to be in need of support. He was standing on his own, but still couldn't believe Draccos had released him from his clutches. The long, hot bath, clean clothes, and a soft bunk helped him calm down, but not enough to definitely get rid of a deep-rooted fear, the fear that all this was a setup, that when he finally demonstrated his joy, the curtains would suddenly go down and he would be brutally returned to the reality of the prison. Whenever he was standing before the door, he had the impression that when he opened it he would see the warden and his henchmen, who would drag him back under the dome of the penal colony with mocking smiles, and throw him into solitary confinement for eternity.

Meanwhile, the hours passed and he was still onboard the courier ship, surrounded by astronauts, who—although keeping their distance—treated him like a human being. He ate a sumptuous meal with them, much tastier than the mush served him for the last three years, then another, only slightly more modest. He slept through the night, waking up many times, and listening with his heart pounding loudly for hateful metallic steps outside the door. He didn't dare put out the light. He feared his heart would not stand another second of complete darkness.

The admirals didn't confide their plans to couriers sent into space; he wasn't, therefore, able to find out from the crew any details about his unexpected release. However, Ursulavinia gave him a headreader with a set of crystals, indicating that he should get familiar with the latest versions of the communication software. It was the only order regarding Henryan that Commodore

Derrick received ... except picking him up from the penal colony, of course.

The next morning, when he returned to his cabin after breakfast, he noticed a red light flashing on the comlink panel. Someone tried to reach him. He hesitated a moment, holding a finger over the display, but in the end his curiosity took over.

He regretted his decision the moment he saw the holographic face of Draccos.

"Don't be too happy, seven two one," the warden said through clenched teeth. "It's just a furlough. You'll come back to us, and then ..."

Henryan turned off the comlink without a word.

TWENTY-TWO

THE XAN 4 SYSTEM, X-RAY SECTOR

09/03—09/05/2354

The basic training lasted three days. During that time Darski not only got familiar with his duties—that is, coordinating all the intra-system communications, mainly with the research outposts on the planet's surface—but he also learned more about Aliens: the first Humankind encountered in the surveyed part of the Galaxy.

What he heard from the scientists surprised him to such an extent that he forgot his own problems for a while. Xan 4 was really a remarkable system. A binary star nursed three circumbinary planets in its orbit: a gas giant nine and a half astronomical units away, a scorched rocky globe orbiting less than seventy million clicks from the system's barycenter, and a celestial body called Beta, circulating between the other two on the edge of the system's ecosphere. Darski understood very little of the scientific gibberish explaining the uniqueness of the planetary system in which he found himself, but one fact got imprinted in his memory: Beta's orbit was very unstable, and therefore every five hundred million years this planet, traveling away from the two stars, would leave the system's ecosphere. This was, however, happening so slowly that the complete glaciation followed only after tens of millions of years of gradual global cooling. During the equally slow return to the ecosphere, temperature increased by tenths of a degree per millennium, and those remains of life that had survived the glacial period evolved, over time conquering the land and sea emerging from the permafrost.

If one could believe the recent study results, Beta had already gone through seven such eras of flourishing life and was now preparing for another departure from the ecosphere. Three or four million years that separated the planet from the beginning of the next Ice Age were, however, an unimaginably long period, especially from the human perspective.

Fortunately for plants and animals living on Beta, the glaciation process spread over eons. The local fauna and flora had time to adapt to the inexorably changing conditions, so some of the species managed to survive. There was of course no question of preserving the advanced life forms; nevertheless, each return of the planet to the system's ecosphere released the spores, hidden deep within the ice, which started new evolutionary processes.

During his ten years of active service, Darski had visited twenty star systems. He was stationed at twenty-eight planets and four orbital stations. Besides, he spent almost thirty-six months in a helon mine located within the asteroid belt traversing unnamed regions of the inter-system void. On most of the visited "stones," as the crews called planets in their jargon, more or less developed life forms awaited him. Sometimes very different from those that can be found in human-friendly places, where the sky is blue, and vegetation green. Darski had seen such a paradise only once, in a remote sector, when he was stationed onboard the battleship *Lem* as a senior expert in the communications section, and under Admiral Dustr visited the outer colonies belonging mainly to large corporations. Delta in the Rubicon System was said to be unique, but even there no intelligent life forms evolved. Many men, seeing this idyllic planet, wished for only one thing: to give up the uniform and get a mining job somewhere in the system. Henryan thought about it, too. Those were the good old days. Back then he didn't know what it is like to drill a gravity-free shard of rock, circulating in the boundless void.

He'd spent most of his service time on red-hot or icebound planets that belonged to the fifth category, or lower, where the crown of creation were bacteria or lichens at best.

Here, things were different. Beta's atmosphere, although as toxic to humans as the water, allowed for the evolution of two intelligent races. Both appeared in the last interglacial period, evolving from the remnants of an earlier era of flourishing life, or rather, from two eras. The scientists studying this world's history suspected that blue-blooded (literally) Gurds were the descendants of the organisms one or even two cycles older than those which developed into primitive Suhurs. The reason for this hypothesis was that it was hard to find any—even genetic—similarity between these two unusual races.

Gurds had a cylindrical torso, thick black skin, four identical prehensile limbs, and a telescopic appendage that grew from the top of their body, whose spherical end was called by the human scientists "a sensory node." The blue-blooded inhabitants of the continent called Gurdu'dihan had no eyes or nostrils, and the external stimuli were imbibed by them—this word was probably closest to the truth—in such a strange way, it was difficult to understand for a xenobiologist, let alone a layman.

These creatures communicated by means of acoustic waves generated in the subcutaneous organ in the front part of the torso. When the class instructor played the converted recording of their speech, Henryan winced, hearing a series of piercing modulated shrieks.

Gurds didn't hunt. It was unthinkable for them to eat other living creatures. They fed on the sprouts of plants they cultivated on a large scale, but their digestive system didn't resemble anything known on Earth.

When Darski saw clumsy Gurds for the first time, they

reminded him of the mythical centaurs. He couldn't say exactly why—their rounded bodies and symmetrically placed prehensile limbs didn't resemble a cross between a man and the noble mount—but nevertheless that was his impression.

This race originated on the swampy plains of the larger of the two Beta continents. Bluebloods settled there twelve thousand local years ago. They referred to years as floodings—from periodic floods occurring at the end of each cold season.

The Gurds' habits were as odd as their appearance. They didn't know the concept of god, they didn't have religions or rituals. It might seem that they didn't understand the concept of the supernatural life. This didn't change even after they'd been confronted with a developed system of beliefs of their primitive neighbors called Suhurs.

Gurds lived in herds, forming dense clusters of even tens of thousands of individuals, but unlike Suhurs, they weren't divided into clans, or tribes. Each stranger who joined or just visited a community was treated on a par with locals, even though he could be coming from the opposite end of the continent larger than both Americas taken together. The basic social unit of Gurds was a family consisting of three adults and their offspring—for Gurds were organisms with three sexes. In order to reproduce, they gave ova and sperm, but the donors of the gametes, the counterparts of Earthian males (called seeders) and females (referred to as egglayers), needed to mate—not necessarily at the same time—with a third partner, or a fetuscarrier. It's in its body that a fertilized ovum nested, and it carried the young throughout all of the thirteen standard months of pregnancy.

The offspring became self-sufficient very fast, which could indicate that in the distant past Gurds, like Earthian herbivorous animals, had been exposed to predation. Interestingly, when people began to observe Beta, they couldn't find a predator anywhere in Gurdu'dihan that might be a threat to these—only seemingly defenseless—creatures. It wasn't until the excavations had been made that the scientists found a compelling evidence that as recently as a few centuries earlier, the life of Bluebloods was nothing like the current idyll. However, no one was able to determine what could be the reason for the extinction of so many species of predators, especially those that prevailed on the greater continent for thousands, and in some cases, even millions of years. According to some scientists, study on Gurds' behavior, and especially on their relationship with Suhurs, was supposed to shed new light on this mystery.

In any case, without natural enemies in recent times, Gurds started to build the foundations of civilization at an ever-increasing pace, and as soon as they reached the level of development of a medieval man and sufficiently mastered sailing the local troubled waters, they reached for the second continent, situated in the northern hemisphere of the planet. So began the conquest of the domain of the more primitive Suhurs.

This warlike race, with thick brown gore flowing in their "veins," created their first communities seventy thousand years earlier than Gurds. Its members gained the title of the Warriors of the Bone, because the skeletons of hunted animals served them to manufacture ornaments, weapons, and even shacks in which the clans lived. Judging from the excavations, Suhurs had colonized their continent thousands of years before the first fire was kindled in Gurdu'dihan. In spite of that, they were currently behind their blue-blooded neighbors in every way. In their case, the evolution stopped centuries ago. If a Suhur from the ancient past could be transported into a modern clan's seat, he would feel there at home. He might not even notice the difference.

The native inhabitants of Suhurta, despite their huge backwardness, did extremely well. They lived in harmony with nature, developing a belief system whose central characters were three gods. Kored and Thub represented both suns of the system —constantly fighting with each other, as cosmology of the

Warriors of the Bone presented the conjunctions of the two stars, which merged together in the sky in an incredibly spectacular way. The history of the third deity, called Yabha, was even more interesting. According to the Warriors of the Bone, he was once the third sun, which in ancient times was defeated by the constantly fighting pair, and after scattering into the myriad debris, hung in the firmament in the form of cold stars. In the lecture on the beliefs, also another interesting difference between the two Beta civilizations was explained to Henryan. It concerned the measure of time. Gurds had a calendar that counted the actual years, or full revolutions of the planet around the sun, while Suhurs counted the conjunctions, which were also regular, but happened four times every three astronomical years.

Almost all aspects of the Suhurs' culture revolved around fighting and killing. Even their units of weights and measures reflected their combative attitude to the world. When a Suhur wanted to describe the distance traveled during hunting, he counted it in bowshots or spear throws. When the clan collected the sagr seeds, they could gather a shield, a helmet, or a hubcap full of them, all of which were the parts of the armor that protected their bodies.

The Warriors of the Bone—incredibly strong, hardy, and ruthless—were natural born killers. What's more, they lived to die in battle, and that was the main purpose of their existence, starting almost from a nestling. And although they seemed more humanoid than Gurds, they were nothing like people.

Warriors of the Bone didn't know such concepts as compassion or love. They didn't know what sex was, either, because nature hadn't equipped them with sex organs. Despite several years of observation and research, the scientists failed to decipher the factors that made some individuals of this species become pregnant. After reaching maturity, a small part of the population formed a kind of fetal ventricles called "pelchavkas." These had a form of bubbles growing out of the upper, mainly "back," part of the body, at the point of contact of the external skeleton's plates, though in some cases they could be more scattered all over the body. Four to seven nestlings hatched in a single brood.

Suhurs called the pregnant individuals a "densha." Each densha was isolated and locked in a special pen in the middle of the settlement, where the nestlings remained until they became self-sufficient. Childbirth, if the ending of the bizarre pregnancy could be called such, occurred after less than four months of pregnancy. When the swollen pelchavkas began to burst, releasing sticky mucus, the clan's priests carefully cut them open with bone blades. The individual freed from stigmatizing pelchavkas shed their remains, and within a few days returned to being a full-fledged warrior.

But sometimes nature played tricks and embryos in individual pelchavkas did not develop properly, or died, and thus, there was nothing to cut open. Nothing flaked off, either. One in twenty Suhurs became a densha, while a dried pelchavka occurred once in every few thousands of successful breedings. A Warrior of the Bone, upon whom this misfortune fell, became a pariah. Being a perpetual "female" meant the loss of prestige and a humiliating—albeit badly needed in the primitive community—function of a lifelong nurse for the other warriors' nestlings. In any clan's seat there could be only one densha. If a new one appeared, the old one was killed—as cruel tradition dictated—by fettering his limbs and leaving him in the killing pit.

The physiology of the Warriors of the Bone was also very interesting. They breathed through the membranes in the upper part of the body. They communicated through the membranes spread all over the body, which could—just like microphones used by people—send and receive almost every sound. Imitating animal sounds was as easy for these creatures as a conversation, which made them unrivaled hunters. With three eyes evenly distributed on the dome-shaped top of the body—and called "head" by some scientists—Suhurs could see all around them. Thus, the concepts such as "front" and "back" didn't have much meaning for them. A Suhur could watch the whole area around him, and sneaking up to him in an open space would be a miracle. A fight against several opponents attacking from different directions wasn't much of a challenge for a fit Warrior of the Bone. Numerous ball and socket joints allowed greater freedom of movement than in humans. The spheroidal equivalent of elbows and knees, of which Suhurs had twice as many as humans, bent equally well in both directions. If they'd known wrestling, a joint-locking technique would not be an effective tactic against them.

A speeding Suhur changed direction without turning back. He could also hit with equal precision both the opponent in front of him, and the one behind his "back."

Two long arms, reaching below the second pair of knees, were equipped with eight claw-like fingers, one of which served as an opposable thumb. A third, and much shorter, upper limb grew from the place where people have a sternum and resembled rather a tentacle than a hand. Only because of it, and the hole leading to the digestive bladder (located in the top part of the body, but slightly below the eyes), it could be determined where the "front" of these beings might be.

The membranes used for breathing were situated between the eyes, spaced out—like the organs of sight—one hundred and twenty degrees from one another, except the largest of them was over the right arm and the other two in front of and behind the left shoulder joint. The Suhurs' respiratory system differed from anything known on Earth so much that lecturers describing Beta's natural environment to Henryan didn't even try to explain the details, saying unanimously that such knowledge would be of no use to someone who was supposed to take care of a technical side of the project "Two Suns." During the training, he was given only general information, and also advised that in case of a serious need, he could turn to the resources of the onboard library.

Henryan heeded their advice, but was forced to stop broadening his knowledge very quickly. He gave up after only a few hours of leafing through the articles written in jargon so hermetic that he could hardly understand anything at all.

The most amazing feature of the Warriors of the Bone was the symbiosis in which adult Suhurs lived with roundworm-like tahars. These creatures were feeding on their hosts, living only in the lower front part of their bodies. There was a ventricle there, filled with not very dense and poorly innervated tissue, called "parenchyma." The Suhurs' skin, extremely hard and difficult to puncture, and further protected by an exoskeleton on the most part of the torso, in the lower front part of the body changed into the circle of fine porosity. It was this way that during the rite of passage tahars came in contact with their hosts' bodies. And that was the way they left them, when the time came.

The role of these symbionts wasn't fully known. However, the scientists established beyond any doubt that by sucking on tahars, which every now and then crawled out of their bowels, Suhurs provided their bodies with the most needed elements, while the "worms" living in their parenchyma, through which all the brown blood flowed, eliminated toxins from the host's body. It was a kind of symbiotic perpetuum mobile. Thanks to this biological mechanism, a mature Warrior of the Bone hardly needed other food—that was one of the reasons this race lacked any interest in agriculture or animal husbandry—and equally important, didn't excrete the waste products of metabolism. A few tiny sagr seeds were quite enough to sustain him for a few days if he didn't have to hunt or fight in this time. Only the nestlings were fed with more nutritionally balanced seeds of redhusk.

On the second day, Henryan got acquainted with the history of Beta, or rather with the history of civilization that arose on it during the last cycle. The first contacts between both races didn't foretell the events of which the inextricably linked suns of Xan 4 had been the silent witnesses over the last millennium. Gurd travelers, once their race got ready for the exploration of the planet, repeatedly visited the Suhurta's coast, often venturing to the heart of the smaller continent, accompanied by local guides. During these expeditions, they drew the detailed maps of the fertile and never before cultivated lands.

The Gurds' civilization was at the time much ahead of the northern primitive warriors in every aspect. Hundreds of circles, as the Quadrupeds called their amazing, shell-like cities, were being constructed in Gurdu'dihan. Arts and crafts were flourishing. The whole continent was one big construction site. Bluebloods, peaceful and weak by nature, didn't know wars. In even the greatest communities, with tens of thousands of individuals, concepts like violence and theft were unknown, and the incidents of causing death or injury, usually inadvertently, were rare.

The Quadrupeds formed a gigantic, tightly knit community, whose members coexisted peacefully and multiplied at an accelerating pace, which was the exact opposite of the Suhurs' civilization. A thousand years before the discovery of Beta by humans, they surpassed numerically the Warriors of the Bone, who—divided into clans—were constantly fighting among themselves. Currently, there were already nearly twenty times as many of Gurds as their fighting neighbors.

The first attempt to colonize Suhurta took place one hundred and thirty floodings after the discovery of the smaller continent. A united fleet brought thousands of volunteers from the south, together with their belongings and farm animals. Earlier, the Gurds' leaders made a deal and "bought" a broad coastal plain from the local clan. They paid with piles of armor and weapons, made of unknown to Suhurs iron.

The peaceful coexistence of the "inkblots" (it was enough to see a dead individual of this species to understand why the soldiers dubbed Gurds this name) and the "savages" (here the association was simple) didn't last long. The warring Suhurs' clans clashed constantly, entering into temporary alliances, and when one of the tribes on whose land Gurds eventually settled lost the war, the new leaders established a new order of things on the conquered territories, including the newcomers. Only a few Quadrupeds managed to escape the carnage. When the news of it reached the Old Land, the Supreme Council of Gurdu'dihan, shocked by the enormity of the crime, decided that the primitive clans of the north had to be punished for their actions.

But first, Gurds had to master the difficult art of warfare, or rather to recall its principles, because that was how they'd got rid of their predators hundreds of floodings earlier. According to the Supreme Council, it was time to dust off the methods used in those days, and apply them again. It wasn't easy in the case of creatures, who were not only terribly afraid of pain and death, but also who avoided violence. The leaders needed multiple floodings to raise a generation prepared to fight and to lay the foundations of a new strategy, based mainly on the analysis of the behavior of the savage inhabitants of the north, fortunately documented in numerous reports of early settlers and earlier explorers. Only later did they start training a powerful army, which was equipped with weapons that hadn't been seen in Suhurta till then.

When the Gurds' leaders finally decided they were ready, they sent their army overseas. Forty floodings after the massacre of settlers, the sixty-four ships—this was the luckiest number known to the race of Bluebloods, who used the octal system—came ashore at the coast of the feral plain and emptied nearly forty-one thousand well-trained soldiers onto the sandy beaches. This time there were no deals. The surrounding clans of the Warriors of the Bone were wiped out before the smaller of the suns disappeared from the sky. No prisoners were taken, even the nestlings in their pens hadn't been spared. It was supposed to be revenge, and also a final solution to the problem. But the enemy didn't know that, because there was not a single Warrior of the Bone on the plains who would remember who the invaders were and what their invasion meant. The clan responsible for the massacre of Gurds had been defeated many clashes of the suns ago. Some time later, the winners of that battle shared the sad fate of the defeated clan, and their successors were routed many more times since then.

The sithu commanding the expeditionary force—a "sithu" being the equivalent of an Earthian general—Gahra'tib, was so enthusiastic about the first victories that he overestimated his strength. The ease with which his armored soldiers defeated the clusters of angry warriors lulled the sithu's vigilance. Not having much battle experience, he wanted a quick triumph, and chasing it, he went too far inland. He trusted that his awesome weapons would work in all conditions and the superbly trained soldiers would meet any challenge. After all, the enemy hadn't employed any complicated tactics yet—whenever they sensed danger, Suhurs attacked frontally without any hesitation. And the invader wasn't going to give them a chance to learn from their mistakes: those Warriors of the Bone who survived the battle with the Gurds' army—mostly wounded—were immediately finished off.

The Supreme Council ordered Gahra'tib and his expeditionary force to capture the beachhead in advance of an invading army. The order was simple: the sithu was supposed to get rid of the Warriors of the Bone from the broad coastal plain near the mouth of the Suhurta's longest river, then build a network of forts along the borders of the occupied territory, and after having deployed garrisons there, wait for the arrival of the main force. Gahra'tib had done this ahead of time, but the ease with which he kept defeating the clans piqued his ambition—a feeling unknown to him before. Since the Warriors of the Bone were losing every battle, he decided to crush them permanently and reach the opposite mainland coast, as planned for the second phase of conquest. The Supreme Council's strategy envisaged the extermination of the primitive creatures threatening the settlers, so that they could destroy the produced weapons as soon as possible and revert to peaceful existence.

And so, day after day, battle after battle, the expeditionary force entered deeper and deeper into the clans' territories. The invaders found themselves in the heart of the continent before the news of insubordination reached Gurdu'dihan. The advantage that the Quadrupeds had thanks to their discipline, training, and modern weapons inspired more officers, who didn't protest when the sithu presented the plans for further bold military measures.

However, this tactic stopped working when the expeditionary force wedged the tens of thousands of wheel revolutions inland and got stuck in the middle of the boundless steppes. The Gurdian soldiers were running out of their basic weapons that looked like Earthian piques; they also suffered from serious shortage of arrows. And far from forests, there was nothing to replace them. The number of casualties increased. Within three weeks, more than four thousand Gurds were killed, a seemingly insignificant number when compared to the total size of the expeditionary force, but still ten times larger than before entering the central plateaus.

Pride wouldn't let the ambitious Gahra'tib turn back when he still had time, although he probably considered this way out quite often in the solitude of his tent. Finding himself in the heart of the continent, he decided that the wisest move would be to break through to the dells, lying much closer than the coast, from which he'd set off. There, the exhausted soldiers would find the wood for piques and arrows. And also more food, since its supply began to slowly run out, despite the fact that the troops were supposed to be stationed at the forts for a much longer period of time.

The plan, although reasonable, wasn't implemented. In a place situated only two days' march away from the edge of the forest, the expeditionary force was met by the powerful army of Suhurs. The clans, having to deal with a foreign enemy, achieved the impossible: they united for a single battle. Even the safe residents of the far north and the equally distant south came with their fists to support the Warriors of the Bone from the plains. Intense enemies until very recently, they stood side by side, trying to ward off the invaders, and at unimaginable expense made sure that none of the blue-blooded freaks would return to the coast.

The members of the Supreme Council of Gurdu'dihan also wanted to end the war fast. Thus, they reveled in the news of their army's winning streak, full of brilliant victories and conquests. However, at some point, the reports sent by the winged couriers stopped reaching them. They quickly figured out what the reason for the silence of the brave Gahra'tib could be. And when a short time later the crew of one of the ships, which miraculously survived the bloodbath that Warriors of the Bone caused also on the coast, passed the information about the defeat of the expedition, the notables began to ask themselves what would happen if the packs of bloodthirsty Suhurs, keeping up the momentum, cross the sea and set out toward the greatest circles of Gurdu'dihan.

The word was spread to the farthest corners of the continent. The preeminent minds began to work on the improvement of existing weapons and the invention of new ones. The training of the invading army was accelerated; additional hundreds of thousands of young Gurds, who had been trained just in case, were recruited. Preparing for the worst, the Quadrupeds began to fortify the coast—especially along the straits separating the two continents. The war, just like it used to be on Earth, gave powerful impetus to the development of both Gurdian technology and science.

At the same time, Suhurs, drunk with success, reverted to their former life. It didn't even occur to any of them to set out overseas. The ships captured off the coast were chopped for wood so that the warriors fallen in the last battles could be burned on pyres worthy of their actions. The world of Suhurs was saved once again. Thus, the alliance of clans ceased to exist as quickly as it formed.

Bluebloods returned after another thirty floodings, when the defeat of Gahra'tib had become only a vague memory in Suhurta. This time the Quadrupeds were much more numerous; they had better weapons and a whole new strategy. Their army would conquer the territories of several neighboring clans in a massive attack, and then end the offensive. Next, they entrenched themselves, defending the conquered territory until the workers, following close behind, raised enough forts and watchtowers. When the troops set out again, the occupied and theoretically safe land was developed; the civilian Gurds built the groundwork for future circles, which Suhurs wouldn't be able to destroy in a sudden raid. These constructions were often surrounded by moats and wide strips of bare ground to prevent a surprise attack of the enemy. Not only were the armed residents able to defend themselves until the arrival of the relief force—which would always come quickly—but they also counterattacked, often with very good results.

An inventive weapon—a firearm—back then still very imperfect, but nevertheless ages ahead of the weapons of the enemy who fought with bone clubs, sowed death and destruction in the ranks of Suhurs even before they could come into direct contact with Gurds. Particular respect was commanded by the first cannons—called "smoldering trunks" by Suhurs—able to fling to a considerable distance the containers with oil, previously unknown to the clans, which caught fire immediately upon spillage.

Remembering the victorious battle with Bluebloods, still famed in songs and stories, the Warriors of the Bone put up fierce resistance to the invaders, but Gurds had such a huge advantage over them that the clans had to retreat. Whoever was left on the disputed land died; even the new covenants between the Suhurs of the mountains and the warriors of the plains didn't help matters. Gurds, also remembering the fate of the expeditionary force, didn't allow themselves to be provoked and slowly but surely wrested the Suhurs' lands from them, taking hill after hill and valley after valley.

It took them forty floodings to reach the place where the proud Gahra'tib met his vanquisher ... and he was able to get there in less than one local year. After another twenty years, the conquerors planted the poles with Gurdian knots on the beaches and cliffs of the east coast, finally separating the northern and southern warriors. Thanks to limited casualties on their side, the continuous influx of soldiers, and good harvests on the occupied territories, the Gurds' armies had no problems with carrying out the subsequent stages of the offensive. They aimed first at the warmer and more accessible south. The clans defended themselves fiercely, but they didn't stand much chance against the indiscriminate use of firearms, even so primitive. Although this campaign ended much faster than the march toward the east coast, the development of vast territories took the invaders four generations.

The decisive act of this drama began when Bluebloods finally purged the southern part of the continent of the last remaining Warriors of the Bone. Only a few of the depleted clans managed to escape into the inaccessible mountainous areas of the north, where they were inevitably doomed to utter destruction anyway. The huge forces of Gurds crossed the previously fortified bed of the Adal Vin, the queen of rivers, which for many floodings had constituted a natural border between the two races. The Quadrupeds attacked on three fronts, which was meant to prevent Suhurs from regrouping and giving a decisive battle, like the one that occurred during the first invasion. However, to their great surprise they encountered only empty settlements. The scouts reported that the clans were retreating toward the mountains. All of them, without exception.

The commander of the army, Sithu Taih'law, started to get wind of conspiracy. The brave and honorable Warriors of the Bone had never given an inch to their rivals. He suspected they were trying to lure him into a trap, as they once did with Gahra'tib, but in the end decided that the new strategy of the enemy couldn't affect the plans of this phase of the campaign. When his troops reached the designated positions, he forbade pursuing the enemy and ordered the construction of another line of fortifications. It was the only stage of the war during which Gurds didn't fight a single battle or lose a single soldier.

Sixteen floodings later, when all the conquered territories had been parceled out and settled by civilian Gurds, Taih'law started the next phase of the campaign. Again, three great armies moved north toward the foothills and the massif of the Seven Pinnacles that separated the invader from the rocky coastal highlands, constituting the last bastion of Suhurs in this part of the continent. The goal was to claim the plateau Tok Keme—the vast plains, beyond which began the wooded hills and the mountains. The foothills were to be conquered in the next phase of the colonization.

The sithu, already in his old age, hoped that clans would once again give up their lands and that he would achieve victory again without fighting or incurring severe casualties. On the first day of the offensive, Suhurs fled as before and this put Taih'law off guard. Although in the very beginning he didn't intend to take any risk, he decided to make his own luck and forced the army to march faster, hoping to once again trick the Warriors of the Bone, who apparently wanted to lure him to the foothills. Thanks to his previous brilliant successes, the aged commander had been the favorite of the Supreme Council for some time and he was this close to the great honor of participating in its meetings, as the only soldier in history. In his opinion, another victory would guarantee him this privilege.

For the next two days, the invaders encountered no resistance, thus the sithu set an even more murderous pace. In just seven days, the Bluebloods occupied as much area as they should claim within three weeks. Far behind, they left the engineering units busy with building forts and fortifications. Despite appearances to the contrary, this was a deliberate move. Taih'law wanted to reach the line designated by the Supreme Council as soon as possible, and then stop his troops a day's march away from the first hills, where he expected Suhurs' resistance. Over the many floodings of his service in Suhurta, he got well acquainted with the customs and traditions of the Warriors of the Bone; that's why he was sure he had their strategy figured out. On the eighth day, however, when all the three troops were again within a short distance of each other and only one thousand wheel revolutions from their goal, countless hordes of natives stood in their way.

On the plain, far from the edge of the foothills, gathered all the clans of the north. Facing each other were a hundred thousand Warriors of the Bone and the Gurdian army, three times more numerous and considerably better equipped. The enemy was rested, knew the area perfectly well, and wasn't going to delay the battle.

In spite of this, the sithu was sure of victory—firearms more than compensated for any weakness. Unfortunately, he forgot one thing: the fast marching pace prevented the purging of the occupied territories. It was his worst mistake. Just before the decisive battle, the scattered clans following the armored troops hit from behind and attacked the Gurdian army, which was preparing for a fight. Suhurs wreaked havoc in the support area. Taih'law fell in the first moments of the attack. With him died the majority of Gurds that stayed in the headquarter tents. As luck would have it, the Warriors of the Bone struck when the sithu called a council in order to discuss the battle plan with the troop commanders. Not a single senior officer survived the slaughter. Soon a horde of battle-hardened natives fell upon the tired, confused, and lacking orders Gurdian soldiers. The largest massacre in Beta's history had begun.

Having no chance to escape, Gurds decided to resist till the last drop of blue blood. They died en masse, but also took whole clans down with them. When the smaller sun disappeared behind the mountain peaks, the grassy plains were covered with a blue-brown sea of gore. Only a few hundred invaders managed to flee, taking advantage of the confusion. Less than six thousand Suhurs returned to the hills after dark. They won, but it was a Pyrrhic victory, which they learned during the subsequent clashes of the suns, when the successor of Taih'law, Sithu Her'hot, brought another, although much less numerous army.

The survivors told the commander about the tactics adopted by Suhurs. It was clear that the decimated clans were not a threat anymore. The new sithu realized almost immediately that he had a big chance of ending this war and defeating the enemy once and for all. As to the training of a new army, he suggested not doing it, because it would take a few or even a dozen floodings, and instead he advised the Supreme Council to concentrate in the north all the forces available in Suhurta, which could be achieved by reducing the number of garrisons in other parts of the continent (at that time the natives' attacks were rare, especially in the central plateaus and the south, where finding a Warrior of the Bone would have been a miracle). The Supreme Council agreed to his proposal.

Tens of thousands of soldiers had been relocated, leaving in place only the troops from the far south, where the clans hiding in the mountains were still a little threat to smaller circles. This allowed Her'hot to purge the territory which Gurds had won in the previous campaign. A young, although ambitious and clever, sithu won the foothills much faster and easier than his superiors expected. Gurdu'dihan gained a new hero.

The penultimate act of the war between the two Beta races ended many years later, when the last clans, defending their seats in the Seven Pinnacles, were driven off. At that time, all the lands south of the mountain range had already been parceled out and settled. The Warriors of the Bone were pushed to the most inhospitable part of the continent, where they had too little space to be able to regain their former glory.

Her'hot didn't get to put an end to the conflict. Although he didn't lose a single battle, he was defeated by the climate and diseases. The time spent in the high mountains, camping in dank caves, all this took a toll on his delicate health. The sithu expired with dignity, transported by aircraft to the capital, where—till the very end—he enjoyed reverence and respect worthy of the greatest hero.

A few floodings later, Sithu Taba'ruk, the new Gurdian commander in Suhurta, marched onto the last highland, leading an army consisting of veterans only. He also deployed the scorched earth tactics, but the territory was more difficult, and the last clans put up a fierce resistance. The Warriors of the Bone finally learned to fight using ruse—which, given the centuries-old history of the conflict, wasn't a huge achievement—and made Bluebloods pay a high price for each occupied rock or shrub.

The Supreme Council had finally come to the conclusion that further bloodshed didn't make sense. The closer soldiers approached the northern, far reaches of the continent, the colder it got, plus the rocky terrain behind the Seven Pinnacles was infertile and, in Gurds opinion, not worth such a high price. Further action was thus abandoned when the armies of Taba'ruk reached the Valt Aram, the last major river of the continent, and stopped less than twenty thousand wheel revolutions from the rocky cliffs, where, according to some ancient maps, the main-land ended. The riverbank was fortified, the fords were deepened, the conquered lands parceled out to soldiers dismissed from service. The Warriors of the Bone had been almost wiped out. As they were no longer able to threaten the new empire, their remnants were left to fend for themselves, and cut off from the rest of the world with the border running along the bed of a wide river that started in the high mountains of the east and flowed into the sea far to the west. Despite all this, Suhurs incessantly stirred up trouble; although they only attacked the border circles, destroying crops and slaughtering the settlers and their livestock, Gurds were forced to maintain a number of garrisons in this region.

This state of affairs lasted for almost thirty floodings, but was about to change. The Supreme Council of Gurdu'dihan, wanting more than ever to get rid of all the weapons, decided that they must settle the matter once and for all.

TWENTY-THREE

THE XAN 4 SYSTEM, X-RAY SECTOR

09/06/2354

It's about time to solve the last puzzle, thought Darski, entering the maglev car.

On the fourth morning, after passing a short theoretical knowledge test on Beta and the project, he started his first watch. The command center, for which he was heading, was located in the sector four, exactly on the opposite side of the rim. The workspace and living quarters of this giant station consisted of eight segments, each four floors high and with a length of almost a mile and a half. Every segment was divided into five smaller compartments that could be disconnected from the rest of the structure.

Sectors one, two, seven, and eight served as living quarters, in the third there was the research center (whose staff lodged in sector two). The fourth sector housed the headquarters, including the command center that was the heart of the entire station. Sector five was sealed off—the Department of Fleet Security had located there their lockups, interrogation rooms, and such other places, of which most people preferred not to know. The last—if a wheel has an end—sixth sector, housed the medical department, and the doctors lived in the sector seven.

The eighth one was reserved for the military, and the first one for technical staff.

Henryan looked around the spacious car. Apart from him, in a brightly lit cylinder were doctors, engineers, scientists, and several gendarmes. *Not a single familiar face,* he thought. Even though he hadn't met many people during the three days of his intensive training, he still hoped to meet the guys with whom he ate meals at the mess hall somewhere on his way.

The express train, the fastest of the three lines available on the rim, stopped at every fifth station, always in the central part of the segment, spitting and swallowing a host of people.

Darski got lucky at the second stop. In the medical sector, thoughtful Valdez entered the car. He was holding a whole bunch of readers under his arm.

"I'll help you," the sergeant said, moving closer to the superior.

The lieutenant looked at him absentmindedly as if he didn't recognize the subordinate, but after a second, he blinked with a gleam of understanding in his eyes.

"Oh, it's you, Sergeant Pry," he said stiffly, but let Henryan take part of the documentation. "Excuse me, Sergeant, I had a rough night."

"A party in the officers' club?" Darski smirked.

"I wish," Valdez replied, keeping a straight face. "Work. If I were you, I wouldn't count on a lot of free time in the near future."

"Are you going to go to perform your duties in such a state?"

"Of course not. I'm going to report to the old man and then go to bed."

The maglev stopped at the additional stop in the sealed-off sector. No one disembarked, but two "esdees"—Security Department officers—got onto the train. If it hadn't been for the huge height difference, they would have looked like twins—shaved heads, black uniforms, gray headreaders, grim faces. The lieutenant stepped back against the wall and nodded to Henryan. Apparently, it was better not to get in their way …

"Why were the other three expelled?" Darski asked in a hushed voice.

"Who do you mean?" the still distracted officer mumbled.

"Those orange ones," clarified the sergeant. At the same time he noticed that one of the agents perked up his ear. The implants gave the bastards superhuman hearing.

"Orange?" Valdez repeated, stupefied.

It was clear he hadn't yet recovered from a rough night.

Another additional stop, unnamed, sealed off by the force barrier. The buzzkills got off the train without speaking even once.

"Arrival, replacement," Darski tried to put the lieutenant on the right track.

"Do you mean Seifert and his guys?"

"Yes, if it was them who were hopping in the direction of the shuttle on which I flew in," answered Henryan.

Lately, he'd often wondered to himself what the reason for the arrest of the previous communications officer was. He hadn't learned it in the first briefing, and the news about Aliens was so shocking that all other issues got immediately forgotten. Later, during the training course, he preferred not to ask.

"They had a whim to play God." Valdez smiled at his thoughts. "And so they were thrown into hell."

"Pardon?" Henryan frowned.

If he understood the lieutenant correctly, his predecessor received a one-way ticket: he was sent to the legendary secret prison from which no one had yet returned. Although this mention of God … No, it must have been just a metaphor.

"You'll find out everything. Soon, too." Valdez looked at him askance.

Henryan sighed. Either his new boss badly needed rest, or he didn't know too much.

"I'm sorry, sir, but I really don't understand any of that."

"Trust me, Sergeant Pry, it is better for you this way. You don't understand anything, you don't know anything, and you are not interested in anything. You follow orders and don't really care about the rest of it."

"Quite a reasonable approach," Darski admitted.

"Especially in your situation," Valdez said. "You're new here, you have no clue about what's going on down there."

"I know a little about the project. For three days, they were making me learn the flora and fauna of Beta. Not to mention the history of inkblots and savages."

"I don't mean Aliens, but our own," Valdez corrected him. "While the scientists are more subordinate than robots, the gendarmes are bored and constantly come up with unfortunate ideas. Like sending a nanobot to some bard to whisper a well-known song, or teaching the inkblots how to make moonshine from local grain."

"Good one!" Henryan laughed, but immediately went silent, having noticed a rebuking glance of his superior.

"Do you really feel like wearing an orange outfit?" Valdez asked, lowering his voice.

"No, sir." Darski was momentarily serious.

"These are alien races, civilizations older than ours, although much more primitive. We have no right to interfere with their lives. It's their world and their history. Do you realize how valuable the results of the observations we take down there can be?"

"I understand the importance of scientific research, but I think a life sentence for such trifles is a bit of an exaggeration."

"If you were really thinking, Sergeant Pry, you wouldn't have spent three years in a penal colony, or said what I just did not hear."

"Yes, sir."

The lieutenant looked him straight in the eyes, and then looked around warily as if to check that no one was eavesdropping. Satisfied, he leaned toward Darski.

"This is not about trifles. Extra shifts, demotion, a month's detention ... Until recently, such antics entailed standard penalty, but a few weeks ago, there was a dramatic escalation of this foolishness." He glanced at his personal reader. They were less than three minutes away from the command center. "Dr. Fukkuya first reported the strange behavior of the savages. On more than one site, he observed that the Warriors of the Bone perform new rituals. Imagine that they ended their customary prayers with the sign of the cross, just like Christians do. This raised legitimate concerns among the scientists. We enhanced the monitoring of the whole sector and after just two days, we knew that one of the Suhurian fisters had had a vision, in which the Spirits of the Mountains—those are minor deities, a sort of the clan's guardian angels—provided the following information: gods turned their back on Suhurs, dooming them to destruction. Of course, the tutelary entities didn't want to accept it."

Darski shook his head.

"That's some kind of nonsense ..."

"Not entirely," Valdez cut in. "The monitoring tells us that the Supreme Council of Gurdu'dihan has recently approved the plans of the decisive campaign. Gurds will set out soon; the orders are traveling by sea as we speak, along with draftees for the sampo-sithu's army. For Suhurs, this means an imminent extermination, which we will watch passively in line with our orders."

"So Seifert's at fault for sending them a warning?"

"The mere warning wouldn't be a problem, especially since we are looking at the last moments of this race. You see—there's no way we could have long-term effects of these antics." Lieutenant Valdez lowered his voice even more. "Two weeks ago, at about fourteen hundred hours orbital station time, the satellites received a signal from the planet's surface. Someone used a plasma weapon on the northern continent. Can you imagine? Can you imagine the chaos which erupted here when it turned out that the savages got Earthian weapons in their sticky paws? The old man lost it. This mission has the highest priority. The scientific department of the Federation's government invests a staggering sum in it."

Valdez nodded at the wall of the car, but he probably meant the whole station.

"Whenever a report on the smallest incident reaches the Central Systems, we have at least three admirals on our back, and the scientists don't idle: when they see an unauthorized interference with the natives, they immediately put it on paper, so to speak. This is not a game, Sergeant Pry. We have to be invisible and inaudible. We observe and research. We never interfere. Come hell or high water. And this—" For a moment, he was lost for words. "This was a terrible villainy. One such shot could change the history of Beta."

"I think you're exaggerating, Lieutenant. How could one … ?"

"Very easily." Valdez looked up at the puzzled subordinate. "The inkblots are launching the last crusade. It will be led by Sampo-sithu Takeli'toko, their spiritual and military leader. Imagine what would happen if just before the battle, or in its course, his tent and all the surroundings suddenly evaporated in the heat of a big explosion, just as it's been foretold? Yes, foretold. This is another trick of our pranksters. Gurds are a more advanced civilization, they've recently entered an industrialization phase, but for many thousands of years—which, incidentally, really puzzles me—they haven't developed any religious beliefs.

"And now, thanks to some moron, they would receive quite tangible proof of the existence of a supreme being. A supreme being which sides with the savages, their longtime enemies. It would change the course of history of not one, but two civilizations!" he hissed in a stage whisper.

"The chosen people …"

"There you go. After all, you get a thing or two."

"But—"

They reached their destination. The doors slid open noiselessly, letting them out into a wide cylindrical corridor. At its end one could see three open armored bulkheads and as many entrances guarded by the shimmering force barriers. The command center lay beyond.

"But me no buts," Valdez said after they'd disembarked. "Fortunately, the savages couldn't keep their hands off the weapon and used it prematurely, even though Seifert repeatedly warned them not to do that. Thanks to their insubordination, we were able to trace the contraband weapon. The Cerberus Orbital Defense System removed the threat immediately. A few seconds after the shot, both the phaser and the shooter were vaporized, and we started looking for the clone-of-a-bitch who'd made this mess. And so we tracked down the bastard, although it wasn't easy, because he had been stealing weapons from our armory for a long time, albeit in pieces. Then, following the clue, we found the one who'd delivered the phaser down, and in the end we got the coordinator of all these actions. It's him that you have replaced, Sergeant Pry. You must wonder sometimes why someone gave you a chance, even though they shouldn't have?"

Henryan nodded, curious about the answer.

"The old man needed for this position someone he could completely and utterly rely on. Someone who can't be bought the way Seifert was. You, Pry, won't give him any trouble. You've already learned the hard way what the punishment for insubordination is. You'd better not forget that you're out on parole."

"I will not forget, sir," Darski assured him sincerely when they'd passed the checkpoint. "I don't understand, however, what the problem is. After all, you've busted the guilty parties and destroyed the contraband weapon."

"The old man will explain everything to you." Valdez nodded at the circular dais of the command station, then patted the documents he carried. "It looks like the Seifert's case was the proverbial tip of the iceberg."

————

"I'll be brief," the colonel said when Henryan reported to him, shortly after parting with Valdez. "I didn't ask for you because you had a level-five security clearance. I could find a dozen better handymen than you onboard the ships stationed in this system, Sergeant. I need someone whom I can completely trust in the position of the intra-system communications coordinator. Someone like you, Darski, Prydewhite or whatever your name is."

"Prydeinwraig," Henryan prompted obligingly.

"Couldn't you come up with something simpler? Either wheezing, or gabble."

He silenced the sergeant, who started to open his mouth.

"Yes, I know what they called you at school. It just pisses me off—" He paused, swallowed hard, and began again, this time more calmly. "The point is that I must have a man here who will be absolutely obedient. Let us be clear: you enjoy the parole thanks to the Admiralty, but I can revoke it at any time. Very easily, with one move of my hand. And I'll do it, if I have even the slightest suspicion of your disloyalty."

"Don't worry, sir. I'm not going to go back there."

"That's what I'm talking about." Colonel Rutta relaxed a bit. "Did Valdez fill you in about the project?"

"Very superficially, sir. He said that you would explain everything."

"Chicken," Rutta snorted with contempt. "The situation is as follows. We have quite a few people onboard, mostly soldiers, who are doing everything to sabotage the mission of the scientific division. They got this crazy idea that they will save Suhurs, not allowing for the final phase of the Gurds' campaign."

He shook his head in disbelief. "Do you know what names they gave them when we showed up here?"

Henryan nodded.

"And now they're playing gods to save these primitive, cruel creatures—"

"In a way, I can understand them," Darski said.

"You can understand them?" The colonel didn't hide his surprise. "Either my hearing is failing me, or you've just asked for the parole revocation."

"I assure you, sir, that's not what I meant." Henryan felt shivers running down his spine. "I understand what drives them, but I don't support their actions."

"Implicit trust, Pry," Colonel Rutta reminded him. "How can I trust someone who shows understanding for the people he should fight?"

"Of course you can, sir. They won't talk me over to their side no matter how hard they try. I am fully aware what my other option is."

"Is it really as bad as they say?" Rutta suddenly changed the subject.

"Even worse, sir."

"Tread carefully then, Pry. Your task will be to block the actions of so-called Gods. The final battle's going to start within a month. Until then, you have to 'caulk' the communications system so that not even one binary digit of unauthorized data could be sent without my knowledge. Let's get this straight: from now on, no man has the right to interfere with the history of Beta. Understood?"

"Yes, sir." Henryan stood ramrod straight. "And what about locating the other ... Gods?"

"You still don't understand, Sergeant!" The station's commander groaned. "Do I speak some kind of a dead language?"

Darski shook his head in terror.

"There are no Gods. And there never were. These unrelated cases of interference mentioned by Valdez ... all were just a silly joke of few bored soldiers. That's how the Admiralty sees it, and so do I. Are we clear on that?"

TWENTY-FOUR

EIGHT HOURS later Henryan was relieved by another soldier, and could return to the residential area. This time he went for the slowest, standard train—a ride on it cost far less than on the express line. Valdez advised him to save credits by avoiding such luxuries, because with his sedentary job he wouldn't get too many extra points for the generated energy, and a sergeant's salary wasn't among the highest, especially that the Admiralty assigned the parolee the lowest possible category. Thus, Darski had to wait on the platform for the fifth train before he was able to crowd in. It was quite an ordeal. Moments in which he didn't feel the pressure and the body odor of his fellow travelers were rare. A dozen minutes later, he pushed his way to the exit, to finally breathe the crisp air of the central corridor in his sector. After a few steps he paused to decide what bothered him more: the dirt sticking to him or the growling in the stomach. A shower or the mess hall ... He chose the former.

He arrived at his living quarters after a short, brisk march. His accommodation was located favorably—everything Henryan might need was within walking distance. He'd begun to undress even before he passed through the door. The kinetic batteries removed from the slots on his belt were immediately placed in the power supply; Lieutenant Valdez was right—during the whole day's work he had charged them just to thirty percent! He unzipped his jumpsuit, slipped his arms from the moist sleeves, removed the boots, took the thick socks off and chucked them into a corner. Soon he reveled in the warm mist filling the narrow cylinder of the shower cubicle. A twenty-second bath. A costly luxury—he used up his daily ration of water.

He wiped himself dry quickly, threw the towel to the evaporator and put on a fresh change of printed underwear. The old pants went to the atomizer. He wasn't going to save energy points on the underwear. It was enough that he would have to wear the same jumpsuit for a few days in a row. He took a tracksuit from the dresser, put it on, looked at himself in the mirror, and started toward the door. He stopped halfway. The meal card was still in a sweaty jumpsuit hanging sadly from the door of the shower cubicle.

He felt the material quickly, and muttered in surprise when his fingers found a hard object in one of the side pockets on the leg. A moment later, he held a microcrystal between his fingers. A clean one, with no signs or print on it. He pressed his thumb to the bottom of the vitreous pyramid, but no hologram identification appeared over its top.

"Interesting …" He weighed the find in his hand.

This data storage device definitely didn't belong to him. So how did it end up in his jumpsuit? It certainly hadn't been there before. He checked the pocket that morning, leaving for breakfast. There should be only the meal card inside it now. He took the thin plastic rectangle. How is it possible that he hadn't felt the inch-tall pyramid earlier?

This could only mean that—at that time—it wasn't there yet …

Darski took the microcrystal between two fingers and looked at it against the light. *Interesting,* he repeated silently in his mind. Whoever planted this data storage device on him must have been very keen on maintaining anonymity. Did he just receive a message from the people mentioned by Valdez and Rutta?

He looked around his quarters. He could read the data in at least three ways. In the corner there was a small desk with a built-in terminal of the central computer of the station. These devices had multireaders as part of the standard equipment, but any operation performed on them was recorded in the station's data banks. Equally well, he could use the holoprojector whose panel hosted a triple-slot chamber adapted for reading different crystals. Henryan could see it from where he was standing. Except that this holoprojector was also connected to the onboard network. Confidentiality was guaranteed only by using a personal headreader.

Henryan dipped his hands into the half-unpacked bag. His fingers found the rounded shape, and he was just starting to take it out when a loud growl in his stomach reminded him where he'd been rushing to a minute ago. He weighed the device in his hand and slipped it into the pocket of his tracksuit. *Fifteen minutes' delay won't make much difference,* he thought, taking the microcrystal, too. Eating dinner shouldn't take more than that.

———

The mess hall was hopelessly crowded. Many soldiers living in this sector had just gone off duty for the day, and it seemed that the vast majority of them decided to grab something to eat before the afternoon nap. Darski was as fast as he could—he had even given up on one course in order not to stand again in a long queue—but he didn't manage to get back to his quarters as soon as he'd hoped. He stood by the scanner after just under nineteen minutes. He put his palm against the cool dry plastic, and when the light faded, he raised his hand to fix his hair, matted and damp again. The hand passed his nose for just a moment, but it was enough to smell the sharp odor of a disinfectant. Before he realized that something was off, the door opened with a quiet hum and he entered the darkness of the cabin.

"Light," he ordered and immediately approached the wall.

A dim glow filled the interior. Thirty percent, he remembered the battery level. The system automatically reduced brightness to save enough energy for the rest of the day.

Henryan stood next to the lighting panel and looked at his hands closely. Then he sniffed them. The left one didn't smell of anything. The right one did, albeit faintly, of flavored chemicals.

What the hell? Someone cleaned the scanner? Why?

He sat down on the bunk, still staring at his own hands in disbelief. Less than an hour ago he pressed a sweaty palm to the scanner by the door. He left a greasy stain on it. He definitely did. He still remembered the characteristic cluck, and the uncomfortable feeling that accompanied it. Now the plastic was dry and clean. Well, and fragrant ...

Darski looked around. His bag stood against the wall, where he had left it. On the table next to it lay a neat stack of the underwear, printed upon arrival, waiting to be put away in the drawers hidden in the wall. The dirty jumpsuit hung from the door of the shower cubicle. Everything was in its place.

I'm paranoid because of this damn microcrystal, he thought, rising from the bunk. Although he'd never heard of the self-cleaning scanner panels, the fact that the plastic was clean didn't necessarily mean anything ominous. Maybe some technician was servicing the equipment ...

He took the transparent pyramid out of his pocket, walked over to the corner desk and sat down at it. He activated the touch panel in the counter with his left hand, and then immediately turned it off. He raised his hands to his face and sniffed his fingertips again. Those that came in contact with the glass smelled like his right hand. He stood up and leaned over the counter. He blew a few breaths on the flat surface, and then crouched. Apart from the fresh prints, there wasn't a single trace there.

He was stunned. He had spent at least ten hours in this corner, if not more, reading the training materials. And he certainly didn't wipe anything. He was going to tidy the cabin at the end of the week.

He walked around the entire room, sniffing everything he could, but only near the holoprojector's panel he had the impression that he could smell the faint scent of the same chemicals. However, he wasn't absolutely sure about it. When he sat again at his desk, he smelled nothing. He sniffed a few times just in case.

Someone had clearly paid him a visit during his absence. Someone who didn't want to leave a single trace behind. If Henryan hadn't rushed back from the mess hall, he probably wouldn't have noticed anything. The question was how the intruder got in and what was he looking for. Darski tossed the transparent pyramid in his hand. The answer could be hiding inside it.

He reached for the headreader he'd received onboard the courier ship, and sat back on the bunk. He examined the equipment closely as if afraid that someone might have tampered with it, but eventually inserted the crystal in the slot, and then put on the headband. Before he activated the message, he leaned back against the wall.

For a moment, he saw only darkness. He even thought that the crystal was empty or corrupt, but just when he began to raise his hand to remove it from the slot, suddenly right before his eyes he saw a three-dimensional lettering. Simple and not very long.

WELCOME TO XAN 4, SERGEANT.

Henryan smiled to himself. Hearing about the antics of Gods, he guessed he was dealing with serious pranksters. Now he had proof that he was right.

TWENTY-FIVE

THE XAN 4 SYSTEM, X-RAY SECTOR

09/07/2354

The next day Henryan reported for duty ahead of time. He'd got up early and took a long walk along the corridors of the residential area to recharge his batteries. He wasn't going to sit in complete darkness as the night before, especially when after curfew the doors were automatically blocked, just like in prison, and anyone who wanted to leave their quarters had to report to the duty officer.

He took his place before a whistle announced the beginning of the watch. Double-checking the equipment took him only a few minutes. He was ready to accept the orders before the colonel had time to sit on his throne.

Lieutenant Valdez sent him a detailed job schedule for the day. The list wasn't long—it contained sixteen locations, most of which were situated on the smaller of the continents. Only one of them had a red priority. Darski started with that one. He ordered the system to disconnect the capsule with vision probes from the closest satellite, and directed the miniature robots to the coordinates given in the table. He tested the cameras twice, taking a series of close-up and panoramic photos. The first target was one of the Suhurian settlements—a typical "bone village" of the savages, with a couple dozen shacks circling the round pen with a few nestlings splashing around.

He checked this item on the list and moved on to the next. It wasn't until the tenth location that something caught his interest. He placed the vision probes over a Gurdian great coastal circle. Treb'aldaledo was the first and the largest Gurds' colony in Suhurta: according to recent estimates, it had a population of nearly seventy thousand inhabitants. When the nanobots dropped below the clouds, Henryan was suddenly speechless. He had never seen anything like it. On the coastal plain, not so far away from the shoreline, shiny shells lay. At least it looked like this from a distance. During his training, Darski heard about the unusual buildings Bluebloods lived in, but now, seeing them for the first time with his own eyes, he was stunned.

In the middle of each circle, as these structures were called, there was a soaring spire made from the same shining material as the surrounding spiral of the proper building. At the end of the last whorl of the building Henryan saw another spire, half the height of the tower, serving as the central point of the "shell." Around the outer wall of the circle stretched a perfectly flat strip of soil, void of plants and stones, reaching the borders of the next "neighborhood." Henryan counted more than fifty of them, but on the outskirts he saw the frames of new ones, which hadn't been completed yet.

Ignoring the alarm signal, he used one of the cameras to zoom in on the nearest shell that was being erected. Scores of Bluebloods swarmed around the frame of the building. They resembled ants, climbing nimbly even the vertical elements, or stretching cobweb-like nets between them. In another section, the workers were planting cambered plates of solidified mass that were being formed in the casts a little farther away, near great "furnaces" where the building material had been melted. The plates, placed next to one another, formed the foundation of the rounded wall of the spiral's first whorl. The gaps between them were filled with the same mass that reinforced the pillars.

Wherever the wall was ready, dozens of Gurds crawled along it, covering the entire surface with a slightly different, oily substance that after being smoothed over, shone like mother of pearl. Despite their huge size, these structures didn't have any openings. Only at the tops of the two spires there were visible circular entrances, through which Bluebloods got inside their "apartments." Looking at the buildings, Henryan finally understood why storming these cities was difficult for the savages. Climbing the smooth towers was impossible, unless someone had lizard limbs. And breaking through the hard walls of this thickness required tools and time, which the Warriors of the Bone with their tactics of guerrilla warfare simply didn't have. It didn't look very g—

"Is something wrong, Sergeant?"

Darski started when he heard Valdez's voice behind his ear.

Without looking up, he directed the camera to the designated position. The red icon on the display of his console stopped blinking after a few seconds.

"No, sir. I beg to report, sir, that everything is just fine!"

"Then why can't I see the full area coverage, yet?" There was irritation in the lieutenant's voice.

"I'm on it," Darski said and immediately got to work, dropping the sightseeing.

———

He idled for the next three hours, glancing at the images from different cameras from time to time. Only twice did the scientists ask him to send probes to the border area, although in Darski's opinion, there was nothing interesting going on there.

At twelve forty-five Valdez passed him the command issued by the colonel.

"Fourteen, full transmission! The highest priority! All switch to the indicated location and a manual control of the selected cameras. The scientific department wants to have the whole picture!"

Finally, something more interesting than the daily routine ...

Henryan assigned the channels to the eight technicians sitting at the consoles below his workstation. He took care of getting an additional set of nanocameras from the orbit, just in case, and when the capsules with the equipment got suspended high over the target, he began to look through the images transmitted from the surface.

The cameras showed a typical settlement of the savages from several different perspectives. The shacks were draped over a skeleton frame—that was the most appropriate term in this case, as Suhurian building blocks were the bones of killed animals. The long, thin shins of the creatures called "tipitas" were joined together with the strings made of dried tendons and guts, and sheets made of tanned leather surrounded the whole structure. In a big square in the middle of the village, around a dozen feet high bone totem, there was a dense fence made of honbuts' ribs connected with ropes, inside which crawled a dozen nestlings—perfect miniatures of the adults.

The technicians ignored the views they were used to, directing the cameras to the biggest hut. This one, in contrast to the others, was surrounded by a row of stakes with the skulls of hrylls, the most powerful predators this globe knew, stuck on top of them. None, however, had jaws—from these the savages made their masticators, which were a cross between a slightly curved sword and a club. Six of the eight cameras entered the hut, and two remained outside. The first one of these two rose up to cover the whole settlement. The other one hovered over the clan totem, ready to approach an indicated object. At some point, the technician's attention caught a fast-approaching savage wearing a full set of armor. He held a thick bone in his hand, all polished and shiny, longer than himself.

———

The Supreme Suhur crouched on the dais in the middle of the kild, the largest of the huts, the location for the meeting of the members of the Congregation, a sort of council of war. He was surrounded by eighteen gorims—the oldest and the most experienced warriors, representing every settlement of the clan of the Triple Pierced Shield. Each of them, as tradition dictated, held an arad; a cane made of hryll bones, which gave its owner a right to make judgments and to participate in the council. Tore Numa-Reh also held this symbol of power, crowned additionally with his predecessor's kotor—the Suhurian counterpart of a heart—sealed in sagr resin.

"I've summoned you to help me pass judgment on the situation," the Supreme Suhur rumbled as soon as the mennites covered the kild's entrance with a tanned skin of a hryll, darkening the room. "Less than thirty sunrises ago, a young fister, Karan Degard, was a witness to epiphany. Although he wasn't a priest, the Spirits of the Mountains let him know that the gods of Suns and Stars intend to abandon us."

Muffled hoarse voices filled the interior; the Warriors of the Bone from the farthest settlements had already heard the rumors about it, but until now no one heard anything firsthand. Tore Numa-Reh silenced them with a tap of his arad.

"Yesterday, on the Holy Parchan Hill, the fister offered the ultimate proof of his veracity. The weapon from the otherworld, which the rebellious and spurned Spirits of the Mountains stole from gods to save the clans left to fend for themselves. Those of you who were there with me have seen what the Thunder Sower can do ..." He still couldn't see well with one eye. Even though he'd stood far from the parchan, the column of a glary light blinded him for many swellings of the membranes. Several of those present had similar problems, not to mention the burns. "The imprudent words of Tikren Da-Deradha made us act against the will of the Spirits of the Mountains, and thus not only have we lost the divine weapon, but perhaps also the kindness of our tutelary entities."

Hika No-Korto, the oldest of the clan's scouts, short but powerfully built, used his arad to tap the stone lying next to the dais he crouched on.

"Open your membranes!" Tore Numa-Reh pointed at him with the sacred cane.

"I will not defend Tikren Da-Deradha, may his entrails serve his tahars as good and nourishing fodder, but I cannot believe myself that the messengers of gods, who for countless clashes of the suns passed their words only to the holiest, would now skip them and choose an ordinary warrior who didn't even have a battle nickname."

A muffled rumble filled the hut; many members of the council were rolling down their palps simultaneously.

"The offerings have been laid on every altar since the very morning," Tore Numa-Reh said, when the warriors finally closed their membranes. "We have shed rivers of blue blood. There are no prisoners left in the killing pits of the clan, but our efforts have been to no avail. Gods still do not answer!"

"Getting new prisoners is not a problem. Let us set out for the plains, and we will bring you more Quadrupeds than the grains of redhusk fill your helmet," the oldest of the scouts assured him. "Our gods have always been happy to receive the tribute of blood," he added, seeing the indecision flash across the Supreme Suhur's face. "Let's give them more of it, and they will surely respond."

"Yes! Yes! We need more blood!" Several other council members backed him up.

"Perhaps there are no longer enough of us," the mighty hunter Kano Kazo-Hota said uncertainly after the last grumbles faded. "At night there are only a handful of fires in the highlands. Before, from the peaks of the Seven Pinnacles, we could see more of them than the stars in the sky."

"Not enough for what?" Hika No-Korto asked.

"For gods to bother with us—"

He was interrupted by someone on the other side of the kild.

"Impossible!"

"Kano Kazo-Hota speaks rightly!" Toreka Kar-Eni, sitting on his right hand, supported the neighbor. "We no longer meet their expectations, so they left us."

"What expectations?" Tore Numa-Reh asked when another wave of turmoil died.

"When the clans were more numerous than the grains of redhusk in a shieldful, the number of offerings made in the sacred land rejoiced the hearts of Kored, Yabha, and Thub. There were days when we pushed whole defeated clans for them down the Steep Scree," Kano Kazo-Hota said, and the other warriors straightened their palps, supporting his words. "We alone gave them a river of blood, and in Suhurta there were a swarm of settlements like the one of the clan of the Triple Pierced Shield. These few altars that remained don't satisfy the needs of the minor deities, and you want them to summon all our gods at once? Not to mention the fact that one hundred helmets of this blue slush is not worth one drop of the brown blood."

"Well said, Kano Kazo-Hota, Hunter Who Has Participated in Countless Battles," Tore Numa-Reh praised him. "So there is no point in shedding the Gurds' blood."

They fell silent, pondering on these words.

"Let's sacrifice the densha and those nestlings who can't bear arms," Hika No-Korto suggested. "Death at the hands of the Quadrupeds awaits them anyway if we don't appease gods."

This time the others were not so eager to express their support. But the longer the silence lasted, the more growls of approval resounded under the kild's vault.

"Why do you insist on further offerings to gods, who decided to abandon us?" Kano Kazo-Hota asked suddenly. "Why don't we try to regain the trust of the Spirits of the Mountains, who are on our side? They've always liked the taste of the Quadrupeds' blood."

"How are we to set about that?" Hika No-Korto snorted. "Do you want us to chip off the rites of Kored, Yabha, and Thub from the altars and replace them with symbols of Lut Se-Ifer and his brothers?"

"I don't mean to encourage anyone to destroy the altars. This way we could only incur more of the gods' wrath, and you've seen what they can do when someone opposes them." He touched his swollen eyelid. "Rather, I was thinking of sending a group of the youngest warriors to the caves where Karan Degard had his epiphany. Let them pay the tribute of their own blood there."

"Be it so!" The Supreme Suhur tapped his arad on a black stone, cutting off further discussion. "We will send the fist of Karan Degard to the caves; we will sacrifice his most faithful comrades. If the Spirits of the Mountains do not speak to them in four sunrises, we'll start laying offerings following Hika No-Korto's advice."

None of the warriors answered. They in turn tap the stones with their arads.

The decision was made unanimously.

"There's something else," Tore Numa-Reh rumbled when he heard the last resonant clatter. "We have to give judgment against Tikren Da-Deradha."

"Hand binding," Hika No-Korto offered immediately.

"Hand binding!" The others supported him.

This time their arads tapped the stones almost concurrently.

TWENTY-SIX

WHEN DARSKI WAS RELIEVED by another soldier, he duly saluted Lieutenant Valdez, who wasn't leaving the command center yet, then moved toward the door in a relaxed manner, mingling with the crowd of soldiers going off duty. A large group of technicians serving in this section of the station was already gathered in front of the elevators. Henryan kept his distance. He wasn't keen to travel in such a crush of people. Although until recently he'd desperately longed for human company, now he couldn't get used to the station's melee. He didn't understand this, but fortunately, unlike most of the staff, he had time to spare.

In a dozen minutes, the corridor became emptier. New maglev cars appeared every fifteen or so seconds. Another two or three seconds, he judged, and rush hour will be over. This time I won't sweat like a pig, thus saving water for the evening. And the mysterious person dropping crystals will have a more difficult task if they want to repeat their trick. He smiled to himself.

"What are you waiting for, Pry?" The lieutenant's voice interrupted his thoughts.

Henryan cast a quick glance at the clock and frowned. He had been stuck on the platform for almost twenty minutes.

"The air conditioning isn't efficient enough during rush hour," he explained. "Yesterday I was sweating so much I had to use the whole daily water ration in the shower."

"We are recently overpeopled," Valdez admitted, standing next to him. "On top of that, in a few days we will have a large delegation here. High-level officials. Half of the Senate and two hundred people of the entourage. The old man's just announced standby state of emergency for the entire technical and operational staff."

"Senators? Here?" Darski was genuinely surprised. "Why?"

"You have no idea, do you?" Lieutenant Valdez laughed before moving toward the stopping train.

Henryan followed. As soon as he crossed the threshold, the door slid shut with a hiss. Apart from them, there were only a few technicians in the car.

"The last days of savages," Valdez explained, lowering his voice. "Who would want to miss such a spectacle? You're in luck, man. It's not every day that an intelligent race disappears from the Universe. Hopefully—"

"But they won't become extinct. I mean, not entirely."

Valdez looked at him strangely.

"What are you trying to say, Pry?"

"I … The eggheads will surely catch enough specimens for further observation and research."

"Naughty, naughty!" The lieutenant smiled and wagged a finger at him. "Bless your lucky star, Sergeant. Because I was already beginning to suspect you are soaked with Gods' propaganda."

"They haven't even contacted me—" Henryan stopped in mid-sentence and frowned.

"Is something wrong?" Valdez asked, alarmed.

"No. I mean, yes. Something strange happened to me yesterday."

"In the command center?"

"No, in the evening, after I'd returned to the cabin ..." He paused for a moment, then told the lieutenant about the whole incident. In detail. Starting from finding the crystal, and ending with the detection of the cleaning agent on both the door panel and the terminal counter.

Valdez listened attentively, but didn't seem particularly disturbed. After Darski finished his story, the lieutenant was silent for a long moment as if wondering how much he could say. He spoke only when they passed sector five housing the Security Department.

"It wasn't just a prank."

"You think so?"

"Let me put it this way: the guys always play pranks on the newcomers, but it's just for fun. Planting a crystal is not funny, that's why I think that Gods attempted to contact you. For the first but not the last time. We expected they would seek to get in touch, but we didn't think it would happen so soon. What worries me, however, is this scanner. The esdees might have had something to do with it—"

"The Security Department? They know who I am?"

"No, but you took Seifert's place," the lieutenant reminded him, changing his tone to somewhat less formal. "It's no wonder they're checking up on you."

"If I were them, I would choose a different time of the day to visit. My brother was an esdee. Even though he'd served in the criminal investigation division since the very beginning, I got to know the working methods of SD agents through him."

"You're right," Valdez nodded. "You'd spent entire eight hours in the command center."

"See what I mean?"

"All the same, I have no doubt it was the Security Department. And I'm not talking about the low-ranking clones-of-bitches in black. Only the counterintelligence officers are pedantic enough, and fucked up enough, to disinfect other people's scanners." The lieutenant looked into Darski's eyes and saw pure fear in them. The fact that the counterintelligence division went after him could mean serious trouble. "They were probably looking for the crystal."

"How did they know that someone had planted it on me?"

"Cameras, wiretapping ..." Valdez shrugged. "Doing this, they're in their element. They searched the cabin after you'd left for the mess hall, convinced that the crystal was still in the jumpsuit's pocket. They hoped they would have more time, but unfortunately for them, you rushed back. Ten minutes later you wouldn't have smelled anything."

"Galacticunt!" Darski felt a cold shiver go down his back. "What am I supposed to do now?"

"Remember my advice?" the lieutenant asked. "You don't understand anything, you don't know anything, you are not interested in anything. Stay away from it all. By next week this whole thing will have blown over. Gods will go on about their business and the whole matter will be forgotten. If you receive another message, on crystal or any other damn thing, just throw it away."

"Okay."

The train began to slow down, approaching the residential area.

"Actually ..." Valdez said suddenly.

"Yes?"

"I have a better idea. If you get another message, bring it to me. Maybe I will be able to work these bastards out. Time's running out on them, and haste makes waste, as the proverb goes."

"You got it," Darski agreed without objections.

"And don't worry. No one else will know about it. If the esdees catch you out, tell them it's a part of the sting we've been working on. I will back you up."

Henryan nodded his head eagerly, then suddenly asked, "Who are they?"

"Who?"

"The people you call Gods."

"That's a topic open for discussion another time," Valdez said enigmatically, looking at the indicator of their current position.

The train was stopping.

"Today I don't have time, I have to run some errands in the medical department," he said, moving toward the exit, "but tomorrow after the shift we can meet on the observation deck and talk."

"Sounds good to me."

The door opened with a quiet hiss, revealing a wide, and completely empty, corridor.

Getting off, Valdez added, "Don't worry, Pry. You won't go back to the penal colony if you do what I say." Stepping on the platform, he turned and said over his shoulder, "One more thing. This is going to be the definitive end of savages. They can't be kept in captivity. A day or two, and they die—"

The door closed, separating them, before the lieutenant could finish his sentence.

TWENTY-SEVEN

DARSKI DIDN'T GO STRAIGHT to his cabin. He was hungry and clean enough to go to the crowded mess hall first. He had to stand in a long queue, but then he was able to load his tray full of food. Finally, he stood in the middle of the room, looking for a free seat. People came and went, no one here lounged and savored the meals. The rations were nutritious and much tastier than the prison mush, but few of the station's inhabitants knew that.

A seat had just been vacated at the end of a long table on the left. A tall and as thin as a pole pilot winked at Darski, who passed deftly by him to reach the place before a girl in a uniform of technical services.

"I'm sorry." Henryan smiled at her, sliding the tray into the hollow tabletop.

The blonde with a crew cut pursed her lips disdainfully and walked over to the next table.

"The law of the jungle." A technician sitting opposite bared his neat white teeth. "Sergeant Pry ... de ..."

"Prydeinwraig," Darski corrected him automatically. "Don't even try to get your tongue around it. Everyone calls me Pry."

"Tregvas," the man introduced himself. "Corporal Tregvas, a

local low-cost carrier ..." Seeing Darski's surprise, he added quickly, "I whizz to Beta in a shuttle."

They shook hands.

"Is it always so crowded in here?" Henryan asked, taking the first spoonful of mush.

The pilot looked at him curiously.

"You new?"

Darski nodded, swallowing a hot mouthful.

"Sector one was closed yesterday; the technicians and army live together now," Tregvas explained. "Additional two hundred mouths to feed had to take a toll on the capacity of this mess hall. Which is particularly visible at the end of each shift."

"Do you know why they took out the entire sector one?" Henryan asked.

"They are preparing it for the guests." The pilot lowered his voice. "Apparently, somebody important is about to pay us a visit."

"Even more than one somebody," Darski said.

"You know something more?"

Henryan didn't answer right away. He chewed on a piece of cell-cultured beef from the onboard farm for a moment, wondering if he hadn't just blundered. Valdez talked about the bigwigs coming to visit as if it were no secret—however, the ordinary staff had apparently no clue about anything.

"In a few days half of the Senate will descend on us," he said in the end, hoping that it wouldn't be a breach of confidentiality.

"Damn, firsthand information!" Tregvas clucked with admiration and, putting the cutlery away, added quickly, "You work in the command center?"

"Yes," Henryan confirmed with his mouth full of food.

"In what capacity, if it's not a secret?"

"The intra-system communications coordinator," Darski answered after a moment's delay, when he'd rinsed his mouth with water.

"When Seifert was here—"

Zaitsev, a black gendarme sitting nearby, looked up from his plate. Now there were two of them staring at him. Darski slowly licked his lips.

"I think I'll go," he said, grabbing the tray with some food still on it.

"Easy, Sergeant," the New Russian said. "We won't bite."

"Louismail … I mean, Seifert," Tregvas started to explain, "played on our gravbasketball team. Most of us knew him." He made a sweeping gesture with his hand, indicating the rest of the mess hall.

"You could say he was popular," the black gendarme added.

"I'm just a replacement," Darski said uneasily. "Not even—"

"But we know that," Zaitsev reassured him. "And we don't have anything against you, Sergeant. It would be a great pity to waste so much food." He pointed to the tray.

Henryan sat back, moving the tray toward himself, but for some reason the next bite stuck in his throat.

"You know what happened to him?" Tregvas asked, apparently also having lost his appetite.

Darski swallowed the spicy beef and drank the water. Now he had a horrible, metallic taste in his mouth that he couldn't get rid of.

They sat in silence for a moment, staring at the tabletop. Henryan, too. He was just wondering whether the two might belong to Gods and try to set him up, when he felt someone's heavy hand on his shoulder. He flinched as if someone doused him with boiling water. The tray with his unfinished meal flew toward Tregvas, splattering him all over. Henryan, standing up abruptly, got hit in the back of the head so hard that his teeth rattled. He hissed in pain and turned around with his hands raised, hoping that the esdees would give up the beating if he surrendered immediately. In the penal colony it wouldn't have worked, but here, with so many witnesses …

He dropped his hands as quickly as he raised them. Before

him stood a frightened fatso in stained overalls, holding a bent tray.

"Easy, man," he gasped reproachfully, looking at the splattered slurry. "I just wanted to ask if you're done eating ..."

Darski looked around the mess hall. There was a complete silence in the room. All eyes were on him. Only Tregvas was looking at himself, trying to clean his sweatshirt. The fatso wrinkled his brow.

Henryan shrugged.

"I'm sorry, buddy. You took me by surprise. Come on, I'll buy you a new one."

He reached into his pocket for the meal card and paled. His fingertips found a cold, hard and damn familiar shape.

———

Again, he had to use the daily water ration to clean himself up after the incident in the mess hall. A good amount of sauce went over his collar when standing up suddenly, he knocked dinner out of the fatso's hands. Despite the long shower he still felt a pungent odor. Eight liters of water, even broken up into a fine mist, were unable to wash all the sauce off.

He fell heavily on his bunk and looked at the desk. The microcrystal was lying where he'd put it. It was bigger than the first one. *I should report it to Valdez,* Henryan thought. He had every intention of doing just that, but not yet. First, he had to cool down. And think his situation through.

Someone was playing games with him, and didn't even try to hide it. The second crystal was put into his pocket in the mess hall. Or in the corridor, which was also crowded with people and, in addition, Henryan was still distracted after the conversation with the lieutenant. So either the corridor, or the mess hall. Which meant half a segment could be suspects.

Henryan's gaze wandered once more toward the microcrystal. Lieutenant Valdez was right—it wasn't just a prank. The initial contact was a test. The first crystal didn't contain any information in case the esdees intercepted it. Seemingly, an innocent practical joke of the colleagues. He was extremely lucky to take the crystal with him. The agents ransacked the entire cabin and found nothing. Since he turned out to be clean, maybe they would leave him alone ... No, it wasn't very likely. Valdez was right indeed.

What's it all about? What are they trying to achieve, jeopardizing my safety and freedom ... ? Darski didn't know the answers to these questions, or to a thousand of others that were whirling in his brain. But he could change that. He just needed to get up, reach for the headreader, and place the crystal in the slot. It took him only a few seconds.

There is nothing worse than uncertainty, he decided, turning on a portable visualizer. This time, the darkness was much shorter. As he expected, an inscription appeared. Slightly longer than before, and more mysterious:

**IF YOU WANT TO KNOW THE TRUTH,
WATCH THIS MESSAGE TO THE END.**

———

The recording showed the interior of a medical laboratory with an autopsy table in the middle. On the gleaming white slab lay a savage, strapped with magnetic ties. Some people in full protective suits stood around it. The scientists were taking samples, connecting sensors, checking equipment.

"Test number three hundred eighty-six," someone said when the camera focused on the Suhur. "Object acquired six hours ago from the killing pit of the clan of the Triple Pierced Shield. Terminal state. We are turning on the internal nanocameras."

A clock appeared in the upper part of the image, and a row of ten windows in the bottom part. Darski placed his finger on one of them. The image of the savage was minimized and replaced with a new picture. Very dark and strange. A fleshy tunnel with a rounded, slimy shape moving inside. Henryan pointed a finger at it, and a box with the word "tahar" and a short description, already familiar to him thanks to the training course, appeared right on cue. The disgusting creature slithered toward the camera, filling almost half of the image. A few hairlike filaments, adorning the end of its segmented body, were clearly visible. The worm spun them suddenly, directing the microscopic head in the direction of a brown drop hanging from one of the many holes. The filaments whipped the walls of the tunnel, and when one of them hit the oily, life-giving liquid, the rounded end of the tahar unexpectedly split into seven parts like a blooming flower, and in the blink of an eye the worm caught the drop of the old warrior's gore.

Darski checked the other windows—most of them showed similar strange organs, except that there were no worms there. He glanced at the clock. It indicated the thirty-sixth minute of the test, but the numbers kept changing very quickly. The information box displayed the words: "The projection fast-motioned twelve times."

He looked at the funnily twitching body. When the convulsions grew stronger, he checked the images from the three cameras labeled "parenchyma." There were no longer any tahars on any of them. He switched to the other images, and very quickly found the worms, but in places where they shouldn't have been. They raged, biting through the tissue of various organs, sucking every drop of brown gore they came across. It looked really awful. After a few minutes Henryan fast-forwarded the projection even more.

The Suhur's body, devoured from the inside, stopped moving after eleven hours of torment. In a monotonous, passionless voice, the scientist commenting the experiment said, among other things, that: "Object number three hundred eighty-six died much faster than the objects of previous thirteen tests, mainly because of the old age and significant weakness."

The picture darkened, but a new inscription appeared immediately against the absolute blackness:

**WOULD YOU RATHER DIE IN A BATTLE,
OR SUFFER SUCH DEATH OF OLD AGE?**

Darski smiled to himself. The answer was simple.

WE WILL BE IN TOUCH, SERGEANT.

Henryan took off his headreader, picked the crystal from the slot and looked at it thoughtfully. They hadn't told him everything during the preparatory training course. He heard a lot about the cruelty of Suhurs, their bloody rituals and primitiveness. Only now did he see the reason why the Warriors of the Bone valued violence and death. If this recording hadn't been fabricated, it put things into an entirely new light. And it explained quite a lot. Who in their right mind would want to experience such terrible agony, especially if painkillers were unknown to them?

He slowly began to understand what Gods were on about. He walked over to the terminal and established the connection with Valdez's number. The holo screen blinked for a few seconds, then it took shape of a sleepy face of the lieutenant, and disappeared instantly.

When Valdez appeared again, his eyes were still swollen, but his look was sober.

"Now it's the secure line, go ahead."

"I've received the second crystal," Darski said.

"I see. Bring it tomorrow to the center. At twelve you'll get a fictitious order telling you to repair the transmitter. You will take the service elevator and go to the hub. Technical sector, level one oh four. The order will contain the access codes to this part of the station. We will meet under the dome, on the observation deck."

"Why there? Can't we talk in the center, or—"

"No one can know about our conversation," Valdez interrupted him. "Take my word for it, Pry, it's the most sensible place that comes to my mind."

"There are going to be a lot of people, I guess?"

"Don't you worry about this."

TWENTY-EIGHT

THE XAN 4 SYSTEM, X-RAY SECTOR

09/08/2354

Sitting under the transparent cap of plasteel, you could see not only the infinite black void, or anchorage of the Fleet's ships, but also Beta itself. The station was placed into a stationary orbit over the equator, on the dayside of the planet. Every crew member could come to the observation deck in their free time, hover over one of the observation posts—the dome did not spin like the rest of the station, so there was zero gravity here—and enjoy the view of the absolute blackness of space, tiny lights of the stars, and the celadon and gold circle of the planet, where shoals of clouds lazily moved over the outlines of the continents.

Darski didn't believe Valdez's assurances, but when he got off the train, he indeed did not see anyone. He thus flew over to the central part of the observation deck, fastened the safety line to the post's handle, and stared at the majestic work of Mother Nature. This planet was very different from his home, Sava. It had a gigantic ocean, continents, dense atmosphere, ice caps, but not a single moon.

"Thanks for coming, Pry." Lieutenant Valdez hung over the nearby observation post.

Henryan reached into his pocket and produced the microcrystal. He took it between two fingers, and then threw it in the direction of Valdez.

"I got it in the mess hall," he said.

The lieutenant grabbed the slowly soaring pyramid.

"Have you already watched the recording?"

"Yes."

Darski knew that the professionals were able to squeeze a lot of information out of crystals. The date of the last reading was one of them. It wouldn't pay to lie.

"What's on it?"

"A recording of"—Henryan was looking for the right words—"of some medical experiment."

"Interesting ..." Valdez pulled an airtight container out of his pocket and put the coldly glittering pyramid in it.

"Who are they?" Henryan repeated his earlier question, not taking his eyes off the majesty of Beta.

"That, unfortunately, we don't know. Seifert and his associates didn't rat out anyone else."

"I didn't mean the names."

"I see." The lieutenant was silent for a moment, taking a more comfortable position. Eventually, he began to speak. "At the beginning, it was just the usual antics of the soldiers. We had almost thirty incidents in the first year of the mission. Fortunately, harmless ones. We managed to cover up most of them—"

"Cover up? How?"

"By eliminating the witnesses. Then, there were several times more savages than now, and inkblots ... You know how many of them there are. Sometimes we staged the attack of one or the other side, but more often than not we simply brought all those who'd seen anything up here."

"To experiment on them."

"Don't be so dramatic, Pry. The scientists needed the live specimens for research anyway. They could experiment on the supplied material to their satisfaction, and at the same time we removed the source of danger. We were hoping Gods would finally understand that instead of helping Suhurs, they sent them to the labs. Anyway, why am I explaining myself? A hundred times more inkblots and savages die on Beta every day than we've killed in a year in the station's laboratories—"

"We were supposed to talk about Gods," Darski reminded him, taking advantage of the moment's silence.

"And who are we talking about if not them? As I said, it was the usual antics at first, and no one saw any harm in that. You know how it is with the army. The scientists complained to the Admiralty, and from time to time they submitted their reports, the old man reacted accordingly, sending the guilty ones to the hole, or demoting them, and somehow it was working. Unfortunately, over time, more and more soldiers got fascinated with savages. Don't ask me why. I often wondered what might appeal to us, humans, in these primitive and disgusting creatures, but have never found the answer to this question. For obvious reasons, we couldn't even think of the full crew exchange. The government is doing its best to keep the existence of the two races discovered on Xan 4 secret. And probably rightly so—" Lieutenant Valdez fell silent again when a loud clatter came from the nearest entrance. Darski, seeing his reaction, realized that he was not the only one overreacting. Valdez reacted as nervously as he did yesterday in the mess hall. "What was I … Oh, yes. At the end of the third year of the mission, things escalated. It wasn't just pranks at the scientists' expense anymore, but much more serious stuff."

"Like what?"

"For example, someone warned the clans about danger. Inkblots were in Treb'aldaledo, considering an attack on some or other settlement, and a few hours later, news of this reached the Suhurian priests and we had a slaughter on our hands. Sometimes we learned about everything much later, when savages praised the massacre in songs. Yes, I know, their buzzing can be hardly called songs. There is neither rhythm nor melody there. A cacophony, nothing more."

"We had so-called 'twentieth-century classical music' a couple of centuries ago," Henryan said with a wry smile. Listening to Suhurian bards, he had the impression of playing one of the crystals collected by his mother. "It was very similar."

"Really?" Valdez muttered, surprised. "Anyway, it doesn't matter ... After a few months, although we were aware only of a part of these activities, it occurred to us that these weren't the usual antics. The guys started playing gods on this planet. And they were serious about it. There was even a special commission sent from the sector's headquarters, which determined after a lengthy investigation that the perpetrators only'd meant to cause greater battles and more casualties. You know, the soldiers were bored and incited Suhurs to fight. This placated the Admiralty for some time. For brass it was a reasonable and acceptable explanation, too. But we knew different. And we were right. But the orders were clear: if the guys limit themselves to warning savages of danger, we shouldn't make an issue of it.

"Finally, about a year ago, something happened that forced the old man to declare open war on Gods. There are a few permanent bases on Beta. We've set them up in mostly inaccessible areas, for example in the higher parts of the mountains or under water, so as not to be too conspicuous. Staying down there, the scientists can spend more time on research instead of traveling back and forth. And we provide around-the-clock protection. A security team consisting of sixteen soldiers is stationed in each base. They have two graviplanes to move around and one heavy shuttle in case they need to evacuate the equipment and scientific personnel. Imagine that one night, two idiots flew over the largest Gurdian circle in this part of the continent, turned off camouflage, and hovered over the central quarters, talking through the speakers about the divine curse which will fall upon any Blueblooded that would cross the Valt Aram. It took us fifteen minutes to take control of the situation. In the meantime, there was such a stampede on the ground that hundreds of inkblots died trampled down."

"Have they lost their minds?!"

"Not really. They were hammered, that's true, but a few days later, we were able to piece together a handful of seemingly unrelated facts. We found out that less than an hour before the incident, the Supreme Council issued a decree commanding the immediate commencement of the final phase of colonization. This took place in the heart of Gurdu'dihan, on the other side of the planet, so at first no one connected the dots. Both the pilot and the navigator of the graviplane insisted it was just a drunkards' jest, they'd made a bet with their buddies that they'd pull it off, and so on, and so forth, but Colonel Rutta didn't believe a word of it. He told us to keep sniffing around.

"Over the next two days, we checked all the databases, but found nothing. Since the information about the new Gurdian campaign against savages, no one from the orbit had contacted Quartus, I mean the base from which the graviplane flew out. The old man was very disappointed. So were we. It indeed looked like a coincidence. We were ready to let go, but someone from the team came up with the idea to check the communications with other receivers, even the most distant.

"Well, we found something strange. One of the routine control radiograms sent to Septimus, on the southern tip of Suhurta, had a mismatch in the control sum. Normally, no one would pay attention to it, because such mistakes happen, but the old man told me to analyze every anomaly, so we analyzed this message and found an extra set within its code. Encrypted. It had been sent seven minutes after the arrival of the message from Gurdu'dihan. It contained summary information about the order issued."

"It's terribly complicated," Darski muttered.

"Wait, Pry, there's more. We already had a foothold. We knew who'd sent the file and who'd received the message. Following the clue, we discovered the next four middlemen, but there the trail went cold. From Secundus, no one sent the data farther. And from there, it was over four hundred miles to Quartus.

Although officially we couldn't accuse the pranksters of anything, we learned that there were people in our ranks who looked at this matter differently than the heads of the scientific department. Now we know that they are willing to do a lot, and even to sacrifice a lot, to protect Suhurs."

"The attack order was countermanded, I gather."

"No, it wasn't," Valdez said. "But there was no one to execute it. For the first time in the history of Gurdian civilization, all sithus shirked their duty to the Supreme Council. That day we changed ... hell, what am I saying ... 'Gods' changed the history of Beta. Do you understand?"

Darski nodded, then realized that the lieutenant might not be looking at him. He added quickly, "Yes. Suhurs were saved for the time being. Maybe even a year. And what happened to the pranksters?"

"Those directly involved went to jail. Those suspected of complicity were demoted and are still scrubbing the johns or patching up the hull of the station. But we hadn't gotten to the bottom of this. Next months showed that Gods were doing fine. The incident with the phaser was the fifth serious violation of regulations."

"Do they really believe Suhurs can be saved from extinction?" Darski asked.

"It looks that way," the lieutenant said.

"But why are they picking on me?"

"Seifert got caught, and they still need someone in the communications, preferably at the level of the command center. Someone who has access to the latest information and the hardware. Without it, they can't respond quickly enough, and the most recent disobedience of savages thwarted their plans at the worst possible moment. If the great sampo-sithu were killed on the battlefield with an unknown weapon, Gurds would consider this a divine intervention. Which in turn—with thousands of eyewitnesses—would force the Supreme Council to revise its policy toward Suhurs. The local inkblots are slowly forgetting about the curse, but one more action such as this would make them flee across the Adal Vin."

"From what you've told me, it's clear that Gods are well organized. They will get their own way with or without me. After all, as you said, one more action is all they need."

"I assure you, Pry, that we don't idle, either. We've put up safeguards and secured the system in all possible ways. We have reduced the surface staff to bare minimum. The communications centers in the bases have been automated or put under strict supervision of the scientists. No soldier can leave the base without the commander's authorization. We've also stripped them all of directed-energy weapons. So, in order to arrange for something that could be considered as fulfilling the curse, they must now really use their brains. Unless they get to have their man in the command center. No wonder they do everything they can to reach you."

"There are a hundred people working in the command center," Darski noted. "Most of them with much more experience than I have, and some of them probably on a friendly footing with Gods. I am the worst possible choice."

Valdez smiled.

"You still don't understand a thing," he said. "The operations on the surface are monitored by eighty-five people working in three shifts, but only four of them have access to the command channel. Me, you, and our substitutes. No one in the center can lift a finger without our knowledge. If an unplanned message appears in the holonet, you will pick it up immediately. If someone issues an unauthorized command, I will see it on my screen before the sender lifts his fingers off the keyboard. That's how it works. Without access to you or to me, Gods are helpless."

"And our substitutes?" Henryan asked.

"Yours has been transferred here from the SD headquarters. You know what that means: the guy is die-hard. Of mine, I am equally sure. It was thanks to him that we were able to detect the perpetrators of most incidents so far."

Darski chewed his lip nervously. He knew he had to help the station's commander, even if he didn't want to. The colonel had this planned very smartly. A few years in a penal colony changes perspective. Irreversibly. An inmate would give anything for the smallest chance of escape, even his own mother, let alone a primitive alien race, which was anyway doomed to extinction. But the memory of the warrior dying in agony still troubled him.

"Isn't it too obvious, Lieutenant?"

"What?"

"My appearance on Xan. I am flying in from nowhere and immediately get the only position that Gods need, and that you should have secured together with esdees. I'm afraid they've known since the beginning what is going on. And they play games with us. There won't be any serious attempts of contact ..."

"There have already been such attempts." Valdez tossed the tiny pyramid in his hand. "Understand one thing, Pry: for them it is a sink or swim situation. They lost their key player in the last minutes of the game, while the score was unfavorable for them. Now they have to make a move, otherwise they will lose altogether. Even time's not on their side. They are really desperate. And that's why they will approach the single man who is the key to the success of their plan. If you don't want to cooperate with them willingly, it can get dangerous. But you will not support them when it comes to a showdown. Do we understand each other?"

"I'm not crazy," Darski assured him. "I'd rather die than go back to the Sturgeon Belt."

"That's the answer I hoped for." Valdez unfastened the safety line and grabbed the railing. "Now listen to me carefully, Pry. If someone plants you a new crystal or contacts you in any other way, engage in a dialogue."

"But ..."

"Don't interrupt me!" The lieutenant raised his voice. "We've pulled you out of the mines, even though we both know you should rot there. The fact that you are relaxing today under this dome instead of drilling another tunnel on some unstable asteroid, you owe to us, and us only. Me and Colonel Rutta. But now it's not me who is pulling the strings. If the old man finds out that you've screwed, you'll get an orange outfit and you'll hop away to follow Seifert the very same day."

He lowered his voice again. "Look, man … I'm on your side, but we're both up this shit creek without a paddle. So, you have no choice."

"I know."

"Then listen carefully, Pry. We don't want that much from you. You don't have to expose Gods. You don't need to submit reports, or rat on anyone. The Admiralty is not interested in revealing the depth of this conspiracy, or its subsequent participants."

"I guess …" Darski muttered.

"We just want to know what Gods are up to, so that we can thwart their plans. I'm not an idiot, I am aware that they will check you. Most likely, for their own safety, they won't even tell you what they're going to do until the last minute. Maybe they will slip you some false leads."

Lieutenant Valdez paused as if pondering over something.

"I want you to understand that the ultimate goal of this operation is to prevent interference with the destinies of the two alien civilizations. We'll give Gods free rein, let them enjoy an illusory sense of impunity. We will ban only their last, decisive move. If inkblots think they need to get rid of savages, so be it. I know it sounds inhuman, and the conspirators will undoubtedly use this very pitch, but you must remember that the matter is not as simple as it looks. In ten years, a hundred at most, restoring Suhurs' population will lead to a new war, and we'll be back to square one. Protracted fighting means millions more victims on both sides of the conflict. By allowing them to live, we will sanction slaughter on an unimaginable scale. Elimination of savages at this stage will obviously be an irreparable loss. We all understand that we are dealing with ... with an old, intelligent race, but look at this problem from a different perspective.

"The Warriors of the Bone are a threat even to themselves. You've recently seen some kind of experiment, no doubt not very pleasing to the eye, but I'll bet that Gods won't show you the holo of making offerings—including individuals of their own species—or mangling nestlings. I could go on with examples like this for hours."

Darski'd had enough by now.

"What am I to do?" he asked.

"You'll make a decision when the time comes, depending on how the situation develops. But remember one thing: you can't immediately agree to their proposals. Let them make several attempts. Keep acting nervously, as you've been doing so far. When they start to press you, avoid answers, deceive them, and ask for more time to think. The longer it takes, the more desperate they will become, and thus, more careless. From now on, we're going to communicate only in the command center, only verbally. No electronics. Starting tomorrow, the old man is proclaiming a state of heightened alert, which means the closure of most channels, and tighter control of the station's traffic. That should help us. Do you have any other questions?"

"No, Lieutenant."

"Excellent. Then sign the documents confirming the completion of the repair for me, and go back to the rim."

"Yes, sir." Darski took one last look at the contour of Suhurta and its narrow northern end.

The Seven Pinnacles stood out clearly from the celadon and gold highlands.

TWENTY-NINE

ZAITSEV WAITED for him in the corridor of the residential area. He was standing just round the corner, behind the bulkhead, where he could watch this level's main intersection. Leaning against the wall, he was typing something on his comlink, smiling to himself as if it amused him. A moment before Darski turned into the leg of the corridor that led to his cabin, the black gendarme stopped what he was doing and leisurely mingled with the crowd. Henryan was firmly convinced that their meeting wasn't a coincidence.

"We need to talk, Sergeant," Zaitsev said indistinctly, not taking his eyes off the comlink.

"I don't think so."

"Esdees are sniffing around you," the black gendarme added quickly.

"I know."

Zaitsev looked at him in surprise.

"Slow down a little," he asked, changing his tone.

"I'm in a hurry." Henryan tried to brush him off again, and not because the lieutenant told him to. He really didn't want to continue this conversation.

"Really?" Zaitsev hissed, irritated. "This time it won't be just a search. They are waiting for you."

Darski shrugged.

"Let them wait. I have done nothing wrong."

"If I were you, I would check all your pockets," Zaitsev advised him, before turning sharply when the corridor forked, and started to squeeze between the first shift soldiers returning to their cabins.

Henryan cursed and, in spite of himself, slowed down. He resisted the temptation to immediately check his pockets. The esdees could have put a tail on him, since they planned open confrontation. A dozen steps away, behind the corner, his corridor began. If he was to get rid of the crystal, this was the only place. He let the crowd swallow him, put his hands in his pockets, as if reaching for something casually, and immediately found the cold pyramid. He grabbed it with two fingers. He wondered frantically what to do with the cuckoo's egg ... that's probably how people once called the sneakily planted objects. In this part of the corridor there were no public atomizers. He could drop the microcrystal onto the floor grating, since no one would probably notice it, but this wouldn't solve his problem. In a moment rush hour would be over and the transparent pyramid would catch passersby's attention. Not to mention the security cameras.

No, I won't be able to get rid of it this way, Darski thought. *Maybe it's better to pass it on to someone?* On second thought he rejected this solution, too. He wasn't as dexterous as the person who bothered him with the Gods' messages. Getting caught was almost certain, and if the "recipient" starts making a scene ... Damn it! Suddenly he felt someone take his hand, the one in which he held the pyramid. It wasn't a strong grip, rather a soft brush, so surprising that before he realized what was happening, the microcrystal changed its owner. He didn't see the face of a woman in a white uniform of a medic, who had just walked confidently past him, saving him a hell of a lot of trouble. Before she disappeared in the crowd, he noticed she had flaming red hair and pale skin on the neck, speckled with freckles.

Thank you, Henryan thought, turning left into a narrow corridor, adorned with two rows of doors with scanners. It was much more quiet here. Several soldiers, off duty like him, were walking toward their cabins.

Putting his palm on the scanner, Darski swallowed loudly. The door slid open with a barely audible hiss. It wasn't completely dark inside, as when he'd finished his shift on any given day. This time, he was greeted by a pleasant twilight. In the dim glow of the lighting panels he saw three bulky figures.

"Sergeant Prydeinwraig?" The man pronounced his name with some difficulty.

Judging by his accent, Welsh was foreign to him.

———

They did not march him to their office. They didn't have to. The fast but thorough search, with the full scan of the digestive system, took them only a few dozen seconds. Then Darski was sat on a chair at his desk. The Security Department officers stood around him, so that he had only one of them in his field of vision.

"Where is the microcrystal?" the shortest of the three men asked. He was still a head taller than Henryan.

"I don't have any microcrystals," Darski said, momentarily realizing that his answer was too elaborate and too quick.

The SD officers also thought that the suspect, taken by surprise, should have asked first what crystal they meant. Everybody at the station used microcrystals. They were the most common data storage devices.

"That we already know," the first officer said, brushing some fluff off his impeccably tailored uniform. "I asked what you did with it."

Darski looked the esdee straight in the eye, and suddenly felt an icy chill crawl up his spine. These were not the eyes of a sane person.

"As soon as I found it in my pocket, it went to the nearest atomizer," he explained after a moment's thought, trying to make his words sound sincere. "I'm not going to get entangled in conspiracy and rescue savages. I'm not Seifert."

The esdees exchanged glances.

"Here, here. For someone who throws away crystals without reading them, you seem to know an awful lot about their content," the interrogator said with amusement.

"I have been instructed not to meddle in the affairs of Gods," Darski explained.

"Who instructed you?"

"Lieutenant Valdez."

"The colonel's bitch," another esdee snorted. This one was standing behind Darski.

"What did he tell you?" the first esdee, standing in front of him, asked.

"Nothing specific."

A hand as big as a shovel rested on the sergeant's shoulder. He knew what this gesture might herald. In the penal colony, he'd been also questioned whenever there was a failure of the armor or the equipment. Human ingenuity knows no bounds. Both when it comes to taking one's life, and extracting truth from others.

"Try to be more precise," the invisible one advised him.

"It seemed to me that the lieutenant is on your side—" Darski began and hissed loudly when the fingers of the giant tightened on his shoulder's tendon. This guy knew how to inflict pain. "I'm telling the truth! It was him who warned me about Gods. He advised me to stay clear of them."

"And to discard crystals in the atomizer?"

"No," Henryan admitted. "He wanted me to pass them to him."

"So why haven't you been doing that?"

"Because of … fear."

"Fear of what?"

"Of visits like this one, of being involved in some scandal—"

"We know what's in your file, Sergeant. Or rather, what's missing."

Does it mean that creating a new personal file and changing the appearance haven't misled the always vigilant Security Department?

Darski swallowed and looked up.

"If you know about the sentence, you should also understand why Rutta fetched me here."

"Some say our intellectual level leaves much to be desired, Sergeant." The shortest of the agents folded his arms. "That's probably why we have to resort to such brutal methods of interrogation."

Henryan took the hint and added quickly, "Colonel Rutta wants me to be bait for Gods."

The esdee smiled. For real. It wasn't a sadistic grin, so frequent on the faces of the torturers when they finally managed to break the suspect, but a normal, sincere smile of an amused man.

"Old fool. If he stayed out of this and let us work, there would be no incidents. What is his plan this time?"

Darski spoke briefly about Valdez's proposal, skipping a few minor details, like giving the previous microcrystal to the lieutenant.

The agents listened to him attentively, and when he finished, remained silent for a moment. In the end, the shortest one said, "I'll be damned, the dogs of war are starting to play counterintelligence."

The two esdees standing behind Darski guffawed.

"Listen to me carefully now, you damn wretched clone-of-a-bitch, shooting decent people." The icy tone didn't agree with his smile. "From now on, you won't discard anything. Every crystal you get you'll immediately play back on this terminal."

He pointed to the desk. "You don't have to watch it. It's enough that the contents will be copied to the system. Then you can give it to Valdez, let him play a detective."

Henryan nodded vigorously.

"Pretend you're still the old man's bait, but remember: from now on, you work for us, not for him," the one standing behind him said.

Darski nodded eagerly again.

"One wrong move, and you're going back where you came from," the third agent threatened.

"I understand. I'll do what you want."

"Great." The first esdee stood with his legs wide apart, folding his hands behind his back. "Rutta won't sweep this thing under the carpet. Not this time. The old fool allowed for the creation of an illegal secret organization. We will eliminate it, and you will help us."

"I've already said I will do whatever you want."

A pressure on his shoulder eased. The esdee standing in front of Henryan nodded slightly, still smiling. The pain that came suddenly was sharp, piercing, unbearable. Darski fell off his chair. He wanted to howl, but only a quiet grunt escaped his mouth. A blow to the kidney made him breathless. He fell to his knees with his eyes bulging. Holding the throat with both hands, he was trying to gasp for the tiniest bit of air. The esdee leaned over him and patted him on the sweaty cheek.

"It's a small advance in case you change your mind."

THIRTY

09/09/2354

Have I just got out of the frying pan into the fire? Maybe not. Maybe I still can play this well and extricate myself from this shitty situation …

Darski sat in front of the communications console, watching people in the huge command center. He didn't see any signs of nervousness, furtive glances, meaningful gestures or smiles. Regular people working regular jobs. *How many of them were involved in the Gods' conspiracy? Maybe all of them, maybe none. No, some of them certainly support the Suhurs' cause,* he decided after a moment's thought. *Lieutenant Valdez must have had a similar opinion when he insisted on limiting contact outside the center.*

"Don't sleep, Pry!" Henryan felt his superior's hand on his shoulder before he heard his voice.

"I'm not sleeping, Lieutenant," he said, turning around. "We need to talk," he added in a whisper.

Valdez's face remained expressionless.

"Show me something on the display," he whispered back after a few seconds, which he spent staring intently at the console.

Henryan pointed to one of the charts visible on the screen.

"I had a visit yesterday," he said in a low voice.

"Who was it?" Valdez asked, opening a hologram with a touch of his thumb.

"Esdees."

The lieutenant closed the chart, and pretended he was looking for some data.

"This was only to be expected."

"They know everything," Darski answered the next question before it was asked.

"From you?"

"No. Yes. Partially ..." he stammered.

"I see." Valdez looked up toward the dais. Colonel Rutta didn't look at them, busy talking to two officers. "What did they want?"

"They seemed to be amused by what we intend to do."

"Amused?" The lieutenant looked at Darski, not hiding his surprise.

"Yes," the sergeant confirmed. "One of them even said that you could continue to play a detective."

"Couldn't you keep your mouth shut?"

"I tried," Henryan snapped angrily, "that's why I still piss blood."

Valdez looked at the screen again, and cursed quietly.

"I should have known they would put the heat on you so soon."

"They have my file. The real one," Darski complained.

"They have their own databases," the lieutenant explained.

"Maybe we should withdraw—" The sound of sirens interrupted Henryan in mid-sentence. He looked down at the console. One of the lights was flashing red. A technician from workstation three was waving his hand at them.

"Galacticunt!" the lieutenant hissed angrily. They attracted the attention of the whole center. "Get to work, Sergeant!" He growled when the room grew silent. "You can discuss the issue of probes failure with the engineers, as long as it is after your shift!" he added, running to his workstation.

Henryan quickly established communication with Beta. In front of him appeared a hologram of a woman's face, contorted with rage.

"What's your name, you moron?!" she yelled as soon as he switched on voice transmission, and continued without waiting for an answer. "Give me a set of cameras in the position eighty-four! At once! If I don't have the full transmission in one minute, I'll report you, you incompetent scum in a ridicu—that is, without a ridiculous hat! You're a saboteur!"

Darski listened to her grumbling, sending commands to the nearest satellites. Twenty seconds later, a swarm of nanobots spilled from the capsule and sped down toward the assigned coordinates.

"We will be ready in two minutes, Doctor … Godbless," he assured the woman when she paused for a moment. "We had a little problem with—"

He didn't finish, because her holographic image disappeared.

"What's going on here?" Colonel Rutta bothered to come down to the lower level.

"Sergeant Prydeinwraig informed me of a technical problem, sir," Valdez reported from behind his console. "We were just analyzing it, when—"

Rutta looked at them both furiously.

"Him, I understand, but you, Lieutenant Valdez, you pulling something like this …" He shook his head.

If looks could kill, Darski would turn immediately into a pile of ash.

THIRTY-ONE

NARO SLOWED DOWN before the next summit. He covered the last spear throw on all fours, maneuvering carefully among the boulders and the tufts of thorny redhusk. He reached the ridge and froze, watching the surroundings.

In the distance he saw the outlet of a wide ravine, and behind it—a vast plain, on which a herd of honbuts, huge like huts, marched majestically. In front of him, at the bottom of the slope, seven members of the Karan Degard's fist were just ending the preparation for the hunt. Old Redu Nizo-Hakra was with them, teaching the youngsters how to properly set a trap for the most mighty predator of Suhurta.

Naro, seeing that he was in time, jumped to his feet. Before he went down to the hunters, he made a shrill, very low rumble of the hunters' clan greeting, which couldn't be heard by the beasts lurking nearby. He preferred to reveal his presence in advance, before the Warriors of the Bone, gathered around the oldster, would fall into a deeper trance.

He crossed the steep slope with a few well-calculated strides, and landed lightly on the soft ground. Redu Nizo-Hakra stood up first. A sharp reprimand could be heard in his wheezing.

"On the fat tahars of greatest warriors, why do you, who do not yet have any nickname, dare disturb us hunting?"

Naro covered his eyes with the thicker eyelids, and hastily ducked his palp.

"Forgive me, great hunter. I am Naro of Daran Toku-Taro's breeding. The Supreme Suhur sent me with a message for Rekne Tare's fist."

The other hunters shifted nervously at his whirring.

"Then open your membranes," the old Warrior of the Bone ordered.

"The Congregation decided that the clan of the Triple Pierced Shield would ask the Spirits of the Mountains for forgiveness. In three sunrises, when the next clash of the suns begins, your fist is to stand at the mouth of the Bor Omot caves to implore gods for another chance with your own blood."

"In three sunrises …" Redu Nizo-Hakra calculated some-thing in his mind. "There is more than enough time both for the journey, and the hunt. The Spirits of the Mountain will enjoy the offering more if the warriors laying it get their own masticators first … masticators made from the jaws of the biggest hryll that ever trod these plains!"

The youngsters supported him with a loud concerted rumble. It was their first hunt for such big game. Each of them hoped for a stunt, earning him the right to a nickname, either the warrior's or hunter's one.

Having fulfilled his duty, Naro greeted the old Suhur by folding his arms in all joints. This way he wished him good hunting, and then, without further opening his membranes, he moved toward the slope from which he had just run down.

"Wait!" Redu Nizo-Hakra ordered, stopping him. "Since you're here, maybe you would like to join the fist I lead? Only for the time of the hunt. Karan Degard died, so we could do with someone in his place, to make it eight hunters."

"It will be a great honor for me," the messenger said. He'd

only left the clan's pen recently, and hadn't had a chance to gain even an ordinary nickname, yet.

The hryll hunt … Few Suhurs his age could boast of killing the beast. He didn't count on getting his own masticators, because there were only eight bones suitable for this weapon in the giant. The best trophies will be therefore gained by four bravest out of the fist's seven warriors, but if he does well, he can get some valuable bones and tendons for his first armor. He squeezed tighter the stabber he had polished in the pen, the only weapon he had, and started toward the circle.

He took the available free spot, and after covering his eyes with the thicker eyelids, soaked up the monotonous drone of a prayer, which also served as the instructions for each of the young hunters. He learned it by heart, repeating sound after sound after the oldster. A hundred swellings of the membranes later he was ready, as were the other members of the fist. He was filled with mystical enthusiasm, shared even by his young tahars.

"It's time!" Redu Nizo-Hakra sprang up from his place in the middle of the circle.

Although the rules were very simple, hunting such a beast was not an easy task. There was only one way to knock down the dangerous giant. First, the hunters had to dig pits, a little wider than their bodies and deep enough to completely disappear in them after squatting. Redu Nizo-Hakra traced a couple of long lines on the ground, measuring them carefully with his spear, then designated two places in each corner of the formed rectangle—that was where the fist members were supposed to hide. For himself he dug a much deeper shelter outside the rectangle, roughly in the middle of the shorter line. When the pits were ready, the oldster told the young hunters to weave the covers for their helmets. They made them with twigs of plants picked on the slopes of the ravine. They were trying their camouflage in turns, vigilantly watched by the old warrior, and rebuked by him whenever they did something wrong.

They needed many swellings of the membranes to become invisible. In the end even Naro, watching the plain, couldn't tell which clump of plants was natural, and which one hid his companion underneath. The pit of the old Warrior of the Bone had also been covered with weaved twigs, although unlike the others, it remained empty.

When the fist disappeared in the prepared hideouts, Redu Nizo-Hakra raised his bow and walked ahead, softly hooting the familiar hunting prayer. After he left, there was a deep silence and total stillness in the ravine. Naro couldn't say how long it lasted. But he knew very well what the experienced hunter was doing at the time. His task was to find a suitable prey, and hrylls were never lacking in this area—especially during the migration of large herds of honbuts. Then the old Suhur had to draw the attention of the predator and draw it away from its almost inseparable companion, which was one of the most difficult and dangerous hunting tasks. Even the whole clan wouldn't be able to overpower the two giants, let alone the fist of youngsters. The Warrior of the Bone had to approach the beasts lurking among the rocks so skillfully that the second hryll lying nearby wouldn't smell the pheromone bait, with which the hunter was going to attract the future prey. Suhurs knew many tricks that allowed them to lure game, and the older and more experienced they were, the faster they led the animal to the place with traps prepared beforehand.

Redu Nizo-Hakra enjoyed a reputation of one of the best hunters in his clan, so it was no wonder he had done his part before the smaller sun stood at its zenith. The youngsters hidden in the pits first felt the tremor of the ground, and soon after they heard the shrill rumble of their mentor, returning in long strides. The braver ones glanced toward the outlet of the ravine, raising the weaved covers a little. Naro was one of them, though in his case one could speak of curiosity rather than bravado.

The old hunter was running as fast as his legs could carry him, and behind him sped a really big hryll. It was several times taller than the Suhur decoying him. Two flexible, long necks, placed not in the front, where the beast had an eye, but on the sides, more or less behind its shoulder blades, were sticking from a long body ending with a bunch of whiplike tails. The muzzles located at the necks' ends, equipped with four jaws, reached every now and then for the nimbly dodging Warrior of the Bone. Redu Nizo-Hakra was still a bowshot away from his hiding place, but no more than two spear lengths separated him from the snapping jaws of the beast.

Naro began to doubt whether the oldster would manage to reach the trap. In just a couple swellings of the membranes, the massive jaws would get him, and then tear him apart, which the young hunters would have to witness. The inexperienced messenger underestimated, however, the skills of the elderly hunter. Redu Nizo-Hakra reached into a bag slung over his arm and without slowing down even for a moment, took out a hollow bone of a honbut. He snatched the stopper with a practiced movement before the beast had time to snap at him with both muzzles at once. Dodging aside, he spilled the contents of the bone gourd over his shoulder. The necks, rushing again at him, curled in a flash as if someone had punched them with masticators. A moment later, the hryll kicked wildly, trying to shake the unbearable smell off. The ground quivered when the mighty animal landed on its feet. It looked really enraged. In the meantime, the hunter ran a relatively safe distance away and, without slowing down, started to chirp like a wounded skaklak so that the confused prey wouldn't give up the chase.

The predator heard him and immediately took up the chase. It rushed madly forward, but it was already too late. Redu Nizo-Hakra was just reaching the trap. Two leaps were enough to pass the first pits; two more lengthened steps, and the old Suhur stopped at the edge of his own hiding place. The hryll also slowed down, seeing that the tiny prey stopped running. It glided now, bending the front paws as if preparing for a jump. It held both its muzzles raised high, ready to capture and immediately tear apart the brazen Suhur.

Seeing the giant come between the lines, the old hunter growled as piercingly as he could, and when the predator's jaws darted toward him, he jumped gracefully into the previously prepared hideout and shielded himself with the two spears that he had left by the pit.

The members of the fist took their cue from him. When both muzzles began to dig in the ground, trying to get to the prey, the young hunters jumped out of their pits and crept up to the feet of the hryll in total silence. The most dangerous part of the hunt was about to begin. Eight hunters had to strike simultaneously in a perfectly synchronized attack. Four of them had to cut tendons in the beast's paws, to immobilize it. A failure would mean a death sentence for the whole fist. The other four Warriors of the Bone had to attack both necks, the bases of which were at this point at their shoulders' height.

Naro's task was to immobilize the right hind limb. The front ones, much more agile, were to be taken care of by the best of the fist: Rekne Tare, the successor of Karan Degard, and Tilu Koru, the strongest of them all. The messenger lifted a snipper, loaned to him by the old hunter, and focused on the tendons vibrating under thick skin. He was waiting for a signal, reacting instinctively to every movement of the animal.

Now every swelling of the membranes counted. The hideout of the old Warrior of the Bone was deep, but the hryll could get to its tasty morsel anyway if the other hunters wouldn't mutilate this colossal, hungry, and furious beast fast enough. To do this, they had to strike at the same time. They communicated in high-pitched whistles, inaudible for the animal, informing one another whenever they were ready to deal a blow. Suddenly, Naro heard three confirmations whistled concurrently, and seeing the right hind limb right in front of him, he answered with a prearranged signal. He lowered the polished and sharpened bone of a tiskut, cut the gray skin in the place where it was most stretched and brightest, bisected the thick as his arm bundle of tendons and—chased by a pitiful roar—jumped back into his pit.

In case of failure, that was the only way to save life. From above came the shrill screeching of the wounded beast. The ground trembled time after time, whenever the giant thrashed convulsively. An experienced hunter could read the prey's condition from the rumbling sounds, but for Naro it was the first hunt of his life, so he could only cower in the pit, awaiting death: his own, of the other warriors, or of the beast. Or all of them together.

A dozen swellings of the membranes later there was a loud thud and suddenly the ground ceased to vibrate. Naro, remembering the old hunter's instructions, tried to lift the cover. He flexed his legs slightly, but felt resistance. He pushed harder—with equally little success. Something was lying on the top of his hideout. Something very, very heavy. The knocked down hryll. *So the hunt was successful,* he thought, taking pride in the fact that he hadn't failed. Following the advice of the oldster, he used his stabber to check whether the beast would react to pain. The sharp end of the bone slid into the predator's body, which immediately shivered and moved restlessly.

Tough luck, I have to wait, Naro thought. The wounded hryll will finally weaken. If there are some smaller predators nearby, it will die before the first of the suns touches the tops of the mountains. If there is no beast in the area willing to finish off and devour the giant, the Warriors of the Bone will have to wait until the bigger sun disappears behind the horizon. And when the hryll's body finally ceases to react to stabbing, they will come out of their pits to skin their prey, and take away all the precious bones that will serve them for making excellent weapons and armor.

———

Henryan didn't see the young warriors skinning the hryll, because Suhurs didn't leave their hideouts before the end of his shift. But he was sure of one thing: the inexperienced Warriors of the Bone didn't manage to hurt the hryll before it got to their leader. The old Suhur was still stuck in his pit, because the predator wasn't able to pull him to the surface, but the massive jaws inflicted so many wounds—people in the command center had an opportunity to look at them very carefully after the scientists took control of the majority of the cameras—that he didn't have the slightest chance of survival. Even if the young hunters had crawled out of their pits earlier, which none of them did, although only three got pinned down by the dying hryll.

Darski, watching the hunt from the perspective of the nanocameras, wondered if the old Suhur had been angry at the youngsters for being too late to attack, or rather proud of the fact that the fist he led defeated the most powerful land predator on the planet. Henryan couldn't tell. Or rather, he didn't want to know … If he checked the records of this session later, he would probably find the transcripts of all conversations before, during, and after the hunt. But what was the point? The old hunter died the way he probably wanted: fighting his most dangerous opponent. He had also managed to pass on his knowledge to the next generation of the Warriors of the Bone, before age and illness sentenced him to a slow and painful death. And the youngsters, remembering him as he'd remembered his mentor and his predecessors, would not allow the knowledge passed on to them to be forgotten.

Henryan left his workstation four standard hours after the beast had been knocked down. At the shift changeover he nodded to the Security Department guy taking up duty, reported his departure, and headed in the direction of the train station. Lost in thought, he waited on the platform until the end of rush hour, and when the first, less crowded car came, he got inside without looking around.

This time he took a seat—mainly in order to make the task of whoever was going to give him another crystal more difficult. Two women stood near him. Both were not very tall; one was from the medical department, the other—somewhat stouter than her colleague—wore the uniform of technical services. They caught his attention because they had headreaders on, and with headphones in their ears they were watching something with flushed faces. They finished only when the train passed the SD sector.

The medic shook her head.

"Horrible," she said, staring into space.

"Horrible, and pointless," her friend added.

"Pointless?" the medic asked, surprised.

"From what I gather," the technician frowned as if collecting her thoughts, "the young savage brought a message to the hunters, saying that they should go someplace and make an offering. Of themselves, of course."

"Really?" the medic asked, then snorted with disgust. "Stupid savages …"

Hearing her last words, Henryan saddened.

THIRTY-TWO

THE XAN 4 SYSTEM, X-RAY SECTOR

09/10/2354

"I'm sorry, Sergeant, I didn't get what you just said." Valdez tore himself away from the reader. Still fishy-eyed, he looked as if Henryan's voice brought him out of a reverie. "Can you repeat that?"

Darski smiled to himself, seeing the lieutenant's red eyes.

"Let me put it briefly, sir. We need to test the identification software."

"Identification software?" The commander's aide still didn't understand. "Why the hell do you want to test it? Haven't we expressed ourselves clearly enough? You are supposed to patch the holes in the system, and not catch the people involved in the incidents."

"I know, sir. I'm not going to go after anyone. While analyzing the security systems, on your orders by the way, I noticed that we were using a very old version of the software."

"What are you talking about, Pry?" Valdez's eyes widened. "We update everything. That is, whenever we receive superluminal transmissions."

Henryan smiled meaningfully, jerking his chin toward the

superior's console. Valdez needed several seconds to reach the appropriate logs.

"Clone-of-a-bitch ..." he groaned, skimming the records. "How did he do it?"

"It's very sim—" Henryan began, but stopped in mid-sentence, seeing the superior's raised hand.

"Yes, I know. I just wonder why we haven't noticed it before."

"Hiding these changes wasn't difficult either, especially that Seifert knew perfectly well how to redirect the data so that the logs contained information on—"

"Don't treat me like an idiot, Pry."

"I thought—"

"You thought wrong," the lieutenant said indignantly. "I may be tired, but I'm certainly not stupid. I know how to do it; I just needed a moment to piece it all together. I was talking to myself, not to you," he added apologetically, and then became even more thoughtful.

This disconcerted Henryan.

"I can perform a random test of the version we have," he suggested quickly.

"What for?"

"To see why Seifert went to so much trouble."

"It's obvious," the deputy commander snorted, irritated.

"And how he did it," Darski added.

Valdez made an urging gesture.

"Sit your ass down, Pry, and get to work. The old man can't find out about this. Perform this random test on ... ten people—that should be enough. Boundary conditions. Progressive gradation. If you notice something wrong, delete the damn thing and install a new, clean version of the software. Can you be done with it before the end of the shift?"

Sergeant Darski shook his head doubtfully.

"I will redirect all ongoing tasks to the guys, who have a level-four security clearance," the lieutenant promised. "Let's hope savages won't do anything that would require the involvement of the whole team today …"

"I'm getting to work then, sir." Henryan saluted buoyantly, immediately making the formal turn so that lieutenant wouldn't notice how happy the order made him.

Not only did he score another point with his superiors, but also gained a chance to improve his negotiation position for dealing with Gods. And he needed it very much right now. Only the conspirators could help him in the realization of a certain risky plan. Without changes in the software, he would have to ask them for a favor, which would mean the need to do something for them, and that, for obvious reasons, was something he would rather avoid. But if he could prove that he was able to trace anybody, the conspirators should understand that it was better not to mess with him. Finding the woman who took the crystal from him was even less complicated—it was enough to lean on Zaitsev, who had to know her. Anyway, he was going to play it his way, so that Gods received a clear warning.

The upset deputy commander appeared at Darski's console a few minutes later. Seeing the lieutenant walking in his direction, Henryan launched a random number generator, with which he selected nine out of ten objects for testing. He had already selected a picture of the mysterious woman as object number ten.

"Can you be done with it before the end of the shift?" the lieutenant asked again, glancing anxiously toward the command post. He wasn't a particularly good conspirator.

Darski nodded.

"I'm just initiating tests on randomly selected crew members," he said. "This is a fully automated process, I don't have to oversee it the whole time. I just need to authorize the subsequent stages of the search, which takes time, so even if Godbless comes up with yet another urgent observation—"

He paused, feeling that he didn't need to add anything more.

"Great." Valdez patted him on the shoulder, then walked

unsteadily toward the exit. "Let me know, Pry, when you are done with the full diagnostics."

"Yes, sir," Henryan said. His eyes followed the superior.

It was time for the station's computers to do most of the work for him.

———

The task proved more difficult than he'd expected. During the first fifteen minutes of the search, the system recognized as many as six out of the ten people selected for the test, although Darski fed it very scanty input data. Each time, he downloaded a single image from the security holocamera, showing—at best—a part of a human silhouette, hardly visible in a dense crowd. To make the search more complicated, he erased all the information about the place where the recording had been made. Another limitation was the exclusion of the vast majority of options, such as checking the IDs of the jumpsuit batteries, or finding the serial numbers of electronic devices that could be seen on selected holograms. According to procedures, a person performing the test should add them gradually, starting from the least important, and only when the software encountered problems.

Henryan didn't make the first adjustments until the twenty-seventh minute of the test, when the system reported the failure to identify the other four objects. The inclusion of another analyzing module increased the number of hits to eight. The third extension revealed the ninth goal in the fifty-third minute of the search. But the last, tenth object—the most important one—still eluded the all-seeing eye of the system, despite using all the available analyzing modules.

Darski recorded the entire session on a microcrystal, and then reinstalled the software and performed a new test, this time without interfering with the random number generator. With it he reached one hundred percent detection rate after the incorporation of just the second extension. He could already send a brief report to the lieutenant half an hour before the end of his shift. The crystals with both tests went to his pocket. He had every intention to upload the contents of the second one to the terminal in his cabin—as the Security Department requested. He wouldn't be able to hide meddling with the software from his substitute anyway, so let the esdees think he was their bitch. It was also a part of the plan.

———

After dinner, he sprawled comfortably on his bunk and, using private headreader, played the recording of the search for the red-haired savior. He was sure the equipment was clean—he'd checked it carefully after the esdees' last visit, and then carried with him everywhere to make sure they wouldn't install a spyware on it.

This woman certainly wasn't an amateur. She had to have a thorough knowledge of the distribution of the cameras, for she moved around the station in such a way that she showed up in their lenses only sporadically. Staying unnoticed was impossible, but she used the shields—such as people walking next to her—extremely skillfully, and was sneaking inconspicuously through the whole sections of corridors. Henryan had only a few fragmentary images of her, but—unfortunately—none of them showed a single birthmark, or other distinguishing mark allowing for identification. Hair color didn't count. Aided by the latest technology, women could make wonders with their hairstyles; widely available nanosprays that enabled rapid, or even gradual, change of hair color were the simplest means of camouflage. Just for peace of mind he checked how many red women served at the station—as he expected, none of the sixteen workers selected by the system resembled the one he had seen in the corridor. The body-build was wrong, the stature was wrong, ages didn't match.

He began his private investigation with a brief analysis of the result. He wasn't going to waste time on procedures—he was a human being, not a machine, so he allowed himself to take non-regulation, but extremely useful shortcuts. Especially that analyzing the failures of the computer wouldn't do any good for him. However, just reading the summary of the last stage of the search was all he needed to find out that Redhead had disap-peared in the first segment of his sector, which could mean that it was there where she changed her hair color and maybe even her attire, and this way she ceased to be the object the system was looking for. The makeover didn't occur in any of the cabins, because their entrances were monitored, just like the rest of public premises, including toilets. While the polarity reversal of the nanospray, taking a few seconds, could take place when the woman knelt, pretending to tighten the Velcro of her shoe, changing clothes in the middle of a crowded corridor would be a much greater challenge.

A person avoiding cameras couldn't do something like this unnoticed. Taking a medical uniform off and putting another outfit on required time and space. Still, Henryan was sure that Redhead was able to do that, although not necessarily in the vicinity of her last whereabouts. He also came to conclusion that kinetic batteries had been removed from both outfits; the system determined that by comparing the three types of data from the places where pieces of the woman's image had been captured: it was about the number of people shown in the indi-vidual shots, the number of signals sent by the batteries from these sites, and the information from the pressure sensor plates, whereby the self-sufficient systems of the station regained a substantial fraction of energy. The Admiralty's policy on saving, implemented only recently, this time served the purpose of which its creators had never dreamed. Henryan smiled to himself when he realized that his idea to add the sensor read-ings as an option of the identification software had proven to be a hit. The analysis of this last factor indicated that there was one person more in the corridor than indicated by the count of the people in the cameras' field of vision. Thanks to it, Darski caught a new scent.

He didn't bother to check how many people hadn't carried batteries at that time. It had to be hundreds, if not thousands at this hour. Going off duty, people recovered the energy worked out during the day by placing their batteries in the wall sockets in their cabins. Many went out later to the mess hall, or to meet up with friends, but very few people carried batteries with them. The Redhead certainly did the same, although for a slightly different reason.

One could draw one logical conclusion from all this: Redhead, as he still called her in his mind, had to do the makeover in the fifth segment of the medical sector, in the corridor, among soldiers, medics, and technicians. But how to do such a thing unnoticed? She didn't become invisible, after all. Although … If she'd had several accomplices, they could have created an artificial crowd and cover their hurriedly changing friend not only from the eyes of passersby, but also from the lenses of cameras.

Henryan smiled to himself again. It was such a simple ploy that the artificial intelligence would never consider it.

First, he checked where the signatures of the kinetic plates began to match the number of people shown on the security recordings. Then, reviewing the records from several nearby cameras, he noticed something that lent credence to his theory. Against the wall, on the edge of the blind spot between cameras number sixteen and seventeen, stood a group of men. Behind them there was a continuous flow of people. Locating this place on the corridor plan, Henryan felt a growing excitement. Although he couldn't see the section of about two feet width—this was the size of the blind spot—he guessed that there was another, perhaps even two conspirators standing there. He became sure half a minute later when the soldiers he observed said goodbye and vanished in the crowd. Camera number sixteen showed a characteristic bulky figure of Zaitsev.

Mystery solved! Five men were enough to dupe the computer system of the latest generation, worth billions of credits. Darski valued himself much lower, and they still didn't manage to fool him.

Earlier, before he left the command center, he'd also downloaded the latest version of the identification software. His private headreader didn't have the computing power allowing for the full analysis, but given sufficient time, a simple task of comparing the faces and silhouettes of passing people should be feasible, and reveal the most important anomaly. If luck were still on his side, he would have found what he was looking for by morning.

He didn't have to bring this search to an end. He could simply ask Zaitsev what the Redhead's name was, since he had no doubt that the black gendarme had collaborated with her right from the start. The emergence of a savior couldn't be considered a coincidence; the whole action was timed too well for that. But he couldn't take the easy route. He had to act according to plan in order to catch Gods with their pants around their ankles. Finding Redhead on his own, without the system's help, should give him a head start in the game with the conspirators. And who knows, doing that he might cut through two armors with one laser.

THIRTY-THREE

THE XAN 4 SYSTEM, X-RAY SECTOR

09/11/2354

Tracking Redhead was much easier than finding her. She worked in the technical department, where she was servicing the robots caring for the hydroponic crops. During a routine inspection of one of the substations on the fourth level, Henryan used the logins, disclosed to him, to check the schedule for the time at which Annelly Lawrence finished work. He also looked at her usual route back to her cabin. With a sufficient amount of data, he decided to make the first approach.

His shift ended half an hour before Redhead's, so he didn't have too much time for preparations. After the shift changeover, he mingled with the crowd of soldiers heading for the train station. This time he went for the fastest connection. After reaching his segment, he intended to change to the standard line. Here, on the opposite side of the rim, past the living quarters, the press of people was lighter, so Henryan didn't have any problems getting on the train. Before the cylindrical car of the express line rose to the height of a dozen feet to disappear in the fastest tunnel, crowds of tired passengers poured out onto the platform from the standard line train. Darski waited until the fetid stream of people passed him, then jumped quickly into the car to travel the last four stops.

He took a seat, wondering whether it was worth it. From now on he had to act stealthily, because his every appearance in the holonet would be recorded and leave a permanent trace, easy to find by esdees. Not wanting to take too much risk, he asked a favor of Zaitsev, of course without any explanation as to why he did it. The black gendarme got on the train at the next station, stood next to him, and when the train started, quickly swapped the batteries, using the few seconds' gap during which the car, gripped by a force field, fell to the lowest and slowest tunnel. It was the only moment when the station's Big Brother went blind and deaf. They parted without a word in the first compartment of sector one, and Henryan, seen by the station's computerized surveillance as Stepandrei Zaitsev, went to visit a friend, while Sergeant Darski (according to the system) went shopping to a nearby canteen. No red light blinked on the esdees' consoles. The behavior of the observed targets wasn't aberrant in any way.

Fifteen minutes later Henryan was in Annelly's neighborhood, which was as jam-packed as his compartment. After almost twenty-five percent of the living quarters had been shut off, the station resembled a sardine processing plant. Yes, the comparison was very apt. The corridors, especially at the end of the shift, were the equivalent to the feeders that delivered the said fish to the cans—here called maglev cars. There was a rumor circulating among the soldiers, saying that lower ranks lost the privilege of having their private cabins, which suddenly became semiprivate. Henryan didn't know anyone who had a roommate, but suspected there had to be a kernel of truth in these gossips.

First, he went to the mess hall in which Redhead usually ate. He noticed her almost immediately: she was stuck in a queue, more or less in the middle of a long line of weary people. He thought that if the customer service here were as bad as in his mess hall, Annelly wouldn't be done earlier than in thirty minutes. Since he was getting hungry, he decided to leave to spare himself the sight of food which only gave him a bad case of the munchies.

The corridor's fork, just under the camera, was the perfect hiding spot for someone who didn't want to be noticed. It was in such a place that a few days ago Zaitsev was waiting for him to warn him about the visit of the esdees.

Henryan pulled out a reader, selected the smallest size of the display, and chose randomly one of the information channels to pass the time. The media were filled with the news about the special session of the Senate, which involved several hundred representatives of the Federation. No one mentioned, however, the location of this extraordinary meeting, the date, or the real purpose, but such things could not be revealed to the ordinary people after all. Why would anyone need to know that the rulers of the known Universe were coming to Xan 4 to enjoy the destruction of an intelligent alien race?

Henryan smiled involuntarily. Yesterday, Valdez told him in confidence that the senators demanded from the Admiralty three hundred antigrav spartans, in which they could fly over the battlefield—of course in full camouflage—watching closely the most interesting, that is, the bloodiest, struggles.

Knowing how things worked, he was aware that even such ridiculous whims of politicians could be met, and that the admirals, as a token of gratitude for this folly, would receive additional grants for secret weapons programs or lifetime positions as advisers on Earth. You scratch my back, and I'll scratch yours, but we both of us still itch …

Darski absorbed the news with one eye, peering at the same time toward the exit of the mess hall. He didn't want to miss Redhead, and much to his annoyance, she still didn't come out. A glance at the clock in the corner of the display told him that he was unnecessarily nervous, because it had been only seven minutes since he located her.

She appeared at the fork of the corridor thirty minutes later, smiling and talking lively. She went past him, arm in arm with a slant-eyed friend, laughing out loud. *This is not good,* Henryan thought. If they are planning a girl's night out, my efforts will come to nothing, and Zaitsev will not be so eager to help me again, especially when he realizes where I've spent the "stolen" time.

He walked two steps behind Redhead and her companion. The two women were clearly heading toward the cabin 1171, where Annelly had been lodged. Another minute and they will be there. Thirty seconds, fifteen … Henryan slowed down. He didn't want Redhead to notice him, because it would undermine his chances of the second approach. A moment later, he saw a sham peck on the cheek, and the two friends finally separated. The slant-eyed woman walked toward the door three numbers away from Redhead's cabin. Darski went past her, accelerating slightly to catch up with Miss Lawrence before she would have time to close the door.

He stood behind her as she withdrew her hand from the scanner.

"Hey," he said in a friendly tone.

She turned in the doorway, still smiling and lost in thought. Her eyes grew large before he found himself together with her in the cabin. The door closed with a soft hiss, cutting out the buzz coming from outside.

Annelly jumped away from him like a scalded cat.

"Who are you?" she asked, turning pale.

"You looked better with red hair, Annelly," he said, pretending not to be offended by her reaction.

"We're not on first-name terms!" she snapped, still backing away.

"So it's high time we changed it, Annelly."

"Seriously, Sergeant … Darski, is it?"

At this point, Henryan stopped smiling, too. He saw a flash of satisfaction in her eyes and decided that he had to pay her back in her own coin, no matter what the cost.

"Is there anyone on this fucking station who doesn't know my real name?" he asked, trying to sound casual.

"Maybe the scientists," she answered from a safe distance. "They are so thrilled with their project that they don't pay attention to anything else. In their eyes, we are all the same. 'Clowns dressed in identical clothes and wearing ridiculous hats,'" she quoted Doctor Godbless, or maybe some other egghead.

He didn't comment on this, letting the silence last. They both needed time to recover after he had surprised her, and she had thrown him off balance. Although Annelly should have been more shocked, she was the first one to break the silence.

"You did us both a disservice coming here, Sergeant," she said, resigned.

Apparently, she was afraid. Not of him, but of being caught. Her three accomplices had left the station in orange outfits. If the esdees tracked her, she would be sentenced, too.

"Don't worry," he reassured her quickly. "I made a swap with Zaitsev at the station."

Henryan regained his good mood. He concluded that his situation hadn't changed much. So what if Gods knew who he really was? If they'd seen his file, they should have been even more careful around him.

"Zaitsev!" Annelly snorted contemptuously, still keeping away from Darski. "I could have guessed he would expose me. This stupid Afroeuropean!"

"He doesn't know I'm here," Henryan said. Seeing her look of disbelief, he added, "I found you by myself, using the identification software. Stepandrei only helped me to go off the grid for a while. I didn't tell him what I was going to do."

"Yeah, right …" She laughed nervously. There was a slight tremble in her voice, when she said, "The software couldn't identify me."

"You are right," Darski replied, moving closer, "although not entirely. We have to talk. It will be a longer conversation, so we'd better sit down. I'm fine with the dim light …"

She pointed to a chair, then walked over to the wall socket and placed the kinetic batteries in it.

A moment later, the main lighting panel glowed with a pleasant yellow light.

"You are a walking enigma, Sergeant …"

"Call me Henryan."

"Let me decide how I will call you, Sergeant," she said haughtily, sitting down on the bunk. She was tense and aware that her quivering voice and body language betrayed her. She tried to control her fear, but without much success.

"As you wish," Darski shrugged. He felt more and more at ease. "You can avoid the cameras, but any good operator with advanced tools at his disposal can easily track you down."

"Not at all," she protested halfheartedly.

"Do you want to know what your mistake was?" he asked politely.

She didn't answer. She sat for a long while with her head down, perhaps thinking about all this, then finally looked up. Judging by the look on her face, she guessed the truth.

"I'm more interested in the purpose of your visit, Sergeant."

Henryan sat back and gave her a friendly smile.

"There are two things," he said. "Firstly, if you know who I am and why Rutta fetched me here to replace Seifert, you must also understand that you can't count on my help. Trust me, I will not do anything that would put me at risk of going back to the Sturgeon Belt. I'd rather die in the cruelest way than spend one more day there."

She nodded as if she knew what a penal colony was like, but he dismissed the idea of telling her the facts. He didn't have time for this. Maybe next time, if there is a next time.

"The esdees are shadowing me …" he continued. Seeing Annelly's restlessness, he quickly raised his hand to prevent her from speaking. "If they put the screws on me, I will tell them everything I know. That's why I will need yours, or rather Gods', help."

He handed her a neatly folded sheet of paper. If Annelly hadn't been one of Gods, she would have probably been shocked at the sight of handwriting. In the era of voice-activated editors and translators, people forgot calligraphy. Even signatures went out of fashion, replaced by fingerprint-, retina-, and DNA-scanners. Only old-fashioned freaks and conspirators still communicated in this way. He thought himself a member of the former group; she surely belonged to the latter.

"It shouldn't be difficult," she said, having read the list. "Except I don't understand ..."

"Trust me, I know what I'm doing," he assured her with great conviction. "Zaitsev will be our middleman. Let him know when everything is ready."

"Whether we will help you, or not, is not up to me," she said, seeing Henryan standing up.

"I know."

"Our leader may think that helping someone who won't serve our cause isn't necessarily—" She paused meaningfully.

"You should care about the neutralization of the esdees more than me." Henryan started toward the door. "Rutta wants the affair to disappear. The Security Department would love to uncover the plot and send us all to a penal colony. The choice seems simple—"

"Wait," she interrupted him. "How can we be sure that you don't do it to turn us in?"

Darski gave her a pitying look.

"If I wanted to turn you in," he said, amused, "I would give the esdees the following names: Gortad, Simmons, Zaitsev, Fourmiere, Ngogo. I hope I haven't mispronounced any. With so many Gods given to them on the plate, they would easily scoop up the rest. They would sit on their asses watching you fly straight into their nets." Seeing her skeptical look, he added, "If you don't believe me, do what I am asking for on your own. You don't have to involve your friends."

This baffled her. She managed to compose herself, however, before he reached the door.

"And the second thing?" she reminded him.

Henryan turned once again.

"I can't get rid of this esdee by myself. I'll need your help."

Annelly opened her mouth in surprise.

"Don't look at me like that. You have a good head on your shoulders. You won't panic if something goes wrong. And you will know how to disappear afterwards. And believe me, everything can go south if I've misjudged this bastard."

THIRTY-FOUR

THE XAN 4 SYSTEM, X-RAY SECTOR

09/12/2354

If looks could kill, Henryan would turn into a sieve, then a bloody pulp, and finally into ash. Zaitsev was waiting for him in the corridor outside the train station with such a look on his face that some of the soldiers passing that way gave him a wide berth. But Darski didn't care.

"Have something for me?" he asked, getting straight to the point.

The gendarme flashed the whites of his eyes menacingly.

"You set me up, Sergeant," he said, and it sounded like a murmur of the volcano waking up.

"No, I didn't. Do you have something for me?"

The black gendarme nodded.

"She told me to say that everything is ready. The meeting's at eighteen hundred hours. Six, B, two, fifteen."

"That's all?"

Instead of answering, Zaitsev—still resentful—looked at him scornfully and walked away without saying goodbye. Darski ignored him. Annelly was really good if she'd done it overnight. He expected it would take her a few days, and here, what a surprise. But then he sobered. Maybe it was a trap? He knew too much, so Gods decided it would be safer to make it look like an accident ... Getting on the train, he shook his head. *No, he thought, they wouldn't risk it, knowing who I am and what I can do. They are not stupid, and only a complete idiot would believe that I haven't taken precautions—!* He laughed under his breath. If anyone here is an idiot, it's only me ...

He had a few hours for correcting his mistake and putting an encrypted file with all the information collected so far in the holonet.

———

He showed up on time for the meeting. Fifteen minutes before the expected arrival of the esdee, Annelly got off the train in the second segment of the medical sector. She looked nervous, or maybe just very unsettled. Henryan asked her just one question, and when she replied positively, he instructed her to take care of the last part of the commissioned task. Then, he went to the end of the compartment. He opened the door with number fifteen on them a minute before the appointed time of the meeting.

He passed the narrow airlock and looked around the room. It was completely empty, just like he wished it to be; therefore he concluded that the Redhead wasn't trying to fool him. He stood against the wall to the right of the airlock, so that the esdee wouldn't see him straight away, and then waved his hand in a prearranged signal. The accomplice, observing him through nanocameras, dimmed the lights to an eye-pleasing twilight. It couldn't be quite dark, because the opponent should enter the trap without any suspicion.

A few moments later there was a soft hiss, then a sound of footsteps and finally ... silence. Darski saw a black coat and a bald head protruding over the collar.

"Galacticunt, is it some silly joke?!" the esdee yelled, surprised to see an empty room.

Immediately, he rushed back to the airlock, but the door

leading to it didn't budge, even though he was standing in front of them like a statue. Suddenly, Annelly increased the brightness of the lighting panels.

"Hi," Henryan said, stepping forward. The esdee gave him a furious look and reached for his weapon, but froze when he saw a barrel aimed at him. "The handgun, taser, baton. Drop all your toys on the floor. The coat, too."

The esdee hesitated only for a moment. The weapons landed on the metal grill with a thud; a moment later, a heavy, synthetic leather coat followed them, flapping.

"You're a dead man," the esdee hissed.

"One graceful pirouette, and we will be done with the foreplay."

The lieutenant turned around his own axis, and the scanner held in Darski's left hand showed a few skillfully concealed knives.

"The penknives need to go, too—all six of them. We won't be whittling roosters today."

The esdee didn't understand this archaic saying, judging by the blank look on his face. When the last blade landed on the coat, Henryan pointed the gun to the esdee's head.

"And now our beautiful, although bald, princess will take off her tiara and throw it to her knight."

"You're out of your mind, Darski. If you think you will get out of here alive, you are fucking wrong," the esdee said, nevertheless reaching obediently for his headreader. He threw it down at the feet of the sergeant, who crushed the device to a pulp with a deft movement of his big toe.

"It isn't important now what I think," Henryan said, telling the esdee to move away from his coat and weapons. "The question whether you survive our meeting seems to me much more interesting."

The lieutenant narrowed his eyes. It was a barely noticeable tic, indicating that fear was just beginning to crawl out of the darkest recesses of his subconsciousness.

"You won't dare touch me," he said with confidence.

Counterintelligence officers were not to be attacked; they were the ones doing the beating and intimidating. Henryan suspected they all secretly considered themselves untouchable. He thus thought that all he needed was to put one in the position of a victim, and he would not have to wait long for the effects. Judging by the drops of sweat that appeared on the esdee's high forehead, he was probably right. He who lives by the fear, shall die by the fear, as another old saying went. More or less.

"I disarmed you, so I can hit you, too," Darski said, amused. "Or burn a few new holes in this tasteful attire. But before we get to the heavy petting, let me start the ball rolling."

Without waiting for permission, he continued, "We are in a hospital room, which was closed three days ago because it's in need of renovation. According to schedule, the work will start in," he looked at the display by the airlock, "twenty-seven hours. This fact is, however, of secondary importance to us, because I took the liberty of disabling all devices in this room, including the air condition shafts' pumps, which means that there is enough air for us for twenty or thirty minutes. Hence the stuffiness ..."

He unzipped his jumpsuit as if to cool himself down. The esdee threw one long look around him that took in the walls and the grills evenly spaced under the ceiling. His pulse quickened every minute.

"This gives us fifteen minutes to finish this conversation. Or less. Anxiety causes faster breathing."

"You'll achieve nothing, Darski," the esdee hissed. "I'll kill you with my bare hands."

"You can try." Henryan took the threat in his stride. He even raised his left hand as if inviting the lieutenant to fight. "But as you probably know, my brother was the SD captain. He taught me a thing or two during the seven years of our training together. Besides, I am the only one who knows the code for the door."

He pointed to the airlock with his gun. "Here we are equals. You don't have bullies at your service, who would disarm the victim for you, so that you could take it out on him. This time you will have to fight alone, and with me, a terrible clone-of-a-bitch, who never batted an eye when shooting his superior in the face, as the Fleet's prosecutor put it, rather poetically—"

He paused for a moment as if in thought.

"Do you even know what I was busted for?" he asked, suddenly changing his tone. The esdee stood motionless, not taking his eyes off him. It was a good sign. "Sure you do. After all, you've seen my file. So let me tell you something you won't find in any records. I spent three years in a place, which compared to Dante's inferno—you've heard of the guy, haven't you … ?—would seem a nursing home. Our warden, a good-hearted soul, when in good mood, organized tournaments for the prisoners. They played something, checkers for instance, and do you know what the main prize was … ?"

The esdee didn't react despite an inviting pause, so Henryan finished his train of thought. "The winner was allowed to commit suicide. He was given only one minute. It's little, very little, especially when you don't have anything at hand that could be used to take your own life. So they usually bit off their tongues or ran and smashed their heads against a wall. You may not believe this, but one guy literally broke his own neck. I still can't figure out how he did it. In any case, you have my word that every winner had been a goner before we intervened after exactly sixty seconds."

"I don't understand why you're telling me all this nonsense," the esdee snorted.

"Maybe because it's the truth, the whole truth, and nothing but the truth," Henryan said. "But keep listening. Well, imagine that our warden, a guy named Draccos, assigned me to be a life-guard. Permanently. I can see that you don't understand … Never mind. He wanted to break me this way. He didn't. I survived three years in a penal colony, being the most hated prisoner. I squelched the inmates' hope of freedom, even if it was freedom in death. I had to, because the punishment for insubordination was unimaginable torture."

He looked at the clock in the corner of the airlock display, then wiped the sweat off his forehead. He did it with a deliberate, slow, sweeping movement of his left hand.

"But enough of all this chitchat; time is running out. We have only eleven minutes left. Then we will begin to feel the effects of hypoxia. Time to get to the point then."

The esdee grimaced mockingly, but the previous cockiness was gone from his eyes. Sweat ran down in streams under the collar of his thick jumpsuit. Judging by the violent movements of the Adam's apple, his mouth went dry. Darski decided it was time for the next, riskiest phase of the plan. He raised his gun, aiming at the esdee. Seeing it, the lieutenant instinctively tried to dodge, but only bumped his back against the wall and just froze there, with his eyes closed and suddenly pale face. At the same time Henryan moved his hand to the side. He shot only once, at an empty metal container in the corner of the room. The container rolled on the floor with a clatter.

A moment later, came another loud clank.

"So in your opinion I'm talking nonsense," Darski laughed, indicating the gun lying in front of the esdee. "Call my bluff. I'm standing before you unarmed."

He spread his hands wide, then spun on his heel so that his stood with his back to the lieutenant.

"There are six bullets in the magazine." Although he could not see the esdee, the characteristic snap told him that his opponent picked up the gun, checking it. "But if you so much as lay a finger on me," he warned, hearing quick steps behind his back, "you'll die here with me. I will not go back to the Sturgeon Belt. No way. I'll rather die right away."

"I know a hundred ways to pry every scrap of information out of you," he heard the esdee's whisper. The lieutenant was standing right behind him, but as expected, did not attack.

"I don't doubt it, but will ten minutes be enough to break the bastard who served three years in the harshest penal colony a man created? Such threats work with people who have something to lose. What can I lose? Where you want to send me, torture is commonplace. They came for us regularly, and each time tormented us for hours. I was given electric shocks, long and painful, until I lost consciousness, and then was revived. They waited until I came to, and started all over again, or used other enhanced torture techniques. So I am not afraid of anything you can do to me, because I know that I can endure it longer than the nine minutes we have left. Or even less than that … That's why, if you lay a finger on me, you'll share my fate. You will die like a dog, fighting for every breath until you use up the last atoms of oxygen. They will find you here tomorrow, livid, bloated, with your tongue lolling out of the side of your mouth, because you've got no balls and will not bite it off like I will."

"Shut the fuck up, scumbag!" A glob of thick, sticky saliva landed on Henryan's ear.

"Eight minutes …"

For a moment he could only hear heavy panting.

"What do you want from me, you clone-of-a-bitch?" the esdee wheezed in the end.

Darski turned slowly and made a few steps back. The heavily panting, sweaty esdee followed him, still training the gun on him.

"You want to talk, fine. So let's start from the beginning. But this time without this whole crazy circus." Henryan lowered his hands. "Let's talk like civilized people."

The esdee still held him at gunpoint.

"You first," he hissed.

"You know who I am, you know what I did time for," Darski said quietly. "You also know that if I wanted to, I could kill you, even now, despite the fact that it is you who is holding a weapon."

"So what are you waiting for?" the esdee snapped, trying to keep a stiff upper lip. His breaking voice betrayed him, though.

"I'm not gonna fight you. This is how we'll do it. You will give me the gun back, answer one simple question, and each of us will go his own way."

The esdee smirked. It wasn't hard to guess his thoughts now.

"What question?"

"First, the weapon," Henryan demanded. The gun landed on the floor with a loud thud. Darski picked it up, slipped it into his holster and only then looked at his opponent. "What was the name of the scumbag who hit me during your visit?"

The esdee looked as if he didn't believe his ears.

"This is the question you wanted to ask me?"

"Yes."

"You really are fucked up, you knucklehead."

"Don't call me names, just answer my question," Henryan said.

The SD officer swallowed hard. He looked as if he wondered what exactly he should do. He got totally lost in the absurdity of the situation. Finally, seeing the light at the end of the tunnel, he went for the option that seemed most sensible to him at the moment. Darski knew very well what kind of thoughts raced through the bastard's mind. He didn't press the lieutenant, aware that time was on his side. He unzipped his jumpsuit maliciously, and then wiped the sweat off his forehead again.

"Poetze," the esdee whispered eventually. "Gunternest Poetze."

Henryan smiled, then walked over to the scanner by the airlock door. The esdee watched him with hatred. Poor fool. Darski turned to face him.

"Did you say anything about me not making it out of here alive?"

The esdee grinned.

"I did."

"Then let me explain something to you. I know from

Liambrose, that is my brother, that those working in the Security Department appreciate loyalty more than anything. They are like brothers, even like twins. Whoever rolls on his partner is fucked—"

At this moment the esdee, collecting his stuff, understood his mistake. His face flushed even more, and he looked around quickly, searching for hidden cameras. He didn't find them, because the ones that were recording him were smaller than specks.

"Good thinking," Darski added, seeing fear in the esdee's eyes. "Our conversation has been recorded, and its last part is already circulating the holonet, replicating itself every few seconds. You won't delete it, no matter what you do."

He took a deep breath and finished quickly. "If I ever see your nasty snout again, or feel that one of you is nosing around, the whole station will see you ratting Poetze out in a short, pleasant conversation, even though I haven't even laid a finger on you. Watch and learn, you wretched scum."

The displays in the room came alive, growing to their maximum size. They showed both interlocutors. The recording began with the words: "Let's talk like civilized people." The esdee watched it in silence, turning paler with every passing moment.

"I'll kill you, you clone-of-a-bitch. I'll fucking kill you."

"No, you creep, I have just killed you. Crushed to a pulp with my heel. You're finished. You live only because I let you breathe. By the way, don't make up excuses that you had to give in, because you were running out of oxygen. The system will show that the ventilation shafts have been functioning normally all the time. I've only cranked up the heating. The doors weren't locked even for a moment, either. It's a hospital room. Here, the door doesn't open automatically. You have to put your palm on the scanner and hold it in place for a moment to authorize the command. The source of all your problems lies here ..." He tapped his temple with his index finger. "Your fear allowed me to deceive you. And now I wish you a pleasant evening. I also advise you not to forget that the inmates are fond of esdees, and the guards know when to look away, because the sight of a prisoner being brutally raped is too disgusting even for them."

———

Henryan left, leaving the esdee, who was swearing like a trooper, in the room. Annelly had already disappeared. Using her skills, she got to the higher level of the segment, where she caught the train to return to her cabin. That was the plan.

Marching hurriedly to the nearest elevator, Darski couldn't hear anything except the blood pounding in his ears. He allowed himself a moment of relaxation only now, after the confrontation. Stress, held in check till now, used this opportunity with its typical intensity. It dug its icy claws into his heart, and made it pound as hard as if it wanted to get out from between the ribs and send the shivering body to the mercy of death, lurking in the shadows of the dimly lit corridors.

Henryan didn't quite understand where this nervousness came from. After all, when planning the tryst with the esdee, he knew perfectly well that he would succeed no matter how the conversation ends. That's why he could play his role with such confidence and calmness. He would have won even if the esdee didn't prove to be such a coward and shot him in the head without hesitation, as he once did to Renaud. A quick death would spare him further torment.

He found his guilt excruciating—even more than the scandal, in which he got mixed up after his arrival in Xan 4. He endured three years in a penal colony—and he would have endured there another twenty—because he was sure he'd done the right thing avenging the deaths of his brother and forty-one other innocent people. But then, when he saw the Admiralty's report in Draccos's office, something snapped inside him …

He still was flabbergasted by the fact that they snatched him from the hell that the penal colony was. Over the past few days, he floated, carried by a wave of elation, as if intoxicated by the smell of the miraculously regained freedom. The visit to the Sector's command had lasted too short for him to think things through. At least, thanks to the confusion there, he managed to keep Commander Derrick's headreader, which proved to be very useful in this situation. After a dozen-minute conversation with some—unknown to him—officers, he received a new assignment and went to the medical center, where he underwent several treatments, permanently changing his hair and eye colors. The Admiralty didn't want anyone to recognize the notorious criminal in him. For this reason he also had to change his name. Straight from the hospital, he went onboard another courier ship, which took him to the big transit hub in a globular cluster, and from there he was taken to Xan 4 by shuttle. Then it only got worse. The information about Aliens allowed him to forget about the fire, which—in the deepest recesses of his brain occupied with work—was systematically burning the last scraps of his soul. The later accumulation of not particularly pleasant events also delayed the moment of discovering the shocking truth.

He had his eureka moment only now. Standing at the maglev station, he understood that more than anything, he wanted to free himself from all the problems. His present stress stemmed from the fact that he had survived the encounter. Henryan realized with horror that he would still have to cope with the increasing sense of guilt.

Unless he finds a way for the redemption. ...

THIRTY-FIVE

THE XAN 4 SYSTEM, X-RAY SECTOR

09/13/2354

"Man, you're really fucked up," Annelly said, shaking her head in disbelief.

As agreed, they met the next morning on a train carrying the staff to their workstations. The men known to Henryan from the recordings created a tight cordon around them, cutting off one corner of the car to give them some privacy and shield them from the ubiquitous cameras. Observing the ease with which this chance encounter of a group of friends was staged, Darski couldn't help but smile.

"Why do you think so?" he asked. "Maybe I'm just as good an actor as you and your friends?"

"I was there. I saw everything." She leaned toward him. "You've made a great impression on someone. This someone wants to talk to you."

"I'm not interested," he cut in before she could add anything else.

The refusal hurt her. Darski understood this, seeing the flames dimming in her eyes. Only that betrayed her, because she was still smiling serenely as if he agreed to the offer given a moment before.

"It's only about a moment of conversation," she said.

"Do you think it is worth discussing the matters that have already been settled?" he asked, looking coldly in her eyes.

She shook her head, even though she clearly had a different opinion on the subject.

"Either way, be prepared for this meeting," she advised. When he shrugged as if he didn't care much, she added, "Let me ask you something … How did you neutralize the other bullets in the gun I'd given you?"

"Why do you think I neutralized anything?" he asked, surprised.

"You couldn't be sure he wouldn't shoot you in the back. Especially that you intentionally enraged him before."

"Maybe I was hoping he wouldn't chicken out and would pull the trigger?"

She laughed tentatively, and gave him a suspicious look.

"Are you serious?"

He nodded.

"Dead serious."

THIRTY-SIX

THE XAN 4 SYSTEM, X-RAY SECTOR

09/13/2354

"Bor Omot" could be freely translated as the Gorge of Death. It was the name of an extensive cave system, recognized by the local clans as sacred. The Suhurs' cult was dark, bloody, and disgusting. Hundreds of clashes of suns before, young Warriors of the Bone used to slip into the abyss of Bor Omot to undergo the final initiation rite in its eternal darkness. They followed a complicated maze of corridors, relying solely on their instinct and primitive weapons. Many never saw the light of day again. The legend repeated since time immemorial had it that Suhurs who disappeared in the Gorge of Death did not die, but joined the monsters lurking in the shadows to check the courage of those who would come there next.

At a time when there were more clans than the stars in the sky, similar rituals were held throughout all Suhurta. Caves and ravines served for this purpose in hilly regions, whereas on plains, swamps or other hostile, inaccessible terrains were used. Each nestling had to prove that he deserved a place by the fire and a handful of sagr seeds. Thus, immediately after being released from the pen, he was sent to such a sacred place, where he underwent initiation rites. The Supremes Council broke with this tradition only recently, when Blueblooded took the bulk of the lands from Suhurs and exterminated most of the clans. The leaders risked the dissatisfaction of the Spirits of the Mountains, knowing that from now on every masticator and stabber would count double. Suhurian youngsters started to prove their value as hunters and warriors. The eternal darkness of the caves was replaced by the darkness of the night, the tribute of their own blood—by streams of gore spilled while hunting hrylls or fighting Gurds.

The Warriors of the Bone did not, however, forget gods inhabiting Bor Omot. Their favor was to be assured by offerings made now almost exclusively of Gurdian prisoners. Dozens of them were rounded up here before each clash of the suns, and even hundreds of them for the more significant occasions; exhausted after several days on the march, wounded in battle, terrified … The caves swallowed this tribute greedily. It was the same with a few Suhurs, who voluntarily sacrificed themselves to the Spirits of the Mountains to ensure the success of their clans in the coming battles.

Karan Degard had been one of these volunteers. He'd gone down to the Gorge of Death to offer his life to gods, but they—to everybody's great surprise—had spurned him. When he'd been whistling his prayers in darkness, listening to the sound of the beasts sneaking toward him, suddenly he'd had an epiphany: he'd received a message from Lut Se-Ifer, the new guardian of the caves. This message could have changed the course of history. If it hadn't been for the intervention of the priest, who ordered to break the word given to the Spirits of the Mountains, the fate of the brave race wouldn't have had to be sealed.

Rekne Tare stopped at the edge of a large well, known by the local clans as the Gorge of Death. The warriors from his fist joined him one by one, standing on his right and on his left on the narrow strip of rock, thus separating the mouth of the cave from the slope, densely overgrown with sykvaninas. There were seven of them: too young to deserve a battle nickname, too brave to refuse the sacrifice. The last one to arrive was the new priest of the clan of the Triple Pierced Shield. Hakrad Redo-Tele was younger than his predecessor. He was entrusted with this honorable function, although many older and more experienced than him served at the altars. He took spiritual authority over the clan, because, as one of the few, he didn't reject the annunciation of the Spirits of the Mountains.

"We've arrived, venerable." Rekne Tare closed his eyes to show respect for the approaching priest.

Hakrad Redo-Tele halted in a place from which he could look deep down into the bottomless abyss. Its walls were marked with blue spots—the signs of the offerings made some time ago. Satiated with this sight, he knocked his arad on the sacred rock.

"I greet you, the bodiless Spirits of the Mountains! I, Hakrad Redo-Tele, the one who spoke with gods even as a nestling, come to Bor Omot to ask you for forgiveness. Let Tikren Da-Deradha be damned forever. Suhurs adore you! The Warriors of the Bone worship you! He, who ignored you, has been punished, as tradition dictates!" In the distance appeared another fist. The warriors trudged through the low brush, leading the Quadrupeds by cords woven from tendons. "We will make a generous offering today! May the blood of these Gurds strengthen your servants crawling in the darkness of the Gorge of Death, so that they could summon you!" He finished, tapping his arad on the rock once again.

"What is your command, venerable?" Rekne Tare asked when the priest got silent.

"Let's not waste time," Hakrad Redo-Tele said, focusing his sight for a moment on the empty pens on both sides of the mouth of the cave. "Begin the ritual as soon as Temeh Dokru-Kume gets here."

The fister opened his eyes wide, and retreated hastily to prepare his warriors. The group of Blueblooded was approaching the edge of the cliff slowly but steadily.

"Tilu Koru, Reme Naro, Kraga Snaro." Rekne Tare pointed to the nearest three. "You take care of the first group."

"As you wish!" came the unanimous reply.

The selected warriors remained in their positions, while the rest of the fist walked toward the pens. There, just below the rim of the gorge, one could see traces of fire, by which the guards and priests once spent the nights.

Kraga Snaro, most heavyset of the selected warriors, reached for his masticators. From a hard grip of each weapon, tightly wrapped around by a thick tendon, protruded a polished jaw of a hryll, slightly curved at the end, hiding six rows of teeth that were longer than an arrowhead and harder than stone.

Tilu Koru and Reme Naro, a little younger and less experienced warriors of the fist, stood a few steps behind him. Stabbers and bone clubs appeared in their hands. The fister and the priest stayed out of the way. They took places on a small ledge, from which they could see the steep gorge of the cave. The tutelary beings had always been summoned from there.

Temeh Dokru-Kume appeared on the rim several swellings of the membranes later. He knew the ritual well, so nobody had to tell him what to do. As soon as he saw the prepared young men, he wheezed, "Bring them here in knots!"

A moment later, two powerful Warriors of the Bone entered the flat terrain, leading seven Quadrupeds. Among them were two egglayers, a fetuscarrier, and four whelps. The loops tightening on their slender limbs and appendages were attached to a long, thick rod. The Gurds were horrified. The young toddled nervously and the egglayers tried to break free, but any stronger movement only tightened the bonds under their breathing slots, cutting off the air, so they quickly stopped struggling.

Tilu Koru and Reme Naro cut off the whelp that was standing in the front from the knot. The black skin of a young Gurd immediately covered with slippery slime—such was a natural defense mechanism of the inhabitants of Gurdu'dihan, but today it couldn't help them in any way. The Warriors of the

Bone grabbed the cords, with which the prisoner's forelegs were tied, and pulled him toward the edge of the rim, where Kraga Snaro was already waiting. The squealing of the young Gurd, inaudible to Suhurs, turned into a yelp when hryll's fangs plowed through his skin. The cuts were rapid, shallow. The young warrior made sure that the victim would bleed profusely, and then shattered his front knees with a single powerful blow. The body of the prisoner struck the ground with a dull thud, and slipped down the smooth sloping rock.

Hakrad Redo-Tele watched the Gurd gliding down, and when the victim disappeared into the darkness at the bottom of the cave, leaving behind a trail of fresh gore, he tapped his arad on the rock.

"Come!" he rumbled, leaning over the abyss. "Rejoice the tribute of the clans! Feed at will, and ask your masters to listen to our request!"

On his mark, Tilu Koru and Reme Naro brought another prisoner to the brink of the abyss. A big egglayer struggled much harder, in spite of the shackles that suffocated her. The strokes of the clubs and whip swishes didn't help. She calmed down only when Kraga Snaro slashed the visible bulge in the front of her torso with a slick movement. The egglayer's tab slumped on her trunk. Foamy, blue gore flowed out from the wide slit.

The ritual was repeated. Three cuts on the sides, where there were no vital organs, so the smell of blood could lure the disgusting inhabitants of the caves, and finally, crushing the joints of the forelegs. Six swellings of the membranes later the crippled creature began to slide limply toward the darkness.

The third one was a whelp again. He went to the slaughter much calmer and quieter. True, he resisted as much as he could when the Warriors of the Bone dragged him to the dying ground, but obviously, the young Gurd was much more stupefied than the previous prisoners from that knot. A blow of the masticators, and the offering was made. Hakrad Redo-Tele looked closely at the rounded sides of the next Blueblooded, focusing on the places where red spots showed under the slippery goo.

"Leave that one for later," he ordered, pointing to the pen with his arad. "It is pregnant; it will be suitable for the ritual of thanksgiving!"

The warriors obeyed his command, passing the fetuscarrier to the guards and coming back for another prisoner.

The second sun emerged from behind a nearby ridge, better illuminating the southern slopes of the Lone Peak and the highlands extending at its feet. In the distance, on the horizon and behind it, columns of smoke billowing toward the sky marked the trail of the clans' recent raid.

"Hurry up!" Hakrad Redo-Tele urged the young warriors. "The Spirits of the Mountains crave blood!"

At this point Rekne Tare noticed some movement on the slope. About two bowshots from the mouth of the cave he saw another zigzagging line of black figures, followed by yet another at a similar distance behind. He knew there were a lot more coming. To appease the Spirits of the Mountains and apologize for treason, the rocks would have to be stained blue in the coming days.

And then they would run with brown gore.

––––––

The colonel ordered to shut down the live feed video projected on the command center's panoramicon before the last prisoner from the first knot was precipitated into the abyss. Not because the images from the caves were too drastic. On the contrary. Apparently, no one except Darski cared about the fate of Gurds. Those serving in the command center had been watching the carnage on both sides for years, so they got used to such sights. Some people talked and smiled, even when the live events were being shown. And the communications guys had too much work enabling the transmission to get emotional about its content.

Darski, too, was brought back to reality in the end. The iridescent picture of Dr. Godbless appeared on the display of his console immediately after the seventh offering had been made.

"I'm going to need another set of cameras," the head of the scientific department said, her voice devoid of any emotion. "Send me some nanobots that can operate in the caves. Spectrographic, preferably."

Henryan checked if such cameras were available.

"I'll send six units in an hour," he said.

"In an hour?" The scientist's face hardened. "I need them now!"

"All spectrographic equipment supports the satellites over Beta's dark side," he explained, sending her the relevant data.

"It's outrageous! I won't stand for it!" Dr. Godbless got purple in the face. "I'll make sure your superior hears about this. Put me through to Colonel Rutta, now!"

Darski followed her command with relief, glancing at the dais of the bridge. From this distance, he couldn't hear the conversation, but the facial expressions of the old man told him that it wasn't pleasant. Henryan switched to the cameras in Bor Omot. The carnage was in full swing. The Warriors of the Bone conducting the executions were blue with the sticky blood of Gurds. Another knot was just brought to them. This time, it contained mostly adult seeders.

"Sergeant!" Colonel Rutta said suddenly, not through the speakers, but from behind Darski's back.

"Sir," Henryan jumped up from his seat and stood at attention.

"Give that bloody woman what she is asking for!"

"I have already sent a command to the dark side, but it will take time," he reported at once.

"Change the coordinates so that at least one capsule of these cameras will be stationed permanently over the Seven Pinnacles," Rutta ordered.

"Yes, sir! I'm on it, sir!"

"And one more thing—" The commander paused. "If this old bag or another egghead-blockhead requests to be put through to me again, you'll get rid of them or redirect them to the control post." He pointed to the wall, behind which Valdez was sitting. "Understood?!"

"Old bag?!" Godbless's enraged voice came from behind Darski's back. "Who do you call an old bag, you misshapen clone-of-a-bitch in a ridiculous hat?!" The woman yelled before the sergeant got to the console. "I wish you—" Fortunately, her further profanities got cut off in an instant.

Rutta went red in the face, raised his hand and pointed his trembling index finger at Henryan. For a moment it seemed he would explode, but he managed to control his anger and just hissed, "Come see me after the shift's over." He jerked his chin toward the bridge.

"Yes, sir!" Darski clicked his heels.

The colonel returned to the dais as Henryan sank heavily into his chair. The stupid hag, still hollering loudly, just fixed him up with several hours of toilet scrubbing, if not something worse. He turned up the volume a bit, just enough to understand Dr. Godbless's words.

"—shitty, clonefucking jarheads! If you think the Admiralty will tolerate such incompetence, you are dead wrong. I'm going to report this even today, and demand that you are all relieved of your duties immediately!"

"The capsule with spectrographic cameras has already been sent from the orbit," Darski said when she paused for a moment to catch her breath. "Is that all you need, madam?"

"No," Dr. Godbless grumbled. "Make an exhaustive reconnaissance of the foothills. I want to know how many prisoners are being led to Bor Omot."

"Can I withdraw some of the less needed cameras from the caves?" the sergeant asked, quickly reviewing the images. At least three nanobots had nothing interesting in their sight.

"Don't you dare, dimwit!" Godbless hissed.

"I see," he said as calmly as he could. "I'm sending a new capsule right away."

The scientist disappeared from his desktop. This time he made sure he'd terminated the connection, and only when he was absolutely positive, he instructed one of his subordinates to scan the area.

The data came a dozen minutes later. He looked through it and routinely sent it to Lieutenant Valdez for approval. All in all, seventy-three groups of Blueblooded were led toward the mouth of the Gorge of Death. The smallest "knot" consisted of six prisoners, the largest—twenty-four.

A considerable stretch of the sloping rock was already stained with viscous blue gore. Kraga Snaro swung his masticators again. Fatigue and slippery ground made him miss slightly. The head of the bone weapon shattered only one knee of the victim. A well-fed seeder still stood despite the terrible pain, and only the kick of another warrior sent him flying into the abyss. That was the last Gurd of the sixth knot.

Hakrad Redo-Tele tapped his arad against the ledge.

"It's time!" he called.

Kraga Snaro straightened up, raising his bloodstained hands to the sky. Tilu Koru and Reme Naro stood at his sides. With great regret, he gave them the murderous weapon that he'd made by polishing a jawbone of the beast from the plains. It was far from ideal, because Kraga Snaro had no time to finish it, not to mention carving the symbols describing his own achievements and valor. They had killed the giant hryll just a few days ago. If Redu Nizo-Hakra, leading the hunt, hadn't died, he would have got the best bones of the prey, as the one doing the baiting. Kraga Snaro had wondered for a moment, whether he should have chosen the tibia for himself. The hryll they'd managed to knock down was really huge, and even the most experienced old warriors didn't have as magnificent blades as he could have obtained from the massive hindlegs of the beast. But when he'd faced the right, half-flared mouth, lying in the dust, he realized that masticators were the most perfect weapon of every Suhur and that it was with them in his hands that he would someday die. Untying the tendon straps, Kraga Snaro regretted that he wasn't meant to achieve great things in the future. However, what he begrudged most was the fact that he wouldn't die in battle, feeling in his hands the coarse grips of the most perfect and most deadly weapon of the Warriors of the Bone.

He took off his clattering armor, tenderly stroked the chipping in those places where enemies' weapons or predators' claws reached it, then carefully placed the intricate plaiting made of tendons and hundreds of little bones next to his masticators and his leather bag. He straightened up again, this time completely naked, and walked toward the chasm, from the bottom of which still came the shrill squeaks of the victims, being eaten alive, though none of these sounds penetrated his membranes. Today he'd sent into the tenebrous abyss over a hundred Gurds. He shed a river of blue blood.

"Are you ready, Kraga Snaro of the indomitable Krute Kon-Toko's breeding?" the priest asked.

"As always," the Warrior of the Bone answered, as tradition dictated.

"Hands!" Rekne Tare wheezed.

Tilu Koru picked up a piece of strap spattered with blue gore. Kraga Snaro clasped his hands together as if in prayer. Several swellings of the membranes later, the ritual knots were carefully wrapped around him.

"Cage!" the next command came from the ledge.

Reme Naro shifted a wooden arm with a bone cage hanging from it. The cage was large enough for an adult Suhur to fit in. Tilu Koru untied the straps holding its door, and then pulled it to the ledge, fitting it in a recess deliberately hewn in the rock. He held it in place so that bound with fetters Kraga Snaro wouldn't accidentally fall into the abyss while crawling inside. The hefty warrior barely fit in a tight cage, but when he finally did, with only a little help from his comrades, the door was closed again.

"Wounds!" Rekne Tare shouted.

"One!" The answer was loud and clear.

The priest shaded his eyes with the thicker eyelids. The young warrior had shown great courage and fortitude. With skillful gushes he would die by dusk, according to the honorary rites. A single wound meant that the tahars wouldn't start their work before three, maybe even four sunrises.

"So be it!" Hakrad Redo-Tele tapped his arad.

Tilu Koru cut the pyroglyph-covered skin between two bone plates on the warrior's back. Respecting his bravery, he made sure that the wound was not too deep. When Rekne Tare gave a signal, he wiped the blade of the stabber, slipped it into a leather sheath, and joined Reme Naro at the winch.

"Lower him!"

They moved the wooden arm over the precipice and slowly lowered the cage. Kraga Snaro hung midway between the rim and the darkness. They couldn't hear his prayers, as they couldn't hear the squeals and squeaks of the victims being eaten alive coming from the bottom, but they knew that from now on he would summon the Spirits of the Mountains. And they would soon join him, because to perform this ritual, at least three Warriors of the Bone were needed.

"Reme Naro, your turn!"

Hearing his name, the warrior shut both pairs of eyelids, and when he heard another tap of the arad, he pulled smooth, shiny new masticators out of the sheath and stood on the rim, slightly to the right, so as not to step in a puddle of blue gore.

Temeh Dokru-Kume came out from the brush once again. Next prisoners arrived at the place of execution.

———

Darski directed the spectrographic cameras to the Gorge of Death, and ordered his subordinates to monitor them. Calibrating the devices, he tried not to look at the displays, but even those fractions of a second were enough for him to lose his appetite. He had seen plenty of death in service and in the mines of the Sturgeon Belt—but never anything like this.

There were piles of half-eaten corpses on the entire bottom of the cave. The dark-skinned creatures, crazed with fear, were scrambling up the sloping wall, ignoring the pain and new wounds, clinging to each ledge, each protruding piece of rock, trampling one another to run away from the blind beasts crawling in the darkness, attracted by the smell of blood and fresh flesh. Multilegged and legless, armored and soft, pale and black—of all sorts of shapes and sizes, but invariably hungry, monsters first rushed to kill indiscriminately; with time, however, after they satisfied their hunger, they began to play with the victims. They attacked slowly and deliberately, pulling still alive Gurds inside a maze of tunnels. From the difficult to forget training materials, Darski knew that some Quadrupeds, before they died entangled in cocoons, would be digested piece by piece for the next few days, or even weeks. Dr. Godbless demanded a greater number of spectrographic cameras because she wanted to have every detail of this hecatomb saved on the crystals. Henryan wasn't surprised, actually. If Valdez was right, this could be the scientists' last opportunity …

When all was calibrated, the sergeant informed Primus of the successful completion of the task. He sent a plain text message instead of holo. At this point he preferred not to see that sullen woman again, and was pretty sure that she didn't have a great desire for further contact with the command center, either. In any case, she didn't even bother to acknowledge the receipt of the message.

As time passed, little by little, only Suhurs conducting the executions changed. By the shift changeover, Darski had witnessed the putting of three more young Suhurs into cages.

Shaking his substitute's hand, he glanced at the dais. Colonel Rutta stood there with his arms folded across his chest, looking in his direction.

One nightmare is over, time to start another, Darski thought, stepping on the wide stairs. Now he understood why this part of the bridge was called a scaffold. Before he reached the command post, Colonel Rutta had already sat in his chair. He also activated the force field, separating his console from the rest of the platform.

"Sergeant Prydeinwraig reporting as ordered!" Henryan clicked his heels and saluted.

"At ease." The old man's voice was less virulent than he expected.

"Thank you, sir!" Henryan placed his feet apart, put his hands behind his back, but quickly let his arms hang by his sides, remembering the images from the caves.

Rutta noticed his embarrassment.

"Don't take it too hard, Sergeant," he said.

Henryan swallowed nervously. He had heard so much about the maliciousness of the old man that he started to wonder whether it's not a trick of some sort.

"Yes, sir!" he yelled, not knowing what else to say.

"Do you know why I called you here?" Rutta got to the point.

"Yes, sir."

"Well, I'm all ears." Rutta leaned back in his chair.

"Dr. Godbless—I—" Darski didn't know where to start. "I am sorry, sir! I thought she had terminated the connection—"

"A soldier, son, doesn't think," Rutta cut in. "We have eggheads for that. Your job is to check, double-check, and then check once again."

"Yes, sir!"

"And you were thinking, instead of checking."

"It won't happen again, sir!"

"I know ..." Rutta smiled to himself.

This tone, that smile ... Henryan felt shivers run up and

down his back. The old man was up to something. The only question was—what?

"I should order you to scrub the toilets, and believe me, Sergeant, we have thousands of those. Unfortunately, I need you here. Well, and here we have a problem …"

"A problem, sir?" Darski asked cautiously.

"Yes, a problem. If I punish you properly, you could screw up on your watch as a result sleep deprivation. But if you don't get punished after this—this—"

"Old bag," Henryan offered.

Colonel Rutta winced at the sound of his own words, and Darski immediately thought it would be better for him to shut up and let the superior finish his tirade.

"—after this old bag," continued Rutta, "made a fool of me in front of everybody, I will lose my authority among the crew."

"I see, sir."

"I'm glad you do, Sergeant, but this doesn't cut it. So—"

"Colonel!"

Both of them flinched when Valdez's voice came from the speaker. Rutta reluctantly activated a hologram of the caller.

"Can't you see, Lieutenant, that I'm talking with Prydewi … Preyd … Prywe … with the sergeant?" he asked, additionally irritated by the fact that he couldn't pronounce the difficult name.

"I am just calling about him, sir!" Valdez replied.

"Yes? Well, tell me."

"We're carrying out the restoration work of sector one and the observation deck before the visit of the Senate delegation," Valdez said. "I supervise all the work done in that area. You could reassign the sergeant to there, so that …"

His voice trailed off.

Rutta rocked in his chair for a moment, silent and somber.

"Both the wolves have eaten much and the sheep have not been touched," Henryan said quietly.

"These archaic proverbs of yours." The colonel groaned

before he turned to Valdez. "That sounds reasonable, Lieutenant." Turning back to Henryan, he added, "You may go, Sergeant."

"One moment, sir!" Darski said.

"Well, Sergeant ... ? You have a problem with that?" A look of surprise crossed Rutta's face. Valdez was no less shocked.

"Not at all, sir! I deserve to be punished."

"What is it then?"

"It's ... it's about what's going on in the caves."

"Do you think, son, that I like this massacre?" the Colonel asked. "Unfortunately there is nothing we can do."

"But there is, sir," Darski assured him.

"Like what?"

"If Suhurs receive a message from the Spirits of the Mountains, they will leave."

Rutta jumped up from his chair, outraged.

"You have misunderstood me, sir!" Henryan added quickly, stepping back.

"On the contrary, Sergeant. You have expressed yourself damn clearly!"

"I'm not talking about a message like the one Gods have in mind ..." Darski tried to get out of the tricky situation. "We'll tell the Warriors of the Bone something ... anything ... that the Spirits of the Mountains love them immensely, that they will win the coming battle, anything that will end this carnage. Colonel, they are going to murder several thousand inkblots in the coming days."

"Gurds, son," Rutta corrected him, gritting his teeth. "Gurds!"

"Yes, sir. Gurds."

"It is not such a stupid idea," Valdez interjected.

"I can't believe my ears!" Rutta dropped heavily into a chair. "Lieutenant, you advocate another intervention in the history of this planet? You?!"

"Yes, sir. I mean, no, I'm not for intervention as such, but the sergeant's idea seems to make sense to me. Let me explain in person ..."

The colonel deactivated the force field momentarily, and Valdez passed quickly to the command post and stood next to Darski.

Rutta turned the energy barriers back on, separating the three of them from the rest of the command center.

"Do continue, Lieutenant."

"The only way to neutralize Gods is to penetrate into their structures. This is what we've wanted since the beginning, right?" The colonel nodded. "As you know, sir, those bastards are pretty damn suspicious. And such a move could inspire Gods' trust in the sergeant, and—"

"I'm afraid I don't follow, Lieutenant," the old man interrupted him.

"If Sergeant Pry stops the carnage, Gods will see him as a potential ally."

"An ally, you say ..."

Valdez nodded.

"But what exactly do you want to do?"

The question was greeted with silence.

"Can this even succeed with the increased security measures?" Rutta waved his hand. "Even if we let go of locating the source of the message, Security Department will sniff it out in a few hours. No. No way. I refuse!"

"Godbless will explode if Suhurs stop making offerings and leave," Henryan interposed casually.

Colonel Rutta winced when he heard the name of the head of the scientific department. And then his face broke into a smile. A spiteful smile.

"Okay. Use your head, but remember: I don't know anything. Figure something out before the next shift starts. Understood?"

"Yes, sir!" they replied in unison.

"And one more thing," the colonel added. "I want a holo with this old bag's face when she finds out."

———

"I think I know how to approach it," Darski said a moment later, when they already stood in the empty corridor, waiting for the train.

Valdez looked at him carefully.

"When taking over Seifert's duties, I made a thorough analysis of the security systems and found something that probably escaped everybody's notice," explained Henryan. "No one pulled back the nanobots sent to the caves by Seifert. They were inactivated, but they're still down there."

The lieutenant's eyes narrowed. A look of embarrassment crossed his face. It was him who was responsible for bringing the equipment back, thus the oversight was his fault.

"Go on," he said reluctantly.

"I could send them a short message."

"How?"

"Using the external transmitter. For example, from one of the ships stationed at anchor."

"No way." Valdez shook his head firmly. "Since Treb'aldaledo, esdees have been monitoring all connections between the ships of the Fleet."

"Then I'll connect directly to the main antenna of the station," Darski suggested.

"How do you intend to do that?"

"If I can get to the technical levels, I will gain direct access to the antenna circuits. Outside the system, you see. The message gonna go straight to the nanobots, together with a command to self-destruct after completing the task. No control will show anything. No message will go through our communications links."

Henryan was confident; a dealer on Epsilon of the New Bolivia System had communicated with his partners the same way. If it hadn't been for his loose tongue, no one would have caught him smuggling drugs into the local base.

Valdez licked his lips nervously. The sergeant just showed him one of the system's vulnerabilities, the existence of which no one even suspected. A vulnerability that Gods could take advantage of …

"Clever, very clever," the lieutenant admitted thoughtfully. "I'll contact you in an hour, after I have something to eat. Then we'll work out the details." He held out his hand.

Darski had not expected this. As a reflex reaction, he shook the proffered hand, and winced immediately. He felt a cold angular shape in his palm.

"Show it to the esdees," Valdez whispered, seeing his worried look. "We'll gain some time and leeway."

"Okay."

The train car's door opened, but the lieutenant didn't get inside.

"I have to discuss the details of your assignment with the old man," he explained before the door closed.

THIRTY-SEVEN

ONLY EVERY THIRD light was on in the closed area, and despite the air conditioning being turned off, there was a pleasant coolness here. Darski didn't sweat with every movement, and the empty corridors gave him a sense of greater freedom, which made a nice change after his visit to the crowded mess hall. If not for the fact that extra duty took almost all his free time outside of the required six hours of sleep, it could be considered an escape from the daily routine.

Henryan stopped next to the five unfortunates like him, taking place at the end of a neat row. The other soldiers looked around the empty corridor uneasily, but he waited calmly for Valdez. Unlike them, he knew what kind of job awaited him. A large toolbox lay by his feet, given to him a moment ago by an obese noncom from the quartermaster's office.

It's a small world, after all, Henryan thought, realizing he could see a familiar face among his comrades. Corporal Tregvas, standing at the other end of the row, was studying the plan of this level with a neutral expression. Could it be a coincidence … ?

The lieutenant was a minute late. He didn't come by train as they anticipated, but emerged suddenly from a side corridor.

Surprised by his unexpected appearance, they stood at attention a second later than they should have.

"At ease!" he said, and immediately began to assign tasks. "Bodko and Ramirez, the main corridor. Stuyvesant and Kimmie, zone three. Tregvas and Pry, follow me."

Reaching for the toolbox, Darski glanced at the corporal. Another coincidence?

They went down the same corridor from which lieutenant had come a moment before. They were preceded by the pair of soldiers walking to zone three until the first fork; then they were alone. Stuyvesant and Kimmie had turned right. The lieutenant led Darski and Tregvas left. He did not say a word until they reached their destination, which was a technical airlock in the heart of sector one.

Valdez stopped by an armored hatch. Farther on there was a staircase connecting all levels of this sector of the rim. Through it, they would reach the airlock at the top level of the station. This room adjoined one of the eight arms extending from the hub to the residential area, and only from there one could go to the technical corridors that circled the entire rim, in order to get to the hydroponics farms, or warehouses and engine rooms, which ensured the proper functioning of the entire sector.

"Corporal," Valdez turned to Tregvas, "you will take care of the settings of the control modules in all the elevators in this arm. The elevator cars are to stop only at selected residential levels, at the observation deck, and at the gate of the spaceport. Lock the doors on all other levels. Electronically and mechanically. Understood?"

Tregvas nodded.

"I'm on it, sir."

Lieutenant Valdez looked at Henryan.

"Sergeant, you'll perform the diagnostics of the technical elevators within this compartment. A pressure suit is over there," he pointed to the hatch.

"I need to wear a suit to check the elevators?" Darski asked, surprised.

"We're trying to save every last credit. That's why we don't maintain an atmosphere in the technical corridors," Valdez explained hurriedly as if caught doing something shameful. "You will start from the rooms on the other side of the arm."

"Yes, sir!" Darski replied duly, and that ended the short briefing.

After the lieutenant left, Henryan picked up his toolbox and went to the hatch. He activated the lock with a card and waited calmly until a small room filled with air. The panel of the lock slowly changed color from red to green.

"Why did they send you to forced labor? What did you do?" Tregvas asked suddenly.

"Nothing," Henryan said, without turning his head.

"Just like we all. Colonel Bruttal has a heavy hand," the corporal summed up, and fell silent.

Apparently, he lacked the idea how to get to the point. Darski decided to put him out of his misery.

"If you gonna approach me again with some kind of a proposal, just skip it," he said when the panel turned dark green and a massive hatch popped off with a hiss.

"A simple 'thank you' would be enough," Tregvas grumbled.

"For what?"

"For the warning, to begin with."

"Seriously?" The sergeant started to walk up the narrow stairs. "I'm to thank you for warning me of the esdees coming to take some shit that you had planted on me earlier? Maybe it's you who should say 'sorry.'"

The corporal looked down.

"We did our damnedest to pass you the crystals, buddy—"

"I'm not your buddy, Corporal!" The last word sounded like an insult in Darski's mouth.

"I'm sorry, Sergeant."

"For the crystals?"

"No, for the buddy."

They walked in silence. When they reached the top level, Tregvas kept his distance from Darski. He stood against the wall, scowling as if someone had hurt him.

"Because of you, the esdees kicked the shit out of me," Henryan said, irritated by his behavior. "I still piss blood. You could apologize for that, too."

"We didn't know, not really—"

"You didn't know that esdees would have an eye on Seifert's successor?"

"We didn't know that esdees would get violent. They never laid a finger on any of us."

Darski examined the data on the airlock's display. Putting a pressure suit on would take about three minutes, so they had time to clarify a few things. After sealing the helmet, he was going to take care of the task at hand. With each passing moment, more inkblots died … Gurds, he corrected himself.

"Say what you have to say. You've got as much time as it takes to put on a pressure suit. Then I'll take the toolbox and disappear."

Tregvas licked his dry lips. Sweat beaded on his forehead, even though it wasn't hot in the airlock. Apparently, the situation was stressing him out …

"I'm just a pawn," he said cautiously, inserting his feet into a spacesuit, stretched on a rack. "One of many. They told me to raise hell in the canteen, so that I would end up here. Just like the other four guys. We wanted to make sure that Valdez wouldn't assign any outsiders to you."

He lowered his voice confidentially. "Soon, you'll be able to talk to someone more important, Sergeant."

"What are you talking about, man?" Darski looked at him like he was crazy.

Tregvas nodded toward the door leading to the technical level.

"There is someone waiting in there who knows more than I do. Someone, who really can apologize."

———

The technical corridor at the top level of the rim was much narrower than those in the residential area. Also—no less importantly—its plasteel walls always remained transparent. Behind them stretched hydroponics and meat farms and evenly spaced oval tanks. The green ones contained water, the white ones —oxygen.

Seeing the enormity of this place, Henryan understood why the command had given up maintaining an atmosphere at the technical level of the station. The plantations were fully automated, service staff appeared there once in a blue moon, usually in the event of a serious failure that robots were not able to deal with. The corridors, circling the rim, were many miles long. Savings on heating and aeration of such a large space had to be gigantic.

Now, however, the Admiralty decided that technical part of the station could make a perfect, isolated transport route for the VIPs. Blocking the access to the elevators from several intermediate levels of the arm was all that was needed to form an independent alternative byway, allowing for fast movement of large numbers of people between the residential area, the observation deck, and the spaceport. The closure of the entire sector created apt conditions for the reception and accommodation of hundreds of tetchy parliamentarians; however, the bottleneck of the project was the elevators—or rather, lack thereof. Only eight shafts had been built in each arm, not enough for transporting at the same time everybody who would like to get from the rim to the observation deck—or to the spaceport, if the Admiralty would agree to send so many spartans over the battlefield.

For this reason, the colonel ordered to cut off two more arms in the sectors adjacent to the closed area. As a result, the visiting senators would have access to another sixteen shafts—which should prevent potential queues in case of the VIPs; the comfort of the crew, of course, was of no concern to anybody. To ensure complete safety of the guests, it was necessary to block all exits leading from the residential area to the technical level—and this was, among other things, what the punished soldiers were doing.

The outer hatch opened soundlessly. A few clouds of steam floated into the cylindrical corridor when Henryan was leaving the airlock. He took two steps, then stopped since a giant humanoid robot stood in his way. One of the machines tending to hydroponics farms, currently idle. Darski looked around uneasily, but besides it he didn't notice anything or anyone.

Tregvas walked past him casually.

"What do you think you're doing, Corporal?" Darski asked, confused. "I'm working in the corridor! You were supposed to take care of the arm …"

The corporal did not even stop.

"Orders from on high. The conversation gonna take a while, and we don't want you to get into any more trouble. I'll do the first of your shafts, and then take care of my own. I can be quick," he added defensively.

"Hold it right there!" Darski warned him. "Don't piss me off, Corporal. Go back immediately!"

"But—"

"But me no buts."

"As you wish, Sergeant." Tregvas shrugged. "I just wanted to help."

"I don't need your help," Henryan grumbled.

The damn fool was close to discovering that the shafts assigned to Henryan had already been secured.

"Where is this 'someone more important' of yours?" he asked.

Tregvas, still sulking, replied after a long pause, "Activate the robot …"

Darski leaned forward, put the toolbox aside, and then pressed the red button on the plastic giant's torso. The displays built into its skeleton began to come to life. Thirty seconds later, the robot straightened with a fluid movement.

"Good evening, Sergeant," a mechanical, impersonal voice came from the speakers in Henryan's suit.

Whoever was speaking through this machine, they took the precaution of hiding their identity.

A smart move, Darski thought.

"I don't have much time," he said. "Let's cut to the chase."

"Do you know why I wanted to see you?"

"More or less."

A strange sound coming from the speakers could have been a sigh. Or anything else, including ordinary interference.

"No more petty games. In four days the orders of the Supreme Council of Gurdu'dihan will reach the most important sithus, and the final stage of the crusade against Suhurs will begin. We can't passively watch the disappearance of one of the three intelligent races in the known Universe. We're prepared to do whatever it takes to prevent its destruction. We can sacrifice a lot—"

"Me, for example," Henryan interjected sharply.

"No, it's not that at all," the conspirator denied in a mechanical voice. "Louismail was one of us. But he worked of his own free will. It was him who came up with the idea of supplying weapons to the Warriors of the Bone, and he put it into practice. Unfortunately, he got caught, and now we need your help—"

The conspirator stopped short and finished after a moment's pause. "Without you, all our work done so far will go to waste."

"Good, my mysterious friend. This will probably be for the best." Darski changed the setting of the servomotors in his suit; he could now sit in it comfortably. "I've got you to worry about, not to mention the esdees and the investigation team of the old man. There is not a single moment when I'm not under surveillance. If you want to talk to me, you have to resort to tricks like this. Can't you see, man, that I'm not able to help you now?"

"You're wrong."

"No, I'm not wrong!" Henryan burst out. "And what's more, I'm not going to be another Seifert."

"It's not what we're after," the conspirator assured him.

"Really?" Darski asked ironically. "Then what is it that you *are* after?"

"Help. Nothing more."

"Right. If I help you, I'll get a one-way ticket. To a place worse than hell. I know what I'm talking about, because I dropped by there once. It was on my way …"

"We'll make sure this won't happen again."

One more of their empty promises.

"You will make sure …" Darski snorted. "And if something goes wrong, you'll apologize sincerely again."

The Gods' leader didn't reply. Darski reached for the keyboard to activate the servomotors. He had wasted enough time.

"Wait." The mechanical voice came from the speakers again. "You don't know the whole truth about us, or about the case. You've heard only as much as the brass has told you, and the bigwigs are not a very reliable source."

"Go ahead, you have an opportunity to enlighten me here and now," Henryan said impatiently.

"I can't."

"You see?"

"By providing you with this information, I would put too many decent people at risk."

"Are you suggesting I should help you, not having a clue what I am doing, and why?"

"I did not say that."

"Is that so? Because I just heard it."

"It's more complicated than you think. Although you are right about one thing. We need your help, and we can give a lot in return. But that's not all. You should know that Rutta doesn't play fair with you."

"Really?"

"I've seen your file—"

"So what?" Darski interrupted him. "Looks like only Godbless has no idea who she's dealing with whenever she talks to the command center."

"Rutta will get rid of you as soon as he doesn't need you anymore."

Henryan laughed out loud.

"Can you prove it?"

"I can."

"But you won't."

"I will."

"Go ahead, feel free to ..." Henryan paused. He had to wait for the reply.

"Tomorrow you'll get a message with access codes to some proprietary databases. You can check the colonel's correspondence yourself. Rutta needed someone who would obey him implicitly, that's why he contacted primarily penal colonies and prisons. This way, he found you. You suit his needs perfectly, but you can be sure that as soon as he is done with you, he'll send you back where you came from."

"And here's where you are wrong," Darski said without hesitation. "I'm never going to return to the Sturgeon Belt."

"Have a look at Rutta's correspondence and you'll see which of us is wrong."

"It won't be easy," Henryan noticed.

"I know. But I trust in you. You figured Annelly out, even though she thought she could outsmart the system. You did well, I have to admit. If you'd pressed Zaitsev, instead of proving to us how good you are, this meeting would be different. I wouldn't be so cautious."

"You hope this camouflage will protect you, don't you?"

"Yes." The answer was short and decisive.

"What makes you so sure?"

"Annelly is like a child: she loves to play hare and hounds, but doesn't see the bigger picture. I do things differently."

"That doesn't mean I can't trace you. Like everybody, you leave a trail. One just has to know how to find it in the information noise."

"So go play detective, Sergeant. I warn you, however, that this time the noise will be overwhelming. You won't hear anything meaningful in it. Let me spare you more sleepless nights. The bot, through whom I'm speaking to you, is connected to one thousand four hundred terminals in six sectors of the rim, not to mention hundreds of other devices in the hub."

"A few days' search—"

"That's right. A few days of hard work would give the answer, but you'd have to harness the station's mainframes, and that you can't do. If you try to trace me using homemade means, you won't discover the truth in time."

Henryan was silent for a long moment. He couldn't deny it: there were only a few days left to the final battle, and Rutta and Valdez would whale into him, had they noticed that he was scheming again.

"We'll have a chat after I've seen the files," he said in the end.

"Fine. Let Tregvas know when you're ready for the next meeting. Just remember: the time is running out."

———

Darski checked the anchoring of the safety line for a third time, and then pressed the red button, opening the outer hatch of the last airlock. One movement of the arm propelled him into the immense black void. The elastic cord, with which he was attached to the hull of the station, yielded and stopped him a moment later. He felt a slight tug, after which he began to approach the rim. The maneuvering thrusters allowed him to turn around, and after a while the magnetic soles of his shoes adhered to the porous surface of the giant hub.

He took a few awkward steps, leaned over and checked the guideways. On the trolley of the third one he saw a symbol of the main antenna. He strapped himself to the handle with a snap hook, and a moment later, released the magnet hook of the safety line. He lowered it gently onto the anchor field, and when the flat base of the electromagnet hemisphere touched the polished metal, he tugged it three times to make sure it held firmly.

Everything was in perfect order, so he could start the propelling nozzle and go. Hovering above a small cart, he glided along the guideway leading toward the antenna several hundred yards away. The ride lasted long enough for him to be able to reflect on his bleak situation.

The conversation with the Gods' leader shocked him to the core; much more than he had expected. It also compelled him to reflect on what he should do next. He was afraid to live further in the shadow of guilt, which was overwhelming him increasingly. But being genetically conditioned to struggle for survival, he couldn't, he wouldn't be able to surrender to depression, although it still got the better of him, like when he stood up to Security Department. He didn't care then whether he would survive—no, he even preferred to die at the hands of this sadist so he wouldn't have to think anymore. He was ready to take a lot of shit if only that would keep him away from the Sturgeon Belt, and he knew that if anyone tried to send him back there— be it Gods, Rutta, or one of the esdees—they would be in for a surprise.

He had thought until recently, apparently very naively, that there was a light in this tunnel, and that the only chance for him to regain full freedom would be to show absolute obedience to the colonel. Instead—if there were a kernel of truth in the words that he'd heard in the technical corridor—even this guaranteed his return to the penal colony, no matter how the confrontation with Gods would go. Getting rid of the esdees had changed nothing. And he couldn't blackmail Rutta in a similar manner.

What options am I left with then, assuming Gods don't lie? he thought. Only to leave, he realized after a moment. If so, I will leave with such a bang that the entire known Universe will hear about me.

But then his voice of reason kicked in. *First*, he thought, *I should check whether the leader of Gods indeed didn't lie …*

He smiled to himself. Despite appearances to the contrary, the conspirators reached him at a perfect moment.

The cart began to slow down. Darski was nearing an oblong base to which a bunch of long antenna masts was attached. The guideway turned ninety degrees here, in a long gentle curve, and ran on up to the top of the longest of the masts. His goal, however, was much lower, just above the base of the structure. When the cart stopped, Henryan loosened the cord slightly, moved over the module of the connector and fastened himself to it with two snap hooks. It was only after he'd triple-checked the safety lines that he turned off the electromagnets supporting a package with the console of a portable comlink, strapped to the left leg of his suit, and he plugged the device into one of the sockets.

He waited several seconds, letting the console perform all the tests, and when a line of green lights lit up, he pressed a square button activating the transmitter. A millisecond signal emanated from the antenna, and raced at the speed of light toward the nanobots left by Seifert in the caves. A moment later, feedback messages appeared on the console screen.

Darski smiled. Mission accomplished. He unplugged the console, looked around, then took a wide swing and hurled it into space.

THIRTY-EIGHT

THE XAN 4 SYSTEM, X-RAY SECTOR

09/14/2354

Hakrad Redo-Tele crouched by the fire to warm up his cold hands. Serving by the altars on the plateau, he rarely had the opportunity to participate in a ritual designed to propitiate gods. Once or twice, he happened to make an offering of a few Quadrupeds, but it never took so long.

The larger of the suns was setting down when the fist of Temeh Dokru-Kume brought more prisoners to Bor Omot. The priest looked at the young Warrior of the Bone, standing on the other side of the flames. Six of his comrades already hung in the cages. The last member of their fist should join them in a moment.

Hakrad Redo-Tele rose slowly, leaning on his arad, and then went toward the ledge. Rekne Tare retreated with respect to the mouth of the cave, and folded his hands behind his back.

"It's time," the priest said.

"Dakko Turi!"

Out of the darkness emerged a hunched and long-limbed figure of a young Warrior of the Bone from the fist that was supposed to replace the immolators. Rekne Tare, stocky, slightly limping with his right leg, and drenched in blue gore, took his clawed gloves off and threw them on the rock next to the six irregular stacks. A moment later, a shining bone armor followed them.

"Are you ready, Rekne Tare of the mighty Mare Deto-Zuri's breeding?" the priest asked.

"As always!"

The arad went up, but before its tip fell on the stone, a loud rumble could be heard from the depths of the cave. Hakrad Redo-Tele froze.

"It's a sign!" Rekne Tare called, running to the edge of the chasm. "Kraga Snaro! Kraga Snaro had an epiphany!"

The fister turned toward the rising warriors. "The Spirits of the Mountains heard our prayers!"

Everyone rushed toward the wooden structure with a cage of Kraga Snaro hanging at its end. Two Warriors of the Bone were already turning the winch, coiling the leather rope. But before they could move the wooden arm and liberate the exhausted comrade, out of the darkness came another rumble.

"It's Reme Naro!" Rekne Tare informed everyone. "Reme Naro also received sanctifying grace!"

The priest nodded at him with the arad. "Free both of them, burn their wounds and bring them to me," he ordered.

He went toward the fire, feeling a tremor in all his limbs. Here was coming the greatest moment in the history of Suhurta, and he was to be its witness and a eulogist, carrying the news to the rest of the clan. He crouched quickly, and put a stronger grip on his arad. He was ready to listen to the revelation.

Kraga Snaro and Reme Naro appeared together, led by the warriors from the Kire Tako-Dote's fist. Both could barely stand on their feet, but they bravely refused to accept help.

"Open your membranes!" Hakrad Redo-Tele tapped his arad on the ground with all his strength, till the rocks echoed back.

"The Spirits of the Mountains have spoken ... *Your offerings have been accepted*," Kraga Snaro, exhausted, wheezed barely audibly.

"*Gods have left you, but in the coming battle we will stand on your side,*" Reme Naro, still wobbly on his feet, added even more softly.

There was silence. For several swellings of the membranes, the crackling fire was the only sound to be heard.

In the end, the priest stood up.

"Free the others," he ordered, gesturing to the fister with a wave of his hand. "I'm off to the Triple Pierced Shield clan's seat, to bring the news to the Supreme Suhur."

"What about the rest of the prisoners?" Kire Tako-Dote asked, looming in the gathering twilight.

Hakrad Redo-Tele focused his attention on the pen, where a dozen fetuscarriers were held. He had hoped to gut them personally to the glory of the gods of Suns and Stars. Unfortunately, the Spirits of the Mountains thwarted his plans.

"Sacrifice them all," he said, pointing to the slope where Suhurs, incessantly, were leading prisoners toward Bor Omot. "We will thank the Spirits of the Mountains for the favor they have shown us."

When he was leaving the hill, wheezes of satisfaction were coming from all directions.

THIRTY-NINE

THE XAN 4 SYSTEM, X-RAY SECTOR

09/14/2354

Darski noticed that something was wrong as soon as he got off the train. The corridor in front of the command center was swarming with people in blue jumpsuits of the scientific department. Judging from their faces, they were very agitated. Many debated fiercely, waving their arms and readers. Also, by the bulkhead there were much more gendarmes than usual. They carefully scanned everyone who wanted to get inside.

Henryan passed through the checkpoints without inquiry and any problems whatsoever, and then headed straight to his workstation. His substitute was sitting by the console, clearly furious.

"What's going on?" the sergeant asked him, but heard only a loud growl in response.

The shift changeover went smoothly. The esdee pressed his thumb on the screen of the reader without even looking at the records. Darski took his place and made a customary equipment checkup. Right after he'd started looking over current transmissions, he felt someone's hand on his shoulder.

"Don't be surprised when you get to site fourteen," he heard Lieutenant Valdez's voice.

Has something gone wrong? Henryan thought, but didn't stop what he was doing to get to the images from the caves.

When he finally got there, he could barely restrain his shock. Three Warriors of the Bone still stood on the gorestained rock. One of them was just taking a swing with his masticators to break the forelegs of a barrellike Gurd. The creature fell on the rocky slope, and began to slide toward the dark bottom of the cave with a piercing squeal …

Suhurs haven't stopped the ceremony, Darski thought frantically. The message hasn't reached them … Then what caused the commotion at the door of the command center?

After he was done with the routine check, Darski produced a short report, and then he leaned back in his chair. Thanks to the sedatives, he made it through the night, but he was exhausted. The information about Rutta's dirty play planted in him a seed of anxiety. He looked at the dais, but he saw nothing, because the energy barriers that surrounded the command post were on. He moved his gaze to Valdez then. The lieutenant stood at the foot of the stairs, probably waiting for the right moment to talk to the old man. Interestingly, he looked relaxed. This could mean that Rutta was satisfied with the result of the mission, even though they failed to stop the ghastly spectacle.

A luminous sphere appeared on the holovision panel, and after a few seconds, took the shape of a bald head with Asian features.

"This is Dr. Fukkuya," a melodious voice came from the speakers. "I need an extra set of cameras on site sixteen. At once."

"Site sixteen, copy that," Henryan said quickly, and leaned over the console. "The cameras will be there in three minutes."

"Thank you, over and out."

The hologram disappeared.

For a few moments nothing happened. The command center was perfectly quiet.

But in just one second, all hell broke loose behind Henryan's back.

"I'll make you regret that!" A high-pitched voice coming from the dais was so loud that even people in the hallway fell silent when they heard it. "Admiral Okonera will know all about it! You're all saboteurs!"

When Dr. Godbless stood on the top step of the stairs, the lieutenant stepped aside, straining not to laugh. He saluted as she passed, but the gesture only seemed to incense her even more. She raised her finger accusingly, waved it in front of Valdez's face, opened her mouth, then closed it again, not uttering a sound. A moment later, she was already behind the bulkhead, where a crowd of scientists immediately surrounded her. The buzz was back, even louder and livelier.

"Pry!"

Henryan tore his eyes away from the throng to look at the bridge. Lieutenant Valdez was inviting him to the dais. Rutta stood there with his hands resting on the railing, clenching his jaw. He didn't look irritated, but this strange grimace … Darski put one of his subordinates in charge of communications, made sure that his absence would not increase the chaos, and only then headed toward the dais. He briskly climbed the fourteen steps leading to the Bruttal's kingdom, stood next to Valdez, straight as a ramrod, and waited for the colonel to turn on the force field again. The energy barrier purred soothingly as soon as the commander sat behind his desk.

"Good job, Sergeant," Rutta said, leaning back in his chair.

Henryan duly clicked his heels first, and then put his personal reader, in which he described the course of the mission, on the table. He tried to behave normally, although the memory of what he'd heard in the technical corridor wasn't leaving him for a moment. Unfortunately, so far he'd failed to verify the message from the Gods' leader. Although he regularly checked all his pockets, he didn't find any crystals in them.

"Too bad it was totally useless," he said, not hiding his disappointment.

The colonel smiled faintly, reaching for the reader.

"Depends on how you look at it," he said.

"I don't understand ..." Darski glanced at silent Valdez.

"From the Gurds' point of view, indeed, little has changed," Rutta said. "But from ours ..." He paused meaningfully.

"Thanks to you, Sergeant, we have eliminated the last weak point in the station's security system," the lieutenant said quickly when the old man immersed himself in the report. "Congratulations. It was a great idea. Even the esdees bought the explanation that it was a surprise left by Seifert. Your substitute checked the entire communications system, but found nothing that would indicate the source of transmission. And Godbless was rightly served. She won't film the suicide death of the young Warriors of the Bone."

But we haven't achieved the main objective, which was to save a few thousand Gurdian prisoners, Henryan thought, listening to the joyful tone of Valdez.

"I always do my best to perform all my duties properly," he recited the threadbare phrase when the lieutenant finally fell silent, and again clicked his heels.

Despite having taken two pills he felt worse every minute. The sight of two jubilant superiors reminded him of the words he'd heard the previous day. If the mechanical voice didn't lie ...

"This is what we were hoping for, offering you a parole," Rutta said, putting the reader on his desk. "Unfortunately, I can't cancel your punishment. Lieutenant Valdez, however, will make sure that you have enough free time."

"Thank you, sir." Darski reached for his reader.

"Before you go," the colonel put his hand on the device, "can you explain what you were doing outside for thirty-seven minutes?"

"I encountered a technical problem, sir. I couldn't detach the magnet of the safety line. In the end, I had to cut it to get back to the station. I haven't mentioned this in my report, because it had nothing to do with the objective of the mission. I don't think we should report it to the quartermaster's office …"

"This time I will let it go." Rutta slowly withdrew his hand. "We'll keep it quiet. In the future, however, I'd rather you provide all the details in your report. Even those that seem insignificant to you."

"Yes, sir."

The colonel turned, reaching for the switch of the force field.

"That would be all. Dismissed."

FORTY

THIS MICROCRYSTAL WAS SMALLER. Henryan turned it in his fingers, sitting on his bunk. He had less than an hour before he'd have to start an extra shift. He ate a light dinner, took a quick shower and sat down to reflect on his next move. The answer to the doubts nagging him since the day before was hidden in this transparent pyramid. He was eager to learn the truth, but he was afraid, too. Finally, he reached for his head-reader. Further delay seemed pointless. He pushed the micro-crystal into the slot, and leaned back against the cold bulkhead.

First he saw the promised codes; a moment later some folders with the colonel's correspondence acquired by Gods appeared in the darkness. Henryan wasn't going to open them. A good techy could insert any content in the copies of the messages, leaving no trace of the intervention, and he didn't have time for tedious analysis. If he was to believe this wasn't another wind-up, he had to get access to the original files.

Suddenly, he saw a three-dimensional map of one of the station's levels—in the area closed for the Senate delegation, according to the description. In several places there were pulsing red dots. Darski zoomed in on one of them. Three adjacent cabins were combined to create a comfortable apartment, assigned to one of the Speakers of the Senate. In the middle room there was a mobile communications center with the top level of security clearance. With such a device, if it could be hacked, one could send any signal, bypassing even the blockades of the station's command. Using it, Gods could order the bombing of the Gurdian capital, if they wished to. However, there was something more …

Henryan checked the other red markers—all pointed to the senators' cabins with similar MCCs, which had the same status. One could reach any files from these terminals. The only problem was getting to them. The rooms were certainly locked up tight and monitored around the clock.

Very clever of you, he thought, addressing Gods in his mind, when he realized that he couldn't possibly use these devices without arousing the colonel's suspicions and—what was now less of a problem for him—the esdees'. You're showing me the correspondence that may have been fabricated, and also a way to reach its source, knowing that I'll never get access to it.

INFORM VALDEZ
OF POSSIBLE HACKING OF THESE TERMINALS.

Henryan flinched when the inscription suddenly blazed before his eyes. The letters faded after a short while, but it was enough to make him realize Gods just suggested a very simple and effective solution. He had to admit that they had planned this action with great care. He was one of the two people able to detect a violation of rules and procedures—and probably the only one whom Rutta and Valdez trusted. It could work …

**INSTALL THE VIRUS FROM THIS CRYSTAL
SEIFERT'S SOFTWARE WILL LET YOU
REVIEW AND DOWNLOAD RESTRICTED FILES
SIMULTANEOUSLY WITH RUTTA.**

Another excellent idea. If the colonel accesses his mailbox, Seifert's software will enable its preview, and even will download the contents of the selected files to the parliamentarians' terminals. The system will not report an unauthorized access to the database, and Rutta won't find a record of the opening of any of these files at a time when he didn't use the network himself.

It's as simple as it is good, Darski thought, taking off his headreader.

He still had twenty-five minutes left.

———

The same corridor, the same team. Only the equipment was different. This time they didn't receive big toolboxes, but portable scanners and analyzers. Again, Tregvas stood at the opposite end of the short row. He seemed much more cheerful and relaxed. He didn't have to take on the role of a go-between, or be ready for additional work.

They saw the lieutenant in time. This time the superior appeared in the depths of the main corridor. They had, therefore, time to prepare for his arrival.

"At ease. Bodko and Ramirez, you two will take the main corridor. Stuyvesant and Kimmie, the branch on the left. Tregvas and Pry, the branch on the right." Valdez pointed to the fork with his hand. "Any questions?"

"Yes, sir!" Tregvas stepped forward.

"What is it, Corporal?"

"Corporal Tregvas requesting permission to start work later!"

"What?"

"I beg to report that I have received a medical checkup request." Tregvas held out his hand with the data card.

The lieutenant came up to him, put the card into his reader, studied the record carefully, and then looked at his watch.

"The checkup begins in thirty minutes, it will take about

forty minutes. You must be back at eighteen hundred hours sharp, understood?"

"Yes, sir!" Tregvas stiffened at attention.

"You can leave your equipment over there." Valdez pointed to the folded chairs standing against the opposite wall. "The rest of you … to your duties, quick march!"

Henryan rearranged the scanner, slipping from his arm, and performed a left face, just like the others. When the lieutenant looked at him in passing, he gave a prearranged signal, and a moment later, disappeared round the corner. The first cabin was located only a few steps away from the corridor's fork.

He plugged the diagnostic equipment into the socket under the panel to upload the new software. The installation went smoothly. He opened the door, then closed it again and made a check mark on his list. It was the first out of one hundred and thirty cabins that he should take care of that day. Fortunately, another soldier had already done this job two days before, as a part of his punishment. Thus, Henryan could instead disappear in one of the cabins for two or even three hours. He decided, however, to wait until Valdez found him. He didn't have to wait long. Apparently, the lieutenant was very interested in what his subordinate had to say.

They met by the seventh door, just around the next corner.

"What's going on?" Valdez asked, after he'd made sure that the other four soldiers were out of hearing distance.

"I think I know what Gods are up to," Darski said excitedly, trying to sound natural.

"Tell me." The lieutenant looked genuinely interested.

"They want to use one of the terminals on this level to override the system."

Valdez frowned. He knew very well that Henryan didn't have access to information about the hardware installed here. Unless he was in touch with the conspirators, who had informed him about everything.

"How do they intend to do it?" he asked.

"Seifert hacked a few of them."

"Bullshit!" Valdez protested. "Seifert was already doing time when we installed them in the senators' apartments."

"And where did you get them from?" Darski asked, not hiding irony.

"From the storeroom," the lieutenant answered, surprised.

"The same storeroom from which the phaser parts had long been disappearing?"

"Galacticunt!" Valdez roared, stepped back, and once again looked around the corner. "Do you know which terminals we are talking about?"

"I have no clue, but I assume that all those with the top level of security clearance."

"Why only those?"

"Because the systems of the station can be overridden only thanks to them."

Lieutenant Valdez knitted his brows.

"True," he muttered, glancing at his reader. "We'll have to check as many as sixteen terminals. How long can it take?"

"Checking anything of this capacity can take, I don't know … eight to ten hours."

"Can't you do better than that?" Valdez pressed him.

"It depends. If I come across the modifications in the first circuits—" he paused, and then shook his head.

"What?" The deputy commander seemed alarmed.

"Knowing Gods, it could be a wind-up. They are really cunning. We need to perform complete diagnostics of each terminal."

"Fine … Let's go."

He grabbed Henryan by the arm and pulled him down a side corridor. They passed several bulkheads, turned many corners. In the end, they stopped in front of a technical elevator shaft. There, Valdez pulled out his comlink and had a brief conversation with the colonel. Aside, so that Darski couldn't overhear him. But it was obvious even from afar that the lieutenant was pretty scared. Another critical oversight occurred right under his nose. First, the cameras left alone in the caves, then the external antennas, and now, to make matters worse, terminals of the most important notables … He got himself into serious trouble.

"The old man is pissed off like hell," Valdez said, returning to the elevator, "but he didn't allow me to let you into the cabins prepared for the senators. This is a restricted area. No one without the top-level security clearance can enter it."

"I can't do it remotely," Darski shrugged.

Lieutenant Valdez sighed.

"I know …"

They were silent for a long moment. Valdez was racking his brains; Henryan pretended to be worried. He knew that eventually, they would let him access one of the terminals; otherwise they would have to remove them all, and this, the authorities would never forgive them.

"We'd better hurry," Darski urged.

"Don't rush me." Valdez once again pulled out his comlink, and walked away.

This time the conversation was short, and his gestures much livelier and more explicit.

He returned after a few seconds.

"You can go in, but you will be working under my supervision. I was told not to take my eyes off you."

"No problem," Henryan agreed immediately. That was it. He'd been waiting for just such an opportunity. "But I won't fix it with bare hands. And probably neither with this clutter."

He pointed to the portable diagnostic kit.

"Make a list of stuff you'll need." Valdez handed him the reader.

A moment later, his eyes widened.

"What's with the chow?"

"It won't take an hour, will it?" the sergeant said. "We might spend here most of the night."

"Galacticunt!" Valdez didn't look happy.

"You told me yourself on the first day not to expect to be cut much slack ..."

The deputy commander didn't respond to these words at all.

———

Darski knew where to look for the modifications left by Seifert. In fact, he would have found them just as quickly, even if the mysterious informant of Gods hadn't shown him all the changes in the diagrams of the compromised devices. The communications software didn't have any secrets from him. Instead of running a full scan—which he was going to do for the benefit of the lieutenant—he would have chosen to examine the three key blocks, and so he would patch up all the holes in the system within an hour at most. But the detection and neutralization of the modifications made by Gods was a prelude to a much more serious task. At some point he would have to install his own software, needed to intercept the colonel's correspondence.

He knew Valdez would keep an eye on him at all times. He hoped, however, that several hours of idleness would lull the lieutenant's vigilance, or at least reduce it significantly. That's why he took his time, and patiently waited for the right moment.

He also realized that Valdez's supervision would let him quickly perform the most difficult part of the task. He wouldn't have to wait for the old man to activate his personal console. It would be enough if the lieutenant placed a call to Rutta on the closed channel to report the success ...

———

"Gotcha!" Darski leaned back in his chair, letting the bored lieutenant look at the display. The red windows reported the detection of a code that wasn't compliant with the standards of the system.

"Great!" Valdez stood up, stretching his lips into a triumphant smile. Glancing at the reader screen, he beamed even more. He hadn't expected such early completion of the first phase. "It's been only four hours, and we already succeeded."

"True, but it's only a partial success," Darski immediately extinguished his enthusiasm.

"Excuse me?"

"That's the first modification, but certainly not the last. I'm familiar with this system, so I know that you need at least three similar modifications to make absolutely sure that everything will work as it should."

"As many as three?"

"Sometimes even four or more. It depends entirely on the scale of the changes the hacker wants to introduce."

"Oh no …" Valdez dropped heavily into his chair.

"Don't worry," Henryan comforted him, "now that I know what to look for, locating other changes will take much less time."

"How long?"

"Sixty minutes, ninety in the worst-case scenario—" Darski paused, seeing Valdez's uncertain expression. "Watching this junk," he added, "won't be necessary anymore."

"It's music to my ears." The sleepy lieutenant grinned. Inaction was killing him; whenever he had nothing to focus on, he slowly zoned out.

"When I detect all the modifications in this terminal," Henryan assured him, "I'll use a tracker, which will automatically search for and block any overwritten pieces of code. This way, we will check and clean all the terminals in this sector in just a few hours. They will work as before, responding to the test signals, but they won't execute any external commands at zero hour. Gods won't know till the very end that we've found and neutralized malicious content."

"Fantastic!" This time, Valdez responded more enthusiastically.

Darski delayed his next move until the lieutenant's swollen eyelids began to close involuntarily. Mindless looking at the display, on which a cascade of lines of code flowed, could dull a person's mind as well as narcotics. The only difference being that drugs worked much faster, and they gave much more colorful visions ...

Henryan snapped out of his reverie. Here, that was the best proof of what such a monotonous job can do to a man. Although he had work to do, he began to zone out, too.

Another glance at the lieutenant, and he knew he could start.

"I'm ready," he said, without turning to his superior.

"Ready?" Valdez mumbled, roused from his stupor. "Can we go now?" he asked dreamily.

"I wrote a scanning program," Henryan clarified, and showed him a crystal, just removed from a portable encoder.

"Right. Right." Valdez tried to concentrate.

"Can we start?" Darski moved closer to the console, looking questioningly at his superior.

"Sure ..."

Before the sergeant put the pyramid into the slot, he'd felt Valdez's hand on his shoulder.

"One moment!" the lieutenant said suddenly.

Henryan groaned loudly, so that Valdez heard him, then slowly moved away from the desk.

"What now?" he asked.

Valdez held out his hand.

"I must see what's on the crystal first." Seeing the pleading look in the subordinate's eyes, he explained, "I don't make the rules, Pry."

"I see." Darski handed him a gleaming pyramid, and it went immediately to the lieutenant's analyzer.

A few minutes later Henryan received the crystal back, and reassured and satisfied Valdez rubbed his eyes, at the same time yawning widely as if to swallow the whole world. That was just what the sergeant had been waiting for. One quick movement of his hand was all he needed to swap the storage devices. An identical pyramid went into the slot, and with it the appropriate software. Five minutes later, the displays showed a message assuring that the terminal is totally secure.

Henryan retrieved the crystal, turned to put it back into its box, but froze in mid-motion, then extended his hand toward Valdez. The lieutenant looked blankly at the crystal that had been swapped for the second time as if he didn't understand what was going on.

"You'd better keep it," Darski said, fighting a yawn. "It will save us further controls."

Valdez nodded, again glancing at the reader screen to check the time.

"Good idea, Pry," he muttered. "Let's go. We need to get some sleep."

Henryan grimaced mentally. Isn't the lieutenant going to contact Rutta to inform him of the success … ? When he looked down at the display, and saw how late it was, he understood why this point of the plan wouldn't work.

Too bad … He would have to wait until morning.

Valdez stood up, reached for the reader and walked unsteadily to the door. He stopped, however, before he crossed the doorstep. He let Henryan leave first, looking at him apologetically.

"Wait in the corridor," he ordered.

"Something's wrong?" Darski faked concern.

"No, not at all. I just need to report to the old man where we stand."

The sergeant shrugged as if he absolutely didn't care.

"Please, hurry ..." he said, leaning back against the cold bulkhead. "I'm exhausted."

Valdez nodded, and went back to the cabin. Henryan smiled slightly when his superior disappeared from sight. Also, he reached instinctively into his pocket and dabbed his headreader. After all, he wouldn't have to wait until morning to verify the Gods' message.

FORTY-ONE

THE MILITARY USED two means of communication. Under normal circumstances, cryptograms were conveyed at the speed of light to the courier ships stationed at the entry points—as the hyperspace gateways were called colloquially—and these delivered them to the target star systems, which of course took time. Scientists, therefore, did what they could to come up with alternative means of information transmission, especially across the distances of hundreds of light-years. Thanks to quantum mechanics they managed to achieve half-success. Using the phenomenon of particle entanglement, they perfected the mechanism of data teleportation—a process known (theoretically, of course) already at the beginning of the twenty-first century. This method allowed for conversations in real time, regardless of the distance. This was all very good in theory, practice, however, had shown that there was one fundamental problem.

The Admiralty spent gargantuan amounts of money on research, the Federation's scientific department kept promising a breakthrough any moment, decades passed one after another, and the hypers, as the quantum communication modules were called, still did not go beyond the initial phase of development.

It was all about the cost of transmission, namely the amount of energy required to teleport data. The principle was simple: the greater the distance, and the "heavier" the message, the more terawatts were necessary for it to reach the recipient. For this reason hypers were used much more rarely than the military would like. They were great for intra-system communications, especially when the messages were sent from the surface of planets, where the loss of a significant amount of energy was not as painful as onboard a ship. This could be illustrated with an example. Let's imagine that we want to transmit data between objects five light-hours apart, since that is more or less the radius of an average planetary system. The reactors of the mightiest battleships, working at full power, allowed less than a minute of holo transmission, five minutes of primitive audio-visual messages, thirty minutes of audio transmission, or five hundred megabytes of text files. And this with redirecting to the hypers a hundred percent of the power of the mightiest ships constructed by Humankind.

Widespread quantum communications between ships located a few dozen light-years from bases and the headquarters was therefore impossible. At this distance, all the power of reactors would be used up to send just a briefest text message. For this reason hypers were used only to a very limited extent, and placed almost exclusively on the surface of planets, where sources of energy needed to power these monsters were easily available.

Henryan was understandably stunned when he discovered that Draccos communicated with Rutta by way of hypers. Only a moment later, after the first shock faded away, he remembered the fact that there were three huge plants processing helon ore in the Sturgeon Belt, which possessed sufficient energy supply to gratify every whim of the despotic warden.

The history of the correspondence between the two colonels dated back to the day when Seifert had been caught and arrested. A few hours after taking him into custody, Rutta sent a cryptogram to the headquarters, describing the situation and asking about the names of communications officers serving long sentences. Two days later, the Admiralty handed him over a short list of candidates. Only three inmates in the Federation's penal colonies had a level-five security clearance—Darski among them. The other two were sent to the mines for swindling and smuggling. Rutta ran a check on all three, and the next day he presented a request to Admiral Okonera. His choice had fallen on prisoner number seven two one.

It all happened very quickly—a text message was sent via hypers, and it reached Xan 4 just when Darski was getting off the shuttle. Draccos demanded that Rutta rethink his choice, and when the latter told him to fuck off, the former sent an overlong screed, the content of which was most interesting to Henryan.

I'm not sure if you know, Colonel, that our institution is considered one of the harshest penal colonies. We are dealing with the worst villains that ever donned a uniform. The man, for whom you asked the Admiralty, is one of them. He is an unscrupulous killer. He shot his superior in front of the commodore and almost the entire officer corps. What's more, he never apologized for this act, neither did he express his remorse, although the investigation showed that he had killed a totally innocent person who, let's not forget, hadn't done anything to earn such a fate. And that's not all, because the list of heinous crimes of this apostate is long. Yes, it's not the only crime that prisoner seven two one can be accused of.

By submitting attached relevant documents, I wish to inform you that while serving a sentence in our institution, the abovementioned inmate committed a series of murders. We are talking here about a very intelligent villain who knows how to plan a murder, and knows how to cover his tracks. It is only because of this that he hasn't yet stood before another tribunal, but believe me, it's only a matter of time. Our investigators are collecting evidence related to three homicides that we can assign to him with absolute certainty. We are also working on six further cases where the perpetrator could have been seven two one.

That's the man you will have to deal with. I don't understand why seven two one was selected, I only know that he was promised an early release if he performs a top secret assignment. This promise is a mistake, a huge mistake, which I'm trying to make you realize. I'm appealing to your sense of honor, and I'm asking you to consider the following:

Within the next week we will submit factual evidence to the Admiralty, on the basis of which it will be possible to charge prisoner seven two one for the first of the three alleged acts (please refer to the attached documents, you will see that the evidence, though circumstantial, is unambiguous). We have not impeached him yet, because initially we wanted to gather enough evidence to press charges in all the cases at the same time, so that the court would finally see him for who he really is (we are also working on the other six cases, but gathering evidence requires a lot of time). Unfortunately, your request to release him prevented us from wrapping up a sting operation that we had been planning for some time, and by which we wanted to obtain the proof of his guilt.

I do not know what prisoner seven two one is up to now, or how much freedom he enjoys, but of one thing I am certain: this man will do anything to avoid a return to prison. Anything. If you stand between him and his freedom, he won't hesitate even for a moment. We are talking about a ruthless sociopath, who will stop at nothing to escape the law. Human life doesn't mean anything to him.

He can't know he's going to get arrested again, because there is a justified concern that he will kill someone or try to take his own life. Prisoner seven two one is well aware of the fact that this time the judges will not allow themselves to be deceived, and will impose the capital punishment, that is determinate life sentence: imprisonment in the harshest penal colony along with forced labor in its helon ore mines.

My proposal is therefore as follows: Please keep prisoner seven two one until a new indictment is submitted to the court, even if he completes the assigned task before that. I have already spoken about this with Admiral Okonera, who has assured me that the command will recall their promise if the evidence proves to be sufficiently reliable, and this should not be a problem. Any day now we expect to get testimonies that will confirm most of the circumstantial evidence discovered so far.

I'm begging you not to do anything that would put you in danger. You must only make sure that prisoner seven two one doesn't know that he will be prosecuted and convicted again. At the time of the issuance of a new arrest warrant, we will send a set of codes to your cell of Security Department, activating a big surprise that we normally offer each of our wards. Only in this way can we be certain that this degenerate does not escape justice. And I can assure you that—if he sensed he was in for trouble—he would give you hell.

As you can see, Colonel, no action is required from your end. Just make sure that prisoner seven two one is busy until my people enter the stage—

Henryan swore internally. From the letter it was absolutely clear that the warden didn't intend to let it go. A glance at the attachments made the sergeant realize that Draccos had planned a really nasty surprise for him. Darski was going to get framed for the death of several suicides. The evidence had been manipulated so that everything pointed to the deliberate act of a third party, which the investigators believed him to be. Interestingly, he was also credited for the perpetration of misconduct in the cases he hadn't even heard of. All that didn't matter, though. The tribunal would perceive him through the prism of these documents, and that meant sure life imprisonment.

Ain't gonna happen, Darski thought, convinced that thanks to access to Rutta's private correspondence he could anticipate every move of the warden. But he soon felt anxiety emerging from the deepest recesses of his subconscious. He read the letter once again, and suddenly he broke out in a cold sweat. What exactly was this big surprise Draccos mentioned? What were the codes for? The ones this slimeball intended to send to the local esdees?

Henryan straightened up, trying to unravel the mystery, but nothing came to his mind.

He got up from his bunk and walked around the cabin for a moment, not knowing what to do with himself. He beamed only when he caught sight of the terminal. With a few flicks of his fingers he contrived a holographic image of Zaitsev.

"We need to talk," Henryan said.

The black gendarme, jolted out of sleep, rubbed his eyes fervently.

"At this hour?" he croaked, not hiding his surprise.

Darski realized it was the middle of the night. This case was really starting to get to him.

"No," he said hastily. "I'll see you in the mess hall. Six hundred hours sharp."

FORTY-TWO

THE XAN 4 SYSTEM, X-RAY SECTOR

09/15/2354

Following the shift changeover, he couldn't sit still. Zaitsev said in the morning that he would do his best, but couldn't vouch for the results. And this was now the most important thing for Henryan.

"Why don't you deign to look where you're supposed to, you gloomy yokel."

Darski flinched at the sound of a familiar female voice that came from behind him. He turned in a flash. The furious shifty little eyes of Dr. Godbless looked at him from above the console pad.

"I beg your pardon, madam, I'm putting you through to the colonel right now."

"To hell with your colonel," the head of scientific department snorted. "I want you to send cameras over all the Suhurian settlements."

"Over all of them?"

"Am I slurring?" she asked someone who was standing out of the holocameras' line of sight.

Both of them, however, heard the chorus-like response.

"This may take a while ..." Henryan noticed.

"Do you, soft willies in ridiculous jackets, know how to count at all?" Godbless bellowed. "What do you mean 'a while'? Five minutes, ten … ? Maybe fifteen?"

"Probably thirty—" Darski began cautiously.

"What?!" she screamed.

"Dr. Fukkuya—"

"To hell with Dr. Fu—" She didn't let him finish, but immediately fell silent, too, noticing that she had gone too far. "I'm not going to listen to any half-witted excuses. Cameras. Over all the settlements. Now!"

"I'll do what I can," Henryan promised, terminating the connection.

He located the available capsules with cameras, and then reassigned them quickly to specific positions. Dr. Fukkuya had asked earlier for a dozen additional nanobots to intensify the observation of the caves, where offerings were still being made. Valdez, who liked taking the easy way out, ordered to transfer the equipment from the nearby settlements, which meant that now Darski had to fetch the cameras all the way from the orbit. It had to take time—the first sets would appear above the savages' shacks in a few minutes, the last ones would reach the designated places after nearly thirty minutes. Henryan couldn't do anything about that. Just in case, however, he prayed that this time Godbless would get it through her head that the military wasn't at fault, and instead of telling him to go to hell, would crack down on her colleague.

FORTY-THREE

THE SUPREME SUHUR stopped in front of the pen, looking down at a dozen nestlings, which crouched under the soaring totem of the clan. Hundreds of almost identical bones had been strung on the long ribs of a zekkel. Each of them had been taken from the body of a warrior, who died a glorious death in battle or was killed while hunting. Commemoration was denied only to those who died in the killing pits or didn't last long enough to undergo the rite of passage. Every other member of the clan left behind a lasting trace: a single bone, adorned with an ornament praising his lineage and heroic deeds. Few smooth bones belonged to the young Warriors of the Bone, who lost their lives soon after leaving the pen, having been killed in the first battle or mangled by animals while learning to hunt.

Tore Numa-Reh, eyeing the nestlings, noticed that the warriors who'd watched the fires burning beyond the circle of bone shacks started to gather behind him, hastened by the densha.

"It's time," he rumbled, lifting his arad. "Prepare the stones! Open the pen!"

The accompanying mennites started to pull the honbut ribs sticking out of the rock-hard ground.

They kept throwing them on the clattering pile, until they made an opening wide enough for the densha to get inside. The warrior stigmatized with dried pelchavkas rushed past the Supreme Suhur, covering his eyes with the thicker eyelids, as tradition dictated.

"Take your pick," ordered Tore Numa-Reh.

The selection happened in the blink of an eye. The four smallest nestlings from the last breeding, deemed too young to be subjected to the ritual cutting, let alone burning, had been separated from the rest. Commending the priest's choice, the chief of the clan called him over.

"The caves or the altar?" he asked.

"The altar," Hakrad Redo-Tele decided after some thought.

Tore Numa-Reh tapped his arad in approval. The densha guided the little ones outside the pen, where the mennites accompanying the priest briskly led them toward the rock on which offerings were usually made.

The remaining nestlings stood in a row in the middle of the pen, with their palps toward the bone totem. The Supreme Suhur gave another signal, and the youngsters left the shelter, in which they had been staying since being cut out from the pelchavkas of their carrier. It was time for them to undergo the rite of passage, after which they would be recognized as full members of the clan and would be able to take part in the upcoming decisive battle.

They were divided into pairs, two per each bonfire. When everything was ready, the Supreme Suhur once again tapped his arad on the rock-hard ground.

The Warriors of the Bone, waiting behind the shacks, removed the carved flat stones from the embers and mounted them quickly to the bone handles. Without waiting for further instructions, they approached the nestlings and pointed the ritual stones at them. Then, after Tore Numa-Reh tapped his arad once again, the nestlings stepped forward as one, pressing their torsos against the hot pieces of rock. The burned skin sizzled, and this was the only sound that could be heard until the next tap of the arad. Afterwards, the nestlings stepped back and froze again. On their bodies, just below the third hand, appeared a clear pyroglyph with the symbol of the clan. The first one of hundreds that would cover all their skin, except the parenchyma.

The ceremony continued, accompanied by the tapping of the arad and the sizzling of the burned skin, which the densha had been hardening for some time, making cuts every now and then, first gently, then harshly. Thanks to this, the nestlings could now withstand the contact with the red-hot stones, although they still suffered pain.

In the middle of the ceremony, after another command of the Supreme Suhur, a thin whistle could be heard over the sizzle. The chief of the clan pointed with his hand to a youngster who could not stand the pain. A mennite standing closest to him pulled both masticators out of the sheath and lowered them upon the adolescent's body in a fluid movement. The massive weapon raked the skin and shattered the still delicate bones, sending brown splashes of gore in every direction. One blow was all that was needed to kill the unworthy. The densha immediately pulled the corpse away so that nothing would disturb the ceremony anymore.

———

"Sergeant Pryde—?"

Henryan looked up from the display, hearing someone's voice behind him.

A slender woman in a jumpsuit of medical services stopped by his workstation. The plaque adorning her flat chest showed a name "Bonicelli."

"Yes," he decided to help her out. "Sergeant Teddie Prydein-wraig. What is it?"

She held out her hand with a reader in it.

"Today at eighteen twenty, you must show up in the medical block 74C for a checkup. Attendance required."

"I think there has been some sort of mistake." Henryan faked surprise, noticing the lieutenant's curious glance. "I underwent a series of tests immediately after arrival."

The medic shrugged.

"Maybe, maybe not. Here is the request. Please acknowledge the receipt."

Henryan pressed his thumb on the screen held by the medic, and then downloaded the document to his reader, glancing at the superior, who had already approached his workstation. When the medic walked toward the exit, Valdez held out his hand.

"I don't understand ..." Henryan said, showing him the checkup request.

"Maybe it's them," the lieutenant suggested.

"Gods?"

"Who else?" Valdez leaned over the console and lowered his voice. "Give it a try. Maybe they want to contact you. Discreetly."

"But—"

"But me no buts, Sergeant," Valdez said loudly, straightening up. "You must show up for the checkup. That's an order."

"And what about my work?" Henryan asked.

Valdez patted his pocket where he kept a crystal with the tracker.

"I know how to install it. I'll be checking the terminals until you come back from the MedDep."

"If you insist ..."

He took the reader from the superior, who turned, heading back toward his workstation.

"Lieutenant!" Darski called after him.

"Yes?"

"Can I ask you something?"

"Sure."

"What's this ceremony all about?" Henryan pointed to the display.

The deputy commander looked at him in surprise, but a moment later, his eyes showed a glint of understanding.

"Right, you haven't seen yet how they make Easter eggs out of them." Valdez turned back, leaned on the partition, and then began to explain, "That's their rite of passage. No Suhur becomes a Warrior of the Bone until he goes through a few rituals. Sometime after they are placed in a pen, their guardian, I mean the one that doesn't get back to—how shall I put it—"

"I know who you mean," Henryan said.

"Yes, yes …" the lieutenant muttered, momentarily distracted, and then continued, "The first ritual is, as we call it, making Easter eggs. A densha cuts the skin, first very shallowly and gently, and then, when the wounds heal and scars harden, again, but deeper and harsher. It may seem cruel, but if you look at it from practical point of view, you will understand they very much need it. Suhurs don't know medicine. A wounded warrior will either get better by himself, before his body weakens enough for the tahars to devour him, or he will perish. Their exoskeleton doesn't develop until later, so this is the only way for young Suhurs to become more resistant, if only to bites, and don't forget that nearly all Suhurian critters are poisonous. At the same time a densha teaches them to control pain. You've seen what happened to the one who couldn't stand it, haven't you?"

Darski nodded. He still had that picture in his head. The adolescent was killed in a flash, and although many Suhurs witnessed it, none even flinched.

"That's how they treat every nestling which is a disappointment to a clan," Valdez concluded.

"And what about the little ones that were taken somewhere?" Henryan asked.

The lieutenant's face darkened.

"They will be sacrificed," he replied after a moment's silence.

"How come? Why?"

"You see, Pry ..." Lieutenant Valdez began, but then stopped as if he was lost for words. "Let me put it this way. They realize that any day now they will have to fight a decisive battle. They are primitive, but not stupid. They know that this time they have no chance of winning, and that the enemy will butcher all survivors. So they prefer to zap the vulnerable nestlings themselves."

"And if by some miracle they win?"

Valdez shrugged.

"If they win, they will live on, not feeling any remorse. Don't judge them by your own standards, Sergeant. They differ from us. Not only in appearance."

FORTY-FOUR

HENRYAN APPEARED in the waiting room of the medical block 74C a few minutes ahead of time. Apart from him, there were several unknown to him soldiers and technicians in the brightly lit room. At eighteen twenty sharp the name "Prydein-wraig" flashed over the door of one of the offices, so he went inside, looking around uncertainly.

An inconspicuous looking blonde with a fair complexion was standing by the diagnostic table. *Dr. Ashnalia Gupta*, the plaque read. She smiled politely, reaching out for his reader. Henryan didn't give it to her right away, but it had no effect on the doctor's attitude.

"Easy, Sergeant Darski. I don't know the password, you don't know the countersign, or the other way round, but you can trust me." This time the reader changed hands. "What's bothering you?"

"I would like to run a full scan."

"What are we looking for?"

"Everything that deviates from the norm. Extra implants, foreign bodies, modifications. Also on a nano-scale."

She pursed her lips, and then bit the lower one.

"It goes far beyond the scope of a routine checkup," she said after a moment's thought.

"Zaitsev must've explained everything to you, right?"

"Have you told him more than you have told me?" she asked, giving him a condescending smile of a medic.

"I can't say more than I know myself," he began anew. In his opinion, he sounded sincere enough. "Thanks to you, I got to know that the warden of the penal colony, where I did time, wants to bust my balls. To this end, he will send some codes to the Security Department. I want to find out what he is going to activate with them."

"Well, well. A bit of intellectual effort and we have specifics. This narrows it down, because we can rule out any biological modifications." She turned to the diagnostic table. "Please undress and lie down."

He took off his jumpsuit, then the underwear, and lay down naked on the cool table. The soft surface of the medical equipment adapted to fit the shape of his body. The blonde stood at the console behind Henryan's head. A moment later the hemispherical cap of the scanner was lowered, and the exam began. Three consecutive scans, each more accurate than the last, took a minute at most. Before Henryan could fully relax, he felt a slight burning sensation in his right forearm, and suddenly the blinding glare surrounding him began to fade slowly.

"You can dress now," the blonde said flatly, when the scanner was lifted to the ceiling.

Henryan sprang down to the floor, and a moment later stood in front of the woman, zipping his jumpsuit.

"There is nothing in your body that shouldn't be there. I'm talking about implants, chips, and so on. At least on a macroscale. To be sure, I injected you with nanoanalyzers that within a day will scan your body at the cellular level. Don't worry; you'll excrete them within the next twenty-four hours."

"But there must be something ..." Henryan insisted.

"Sergeant," the doctor pouted, "I am not blind, and this

station is equipped with the latest-generation scanning equipment. Nothing can hide from it. The only foreign body in your
organism is a standard medical chip that—"

Darski grinned.

"Can you run diagnostics on this little sucker?"

She eyed him as if he'd asked if she was hiding a third breast
in her armpit.

"Yes."

"Shall we … ?"

"We shall."

"Do I have to undress again?"

She burst out laughing.

"If you feel the need to expose to women, then go ahead.
Although it would be strange with the high doses of sex-
suppressors they give the employees and soldiers here."

He shook his head.

"I'm not an exhibitionist," he declared.

"In that case, just sit down over there and tilt your head." She
pointed to another piece of medical equipment.

Henryan settled in a high-back chair, which after activation
forced him to touch his chest with his chin.

"Just a minute …" the doctor said. "One more second …
There."

"Got it?" Darski asked, still doubled over uncomfortably.

"Yeah …" she said.

"And?" He tried to move, but the stronger he pressed the
headrest, the greater resistance he felt. "Hey! Can I get out of
here?"

"Oh!" The chair straightened simultaneously with her sigh,
releasing the patient. "I'm sorry, I switched off for a
moment—"

"No worries." Henryan shook his head as if to check he could
still move it. A moment later, he saw the woman's face and
paled, too. "What is it?"

The blonde swallowed loudly before she spoke.

"What you have in your head looks like a normal medical chip, but it's certainly not that."

"I don't understand."

"I got hooked up to it, but when I turned on the analyzer ..." Her voice faltered. "This thing not only didn't allow to be explored, but also blocked access to my equipment for me."

"How is this possible?" Seeing that the doctor shakes her head, deep in thought, he repeated a little louder and more forcefully, "How is this possible?"

The second time, he pulled her out of her stupor.

"It must be some kind of top-secret military technology. I've never seen anything like this."

"What does it do?"

She looked at him mockingly.

"Reads your mind, washes, cooks, and if you are naughty, it will turn your organs into jelly."

"Are you making fun of me?"

"You have started this!" she snapped. "I said clearly that I had never seen anything like this."

She was right; he acted like a fool.

"I'm sorry ... But I need to find out what it is and how to block it."

"I can't help you with that." She shrugged.

"Perhaps you know someone who could help me?"

The doctor thought for a long moment.

"Maybe—"

"Who?" Henryan cut in.

"One of our technicians," she answered after a moment's hesitation. "You can trust him. I'll arrange a meeting for you."

"But when?" Darski burst out. "I can't get away from work again. Especially to go to the technical department. Or should I ask the superior for a day off, because I have to change the oil in my head? I don't think it would work. And in my free time I have extra duties to perform as punishment, also under the supervision of Lieutenant Valdez. He might get suspicious."

It was only part of the truth. He wanted this to be done as soon as possible.

"In that case I'm very sorry, but—"

"It's one of the med techs, if I understood you correctly?" When the doctor nodded, he asked her, "Call him in to repair the analyzer."

"He is off duty now," she said.

"So what?" Henryan was not to be deterred. "All other technicians are certainly busy, and you have a patient on the table and can't complete the examination …"

She looked at him strangely, as if he was inducing her to commit sin.

"Are you always so resourceful?" she asked, reaching for her comlink.

"Only when I'm in a tight spot," he answered, knowing that the woman wouldn't understand this archaic saying anyway.

———

"It's a no go," the technician summoned by Ashnalia threw in the towel.

This one was white for a change, even though he had a New Russian name. A big blond man with a round face and large hands darted his fingers across virtual keyboards with such grace as if he were a virtuoso giving a laser-harp concert. All his efforts were, however, in vain. The chip defended itself against every attempt of interference with its contents. And counterattacked, if only it was given a chance.

"Are you sure?" Henryan asked, although he knew the answer.

"I'm positive," Makarkady confirmed. "Someone went to great lengths to protect this little gizmo. Someone with a lot of money and a lot of time, or many clever people at their disposal."

"You mean the government," the doctor concluded.

"Or the Admiralty," the technician added, picking up his equipment.

"Fry the damn thing," Henryan asked the man, grabbing his arm.

The technician looked at him, amused.

"Have you seen the chip?" he asked, when the grip on his arm grew stronger. Darski shook his head. "Show him, Ashnalia."

The medic stretched the scanner's display and a moment later, all the three of them saw a holographic image of the inside of the patient's skull. Zooming in limited the field of vision to the occiput and a cylindrical object stuck inside it, from which dozens of thin tendrils protruded, entangling a large part of the lobe of the brain.

"You fry the chip, you fry yourself," the technician said.

"I'd rather fry myself than wake up in the Sturgeon Belt again." Henryan looked at him pleadingly.

"I'm sorry, my friend, I don't know what belt you are talking about, or who this Sturgeon person is, but I'm not able to help you. This technology is vastly superior to anything I'm familiar with. If it weren't for the serial numbers, I could think Aliens tagged you." He turned to the medic. "Time for me to go," he said, and walked out, leaving her alone with the desperate sergeant.

Ashnalia walked over to the diagnostic chair.

"You should go, too, Sergeant. You've been here much longer than necessary. If the esdees keep an eye on you, they will notice that."

"Sure, I understand." Henryan jumped down onto the floor grid, and walked toward the door with no word of farewell.

———

He dragged himself to his cabin just before the curfew. He hardly ate anything in the mess hall, because whenever he thought about Draccos, appetite always left him.

The warden wants to get me at any cost as if he made it a point of honor. And he made sure beforehand to have the advantage over me … Henryan thought.

He felt powerless. Every time he thought he saw a light in the tunnel, the brightness turned out to be a sign of another, even greater threat.

Why is the fate out to get me? Darski thought, opening the door. *Is it just because I killed an innocent man—?*

Suddenly, he realized that something was wrong.

The lights were on in the cabin. He gulped and stepped over the doorstep. By the computer console, he saw a familiar figure of a bald man in a black suit and synthetic leather coat. The surprise guest leaped to his feet, raising his hands in an apologetic gesture.

"What did I tell you, you clone-of-a-bitch?!" Darski hissed. "By coming here, you sealed your—"

"It's not what you think!" the man interrupted him.

The esdee's plaintive tone surprised Henryan. He would have expected anything but such reaction. But then his nervousness returned.

"I said clearly that if I ever see your snout again …" He took out the headreader from his pocket.

"Wait, let me explain," the esdee begged.

"And what is there to explain?"

"I didn't have a choice. If I hadn't showed up, starting tomorrow you would have another investigative team to worry about," the esdee answered, clipping his words.

"What?" Henryan was too confused to understand him properly.

The esdee repeated everything slower, and added at the end, "If I suddenly let you off the hook, my superiors will realize that something is wrong. Contrary to what you might think, they are not stupid. That's why we have to see each other from time to time, so that they won't get suspicious. We don't have to talk if you don't want to. I'll wait a few minutes and leave."

Darski lowered his hand, and the headreader went back to his pocket.

"If it's another of your bullshit stories, whatever you're up to, I will bust your balls no matter what."

"I don't bullshit you. I want to play it as calmly as possible. The battle is only a few days away, and then each of us will go his own way."

Henryan shuffled to the bunk and fell heavily on it.

"A few days? How many exactly?" he asked, feigning indifference.

"It seems that the sampo-sithu's army will reach the Valt Aram in six days, so the final battle can be expected as soon as next week."

A week. Draccos will get the warrant in—Henryan recalled the correspondence he'd been reading last night—in two, maybe three days. A day later the esdees will get the codes, with which they will be able to activate the chip, and take control over his brain at the first opportunity. In any case, one thing was certain: they won't bust him until the colonel needs him.

Henryan wondered briefly whether he should blackmail the esdee further and force him to give away the codes, but on reflection he realized that he wouldn't gain much this way. Dodgy Draccos would contact the commander of the local SD and not the subordinate officer, even if he'd been appointed as the guardian angel of his victim. The dumb, bald esdee didn't need to know about the existence of the codes till the very end; the station's network was omnipresent, thus activating the malicious chip could be done from anywhere, also from the command room of the Security Department.

He considered a number of scenarios for some time, but always came to the same conclusion: he was screwed, finally and irrevocably. Sitting on the bunk and staring at the grim, silent esdee, he made the final decision. He knew which solution he would choose. He also knew how it all would end.

"Time for you to go," he said, standing up.

The esdee nodded, and immediately headed to the exit. However, he stopped in front of the door, then glanced fearfully over his shoulder. He looked dejected.

"Can I ask you something?" he said, a little shakily.

"Don't push your luck—"

"Just one question. Unrelated to the case."

Darski nodded. He would do anything to get rid of this scumbag. Not only from his cabin, but also from his life.

"Rap it out, and then get the hell out of here."

"I wonder why you hate esdees so much. After all, your brother—"

Henryan's face flushed hotly.

"Never, I repeat, never mention my brother, you wimpy clone-of-a-bitch. He wasn't like you and your minions from counterintelligence. The fact that you are wearing a black coat doesn't make you a true SD officer. Do you want to know how I see you? You're just an informer, a rat who loves to torment the defenseless, so please be so kind as not to desecrate the memory of the hero, who died on duty, fighting the real bandits."

The esdee, red in the face, slipped out through the door without one word.

FORTY-FIVE

THE XAN 4 SYSTEM, X-RAY SECTOR

09/16/2354

The next morning Henryan jumped out of his bunk as the reveille was sounded. He felt strange, but it was not until much later that he realized what had changed. He felt surprisingly well. Although he couldn't say that he exuded humor, all the tension was gone, having dropped like the pressure in an open airlock. The horrible, depressing thoughts had also left him. No, actually, they hadn't. They were still embedded in his head, but no longer crushed him with their weight, nor caused depression.

He was so relieved because he had made the final decision. So far he had been flailing in the dark. Wading through the maze of fate, he found himself caught in one dead end after another, turned back and continued looking blindly for the way out, because he firmly believed that against all odds he would find it, that it was out there somewhere. Today, he at last woke up in a place that looked like a long straight alley, where there were no spurs, or turnoffs. He didn't need to strain anymore. The destination of his life journey was clear, and for the first time in a very long time it was within sight. All he had to do was to go straight ahead, without worrying about anything ...

And that was exactly what he was going to do. But he was still missing one crucial piece of the puzzle. As soon as he found it, his explosive surprise would be all set.

FORTY-SIX

THE XAN 4 SYSTEM, X-RAY SECTOR

09/19/2354

Three days later the punishment was over. As promised, Valdez assigned him to jobs that had been done previously by other soldiers, so Henryan could laze in the afternoons, disappearing in the lower-level cabins prepared for minor parliamentarians, or—if he didn't want to sleep at that particular time—he could work his way through the allocated area and check whether his colleagues had done everything right.

A few hours before the end of the last penal shift he fell on a soft bunk with every intention of sleeping through the rest of his sentence. Before he could close his eyes, though, he heard a melodious signal coming from the corner of the dim room. He leaned on one elbow, squinting, as if that could help. A buzzer of the comlink mounted in the console? Here? Impossible. This level was uninhabited, and everyone at the station knew it perfectly well.

Henryan walked over to the console, surprised, but curious. He hesitated, but after another importunate buzz he put his thumb on the cool glassy sheet. The holopad came alive, and soon an iridescent familiar bust appeared above it.

"Hello, Sergeant," a mechanical voice said.

A robot called him. That is, the robot! Or rather, one of Gods …

"You're out of your mind!" Henryan muttered in disgust. "I bet the esdees can already see this connection—"

"Don't be so quick to make a new bet," his interlocutor cut in. "You lost the last one. Do you even remember what the stake was?"

The mechanical voice remained neutral, but Darski was pretty sure that whoever was using a voice changer had a good laugh at his expense.

"There was no bet," he grumbled. "What do you want?"

"You know what. Your time is up. I'm waiting for your answer. You've seen Rutta's correspondence. Now you know what awaits you." Henryan nodded. "All right then, in that case help us. It won't change your situation, but—"

"No." Henryan's answer was short and sweet.

"No?"

"What do you expect to accomplish by sabotaging Gurds' actions?" Darski asked, barely hiding his irritation.

"We're going to stop the destruction of one of the three intelligent races that exist in the known Universe," the conspirator said.

"Propaganda bullshit."

"And at the same time, the purest truth. These beings did nothing to deserve extinction."

"The same sad fate awaits all species. Us, too. Maybe even sooner than we think."

"Maybe …" the mechanical voice admitted after a moment's thought. "But—"

"But me no buts," Darski cut in. "Suhurs will be erased from the surface of Beta. If not today, then tomorrow, in a month, or in a few years' time. Saving them now, you'll cause a hundredfold greater suffering on both sides of the conflict.

"As it happens, a few days ago I tried to intervene, with the commander's knowledge and consent. Before we secured the external transmitters, I'd sent a message to the savages in the caves, hoping that this would terminate the carnage going on before our very eyes. You know how it ended. I saved a few youngsters who would anyway die in a few days. Thousands of inkblots were turned into food for some horrendous creepy-crawlies. Do you want to watch holos of this feast? As far as I know, it hasn't finished yet, and it's going to continue for a long time, because some of the creatures living in the underground tunnels don't kill their victims right away ..." He paused to take a breath.

"Yes," the conspirator said, taking advantage of the moment's silence. "It's true that Suhurs are disgusting, cruel, ruthless, and devoid of higher-order emotions known to humans. But this is just one side of the coin. You are looking at the problem from a human perspective. And that's a mistake. A serious mistake."

"And what perspective are you looking from?"

There followed a prolonged silence. In the end, the robot spoke again.

"From the perspective of a doomed race."

"And why not through Gurds' eyes?" Henryan asked, perfectly serious.

"Maybe because Gurds don't have any eyes," the conspirator answered, and before Henryan could attack him, he added, "It was a joke. A sick joke. Seriously speaking, though, it's Gurds who are bad guys here."

"In your opinion their conquests differ substantially from the conquest of the Aztec Empire or colonization of North America?" Darski pressed his point.

His interlocutor hesitated.

"I don't get you," the conspirator said in a mechanical, neutral voice.

"And therein lies your problem, or rather the problem of your whole group." Henryan snorted. "You react automatically, not thinking in a broader context."

"Explain to me, then, what this broader context is."

The sergeant laughed.

"I'm afraid this time I won't be able to meet the challenge. Although it is not entirely my fault—"

"Try anyway," the mechanical voice encouraged him.

"Well ..." Darski sank into a deep chair provided specifically for some VIP. "For starters, let me just explain one thing. My father taught history at the sector's academy, hence my knowledge of the antiquity and quite unusual perception of the problem. With the knowledge of history, I have a broader view. I know, for example, that similar cultures existed on Earth at some point."

"Let's not go back to prehistoric times."

"I didn't know that the nineteenth century was 'prehistory,'" Henryan mocked him.

The hologram still showed the robot's blank face. Darski regretted that he couldn't see his interlocutor at this moment. Trying to recover from shock, they must have had this look on their face ...

"What are you talking about?" the Gods' leader asked.

"Aboriginal peoples of Australia. Look it up on Galactopedia, it's worth it."

This time the silence was even longer. Eventually, however, Henryan again heard the same mechanical voice.

"I can see some similarities ..."

"Etruscans, Tasmanians ... In the history of Humankind you will find dozens, if not hundreds of peoples that became extinct, or were wiped out by their better adapted neighbors."

"That's true, but they were all human beings, belonging to a single species that has survived to this day."

"That's why I didn't say you were wrong, but that you lack a broader perspective. If you knew what I do, you might realize that the fall of Suhurs is inevitable. They will share the fate of dinosaurs, saber-toothed tigers, mammoths, and millions of other species that once inhabited planets known to us."

The leader of Gods was silent.

"But given half the chance—" he began after a long pause.

"You can't uproot tens of thousands of years of tradition in an instant. It would have to take many generations, and no one's going to give Suhurs that much time. They will share the fate of the Tasmanians, except that they won't be able to crossbreed with the invaders, so they won't melt away in the new society, but rather get annihilated. If you stop their destruction today, Gurds will finish the job in a few years, when we finally take off, leaving them to their own devices."

"What you say makes a lot of sense, but—" The person hiding behind the mechanical voice suddenly paused.

"But?" Henryan asked encouragingly.

"We didn't do all this so that Suhurs could keep slaughtering Gurds. Frankly, we have a great idea how to solve the problem."

"Would you like to tell me more about it?" Darski thought he would be brushed off once again, but he was mistaken.

"We are going to talk some sense into both sides. Create a huge hologram of gods, who will order the two races to stop warfare … Religion is a powerful force offering leverage over all areas of life. Maybe this would stop the Warriors of the Bone from attacking inkblots—straight away, not in a few generations."

"You forget one thing. Gurds don't believe in supernatural beings. That's why I don't think they will respect the order of 'gods'—especially those who won't be able to do anything to them if the conditions of the truce are violated."

"I know. Some of us share your doubts. We decided, however, that it is better to do something, anything, than passively watch the destruction of Suhurs."

"The road to hell is paved with good intentions," Henryan said sententiously, rising from his chair.

"You won't help us, then?" the conspirator asked.

"On the contrary," Darski said. "I am doing you a huge favor by protecting your asses from spending the rest of your lives in orange outfits."

"Don't exaggerate. Seifert got only six months in a minimum security penal colony."

That was something new. Henryan looked at the hologram through half-closed eyes. Seeing the prisoners in orange overalls, he assumed that all of them got long prison sentences and ended up in a place resembling the Sturgeon Belt. Apparently, he was wrong.

His interlocutor noticed his surprise, and added, "Rutta made us all to watch the sentencing."

Henryan pulled himself together.

"Intervention in the fate of the upcoming battle will be judged by Security Department, which means zero tolerance and longer sentences," he said.

"What do you care?"

"Right. Whichever way you turn, your ass is always behind you," Henryan admitted.

"Indeed, picturesquely termed. And very accurately …"

"Don't try to outtalk me," Darski cut in. "I said no."

"And if I said that I am able to capture these codes—"

"I would consider it a lie. We both know that Draccos is going to send the codes to the local head of the Security Department, and you don't have any leverage with him. You can't do a thing. The verdict is hanging over me, and I know it. That's why I'd rather spare you all my fate."

"You will make things harder for us, but that's it. You can't stop us—"

Henryan laughed.

"I've stopped you already. This conversation proves it. There won't be any holograms appearing over the battlefield. For your information: the old man has deployed several jammers over the Valt Aram, so even if by some miracle you manage to send a signal to the devices, which you have hidden there earlier on the quiet, you won't activate anything. Give up playing God; even He didn't create a sensible world."

With these words, Henryan reached for the switch.

The hologram vanished into thin air, when the robot was beginning to say something. To be sure, Darski disconnected the power supply. Going back to the bunk, he smiled to himself. Thanks to this conversation, he found the last piece of the puzzle.

FORTY-SEVEN

THE XAN 4 SYSTEM, X-RAY SECTOR

09/20/2354

That day was supposed to be the beginning of the end. If Draccos hadn't been bluffing, the warrant should appear in the colonel's mailbox with the next message bundle. Courier ships reached the entry point of Xan 4 twice a day: at oh six hundred and eighteen hundred standard time. The transfer between the entry point and Beta took another two hours. There was nothing of interest in the morning mail, though; therefore Henryan could calmly wait for the end of his shift, observing the situation on the planet. And there was a lot happening there.

The sampo-sithu, or the leader of all leaders, arrived at Treb'aldaledo two days earlier and was now leading the Gurdian armies toward the Valt Aram. He wasn't in a hurry, knowing that the victory was certain. One hundred thousand inkblots armed with the most modern firearms could not lose to three times smaller forces of Suhurs.

The clans, alerted by the scouts, gathered slowly on their side of the river. The Congregation, deliberating almost constantly, finally decided that the enemy had to remember how the last of the bravest departed from this world. Making Gurds cross the riverbed seemed the ideal way to inflict heavy losses on them.

Suhurs could not know, however, that the enemy wasted no time, and that their latest-generation weapons had now a much greater range and accuracy than the previously used firearms. From a human point of view, the Gurdian weapons were still primitive, but many Earthian armies of the mid-nineteenth century would give a lot for the rifles and cannons constructed in Gurdu'dihan. That's how they had been classified, although Darski couldn't see any similarities with the archaic products of Mauser, or Springfield Armory.

The riverbed, though wide, was no longer an obstacle to shooters, especially that Gurds possessed aircraft—a kind of zeppelins, or dirigibles—which floated thanks to the fruit of the lek'ter, one of the most common plants in Gurdu'dihan. Before the flight, large leather hulls were filled with tens of thousands of these strange fruits. The sectional structure of the lifting part allowed inkblots to survive even the heaviest fire. Lek'ter fruits were very durable, and the arrows released in the direction of airships pierced only a few at a time, not doing much harm, as it had happened in the case of Earthian balloons. The only problem was that lek'ter fruits maintained airtightness only for several hours after picking, so the aircraft filled with them couldn't harass the enemy for too long. Just filling the hulls took the airmen almost half of the available time, and then they had yet to reach the front line and retreat behind their own lines. Nevertheless, thanks to the plantations of lek'ter trees that savvy Blue-blooded had started on the plains on their side of the river, alag'terysms—as these pseudo-airships were called—would certainly create havoc in the ranks of the Warriors of the Bone.

Suhurs were screwed, just like Henryan, but their fate was not sealed yet, even if the probability of a turn of events favorable to them seemed very small.

Darski, fascinated, watched the march of long columns of Gurdian soldiers, who looked like characters from the pages of a ghostly fairy tale. The incredible ecosystem of Beta was so different from everything that people had found on the planets discovered so far, that he wasn't surprised by the enthusiasm with which Godbless and her colleagues explored the mysteries of both continents. Especially that the recently started excavations began to provide scientists with the evidence for existence of other, not less developed civilizations here in previous cycles. Henryan regretted that he would not be able to see the results from these studies. As recently as yesterday, Valdez told him that Gorelic, the head of the archaeological department, had made some breakthrough discoveries during excavations conducted in Gurdu'dihan. Everything pointed to the fact that in the previous cycle, the two continents were inhabited by a highly advanced race that could know technologies enabling interstellar travel, and all this more than five hundred million years before the first hominid stood upright.

Although the mission of this station wouldn't come to an end anytime soon, Henryan had no illusions: his fate was inextricably linked to Suhurs', and maybe not so much to them as to the upcoming battle, which would end the stage—of red flickering?

Henryan blinked, coming back to reality. Indicators on the hyper's panel flashed like mad. A quantum message … High priority … He glanced at the display. Quite a few hours remained till the evening transmission, plus this message had been sent from the Admiralty. A couple of gestures later he was positive that he was right. It was a cryptogram from the central sector's headquarters. He preferred not to think how much energy had been used to transfer this data packet over a distance of a thousand two hundred and sixty light-years.

For a moment he wondered if it was Draccos's doing, but soon rejected the idea. The scrooges from the Admiralty wouldn't support the crusade of a mad warden so generously. Especially since it was about an insignificant man, whose name didn't ring any bells, and who wouldn't have threatened the cushy jobs of the bigwigs, even if he had slaughtered half the crew of the station.

Henryan glanced at the lieutenant. Valdez looked surprised, too. The old man disappeared behind a wall of the force field as soon as he received the information about the transmission. For thirty seconds only the murmur of routine exchanges could be heard in the command center. None of the crew knew about the arrival of an urgent message. Only two people handled transmissions at this level: the deputy commander and the communications officer, which in this case meant Lieutenant Valdez and Sergeant Prydeinwraig.

It was the last thirty seconds of the lull before the storm, but for the time being only Rutta knew this.

Then, suddenly, came the sound of sirens, and red lights flashed throughout the room. Everyone broke their eyes from the displays. Red alert?

"Pry!" Valdez shouted a moment later, calling Henryan over. "The colonel wants us."

They ran up the stairs shoulder to shoulder, the barrier of the force field switched off when they reached the penultimate step, and turned back on when they barely passed it.

Rutta's face was gray. He looked at them as if he couldn't believe the message he had been sent.

"Is there a problem, sir?" the lieutenant asked him.

The colonel looked at him strangely.

"There is," he muttered. Then he swallowed loudly, and added, "A big one ... In a moment I will proclaim evacuation. Make sure the dunderheads serving under you don't panic and take care of all the procedures."

"We're evacuating the station?" Valdez asked.

"We're evacuating the whole system," the old man growled, turning his back to them. "You will soon receive the schedules sent by the Admiralty. Distribute them among your men according to the attached clearance key. And one more thing ... I don't want any delays, understood?"

They clicked their heels, saluted, but before they left the dais, the lieutenant asked again, "Is this an evacuation drill?"

Rutta turned slowly. He looked as if he wanted to curse them, but eventually he did not. When he spoke, they could barely hear his words.

"No. It's a war. We have been attacked by Aliens."

———

Returning to their workstations, they were as pale as their superior. The sirens no longer howled, but the emergency lights were still flashing. The confused crew looked in their direction, not knowing if these were unplanned maneuvers, or perhaps a disaster had happened. Darski and Valdez couldn't afford a mistake. They had two minutes to transfer the orders to their subordinates so that they could start implementing the evacuation procedures as soon as possible, which was not at all easy in the station of this size.

Henryan was done with his duties a few seconds before the deadline. He glanced toward the still busy lieutenant, and then looked at the dais surrounded by an opalescent wall of the force field. The chatter around him gradually faded, as the surprised soldiers were getting acquainted with the orders. All at once, pandemonium broke loose. Few men remembered to isolate their workstations, so in a moment they began to shout over one other in panic. Valdez had predicted as much. With one gesture he made all the workstations disappear behind the glittering energy barriers, and blissful silence returned.

Darski looked at the list of tasks, assigned to him. For the most part, they were of a technical nature. The transports of the Fleet were supposed to leave the anchorage in four hours. By this time, all equipment from the Beta's orbit would have had to be sent onboard them, including the Cerberus. Henryan kept checking off each item on his list, sending the codes and commands, and then making sure the devices reacted properly and moved toward the ships. The evacuation plan for this system had been developed many years before, when the observation of Beta's both civilizations began. The military liked to have procedures for every eventuality—and although they were rarely used, on that day they turned out to be really useful. The Admiralty bureaucrats had it worked out down to the tiniest detail, and the station's computers quickly generated the schedules for smooth execution of orders within the time limit. The only uncertain factor was, as usual, man. Specifically—Sergeant Darski.

The alarm messed up his plans. The elaborate scheme to leave with a bang would come to nothing if the evacuation went as smoothly as could be expected. But Henryan couldn't do anything about it. Any derogation from the schedule would be noticed by the system and reported to the superiors. He had to come up with something before the equipment he needed disappeared from the Beta's orbit—

Suddenly, the lush green light lit up on his console. He glanced at the display. Godbless. No wonder she began storming the center. She got cut off from Beta as soon as the first orders came. Henryan reached for the key, but he didn't touch its surface, shimmering in the air. He withdrew his hand, smiling to himself. This might be interesting …

She appeared in the command center a few minutes later, marching unusually briskly for almost three hundred pounds of flesh and fat. She was followed by her inseparable entourage in blue jumpsuits of the scientific department. Her arrival was announced by dreadful racket at the entrance. The gendarmes quickly gave up when throwing insults, she made them realize that it was her who commanded this operation, including the military. However, she soon felt the bitter taste of defeat when it came to climbing the stairs, although none of her ass-kissers dared to overtake their boss. As soon as she paused to rest about halfway up, Rutta deactivated the force field. He stood with his legs wide apart, blocking access to the dais as if he wasn't going to let the scientific plague into his sterile kingdom.

Henryan didn't know whether Godbless got red in the face with effort, or rather with rage.

"Are you out of your fucking minds, you clowns?" she gasped venomously. "What's the meaning of this? I demand—"

"We've received an evacuation order," the colonel interrupted her unceremoniously.

"Get lost then, even to the neighboring galaxy, but leave me my equipment!" Godbless immediately went on the offensive.

"The equipment is owned by the Admiralty." Rutta couldn't let her have her way, even if she begged him on her knees, and he was not going to.

"You got your shit mixed up, you dingbat in a ridiculous hat!" Godbless roared, apparently not realizing that the war with Aliens completely changed the balance of power, and her situation.

But Colonel Rutta knew exactly what was coming. And that day he had a stronger hand. He thus decided to put everything at stake. He raised his hand, momentarily silencing the head of the scientific department. She paused, surprised, but immediately opened her mouth again to start another tirade.

"According to you, saying that I am old, ugly, and not very bright, would be an insult or rather the confirmation of the truth?"

His question was so absurd that she needed a moment to understand what he meant.

"Answer, Dr. Godbless. Please …" he urged.

"What is this nonsense?" she grumbled, still confused.

"I would like to hear the answer to my question." Rutta seemed the epitome of tranquility, which further enraged her.

"According to me, this description fits you perfectly!" she snapped, turning to her entourage.

The scientists behind her laughed unconvincingly.

"Excellent!" Rutta was pleased as if he'd heard a compliment. "Then you won't be offended, Dr. Godbless, if I tell you to get your old, fat, and sagging ass out of here! Get the fuck out of my command center!"

She just stood there and boggled. Henryan had never seen her speechless before. Dr. Godbless's face turned purple, then blue in the blink of an eye. He even began to fear that this was the first sign of a heart attack or a stroke, but the med on her forearm was still green, although now much paler than a moment before.

"What ... ?" she gasped. "What did you say, you twerp?" She was getting her groove back with each word. "Admiral Okonera will know all about it!"

"About the fact that you call him a clown in a ridiculous hat, too?" the colonel scoffed. "This will do you more harm than good, you old bag."

"It's outrageous. Outrageous!" Godbless shrieked. Her entourage looked equally indignant. "You will not get away with it, you turd! I'll destroy you! I will!"

"You have ten seconds to leave the command center." Rutta said casually.

"Or what?" she mocked, albeit a little less confident.

She was surprised by this sudden change of attitude of the usually docile colonel.

"Or you will be arrested and accused of sabotaging the important military operation," he explained, pointing to a platoon of gendarmes entering the command center at this very moment.

"But ... but ..." Godbless completely lost her head. "But we are doing extremely important research here. You can't ... I'm in charge here—"

"You were," Rutta corrected her. "With the outbreak of the war, the Fleet has taken over the command of all operations in deep space. That makes me commander in chief. We have to leave the system in eighteen hours."

"It's enough to deploy equipment to—"

"Get your head together, you dumb hag!" The colonel yelled at her, gesturing to the gendarmes to lead the intruders out. "Your … *our* equipment is going to the holds of the transports as we speak, because all our ships need to leave the Beta's orbit in less than four hours if we want to disappear from this system in time."

"And what about Suhurs?" she groaned before two gendarmes took her elbows.

"Who cares?!" Rutta snapped. Had it not been for the outbreak of the war, this evacuation would be his salvation. He no longer had to worry about Gods pulling a stunt on him at the end. He looked down at her triumphantly. "You have freezers full of their bodies and storerooms stuffed with artifacts. What else do you want? Haven't you seen enough death for the last six years? Let them at least die out in peace."

"It was you, you bastard!" she yelled as she fought to free herself from the gendarmes' grip. "I knew it!"

"Shut the fuck up, you moron!" he shouted, giving her tit for tat. "I had nothing to do with this asinine game, but I'll be honest with you: with your every visit here, with each rebuke via holo I was losing any will to catch the jackasses who were screwing with your research. Take this crone away!"

"Let me go!" she yelled when the gendarmes tried to get hold of her again. "Up clone's—Get off my ass, you—"

Rutta didn't let her finish.

"That's right, if you didn't have your head so far up your own ass, you would fit in a normal chair! Take Dr. Godbless to her cabin, pack her things, and put her onboard the first shuttle. And after reaching the *Nexus*, immediately lock her up in the brig."

She struggled and swore when she was being escorted away, and he followed her with his eyes, smiling as if he'd just won the first battle of the coming war. He nodded, looking in the direction of Valdez and Darski. Henryan decided it was the perfect moment to push forward his own agenda.

"Sir!" he called out, before the satisfied colonel returned to his seat.

"What do you want?" Rutta was once again the caustic, demanding jarhead he was.

"I have a little problem with some equipment, sir …"

"Report directly to my reader. In short order."

Darski had been prepared for it. The colonel received a short list, which contained one of the Cerberus's satellites and one capsule with nanocameras. In both the maneuvering thrusters couldn't be started.

A moment later a bust of the old man appeared on his holopad.

"The equipment which fails to reach the transports must be destroyed. See to that, Pry. No trace may remain of it."

"Yes, sir. Shall I report if I come across another failure?"

Rutta thought for a moment.

"No. I won't have time for this crap. Neither will Valdez. The Admiralty is prepared for some equipment losses. The priority is to evacuate people, ships, and the station itself. Understood?"

"Yes, sir!"

Henryan was delighted. He couldn't have heard better news. There was still a lot of equipment in orbit that he would need. His only regret was that the senators wouldn't see the surprise being prepared for them.

FORTY-EIGHT

TWO HOURS LATER, he got off the train. The corridors in his residential area were almost empty. Most of the staff had been evacuated to the hub, where all were now waiting in long lines for the shuttles, moving back and forth between the anchorage of the Fleet and the spaceport. The operation was running smoothly; if nothing disturbed it, in seventy minutes the observation deck would be automatically ejected, and replaced by a drive module, until now orbiting near the station. The gigantic structure will embark on a journey to the entry point before the last ship of the Fleet leaves the anchorage, except that before that, its deserted interiors would become the scene of the last act of a one-actor drama: the former captain, now a sergeant, who will do anything not to give satisfaction to his pursuer.

Walking along the corridors, Henryan smiled at his thoughts. Almost three centuries of space exploration. Several thousand star systems surveyed, more than a thousand inhabited planets, and no trace of alien intelligence. Then suddenly, in just a few years, and for him in less than two weeks, three civilizations appeared on the horizon. Two totally different and still quite primitive and the third one, about which virtually nothing was known—except that it was powerful enough to declare war on the race in command of the fiftieth part of the arm of the Galaxy.

Passing the entrance to the mess hall, he slowed down, then turned back. He still had a lot of credits on his card, and since he didn't have to spend them on extra energy, he could at least eat well. Unfortunately, it turned out that shutting down the station began with disconnecting the least necessary systems, which included food dispensers. *Tough luck,* he thought. But then again, I won't have time to get really hungry anyway.

Finally, he reached his cabin. This time he had to use an emergency code that the command center had issued to all crew, so that they could bypass the blockades activated by the evacuation procedures. Lost in thought, he didn't notice that it wasn't dark inside. He stopped only when he saw the esdee sitting at the console, as before.

"You again ..." Henryan muttered, feeling a hard ice ball starting to form in the pit of his stomach.

They're still after me, he thought. In the mad scramble during the evacuation, no one will notice that one of the soldiers disappeared without a trace. Damn them all! he cursed internally. I was so close ...

He glanced around quickly, looking for the other agents, but the esdee had come alone. Despite this there wasn't any trace of fear or humility in his face. Apparently, he planned to take his revenge for all the humiliation he'd endured.

"Where are your bitches?" Darski snapped, grabbing his headreader.

The esdee didn't respond. He just smiled friendly—friendly! —and indicated a chair.

"Time to talk openly," he said.

Darski didn't sit down. Instead he leaned out the door to see if Gunternest Poetze and the third esdee might hide in the corridor. He didn't see a soul.

"What do you want?" he asked, wondering frantically if he

could bite his tongue off like the prisoners, who were given a minute to commit suicide.

I have no choice, he thought. I'll have to do it, and do it fast before the esdee manages to activate the codes. I can't flee now because it would provoke his immediate reaction. But I can try to get him talking, and when he drops his guard for a moment—

"I told you." The esdee laughed sincerely, even cheerfully. "It's time to show the cards."

"If that's what you want …" Darski licked his lips. "Just remember: if something happens to me, some people will distribute the holo with your ratting snout."

"Do you think Annelly would do that to me?" The esdee looked really amused. "Sit your ass down and stop racking your brains how to finish yourself off before I immobilize you with the codes, abduct, and turn over to Draccos." Henryan was dumbfounded. Redhead worked for the Security Department? They led him by the nose from the beginning? All of it was just a wind-up? "You still don't know who I am." The esdee eventually sobered. "Haven't you figured out why you had to talk to this unfortunate hydroponic robot?"

"You didn't want me to recognize your voice," Darski answered, still clutching the headreader.

"You're finally starting to get it. And why didn't I want you to recognize my voice? Sit down before you reply. You have nothing to fear from me. If I'd wanted to use Draccos's codes, I wouldn't have waited until you came up with a way to kill yourself."

This time Henryan obeyed. He collapsed into the swivel chair in front of the esdee and lowered his right hand, which held the headreader with the recording discrediting his worst enemy at the station.

"If I'd recognized it, I would have thought it was a provocation."

"Warm, but still cold … All in all, you're right, but not

entirely. True, you would have said it was a provocation, but you would have been wrong."

Darski looked at him closely. He liked this conversation less and less. Either the esdee was playing games with him, or ...

"No, you can't be the leader of Gods," he whispered involuntarily.

"Why not?"

The sergeant didn't answer. He started getting confused.

"I don't know," he said helplessly.

"Haven't you wondered how I had access to the private correspondence of the old man? You're a better techy than Seifert, but you wouldn't have done much without my hints."

Henryan nodded absently. Suddenly, it became clear to him that all this must have been the work of someone who was not only good at what he was doing, but also well-connected. For example, the SD officer, investigating the colonel's case.

"What do you want?" Darski said, a little less aggressively.

"First, let me introduce myself. My name is Gunternest Poetze. Lieutenant Gunternest Poetze ..." He produced his ID. "Now you know that your little blackmail scheme wouldn't quite work if at some point you decided to do me harm."

"You knew ... you knew from the start," Henryan muttered after the first shock faded away. "Has Redhead been in on it, too?"

"Who?"

"Redhead. Annelly."

"She's not ... No. No one recruited by Seifert had any idea who commanded this operation. It was safer this way."

"For you," Darski said.

"Yes. Mainly for me. But for them, too. If they knew they were working for someone from the Security Department, they would probably shit themselves with fear. Pardon me, but you know how people react to us."

"Why?" Henryan asked, lowering his head.

"I'm not sure I understand your question."

"Why did you threaten me as an esdee if you wanted me to collaborate with Gods?"

Poetze didn't answer immediately, and when in the end he opened his mouth, he chose his words very carefully.

"I'm sorry about that. At first I thought I was dealing with a common criminal, a murderer, a degenerate. That's why you've been roughed up. Too hard, I have to admit, but you know how it is. I wasn't sure what Rutta was up to. I couldn't let him talk you around. But then, when I looked through your file and learned a bit about the Sturgeon Belt, I changed my mind. You are a very wise man, and a formidable opponent. Take this action in the medical sector for example. You planned it and executed it masterfully. If I hadn't known what you were planning, I'd probably have shat myself with fear."

He shook his head appreciatively.

Darski had been trembling all over for some time. The mention of the penal colony turned loose the demons in him.

"I've had enough, let me go …" he asked, his voice breaking.

"I'm not going to just stand there and watch you commit suicide," Poetze protested.

"You'd do me a huge favor—"

"Man, a war broke out. Aliens attacked several systems in the outer sectors, and here you are trying to feed me bullshit? You're an excellent soldier and communications expert. We will need people like you."

"I'm a murderer. I killed an innocent man."

"What the hell are you talking about?" the esdee moaned. "You took out one of the worst bastards that had ever worn the uniform of the Fleet."

"I've seen the report."

"What report?"

"From the investigation carried out by the Admiralty."

"Well? What was so bad about it?"

Darski shrugged.

"Read for yourself."

"I have. It was in your file."

"I don't understand …" Henryan looked at him suspiciously.

"The investigation against Renaud had been discontinued for lack of evidence, which had unfortunately flown away into space, but everything pointed to the fact that he was stuck up to his ears in drug trafficking. I also heard through the grapevine that the Admiralty considered reducing your sentence. But the case had been too strongly publicized by the media. Our admirals don't particularly like to admit their mistakes."

"You're lying."

"No, I'm not. I swear they are hard-boiled clones-of-bitches."

"You're lying about the report. I've seen it."

"Where?"

"Draccos showed it to me."

"And you believed him?!"

"I checked the logs—"

Henryan straightened up suddenly. He had checked the logs, but only the ones regarding the Admiralty's messages, not the report itself.

"Galacticunt!" He looked at Lieutenant Poetze. "What about the codes?"

"They arrived this morning along with the documents for the colonel," Poetze replied calmly, but seeing Darski's nervous expression, added immediately, "You have nothing to be afraid of. I deleted the documents, and secured the codes."

"But why? I said 'no' to you—"

"Who's 'you'?"

"Esdees … Well, Gods, too."

"It doesn't matter anymore. Especially to us … I mean, Gods," he clarified quickly. "You were quite right. I didn't see a broader perspective. Now I understand it, thanks to you. We are only human beings; we shouldn't play God."

Henryan shook his head.

"I learned a great deal from our last conversation, too," he admitted. "But to get back to these codes …"

The news of the fabricated report, which he intended to confirm at the earliest opportunity, once again changed his attitude toward life. An alley leading straight to death suddenly gained a lot of promising new turnoffs.

"I've intercepted them. You don't have to worry about them anymore."

"But I do. Draccos accused me of other murders, as you well know, since you've read his correspondence with Rutta. You want to let me go, but soon someone else can take your place. Someone who thinks differently."

"Relax. Although, in your head, you carry the technology developed by the Federation, we—I mean the Security Department—also know quite a bit about it." Poetze stood up, and started toward the door without waiting for Darski. "Get your stuff. After you've been transferred to the ship, you will report immediately to the counterintelligence cell of the DFS. We will deactivate the damn chip, since it's giving you the shits. We have another war to win even if we haven't managed to save Suhurs."

Henryan smiled to himself, but the esdee couldn't see it.

EPILOGUE

THE XAN 4 SYSTEM, X-RAY SECTOR

09/25/2354

That day, both suns of Beta rose one right after the other. First, the smaller disc of Thub emerged from the horizon, and a moment later the edge of the hotter Kored appeared over the hills. This was a sign that both sides had been waiting for. The Warriors of the Bone left the encampments set along the river, gathering together in fists that would stand behind the Supreme Suhurs of their clans. All were present. In the abandoned settlements, not watched by cameras anymore, remained only cleaved corpses of the sacrificed nestlings.

As the previously adopted strategy dictated, Suhurs gathered on their side of the river and silently watched the approaching army of the enemy. A swarm of blue-blooded soldiers marched staggeringly through the plains, in armors that shone dazzlingly in the rays of the two suns. It was a beautiful view, but only for people—Gurds didn't have eyes in the strict sense of the word, and the Suhurs' organ of vision registered totally different wavelengths. Neither party could therefore admire the sight. And even if they were able to, they would unlikely feel like it in the face of the upcoming battle.

Takeli'toko, the Quadrupeds' sampo-sithu, was approaching

the Valt Aram to end the war with the savage inhabitants of the conquered Suhurta; war that had been going on for a thousand floodings. Absorbing their chaotic ranks, stretched across the river over the distance of many wheel revolutions, he did not feel fear. His orderly troops possessed weapons that would crush the proud, though primitive natives. Cannons pulled behind the infantry, and bombs carried onboard alag'terysms would decimate the army of the enemy, and when the Warriors of the Bone eventually fell into disarray, he and the bravest of Gurds would traverse the river on rafts, prepared in advance, to vanquish those Suhurs who fought till the end. His only fear was that the enemy would give up and flee, seeing the overwhelming forces of Gurds, which would unnecessarily prolong the battle. But the final result was certain: a hundred thousand soldiers he led were followed by even more numerous support troops, brought over to the Valt Aram from other parts of the continent. The sampo-sithu left nothing to chance.

Takeli'toko would have been happy if he'd known the thoughts of the Supreme Suhurs. The Warriors of the Bone were well aware of their unfavorable position, but did not feel fear. And not because of the promises made to the young warriors by the Spirits of the Mountains. Seeing the mighty army, they quickly understood that this impending battle would be their last. All proud clans were prepared for it. None would step back. If they had to die, they would die with joy, taking with them so many enemies that the invader would remember their resistance long after the last skeletons of the fallen warriors would gray in the sun and become overgrown with knel.

Gurds had completed the preparations for the attack before the twin shadows of the sagr trees, growing on the riverbank, moved to the waterline. Rafts made of thick logs had been laid on the brink of the riverbed, and huge thunderous trunks had been positioned behind the first line. Also, the bulbous shapes of flying machines appeared in the sky, floating slowly toward the river over the infantry positions.

Both armies were only waiting for the attack orders. The piercing screech of the sampo-sithu was repeated by the commanders. The infantrymen aimed their weapons at the crowd of Suhurs waiting in silence on the other side of the river. The big hammers of the gunlocks were pulled away. The second screech of the commander in chief was drowned by the roar of multiple thunders.

Fifty-three thousand bullets and almost one hundred large-caliber missiles filled with flammable oil sped in the direction of the Warriors of the Bone, who stood motionless just like moments before. Fired from such a close range, the projectiles should have culled the proud clans. A single salvo could amount to thousands of casualties, death and wounded. And every Gurdian soldier would shoot another ten rounds before he was forced to reload.

That something was wrong both armies realized when the large-caliber missiles shattered midway, over the riverbed, as if they hit an invisible wall there. Oil splashes immediately took fire, and began to slowly flow down to the water, as if weightless. The second salvo met a similar fate. So did the third one. Not a single Warrior of the Bone was hurt, even though an avalanche of iron bullets continuously sped in their direction.

The sampo-sithu ordered a cease-fire when the first alag'terysms reached the river. The inconceivable barrier startled him, and frightened many soldiers who till now had believed implicitly in the effectiveness of their new weapons. Takeli'toko didn't understand how the primitive hunters could have erected an invisible wall capable of halting so many bullets, but he was certain he would find a way to overcome this obstacle. For example, over the top.

Gurdian aircrafts cautiously reached the place, where the oil was still burning, flowing slowly to the water. They passed the invisible wall effortlessly, and drifted farther toward the compact mass of the Warriors of the Bone. In just a moment the crews would be able to drop even more powerful bombs on the serried ranks of the enemy. The sampo-sithu closely watched their every move. Now! Rounded shapes broke away from the nacelles and began to fall on top of Suhurs, who were looking up, still motionless.

And again—halfway between the aircrafts and the ground—all the missiles cracked, the oil inside them took fire and hung over the clans, spilling wider as if Suhurs were protected by a solid roof, cast in a transparent material. At this point Takeli'toko thought that he might not win this battle at all. Something beyond his understanding was happening here; something heralded by the voices heard at night over Treb'aldaledo. Could it be true that the rumors of the Suhurs' powers weren't just a figment of imagination of the panicked farmers? Then why Gurdian armies, which had fought the Warriors of the Bone many times, had never encountered anything so inexplicable?

Seeing that the bombing was hardly effective, the commanders turned the alag'terysms back to their own riverbank.

———

Suhurs watched in silence as the hostile missiles crashed, first at one, then at the other barrier, as if they were stopped every time by gods or the tutelary beings. Tore Numa-Reh—entrusted by the Congregation with command against Gurds, as the battle was to take place on the land belonging to the clan of the Triple Pierced Shield—lifted his arad and struck it with all his might against the ground. His gesture was repeated by all Supreme Suhurs.

"The Spirits of the Mountains have kept their promise. They protect us with their supernatural power. Let's prove to them that we deserve the grace extended to us." He pointed with his arad to the opposite bank, reaching for the masticators with the other hand. "Let's attack the enemy! Let's see their blood stain the sacred river from here all the way to the sea!"

The gorims relayed his command. Thousands of Warriors of

the Bone moved toward the Valt Aram. The waters in this place weren't deep or fast-flowing, so Suhurs, twice as tall as their enemies, were confident they could reach the other side quickly. However, before the first ranks of the army of the united clans stood in the shade of twisted sagrs and parchans, the river was hit by a strange, straight lightning, similar to the one that had destroyed the Thunder Sower. The warriors stopped dead, unsure how to interpret it. Was it the continuation of the display of power of the Spirits of the Mountains, or rather a warning sent down by gods?

———

The consternation didn't last long. In the sky, high above the pinkish waters of the Valt Aram, appeared a giant, bizarre, semi-transparent creature. It didn't resemble anything that Gurds had absorbed so far, or that Warriors of the Bone had seen. It was surprisingly supple, had two different pairs of limbs and a strange spherical tab above the trunk. Suhurs standing by the river heard a melodious rumble as if someone spoke right next to their membranes.

"I am Hen Ra-Yan, the god coming from the dark abyss, where the suns pale and the stars fade out. From now on, you have to worship me, as the Spirits of the Mountains, the Plains, and the Waters already do. I defeated Kored and Thub, but haven't broken their discs as they did with Yabha, so that they are able to bestow life-giving warmth upon you. Presently, I'll make Blueblooded go away beyond the Adal Vin, and leave all the lands on this side of the queen of rivers to the clans, where the Warriors of the Bone, to my glory, will again become more numerous than the stars. No one will ever take these plains from you; they will remain yours till the end of time.

"But I forbid you to enter the Gurds' grounds without their consent. My sacred lightnings will incinerate anyone who breaks the covenant established by me. I am the one who gives and takes life, thus don't you dare make any offerings of prisoners or nestlings. From now on, the only sacrifices I will accept will be the kotors of the dead and the zregs of the hunted beasts. And now I urge you to depart immediately and put your weapons away."

————

At the same time Gurds were absorbing a squeal. It was reaching every soldier and every commander, including the sampo-sithu. However, the words intended for them sounded very different.

"My name is Henryan Darski, I am a human, an intelligent being belonging to another highly developed race, inhabiting distant star systems. I came to you in peace, but when I've seen your actions, *I am become death, the destroyer of worlds.* I have powers your scientists haven't yet dreamed of. I tame the suns, I annihilate the planets, I bring whole races to ruin. I will defeat your armies with a single flick of my finger, I will make barren the fields you sow with a single breath, I will crush all the circles that you have built since the beginning of time with a single look. I will do it without hesitation if you don't obey my orders! Hear, therefore, what my will is:

"You will depart to the other side of the Adal Vin, and you will stay there forever. From now on, the longest river of Suhurta will be an impassable border for you and for the Warriors of the Bone. You have my word that no Suhur touches the southern bank with his claws if you don't allow him. I will burn to ashes every warrior who opposes me, and I won't leave a single bone of him that could end up in the clan's totem. If you don't listen to me, I will ban you from Suhurta for good, and then I will lead the countless clans to the fertile plains of Gurdu'dihan so that they can turn it into desert. Go away immediately, and you will be spared."

After these words, strange lightnings began to shoot from the cloudless sky. They struck the water, turning it into steam, hit the ground on both riverbanks away from the armies gathered on them, plowing huge craters and stirring up fires. The sampo-sithu, belonging to the greatest sages of his race, realized imme-diately that Gurds couldn't compete with the giants who came from the stars. He also knew that the members of the Supreme Council would share his opinion when they received the detailed reports.

The conquest ended on that day by that river, but not the way it had been planned in the main circle of Gurdu'dihan. The Warriors of the Bone were already retreating to their settlements. Takeli'toko, having no choice, gave the order to retreat and began the long march toward the Adal Vin, so as not to draw the wrath of Humankind on himself.

———

Both sides won this war, although the absent creator of their success didn't doubt that it would be a long time before Suhurs and Gurds came to terms with the new reality. Until then—or until people returned to Xan 4—the peace on the planet would be kept by combat satellites, and hundreds of nanocameras connected to them, observing from a low orbit whether both races complied with the conditions of the truce.

The new God was going to make sure that His words weren't treated as just an idle threat.

AUTHOR'S NOTE

Rest assured that Nike Stachursky and Henryan Darski will meet again in further installments of *The Fields of Long-Forgotten Battles,* and all the subplots will closely entwine eventually. Look out for Book Two in the series. *Escape from Paradise* is coming soon to a bookstore near you!

ACKNOWLEDGMENTS

I simply can't help myself and must thank several people who have made the impossible possible.

Dear Reader, you wouldn't be holding this book in your hands, and you wouldn't have an appetite for more if it weren't for the great SF masters—Kevin J. Anderson, Jack Campbell, Nancy Kress, late lamented Mike Resnick, and David Weber—who all were kind enough to read *Easy to Be a God*, made helpful comments and praised my work. Thank you, Kevin, Jack, Nancy, Mike, and David!

David French, let me express my appreciation for your craft and talent. My original work very much benefited from your skills, especially in creating neologisms which are essential in science fiction. I have no doubt that *clone-of-a-bitch* will become a part of the vernacular.

Also, I am immensely grateful to MaryJane Stricklin for her positive opinion on Book One of the series, my two eagle-eyed proofreaders: Aysha Rehm and Angela Grant, for an excellent job they've done, Marie Whittaker's for her commitment throughout the whole book production process, Michelle Corsillo for making it happen, and Kevin J. Anderson for his favor and mentorship along the way. Last but not least, I'd like to thank Rebecca Moesta, the good spirit of WordFire Press. Thank you all for the one in a million chance. You've given Nike and Henryan a second life, which is more than I could hope for.

ABOUT THE AUTHOR

Robert J. Szmidt is a novelist, translator, and a former editor in chief of the following monthly magazines: *Video Business*, *PlaySta-tion Plus*, *Science Fiction*, and *Science Fiction, Fantasy & Horror*—  all of which appeared between 1992–2012.

He made his literary debut in the 1980s, then his career path veered into other areas and yet he has never forgotten his roots. At the turn of the century, he went back to writing and founded his by now cult *Science Fiction* magazine, thus initiating a revival of interest in Polish SF.

He has published more than twenty novels, a few novellas, and over twenty short stories. He's also made an appearance in a number of anthologies.

A wiz at post-apocalyptic fiction, he is—not without grounds —called the Destroyer of Worlds.

In *The Apocalypse According to Sir John*, first published in 2003 and in response to its significant popularity reprinted multiple times since, Robert J. Szmidt foretold the Ukraine crisis and its likely consequences.

His other post-apocalyptic fiction works include a novel titled *Solitariness of the Angel of Doom*, which was written well before McCarthy's *The Road*, but in the same vein; its action takes place in the USA and tells the story of the last man on Earth.

In 2015, he revisited the topic of a zombie apocalypse in *The*

Rats of Wrocław: Chaos. This book is in the vein of Max Brooks's *World War Z*; however, Robert J. Szmidt has created totally new zombies, different from George A. Romero's and Danny Boyle's. Book 2 of this series—*The Rats of Wrocław: Prison Bars*—was published on January 30, 2019, and *The Rats of Wrocław: Hospital* on July 31, 2019. A 13-episode audio series, with many movie stars, has been created, based on *The Rats of Wrocław: Chaos,* and it was nominated to EMPiK's Bestseller Award as one of just five bestselling titles in 2019. Full length audiobooks of *The Rats of Wrocław: Prison Bars* and *The Rats of Wrocław: Hospital* were released in January 2022. Book One (*The Rats of Wrocław: Chaos*) is going to be published in South Korea in 2023.

His flagship series is a five-part space opera, a huge bestseller in Poland: *The Fields of Long-Forgotten Battles,* which comprises the following books: *Easy to Be a God, Escape from Paradise, Edge of Extinction, Victory or Death,* and *Asgard's Last Mission.* Due to its huge popularity, the series is continued with further installments: *Per Aspera ad Astra* (2020) and *Pre-emptive Strike* (2022.)

He has also written a trilogy for the Metro2033 Universe project set up by Dmitry Glukhovsky: *The Abyss, The Tower,* and *Riese* (Book One has been translated into Russian and Hungarian and published both in Russia and Hungary; Book Two is to be released in both languages soon.)

Robert J. Szmidt has traveled widely, crossed three oceans, and visited five continents. He is a prolific translator with a dozen video games as well as almost one hundred books under his belt.

He created two science fiction awards and founded a website (www.fantastykapolska.pl) offering free access to the library counting nearly one thousand Polish SF novels, novellas, and short stories, not unlike Baen.com.

Robert has Austrian and French roots. His paternal great-grandfather was the director of the Warsaw-Vienna Railway at the turn of the 19th and 20th centuries. His maternal great-grandparents lived near Albi, a well-known town in the south of France.

He is married and lives with his wife in the bucolic region of Poland called the Polish Jurassic Highland, at 1,600 feet above the sea level, where he can admire elegant ammonites in his back yard. He says, "When you commune with the past on a regular basis, you must have your mind on the future—for anyway, a hundred fifty million years is no more than the blink of an eye."

IF YOU LIKED ...

IF YOU LIKED *EASY TO BE A GOD*, YOU MIGHT ALSO ENJOY:

Beasts of Tabat
by Cat Rambo

Devils & Black Sheep, A Novel of Wild Space
by C.S. Ferguson

Selected Stories: Science Fiction, Volume 1
by Kevin J. Anderson

OTHER WORDFIRE PRESS TITLES BY ROBERT J. SZMIDT

Escape From Paradise
Edge of Extinction
Victory or Death
Asgard's Last Mission

Our list of other WordFire Press authors and titles is always growing. To find out more and to shop our selection of titles, visit us at:

wordfirepress.com

[f] facebook.com/WordfireIncWordfirePress
[t] twitter.com/WordFirePress
[o] instagram.com/WordFirePress
[BB] bookbub.com/profile/4109784512